THE RISE OF DERAGON

THE RISE OF DERAGON

Edited by Caitlin Lengerich
Cover by Bianca Bordianu

ISBN 979-8-9895332-3-7

Published by Sydney Applegate
Learn more at www.booksbysydney.com

To my mom, for showing me The Phantom of the Opera back in 2016.
So much of who I am is because of you.

Content Warning

The Rise of Deragon is a heart-stopping romance-fantasy story that touches on plotlines that might be difficult for some readers. Subject matters in their story contain violence, gore, some foul language, death, murder, and references to sexual content. Readers who may be sensitive to this kind of material, please be advised. Otherwise, brace yourself for what can *really* happen when you open Pandora's Box...

THE RISE OF DERAGON

Prelude
Pandora

Mother says that I am the best of us: a perfect mosaic of all three Deragon girls.

The Saints never blessed me in a supernatural sense, but I suppose they found enough favor with me to let me inherit their key characteristics.

From Aunt Calliope, my voice.

Even as she bore children of her own, it was I who inherited the gift of song. And in an effort to honor that fateful coincidence, I've grown up under her faithful instruction. But in the process of doing so, I have discovered that we speak alike, too. As easily as our words can sow sweetness into one's soul, they can also pierce deep.

From Aunt Venus—Queen Inherit of the Damocles—my skillsets for survival.

"When you control the sea, you control everything," Venus had told me once, and while I didn't understand the gravity of the concept at the time, the look in Uncle Jericho's eyes told me that I ought to remember it. And so, I did. I remembered *everything* and kept a record of all her queenly knowledge through the years, knowing one day, it would be my responsibility to emulate the formidable reign Venus Deragon established.

But it was what I inherited from my mother that was in direct opposition with the strength that Venus was aiming to instill in me.

Mercy.

"You show someone mercy once, and they'll have a hold on you for the rest of your life," Venus told me once. And while the sentiment was meant to encourage me to hold my ground, there was an underlying darkness that stirred within me—like my aunt detested the idea of extending grace because of some lingering ghost from her past.

I was ten, and the idea of seeing my aunt so upset for being good-natured towards someone gutted me—especially considering her hostile reputation in the eyes of those she conquered. Tears had burned within my eyes, and Venus did her best to console me. Her embrace single-handedly willed them not to spill over.

"To be vulnerable is to willingly walk into danger. But fear not, we will teach you which paths are safe," Venus murmured, placing a tender kiss on the crown of my head as Uncle Jericho smiled down at her. "Won't we, love?"

"Of course, we will," Jericho answered, his eyes glimmering with compassion. "We have plenty of time to prepare you for your future."

Yes, there'd be several years ahead of us wherein I would learn what being the Crown Princess of the Damocles truly meant. I would learn about political campaigns, war strategies, the impending prospects of finding a suitor, and worst of all, the threshold on which my mercy must expire and be replaced with wrath and punishment. But all that my mind could focus on at the time was my aunt's tone of voice.

"Have I disappointed you?" I whispered pitifully in return.

"Nonsense!" she cried out, clutching me tighter. "You are an excellent Princess, and you will grow into your power."

I wanted to believe her, but the subtle, pained look on Uncle Jericho's face proved to be another warning sign, one I chose not to ignore.

That day, I feigned an illness that allowed me to sleep away the afternoon, and by nightfall, I slipped through the trick door in my suite and crept through the tunnels towards their rooms. Venus and Jericho had made it their personal mission, once I was old enough, to guide me through the labyrinth of Broadcove's catacombs. I knew the routes like the back of my hand by then, but the moment I tiptoed up towards the King and Queen's entry point, I wish I had lost my way.

I listened as Jericho broke the news: he had seen something disturbing in his sleep. Something that just so happened to have been haunting Venus for the last ten years.

PART I
OVERTURE

1
Pandora

Queen's Feast sets everyone on edge.

The event has been an annual tradition since the year after Venus was crowned, but all of Urovia knows that this year's Feast holds detrimental significance. Specifically, to Jericho.

I never got to grow up with grandparents, so all the stories my uncle would tell me of his mother made it feel like I knew her personally—her kindness, her compassion, her love of the arts. Secretly, there were many times when his shared memories made me feel like I'd grow into a ruler with *her* merits rather than Venus's.

But now, Venus has reached the oldest that Merrie Morgan ever was, and everyone is waiting to see if she survives the year ahead.

As such, the King's Guard has tripled, if only because Venus refused to install a Queen's Guard, despite her husband's fervent requests. Still, I know that if the tables were turned, Jericho would act the same way. The years I spent learning Urovian history—

including *their* story—taught me all I needed to know about their relationship: their lives meant nothing to them in comparison to that of their partner's. Which is crazy to me, considering their bond was once tied together through deep-seeded hatred.

I never voiced much of an opinion on it to Mother, for she always seemed to have a tender spot for the two of them and what they built together. But I would periodically bring up my disbelief to Aunt Calliope during our vocal lessons, to which she'd always smile and say one of two things. In my younger years, it was, "The truest loves in our lives have a secret knack for softening the coldest parts of our hearts." Which felt incredibly ambiguous. Now, in my twenties, Calliope never shies away from bluntly sharing what she was really trying to get at.

"Loving someone who has the capacity to hate you certainly has its merits. When the doors are closed and it's just the two of you alone together . . . having them flip the switch on you can be rather exciting."

From what I've gathered about Uncle Eli, Calliope had him wrapped around her finger from the start. She entered Broadcove Castle, and the poor guard was absolutely smitten. Even now, after three children together, it's clear that Eli would do anything for her, including cater to her various, implied whims. I try not to grimace at the thought.

Instead, I direct my attention to the grand ballroom, eyes passing along every staff member dutifully hanging garlands or dusting the chandeliers. Down the hall, the distant aroma of seasoned meat starts to waft into the room, and before my stomach has a chance to grumble in response, I turn and see myself out of the action.

Heading for my suite, knowing I am past due to meet with my lady's maids and begin dressing for the night's big event, I take the shortcut. Guests already begin funneling in through the main doors, bearing gifts we're far too rich to be receiving, and bidding warm welcomes to the guards that collect them. Meanwhile, the pleasant summer air beyond the observation terrace caresses me like a lover's touch as I pass through its wisteria-lined tunnel and into the East Wing.

This part of Broadcove Castle very quickly became the children's sector, given my three cousins and I were known to be quite the rowdy bunch in our youth. Mother and I originally had rooms nestled towards the southern edge, overlooking the gardens Venus and Jericho tended together with their team of topiaries, architects, and various landscapers. But when Calliope had Flora and Samuel—and the two of them fought like cats and dogs—the adults understandably wanted their space from us kids.

Even now, with most of us at ages above or near adulthood, we're not exactly tame. We may not be tracking muddy footprints through the property and drawing pictures on the castle walls anymore, but we still have our tendencies. For instance, Venus and Jericho aren't always the fondest of my random musical outbursts. But more than that, they cannot tolerate Flora when she feels the need to join in and harmonize . . . poorly, that is.

What Flora does have going for her, however, is her time-efficiency. She's orderly and polite and graceful and—unlike me—fully dolled-up for Queen's Feast.

"You look *marvelous*," I rave, drinking in the full glory of her strapless emerald gown.

Her dark hair is unbound and on full display—a secret indication of where she hopes the night will go, which is with a man's fingers tangled up in it.

As the royal spare, written into the line of succession after Mother assured Venus and Jericho she would likely not have any additional children, Flora has been able to live somewhat of an entertaining, double life. She must be educated enough on the empire's military movements and policies to function in my stead, but she's nowhere near as restricted as I am on certain matters. Like tonight: a man could press her up against the wall in front of the whole crowd and it'd be acceptable, while I would certainly have to have a death wish to even contemplate kissing someone.

"You've looked better, Pan," she chides. "Seriously, Jericho's already off his rocker today. *Don't* be late," she urges me, pointing towards the door to my suite, which is already open.

The conversation ends there, with Flora stomping her feet deeper into her heels until her feet feel snug in her shoes. As I turn to face whatever fate awaits me in my room, I hear the rush of fabric, and the tiny beads along her gown travel across the floor. I try not to dread the fact that I'll be stuffed into a gown equally as ridiculous as hers within an hour's time.

The only thing that cushions the blow is Mother, perched on the end of my vanity chair as a lady's maid touches up the finishing powder beneath her eyes.

"Good, you're here!" she rejoices, rising to her feet. "I was worried you had tried to make a break for it and bolted through the tree line."

Never in my life has my mother ever reproached me for my lack of enthusiasm regarding balls and parties, specifically with the clothes I don for them. In fact, she's the one person that I can truly be myself with about *anything*—the depletion of energy for large gatherings like tonight, the pressure of other's expectations of my future reign, and, as of lately, the selfish hopes of a romantic partner. Or, at the very least, an encounter.

My preselected gown hangs from one of the lower rafters of the room, the grand, deep violet garment revealing an open back, snug fit, and conservative neckline. The portrait of sophistication and power—but not desire, nor youthfulness. Not like the free-formed dress that Flora gets to greet the world in.

I feel my mother's embrace before I fully register that she's crossed the distance between us. Her perfume wafts beneath my nose, but it only partially alleviates the knot in my stomach as I dwell on tonight—not just because parties bestow unreasonable pressure on me, but because of the danger that may be lurking around Broadcove as we speak. "This always helps," I find myself saying.

"I know it does, dear," she hums. "Why don't you tell me what's on your mind while I fix your hair?"

Time alone with Mother always seems to steady my soul, even as I come clean about everything—mainly the jealousy and the urges that come with watching Flora get to live her life without reservations. All the longing I've stomached in solitude for a long while. It feels like the single breath they flow out from lasts five hours.

"What you're experiencing is totally understandable," she says as she secures the final pins into my hair. "You are young and lovely and beautiful. Not only that, but you are also *free* to explore any connection in those parameters, albeit discreetly. Venus and Jericho have never expected you to remain pure for your eventual consort, but I deeply respect that you only wish to share your soul with one person. That, and I see the many pressures the future crown has laid on you and how that affects your perspective on intimacy."

The word *intimacy* makes my skin crawl, but she's not mistaken.

I'd love to be a loose cannon. I *crave* connection to the point where I think I could implode, like I'm outgrowing my own skin by the second. But traitorously, I possess a romantic heart, and I know that if I grant a man access to the most sacred parts of me, I won't want to let them escape me. Ever. And with the duty I bear to marry wisely, I've chosen an existence of touch starvation over emotional devastation. Some days, it's harder to stick with it, though.

"It's not like I've never kissed anyone," I say, blushing at my sudden surge of honesty. "And I'm not *afraid* to be with someone. It's just . . ."

Mother senses my hesitance and eyes me through the mirror. "Whatever it is, you can tell me. I think I already know what you're leading up to."

I release an uneven sigh. "I'm older than you were when you came here . . . when you had me. Can I ask, what was it like?"

"Giving birth?" she asks humorously.

"*Saints* no." I chuckle, though, I've never feared the idea of having children like Venus and Jericho seemed to have. I only fear the thought of doing it alongside someone I don't truly love. "I mean, what was . . . being with Father like?"

Mother's eyes turn watery, and I glance away long enough for her to fight off the spontaneous rush of sadness my question brings. I don't ask much about Father, mainly out of respect for Jericho more so than Mother. She always answers my questions whenever my mind wanders, but considering he had passed away before ever learning that he fathered me, her answers are minimal. Condensed. It always circles back to, *"I'm just thankful that you have Jericho. Wouldn't you agree?"* to which I would nod my head in earnest.

As far as royal fathers are concerned, Jericho falls among the ranks of the more honorable lot.

"I won't speak about his company, as we were a bit of a well-kept secret at the time. Sneaking around, staying quiet—you could say it felt a bit like a forbidden affair. But what I will say is, in those hidden moments we were afforded together . . . I felt like the center of someone's universe."

The sentiment resonates with me somewhere deep in my core, and I try to imagine even *one* person in my life that remotely makes me feel that way romantically. I fail.

"Do you ever get lonely?" I ask, fighting against the feeling myself. "I mean, did you ever consider settling down with another man, like Venus and Calliope did?"

"Loneliness comes in waves," Mother returns, taking her time to answer both of my inquiries. "And sure, in those shifting tides, I considered looking for lasting love. But I soon came to learn that, for me, men are simply that. Just men," she says in a soothing tone, gently squeezing my exposed shoulders. "*You*, my dear, will always be the great love of my life."

With that, my mother steps aside to unveil her creation in the mirror. The apprehension in my bones starts to settle the longer I stare at my reflection, still able to see the ordinary me beneath the woven crown Mother tied my hair into.

"Are you ready for your performance tonight?"

"As ready as I can be," I return, trying not to think about approaching centerstage with only my voice instead of my harp. This was to be my vocal debut. Jericho himself requested that I sing tonight, knowing Venus secretly loves my voice. But I know what comes with putting myself out on display like this. This performance is meant to make noblemen and other approved guests of the King pause and view my gifts in wonder. View *me* in wonder.

I have always found comfort and security while playing my harp, whether in private or in public. Something about plucking the strings and sitting perched before the massive, wooden instrument made me look delicate and protected at the same time. Any eyes that fell on me were only there for a moment before watching my hands work through the multitudes of wires.

But to sing in front of hundreds. *Thousands*, even.

Every eye will eventually meet my own, and I'll have to act like it doesn't intimidate the hell out of me.

"Don't worry," she croons. "You won't be at it totally alone. No doubt, if you concentrate hard enough, you'll hear Calliope harmonizing with you from her seat."

She kisses my temple then quietly sees herself out, nodding to the guard that stands outside my door. He peers in, as if to make sure I'm on track to arrive at the ballroom in a timely manner, and I wave at him more with my fingers than with my full hand. He smiles in a way that subtracts a few years, a dimple pearling near the right corner of his mouth. The sight floods me with a bizarre sense of need, which I fight to ignore.

"I'm just going to run through some warmups and then I'll be out."

The guard nods shyly before closing the door and leaving me to my own devices.

As promised, I take a generous sip of the herbal tea I've left sitting out for the last hour or so and slowly begin my exercises. Arpeggios, a few scales, and lastly, I track through the most difficult measures of the aria Calliope had insisted I sing for the Feast. It's not that the notes are out of reach and I must strain my vocal cords, but the intonation of my vowels could be better. I try for rounder O's and add a vibrato to the words that end on an A vowel to hide any unsteadiness.

And maybe it's just the nerves and the voices in my head, but after five or so attempts at the same three passages, I almost believe I hear a ghost's harmony singing along with me from somewhere hidden.

2
Pandora

For as long as I've known her, Venus Deragon has remained a composed and calculated woman. Lethal grace lingers wherever she goes, as if imbedded in her very shadow. And with merely the glimmer of her eyes, she causes her enemies to crumble. Mother told me that Venus always possessed the quality, but that her choice of prey grew in magnitude as she grew older. The idea startled me at first—to imagine a woman in my sphere of influence being perceived by the masses as foreboding and ruthless.

But looking at her now, her diadem perfectly settled atop her head as if there isn't a bounty on it, I see her strength. Her defiance.

She's giving the nightly rundown once more to members of the King's Guard. Most of these men are young, burly, and heavily armed, but one of them catches my eye—the same one that stood outside my rooms only moments ago—and winks at me when my gaze lingers. The blush begins to fill my cheeks as someone steps before my line of sight.

"You look lovely this evening."

The crimson uniform blocking my view of the guard is simple enough to register, and I draw my eyes up towards my uncle's face. "How kind of you to say," I whisper, even though Jericho's assessment of my beauty suddenly makes my dress feel more constraining.

"Is something wrong?" he asks, noticing my discomfort.

I know better than to tell him it's stage fright. He has always been able to see through people's lies, even the ones that are told to dismiss any worries. "It's not that I'm fearful, per se," I begin, trying to find the most appropriate wording for this subliminal, uneasy feeling. "But I can sense the immense pressure of this night. It's . . . crippling."

Jericho nods, understanding the feeling well. Were his hands not already stuffed in his pants pockets, I wouldn't be surprised to find them white-knuckled and in the forms of clenched fists. "You are a mesmerizing musician," he tells me earnestly. "And every time I walk through the East Wing, the sound of your voice fills the castle with tranquility."

I bite down on the inside of my lip, regretting the words even as I let them spill out.

"You asked me to sing tonight," I whisper, "because it will allow people to take their eyes off Venus and look at *me*. But what if the only way I can get people to see me, to *respect* me, is in song? What if, apart from my voice, these people do not have the confidence in me to one day continue your legacy?"

Jericho pauses at that, pondering my perspective in contrast to his own. In the end, he still appears too baffled by my line of questioning to further dissect it. "Do the pressures of being our heir affect you this deeply?"

"I'm not scared to rule," I clarify. "I'm only scared of disappointing you."

The words hang over the two of us like a suspended blade held by a single string—dangerous and unsettling. Jericho runs a hand through his dark hair that has given way to hints of silver, unable to look at me for a moment, then finds the will to draw me closer to his side. A sudden sternness absorbs all the kindness in his face—the kindness I know he worked for years to obtain. He casts an assessing glance over the room, as if ensuring Venus's presence isn't lingering nearby.

Then, we stride down another hallway, and I try to quell the hurried heartbeats threatening to break through my ribcage as we finally settle upon a shadowy spot. His gaze descends onto my own once more, and the intensity of it nearly makes me shiver.

"Every example of family your aunt and I have known is one we don't wish to replicate. Traitorous fathers, children who lived for the benefit of their parents, mothers whose deaths felt so unnecessary. And so, we are perfectly happy with the family that lies before us. Her and I. You and your mother and Calliope. It's enough for us."

His eyes seem to hint at a lingering sadness in the silence that follows, and I choose to call him out on it. "Is it, though?"

His lips thin into a line. "When royal blood runs through your veins, children secure your legacy just as much as they weaken your stability. Venus and I have seen our fill of the latter, so when Genny had you, we were more than content to install you into our line. To let her sisters bear the weight of expanding our lineage so that Venus and I could just *be*."

His eyes glimmer with hesitation, but he clears it away with a few, fast blinks, the same gesture one would see from someone fighting back tears.

"Still, you know of my blessing, the way I foresee things in my sleep. Most of what the Saints grant me insight on happens soon after I encounter it. But one day, I foresaw a scene that had been haunting Venus for nearly a decade. Each day felt less and less like borrowed time that we were being mercifully granted, and when I came around to the notion . . ." He drifts off, as if in memory. The most somber smile tugs at his lips, framed by the beginnings of a thin, graying beard. "Well, we realized that having a child of our own was nowhere as scary of a concept anymore as losing one another was."

Jericho paces about the room to avoid the full weight of the sadness that follows. "We tried for years, but your aunt endured a grave illness in her youth, and eventually . . . we felt helpless. We had *everything*—power, security, wealth—and yet, I couldn't give her the one thing we had finally come to long for most. I tell you this so that you know the truth; that we've experienced plenty of disappointment together. But you? You've never once come *close* to disappointing us. So long as you're alive, you stand as the embodiment of the years the Saints have granted me Venus. Your very existence, Pandora, is a gift."

Jericho's never been affectionate in a physical sense. A pat on the back or a quick clutch of one's hand is about all the affection he spares for anyone apart from Venus. But his words have always carried insurmountable power, and as I throw my arms around him, nestling my head into the dip of his shoulder and whisper the words, "Thank you," Jericho doesn't fight it. Doesn't try to pry me off.

His hand cradles the back of my head and I feel his pulse thrum within his neck. "Always," he tells me.

I pull away and grant him his space, but my uncle catches my hand in his, briefly pulling me back towards him. "Just a moment," he says as his eyes catch something amiss about my hair. His fingers adjust one of the pins there, and with a curt nod, he approves his handiwork. "All right. You're all set."

I smile at the sentiment, remembering the days when Jericho would bargain with me to get me to do self-defense training. I hated the idea of possibly hurting anyone, even if the instructor was brought in for the sole purpose of taking my practice blows. Eventually, I only conceded if Jericho agreed to braid back my hair before each session, and he did so faithfully. The longer he did it, the better he got at it—soon incorporating more complicated, woven patterns.

And I see now, as Venus rounds the corner looking for him, that he keeps the habit up. Plaited to perfection, Venus's dark hair whips with sudden motion as she halts, spotting us mid-sentence. "Oh, there you are. Is everything—"

"Just as it should be," Jericho returns calmly, easing the tension so obviously creeping over her normal, relaxed demeanor. Even though she's the one supposedly under fire, Venus's primary worry continues to be him. "Shall we?"

3
Pandora

Unlike most events we host in the grand ballroom, this one starts off on a very distinct, sobering note, with every guard manning the room's perimeter, adjusting their weapons in unison. The echoing *click* of crossbows rings out upon the proclamation of the King and Queen's entrance, so it wouldn't surprise me if all the cheers that roar through the room come from a place of terror rather than excitement, worried they'll face a slaughter if they don't applaud.

Following them, enter Calliope and Eli. It's customary to have the adults enter first, a presentation of honor and respect, while their children file into the room in reverse birth order. Ten-year-old Dorian, and his bashful smile, leads the way, with seventeen-year-old Samuel and eighteen-year-old Flora trailing close behind. From the shadowy alcove I hide in, I see more than enough men and women assessing Flora's appearance with either gleaming smiles or envious glares. Naturally, I try to block out how many more will look at me when it's my turn to step out. After them, my mother waves to the crowd, and then, with a gentle gesturing motion, she turns the room's attention towards me.

I'm suddenly hyper aware of what skin my dress doesn't conceal, or how my right eye begins to minutely, frustratingly twitch. Worse, I can feel myself beginning to perspire under my arms and along the backs of my knees—but by some mercy, the revelry only grows louder in the room as I appear.

That mercy being Ardian Asticova's voice introducing me.

The poor man is withered and old and borderline senile—but the smile beneath his scruffy, gray mustache is heartwarming. From all the histories my aunt and uncle educated me on, Ardian's was always one that baffled me. Once a native of an opposing territory, he brought his orphaned niece to Broadcove Castle to serve Jericho's parents as a foreign ambassador, but when Jericho ascended the throne, Ardian didn't cut ties and run home to Mosacia like most people would expect him to. Instead, he stayed to help the bereaved prince find his footing as king and keep his continent secured from anyone with ill intent. Unfortunately, his niece he took responsibility for happened to be one of those dreaded underminers, and when Venus herself annihilated her for her treachery, Ardian *still* stood by Jericho.

It's like the old bat can see those recounted memories in my eyes, and suddenly, he feels the need to glance elsewhere and abandon the stage in slow, staggered movements.

I'm halfway to the steps when I begin to register the amount of attention poised on me. *This is good,* I try to tell myself. *Less people looking at Venus. You can handle it for one night.*

It's not that I loathe being the center of attention. I'd be more than charitable to do these sorts of events, so long as I had someone that loved me at my side to undergo them with me, to make small talk with guests, or even to help bail me out of conversations that drag on. To lay their hand on the small of my back when the hour gets late and tell me, *"Why don't we turn in for the night?"*

Instead, it's me, alone, against everyone. Against every preening gentleman, refined lady, and potential threat to my aunt's and uncle's lives.

I ascend the stairs onto the dais with feather-light steps, my shoulders rolled back and my chin high as I approach center stage. I dip into a low curtsey, placing my hand over my heart in humble acceptance, and then proceed to the chair set before my elegant harp.

I've played my harp for audiences before, casting a dreamlike mood over the room while guests wait for their plated dinners to be brought out by the staff. So the customary routine flows as expected. The string ensemble surrounding me helps pick up the pace when my fingers start to cramp up, each of them incorporating little featurettes to highlight other solo performers. I try not to let the red meat smell that wafts towards the stage make my stomach gurgle, if only to keep from feeling another unsettled emotion in the pit of it.

Just as I consider asking a guard to smuggle me a dinner roll, members of the kitchen staff come around to clear entrees from the table and Jericho strides up to the lip of the stage. The crowd's voices hush before needing to call for their attention.

"Thank you, everyone. I am honored to have so many of you gathered here to celebrate another year that the Saints have blessed my love, my Venus."

All I can think about as the crowd swoons and applauds again is how I ache for someone to acknowledge my presence with even a fraction of Jericho's reverence.

"As a gift to her," my uncle continues, "as well as to all of you,

I've arranged for Princess Pandora to sing a song for us. Please welcome her, now."

I drink in the bemused and surprised expressions of the masses, who now deliberately turn their banquet chairs towards the stage. Then, to steady my heart rate, I look to Mother and Calliope, both of whom flash me toothy, encouraging smiles. It's the push I need to crane my neck once towards the conductor and signal the music to begin.

Despite not having a full orchestra at this gathering, the strings still manage to replicate the triumphant start of the Urovian anthem.

Brought up from roots of infamy
Delivered 'cross the Sea
Reborn from ribs of the enemy
The Saints we thank for thee!

The first few onlookers start to gape at me. Even the staff members portioning the dessert pastries in the back stop their duties to watch in awe.

Crimson blood we spilled so that
Our suffering would cease
This castle stands, thanks to our dead
The Saints we thank for thee!

As I glide through the next two verses, I think about how I've always been enamored with Urovia's anthem. The song is simple, and antiquated by its hymnal refrain. It's the perfect song for operatic women, middle-range harmonies, and men with velveteen vocals. There could be one singer for each part, and yet, the song and its melodic structure could make the room feel infinitely full. But perhaps more than that, it captures the hope of people that aren't alive to see what their humble Urovian roots have grown. That, and when Jericho first took the throne, people feared that the dynasty would deteriorate, and the land would be reclaimed once more by the Mosacians.

But a viciously brilliant queen, with a love for a once-loathed king, managed to thwart a massive empire. Two people against the entire world, it seemed, came out victorious and in love. And *that* was worth singing about.

With everything in me, I lead the ballroom through the final, jubilant chorus.

Land we love, we defend
This legacy we leave
And blessed be the King and Queen
The Saints we thank for thee!

When I finally release the sustained final note, the world erupts with a thrilled, collective sound. It's unlike anything I've ever experienced directly, and as I take it all in—a graceful, polite smile plastered across my lips—I understand why Venus and Jericho host these sorts of events. To have this many people applauding for them, I have no doubt it goes straight to their head. It's certainly starting to do the same to me, the feeling further cemented as a couple men dare to pull individual roses from their tables' centerpieces and toss them towards the stage in honor.

I drop into my final curtsey before the throng of excited congregants. "Thank you. Really, thank you." I beam, delivering a delicate wave to the crowd. "You are all too kind—"

"*Encore!*" an unseen voice among the masses fervently cries out.

The agreement among the crowd is unanimous and resounding, and while I was only meant to serenade the crowd with the anthem, Jericho's eyes go wide with prompting encouragement. *Go on*, they say, and I know that the words are not those of my uncle, but instructions from my king, who I know better than to disobey.

Quickly, my steps carry me over to the maestro, and I whisper the aria I'd been practicing in case of this exact moment. He obliges, rounding up his musicians in a hissed whisper as I once more return centerstage.

"And now, for this next song," I proclaim. "I'd like to invite all the lovers onto the floor."

Before anyone else among the masses has the idea to do so first, Jericho tips his head in charming acknowledgement towards his queen. His dearest love takes his hand with a smile that reminds me of how young she was in their first, shared royal portrait, and on featherlight footsteps, they approach the dancefloor together.

As the king leads them through the dreamy waltz, I begin to sing them into whatever world their souls drift off to. The pianist plinks the ivory keys with a wistfulness that makes this moment even more touching, and I will the knot in my throat to sink into my stomach. Because Saints, watching Venus dance with Jericho almost feels like intruding on a private moment—like two very different dimensions of human happiness exist in the same room and somehow don't cause an explosion.

History has recorded the two of them doing such heinous, unimaginable things together, and yet, to know that most of them were done in the name of true love . . . I am almost able to look past it all.

And perhaps that's another reason why I feel like a disappointment to them.

Because as the bodies piled up over time, their eyes never left one another.

All I fear I can give them is my music.

It's more than enough, some mythical voice in my head tells me, and for the sake of getting through this performance, I heed its words.

Letting my voice soar through the gilded gathering, I watch longingly as fine gentlemen spin beautiful ladies and young maidens across the sweeping palace floors. Revolving in a pattern that allows Venus and Jericho to have their space, I scale through a complicated run and structure my breathing as seamlessly as possible. The song comes to a soothing end, drawn in by soulful chords across all the musicians, and when I expect the world to clap for the king and queen's dancing, I find that every eye in the room remains geared towards me.

I exit the stage amidst the continuous praise.

"Bravo!" I hear a herd of men holler.

"So moving!" an elderly woman remarks kindly.

"Who knew the princess had such a lovely voice?" a few others murmur to one another.

And then, from behind me, I hear, "Stunning. Absolutely stunning."

I try to suppress my blush in time for me to lock eyes on the guard from outside my rooms. "You flatter me, but I owe my voice to my aunt's faithful training—"

"I never said anything about your voice," the guard says, his grin deepening.

The words would normally indicate flirtation, but something about the tone of his voice makes the compliment feel delicate.

"I'm Heath, by the way," he blurts.

"Pandora."

His gentleman's smile is likely nothing more than polite, yet it floods me with the heat of the already-set sun. So much so that, when a server comes around with a tray of alcohol, I blindly reach for a glass and pour the liquid down my throat. I assume it's champagne, but I assumed incorrectly, because the moment the bourbon hits my tongue, I shiver. With Heath's eyes on me, I certainly can't spit it back into my glass, so try not to make a face as I swallow it down, and Heath laughs at the bravery it takes me to do so.

"I didn't know you were this nervous about your performance," he says.

Yes, sure. The performance.

I nod pitifully and attempt to turn the focus back on him. "It's sort of my obligation to make the king and queen happy," I say, only half lying. "So it can be stressful."

"I'm sure," Heath says through somewhat of a sigh, as if steadily running out of words to say to keep the conversation going, but not wanting to be disrespectful about it.

And as I ransack my brain for anything smart or endearing I could say to make him stay longer, the liquid courage starts to run its course, intermingling with the word *obligation*. I've done my job for the evening. I've sung for the guests, and aside from the one dose of bourbon, I kept a sober head on my shoulders. Why be a slave to obligation when no one is looking at me anymore?

"You know what helps relieve my stress?" I dare to ask.

Heath must be able to read the mischief in my modesty, because he tugs me towards the door, and as we head for the hallway, I contemplate the best way to take off his belt.

4
Pandora

For decorum's sake, Heath and I walk without touching. He trails silently behind me to make it appear as though he's covering my back—but when he opens the door to my suite and flicks one last glance to the vacant hallway, all facades fade away. The minute the door closes behind us, Heath captures my mouth with his own with a force I've never encountered before.

A rush of blood to the head nearly throws me off balance, and Heath catches me with ease. In fact, from there, he scoops me off the ground altogether.

I half expect him to lead us to my bed, but Heath carries me to the chaise instead. Then, when I prepare to lay flush against the cushion and have him clamber over top of me, he sits me down in a way that keeps me upright. Still, his lips never leave mine. "This makes no sense," he murmurs.

"What do you mean?"

Heath's hair is silken beneath my fingers but cropped just short enough to keep me from fully clutching onto it. He's hesitant to rake through mine, though. "I've never seen a man on your arm, let alone in your rooms."

"You've been keeping tabs on me?"

His mouth drags across the side of my face, his teeth pulling a desperate sound out of me as they tug my earlobe. Who knew that kind of touch along my *ear* would make my composure turn to dust? Heath doesn't answer my question, though, saying instead, "How could anyone pass over your beauty?"

"That doesn't matter now," I say, and capture his mouth once more.

I start to move against him, aching for friction I know to search for despite having never felt it firsthand, but his hands don't venture anywhere I want. Rather, Heath immediately goes for the buttons on the back of my dress, and my breathing hitches in a manner I don't expect.

I should be excited. The anticipation should be making my body turn warm and supple—but all I suddenly feel is discomfort.

Where's the touching and the sweet nothings and the build up?

"Wait," I gasp. "This is all too sudden."

"I thought you wanted—" he begins, then pauses, assessing his words. His face contorts in confusion, then hardens into frustration. "Do you want me or not, princess?"

My insides lurch at the question, at the rough implication in his tone. There's no love, not even an ounce of adoration, only release—and likely for his benefit as opposed to mine. Holding out for a man that wants to please me might just kill me.

"Get out," I groan, my original pursuit clearly unsuccessful and rather embarrassing the longer it sinks in. "I can't be with a man that won't even say my name as he kisses me."

Fear flashes across his brown eyes, and for a sliver of a second,

I think he feels contrite. Perhaps the harsh question was meant to be seductive, not demeaning. Still, even as he registers the mistake, he's stupid enough to call out, "Wait, Princess—"

"It's *Pandora*."

In an instant, all the light leaves his eyes as if I just snuffed out a candle. I regret it to an extent, but I don't say so aloud, nor do I apologize. The guard refastens his jacket and hurries out the door.

Slumped over the chaise in sudden self-pity, I heave a sigh of annoyance and wonder how it could've gotten to this point. Since when did feeling lonely turn into *this*? And hell, the guard seemed nice enough this morning, but not nice enough to be such an airhead. *Bleh!*

I track the sound of his footsteps dissipating down the hall before I scream into a pillow, the material diffusing the sound of my humiliation. Once my breath runs out, though, I throw the pillow back to its previous spot and stare at the ceiling. Silence descends, and as I prepare to soak it in fully, a new sound catches my attention.

A subtle creak.

My eyes drop to my feet, wondering if a floorboard is loose and I put too much pressure on the ground, but I shucked off my heels the moment I entered my sacred space.

The creak sounds off again, and this time, my head snaps towards the door that the guard just departed from. Maybe Flora tiptoed down the hall and is playing tricks on me, waiting to chastise me for a failed fornication attempt. And yet, when I narrow my eyes, I see the latch within the strike plate of the door.

I'm closed in.

Alone.

And then—

"The voice of an angel," a male voice I've never encountered drawls slowly from behind me. "With the face of an enchantress."

I almost wonder if I'm imagining it—that is, until he finishes his phrase.

"And the spirit of a goddess."

As calmly as I can manage, I turn to glance myself over in the mirror, but the sight of black-gloved hands creeping around its gilded frame—opening the trick door to the castle's secret tunnels—unravels my composure.

My hair stands on end, like I'm seconds away from being struck by lightning, and as I shape my mouth into a scream, the intruder does something unexpected. He extends his hand towards me, his palm up in offering rather than gesturing me to stay quiet.

"Come with me," he whispers.

His *voice*.

Something stops me in my tracks about it, the sound almost otherworldly. Like somehow, his words are sung rather than spoken. Like he's a sorcerer reciting a spell meant to disarm me—and I almost fear that it's working.

"Who *are* you?" I find myself asking faintly.

He pries the trick door open just enough to reveal his face.

Only it's not a face at all, but rather one hidden beneath a mask that resembles a human skull. The heightened cheekbones cut the shape of his face, and the hollowed eye sockets give way to storm-gray eyes that draw me closer just as much as they terrify me. If the eyes are the window to the soul, then staring at him is no better than standing in the midst of a blizzard. The only skin unguarded by bone is a stern chin and soft lips that starkly contrast one another, and I catch myself staring at them for too long.

"I won't ask again," I find the willpower to restate. "*Who are you?*"

A wicked smile curves along those lips. "A fool," he answers mystically. "For I came here to kill a queen, but one look at you and I'm willing to trade you for her."

I reach for the knife strapped against my thigh, an essential that my Aunt Venus insisted I always keep on me—and the stranger watches me. He doesn't move a muscle other than the ones it takes to deepen his smile, as if my intentions of fighting back are adorable.

"Perhaps you aren't your mother's daughter after all," he whispers, his words coated in dark, secret pleasure that makes my stomach turn.

Fury brews within my blood, thrums against my bones.

It's always been a secret—that I'm the daughter of the unwed Duchess, not the wedded Queen Inherit. It was the role I agreed to take on to be installed as the royal heir. But the fact that this stranger—this *assassin*—somehow knows the truth . . .

When I subtract the logistics from the equation, my anger still brews. Because I *am* my mother's daughter. I am merciful and kind and gentle. I'd pick flowers from the gardens before I'd pick up a blade. But I'm also incredibly wise, and it's *that* realization that allows my hands to fall back to my sides, forgoing the knife.

My intruder probably sees the movement as weakness—that I am fragile and naive enough to allow his magnetic force to lift me from my chair and guide me towards the mirror, the coldness of the catacombs already creeping over my skin as I draw near.

But he couldn't be more in the wrong—because it takes the same amount of strength to strike as it does not to scream. It takes strength to mimic awestruck wonder as opposed to displaying terror; to let him believe that he has lured me to him rather than reveal the conscious decision I make to step into imminent peril. There is strength in knowing that I may never come back from this.

"How is it," I murmur, praying to the Saints that this stranger cannot read the lie in my body language, "that you make it so easy for me to step into someone else's death sentence?"

I already know the answer, though. It's what I've been trained to understand until the crown on Venus's brow finally adorns my own: I am their final line of defense. Wearing the crown isn't just a symbol for civilians to revere, it's a reminder to me that should things go up in flames, it's my job to secure their safety, even if it means ensuring my destruction.

To be vulnerable is to willingly walk into danger, I remind myself.

But perhaps the man is attempting to be vulnerable, too, because his smile falters and his outstretched hand faintly trembles.

"Because it's not death that I will deal you, Pandora. It's captivity."

The fact that he says my *name* as opposed to my title is not lost on me. It may be a tactic to him, something to push me over the edge. To know that he watched with bated breath as I turned Heath away for that very reason.

But to me, it's the only scrap of reliability I'm able to cling to as I place my hand into his.

The leather concealing his fingers grasping mine drastically shifts something in the atmosphere. His touch halts my heartbeat and turns my skin to ice. With a quick tug, the masked intruder pulls me flush against him, brings his other hand down upon a tender spot in my neck, and as I'm pulled into the catacombs, the mirrored door clicks shut and darkness descends.

5
Pandora

By the time I come to, I hear the faint rippling of seawater at the base of Honeycomb Harbor, which remains empty save for one, ominous ship.

The Hive never docks all at once, and with how many precarious whispers spoke of a targeted attack on the king and queen, the fleet is likely spread out across every territory Venus and Jericho have accumulated. Close enough to strike by water, cornering any escapees, but leaving the bulk of protection to the ground forces. Forces that this masked stranger—who I discover carrying me in his arms towards the lone vessel—seemed to evade with ease.

"You didn't need to knock me out, you know," I say under my breath when my vision fully restores.

He must've felt me stir awake because my words don't jolt him. "You might've screamed," he mutters gruffly.

But I'm not so sure that's his true answer, because he looks at me with a bizarre sort of confusion. He's *literally* taking me hostage right now, and yet, the first thing I dared to ask him about is why he felt the need to render me unconscious through tunnels I could've *helped* him navigate.

Then again, we're out of the castle, aren't we? He must know a great deal without my help.

His steps falter, and he sets me on my feet with a tenderness that makes my stomach lurch. "Alright, angel. We'll try it your way. But the second you cry out, I will have no choice but to make you suffer. Understand?"

I nod my acceptance, and even though my captor has given me the independence to walk my way towards his boat, he still feels it necessary to set a gloved hand over the small of my back and guide me in his desired direction. It takes strength not to resist his touch just as much as it does not to lean into it. Saints damn me, but something about him feels eerily comforting. He's a fugitive that feels almost like a kindred spirit somehow—and were it not for the leather covering his bare hand, I think I might have shivered beneath him.

"What's your name?" I whisper into the wind.

The only sound between us is the tide, and when I clear my throat in an effort to get his attention, he merely shakes his head. "I heard you, angel."

I'm rattled by the fact that my prisoner nickname is so . . . endearing—but I stay focused. "Who am I going to tell? The moon?"

He smirks at that. "Most people call me Madman."

"*Madman*——"

My captor pulls me close, one hand glued to my back as he hauls me towards him, the other covering my open mouth. Being this close to him . . . he smells like lumber and flames, and he sets my senses on fire in a way that deeply alarms me.

"What did I say about being loud?" he reminds me, his voice surprisingly gentle.

I find enough common sense to wrench his hand away. "I cannot possibly call you that."

"Why not?" His eyes are still assessing our surroundings as we approach the gangway. "I traded Venus's certain death for your capture. Seems mad to me."

I don't care to rehash the critical detail about why that is . . . because I *fascinated* him.

"I . . . I don't wish to call you that."

"But you will."

"It seems unkind."

"Careful, angel," he taunts. "You may find that naming me something other than my worst intentions might have you forming an attachment to me."

I narrow my eyes at him, holding my ground. "I'll run the risk. You're keeping me alive, after all. I see no point in being rude."

"And what if I preferred that you call me by this name?" he challenges, crossing his arms to where they part his midnight cloak.

"You *want* me to call you Madman?"

He doesn't answer, gesturing me to quickly and *silently* walk up the gangway, which can only mean one thing.

Someone has discovered my absence.

I scramble towards Madman with my head tucked down, but even hiding my face cannot prevent the whisper of a cry I hear coast through the air. I pretend not to notice, but Madman's eyes narrow, assessing the source of the sound and how it could've crept up on him. I reach for him, hoping to draw him away from whoever it is, but he relents, and I dare to cast a passing glance over the docks.

"Pandora?" the figure calls out.

Oh Saints.

When my eyes see Ardian struggling to catch up to us, hands extended towards the distance between us as if he could pry me away from this fate, my heart plummets into my stomach.

"PANDORA!"

Ardian stumbles on uneven ground. I almost think I hear his kneecap crack on the stony path. He's a harmless old man, and yet, I can feel rage rippling through Madman's build.

"No!" I find myself gasping for air, knowing that his unexplainable leniency surely won't extend to anyone beyond me, let alone towards someone attempting to liberate me from him. "*No*, don't hurt him—"

"It doesn't work like that, angel," he whispers sternly.

Even amidst what should be a sizeable injury, Ardian persists, calling after me again. "Pandora, who *is* that? Where are you going?"

Scrambling for a way to stall time, to distract Madman from Ardian's discovery, I ransack my brain for anything of use. My nails are manicured and not sharp enough to do damage. Even if my solution was to attack him, the mask on his face looks thick enough to give me trouble if I tried to gouge his eyes out. But I'm not a fighter, I'm a nurturer, a lover—

That's it.

I throw caution to the wind and crash against Madman's sturdy frame, playing the part of a silly girl fawning over a handsome stranger she met at the Feast. Because maybe, if I pretend to be sneaking off to a lover's affair, Ardian will leave us be. After all, everyone always turns a blind eye when Flora does it. I fling my arms around his neck and pull myself closer to him, hoping to capture his attention away from any violence. For good measure, I plaster an easy smile across my lips, and Madman responds in turn by caressing a hand over the middle of my exposed back.

But it happens before I think to ward off the inevitable.

I make the traitorous mistake of inhaling the air between Madman and I, and his scent hits me like a load of cinder blocks—like I've just caught wind of an imaginative, undiscovered world far away. A soft, surprised sound escapes me at the discovery, and Madman's other gloved hand drifts lower in order to steady the sudden weakness in my knees.

The touch is so sensual it distracts us both.

It feels *real*.

For a single, suspended moment in time, I think I see the fury in his stormy eyes slacken.

And then, Ardian is screaming.

"Don't touch the Princess!" he growls with more bravado and deep-seated rage than I've ever heard out of him, his voice closer now.

Despite whatever fascination he has with me and how entranced he was all of two seconds ago, it vanishes at the sound of Ardian's insistent voice. Madman heaves a disappointed sigh. "You'll understand later."

Next thing I know, Madman shoves me, *hard*, and I go scrambling onto the main deck of his boat. I try to grapple for balance along the center mast, but I tumble onto the ground. I hit my head on the way down, but not even the force of the blow can keep me from desperately careening upward, making one last attempt to settle him.

But in a single, fluid motion, I see Madman reach for something in his cloak, brandishing the item like one would a sword, and—

A petrifying, loud noise rips through the serene night, ringing through my ears in a malicious echo. It seems to rattle the constellations overhead, too, and faint dots line my vision from the shock of its ferocity. Then, there's the faint presence of leftover smoke.

And when it dissipates, it gives way to Ardian Asticova's body laid to waste on the floor, blood pooling from the cavity of his chest.

6
Pandora

I've never seen a weakness in crying. Expressing emotions is a healthy and appropriate response in any catastrophic situation. And yet, the moment Madman turns back to me after murdering Ardian—after embracing the namesake I didn't wish to believe in—I go into shock. At least outwardly. I almost begin to fear that I have gone numb to the sight of such sudden violence, but then, little by little, the unmistakable chill of terror creeps up my bones.

The windless summer night promises to make this discreet voyage longer than it should be. That, and there's scarcely any food on this boat, which I remind myself is because Madman didn't intend on taking hostages.

"Why call me 'angel'?"

Madman's head faintly perks up at the question. "Oh. We're talking again?"

His voice is smooth as velvet and his smirk is as dreamlike as it is precarious.

"Answer the question."

Madman laughs to himself, just once. The sudden change in my otherwise airy disposition takes him by surprise. The low sound of his next words burn through me like unanticipated heat.

"Am I not allowed to address you by a term of endearment?"

"I have no problem with your kindness." I don't feel the need to add, *limited and volatile as it may be*. "It's the word *angel* I'm not sitting well with. After all, you somehow know the truth that no one else does. If you had intentions of killing my aunt, and threatening my mother's safety were I not to have cooperated earlier, then you can't possibly be Urovian. Which means you don't believe in angels at all."

Urovia's homeland religion is complex, but it is rooted in supernatural wonder. Saints, angels, prayers, and—in the case of the blessed, like Jericho and Venus—astounding rituals. Ever since the Deragon Dynasty superseded the former era, our present circumstances have intertwined well with the history of the past. Urovia came into existence as a result of liberation from faithless trust in deities of fallen empires, but it came into *power* as a result of divine retribution.

My family's armies sacked the once formidable Mosacian Empire just days after I was born. They struck Sevensberg Palace—once a pinnacle of power and domination—and according to record, the place caved in like a house of cards. When the people saw that their stronghold had been toppled, very few took the opportunity to be defiant against the Hive and die for a nation that had antagonized their allies for several, bitter years. That doesn't mean that there weren't *any* Mosacian loyalists, because there were definitely a fair share of them—as proven by my current capture—but Venus in particular didn't bat an eye at their fury. She and Jericho shut them up swiftly . . . and eternally.

Where they did show sympathy, however, was in allowing the collected territories to continue their preferred religious practices—although even I am inclined to believe that the decision wasn't a kindness. Rather, it was a sleight of hand, a way to gatekeep the supernatural beauty of sainthood, and a treasure only Urovia would get to inherit.

It brings a tinge of sadness to my voice as I finally say, "You're a foreigner."

Madman scoffs. "Yet, you say the word without blatant aversion."

"Does that *upset* you?"

"You're just so—" He stops, shaking his head in frustration. "*Not* them. You were raised by a married couple that wiped out an entire empire and collected its smaller countries like children's figurines. You lived in a golden prison that taught you to be *heartless*, and yet—"

"And yet what?" Nevermind that he just insulted my home by calling it a prison.

Madman works his jaw. "You traded your life for their *filth* to live on."

I try to keep the words from sinking in too deep, but my first instinct is to retaliate. "Well, you would've killed me if I denied you, so it's not like I had many options."

The statement rattles him, and with a huff, he abandons his spot along the ship's steering wheel. Boots clicking as he stomps towards me, I don't have time to apologize or make a break for it before he sweeps me into his arms, trapping me in what should be an embrace but feels more like a constricting cage.

Then, he reaches into his cloak for the weapon he killed Ardian with.

I scream, the sound shrill and unlike anything else I've ever produced, but Madman doesn't bother smothering the sound. We're too far from shore to attract any attention other than whatever fish bob towards the surface of the Damocles Sea.

Held tight against his front, my lips tremble as he presses the weapon against my temple. The metal is cold and heavy against the skin there, and I swallow hard as Madman's mouth careens towards the other side of my face.

"Broadcove Castle is protected by hundreds of guards, settled along a coastline safeguarded by fleets of warships, and nobody's dared to attack their lands since the Hive swarmed Mosacia. The last thing on the king's and queen's mind would be possessing a handgun," he whispers shrewdly, his smile tweaking upward in one of the corners. "The enemy they're *expecting* is a massive army, not a lone vigilante in a mask."

The words are uttered humorously, and the message is clear— he is *not* the good guy. I knew as much when he crept in through my mirror.

"But between me and you, angel, you should trust me when I say that I don't plan on killing you. Not now. Not ever."

The small mechanism clenched in his hand did such unforgivable damage, and yet, Madman holds it with effortlessness. The obsidian gleam of it unsettles something deep in my core, and the featherlight touch of his fingertips grazes the body of it. "Remind yourself of that when you start to contemplate who you should place your faith in. The people who may attempt to ransom you, the same people who let one man slip through their defenses and steal you away without a scratch . . .

"Or me. The man who could've blown your pretty brains out by now—the man who could've killed you years ago but held off, all because he wanted to know you."

The things he says are sincere, and maybe, in some deranged

way, they are meant to be reassuring. Yet terror chills my blood at the revelations his words provide.

I don't know how, but Madman has been watching me . . .

For *years*.

Dissuading guards, surviving in the catacombs and decoding its labyrinth, and observing the dynamics of the castle's inhabitants. He's spent so long in the shadows, watching and waiting—and now, he intends to take what he wants. To take *me*.

Him taking me alive will not prove to be as merciful as I may have originally thought.

Madman's gun apparently has a name: Whisper.

A particularly moronic name for a weapon that nearly shattered my eardrums.

Though Madman essentially threatened me at gunpoint, he takes the time to show me exactly how Whisper works. Dutifully, he unloads and reloads the chamber, shows me how to hold it for maximum stability, and I try not to think of the way sparks go off beneath my skin as his gloved hands guide my fingers over the lines of the pistol. If only to escape the sensation, I squeak out a lie that comes out as, "I'm quite tired," and he casually re-holsters his gun.

Madman heads for a lockbox stored near the wheel, and after keying it open, reveals a meager supply of crackers, some sort of meat wrap, and a tin of soup. "It's all yours," he says gruffly, even though he passes me the objects without any hostility.

I nod graciously towards him, but I politely pass on the wrap. The slight rocking of the boat on water, not to mention all the events of today, have started to take their toll on me—and it looks like Madman can see it on me. He pushes the wrap back towards me. "You need to eat."

"I ate at the Feast," I say, but I realize it's a lie. I sang during supper.

"Pandora."

"No, thank you. You eat. I'd prefer not to deal with you when *you* are hungry."

His smirk reappears. "Was that a joke?"

Unsure if I've offended him, or worse, endeared myself further, I make myself busy by giving in to my secret hunger. I drink the soup like water, not caring about any obnoxious slurping sounds I make as I gulp down the broth, or the unladylike way my jaw works to nibble at the stray noodles and cut up carrots. Once that's gone, I choke down a few crackers. "Happy?"

The ship bobs along a stray wave, and on cue, Madman hands me a steel cup. He must have pulled it from the lockbox when I was shoveling the soup into my mouth. "This should settle your stomach."

As I tilt the cup upwards, consuming the herbal mixture slower than the soup, I catch the first hints of sunrise in its reflection. The dark indigo dims into something warmer, something new. Halfway towards the base of the cup, I realize that Madman is right. It *is* helping my stomach—soothing the unease there in a way that makes the rest of my body feel balanced and loose. And alarmingly fast, at that . . .

Just as the warmth of my drink begins to race through my veins so that I feel it through my fingers, I hear Madman tell me, his voice perfectly calm, "We need to get you out of your dress."

His words set fire to my brain. "Like hell *we* do," I try and argue. But as I hear the words disjointedly fall out of me, I stare into the tin cup like it bit me. "You coward. You *poisoned* me?"

His tone doesn't sharpen, even as spit flies off the end of my bottom lip and lands on the hard boning of his mask. "I only gave you a tonic, angel."

"*Don't* call me 'angel' right now."

"You won't die, you'll just sleep through your seasickness—"

"I didn't ask you to give me anything," I snarl.

"It's fast-acting." He ignores my interruption outright. "So unless you want to sleep in that uncomfortable, purple monstrosity, you should let me help you into some normal clothes."

My eyes turn glassy. "You think my dress is ugly?"

Madman huffs, placing a hand to his concealed forehead. There's an argument festering beneath his stormy eyes, but he wards it off, his voice guttural as he tells me, "Turn around."

"*No.*" The word is vile on my tongue.

"I get it. You don't trust me yet. It's why you haven't let yourself sleep, because you think I'm going to kill you the minute you let your guard down. But I know you're exhausted and nauseous . . . and scared," he adds for good measure.

All I can do in response is pout because it's the truth. Yes, I took his outstretched hand, and I went to him willingly, but each passing second with him, I wonder how deeply I've doomed myself. Even if he has no intention of hurting me physically, my gut instinct is sounding silent alarms. And yet, there's no way to flee. No point in fighting. I'm simply frozen in fear unlike any I've ever experienced.

"So let's get this over with before I have to strip you down unconscious. Turn. Around."

Against my better judgment, I do, fighting the sudden sinking weight of my eyelids and the terrifying realization that him helping me out of my clothes doesn't scare me half as badly as it should.

His fingers work against the few buttons along the top of my dress's keyhole cutout, and when they split apart, I shiver at the touch of his leather gloves coasting towards the zipper at the small of my back. I start to stumble over myself, and Madman steadies one hand where the fabric starts, the other higher up on my bare back.

"I've got you," he whispers, lowering the zipper to the notch. Gently, he situates me on the ground, propping me up against the mast so that I'm sitting up. "Keep your eyes open."

Dashing for the lockbox once more, Madman yanks out a spare set of clothing, which only consists of an oversized shirt. When he returns, eyes wide and hands steady, I'm at least grateful that it's soft. It's enough of a distraction to keep my mind from dwelling too long on the fact that Madman's weaving my arms out of the dress fabric and easing the shirt over my head before pulling me out of the gown entirely. I'm exposed for all of two seconds before Madman yanks the shirt fully over my bare flesh. "Arms up," he prompts.

Pathetically, I reach up towards him like a child longing for parental comfort, and he lifts me from the floor. His arm captures the underside of my knees, the other idly stroking my back, and damn me for wanting to know what his bare hands would feel like as opposed to his gloves.

"You can rest now," he tells me.

A fraction of my will still clings to reality, fighting against the sleeping tonic. I don't want to descend into the blackness, unsure of how long I'll be under. "Give me something . . . to dream about."

Madman sighs, the sound warm and not at all like anything I expected from him. My lashes drift towards the skin beneath my eyes and my head lulls towards the crook of his neck.

"We are not as different as you think . . ."

Only his words aren't spoken.

They're *sung*—all in the loveliest baritone that has ever graced my ears.

7
Pandora

Madman is nowhere to be found when I wake, but judging by the steadiness in my head and stomach, we're no longer at sea.

The room has a distinct smell that I can't place, like there is a vague presence of unknown chemicals, and a steady dripping noise sounds off from somewhere in the hall. Another passing glance around the room reveals that the only light source in sight is a rusted lantern, the flame within slowly dwindling. The bed I'm lying on is no more than a flimsy cot, and the walls caging me in are made of aged stone.

"Madman?" I find myself calling out, though the sound of his name is only whispered.

I almost expect him to be sitting in the shadowy corner of my room—which, come to think of it, feels akin to a prison cell. No furniture, no windows, no way out. I'm entirely alone, shivering at the sudden realization that the cot I wound up in did not come with a blanket to keep me warm. Or a pillow, for that matter.

Yet the tonic Madman gave me worked like magic. Near dreamless sleep took hold of my faculties and carried me through a river of beautiful, fragmented thoughts—Madman's confession of how long he'd been watching me, the piercing gray of his wary eyes, his *voice*. Most of what kept me company in that unconscious realm was the sound of our voices intertwined in a strange duet. A collage of minor-keyed melodies that never sounded quite right when I would perform them solo suddenly made perfect sense with his harmony coursing beneath. Flashes of memories crept over me, too. The voice that called for my encore at Queen's Feast. The lilting voice that drifted into my mind while I warmed up in my rooms.

It was *him*.

And I have a sinking feeling that countless other moments throughout my life have been observed in secret by Madman—far more intimate ones than those that I spent making music.

A knock sounds at the door, and my heartrate gallops on instinct.

Considering Madman is the only soul I know within a reach of hundreds of miles, the last figure I expect to walk into my cell is a *woman*. A fair and lovely one at that, with chestnut hair slowly fading to fine silver tied in a knot at the base of her neck. Crow's feet frame soft, brown eyes—cueing me in on the fact that her life has been either consumed with smiles or filled with concern—and she startles when she finds me clutching myself on the cot.

"You poor thing!" she gasps. "How long have you been here?"

"Not long," I answer, even though I have no concept of time regarding how long the tonic transpired. "I just . . ." *don't know where I am, or what time it is or how far from home I am.*

"I understand," she says reassuringly. However, her eyes glimmer with a similar sentiment of unease. "Still, I must confess,

I'm rather confused. No one forewarned me that I might stumble upon . . . well, *you*. Or anyone else for that matter."

I'm not sure how to respond to that. "How did I get here?"

Her bright disposition falters. "I'm afraid I don't know, dear. Worse, I doubt the master knows you're here either."

The use of *master* makes me feel queasy. "You're not . . . his slave, are you?"

"Heavens, no!" she exclaims. "I simply help tend to all those who occupy Andromeda House. I'm Maia, but with the estate bearing my family name, most people call me Andie."

As kind as Andie proves to be, I do not extend my hand in greeting, still shaken up by my surroundings. "I'm Pandora. It's nice to meet you."

"What a lovely name!"

"Thank you. My aunt named me, but my mother adored it."

"Your aunt must be fond of the history behind it." Andie sighs sweetly.

I try not to let my blatant confusion show. "The history?"

"Yes, dear. The maiden Pandora and her ill-fated box!"

I've never heard of another Pandora in my life. Its uniqueness always made me stand out, and it carried an unknown elegance when people would reference my future reign. But the fact that there's a Pandora who stands as a prominent historical figure outside of Urovia . . . I'm intrigued, as well as inclined to ask for the full story.

"Is she still alive today?"

Andie laughs at that, the sound deep and hard to overcome before she says, "Is she *alive*? You must be pulling my leg right now—of course not! Pandora lived hundreds, if not thousands, of years ago. Gods above, had I known any better I'd say you sounded—"

She stops mid-phrase, as if the air gets ripped from her lungs. The hand she raises over her lips trembles slightly.

"Andie?" I ask, unsettled by her fearful gaze and trembling hands.

Urovian, she didn't say. *I'd say you sounded* Urovian.

And that's when Andie starts to look at me—*really* look at me. I see her assess the shape of my eyes, the tone of my skin. I see the way her eyes track the length of my limbs and how she mentally replays whatever compartmentalized knowledge she has about me in the few moments I've gotten to know her—and I dread it. The emotion takes over me like an unrelenting itch, and in efforts to keep the silence from becoming downright unbearable, I try to change the subject.

"I still don't understand why the master of the house wouldn't inform you about my presence after going to the trouble of bringing me here."

Obviously, I seem to have said the wrong thing. Again.

"I can assure you, Kit has not left the estate in four days. In fact, he's—"

"Kit?"

Andie stops moving altogether, catching her breath and smothering whatever drawn out explanation she was about to give me.

"Is that his real name?"

She stares at me in utter bewilderment. "*Whose* name?"

"Madman's," I reply, wondering if the woman standing before me has a screw loose. I heave a sigh and cast out my hands in pent up aggravation. They slap against my bare thighs. "What is going on? Am I missing something here?"

"Am *I*?" Andie returns, raising her voice ever so slightly. "Who *are* you? How do you not know the stories behind your namesake?

53

And who is *Madman?*"

Oh shit.

Madman is not the Master of Andromeda House. He's not even a *member* of it.

I am utterly alone, and, given the look of grave understanding on her face, at her mercy.

"I must alert Kit of your presence," she says quietly, regretfully.

"No . . ." I begin, and in a flash of movement, Andie bolts from the room, leaving the door wide open as she disappears. "No! *Please!*" I scream. "Madman promised he wouldn't hurt me!"

Deafening silence.

I'm a fool. Of course I shouldn't have trusted a *masked assassin* that told me his original intentions were to murder my aunt. I shouldn't have banked my odds for survival on nothing more than his word. I shouldn't have taken his hand or kept quiet or, hell, even kicked Heath out of my rooms to begin with.

In this moment of complete panic and desperation, I start to think that I should've let that guard take my virginity, because at least he wouldn't have taken my life.

Oh Saints, now I'm *really* crying. The ugly kind that even the prettiest of women cannot pull off. I'm mouth breathing, and I can feel the snot building up in my nose before it loosens from the center of my head. Spit gathers in my mouth. I'm about to claw at the concrete to feel physical pain more tangible than the trepidation in my soul until footsteps sound from down the hall.

I close my mouth, crying in petrified silence, my head bowed towards the floor.

From his shoes alone, I know for certain that my cries for Madman were in vain—that the master of Andromeda House stands above me, now.

"Well, I'll be damned," he muses. "You're not some babbling, stranded damsel. You're a *Deragon*."

The way his words carry an air of wrath only magnifies my distress. But I dare a glance upwards, tears drenching my face, and my heart stops beating. Instantly, I begin to understand why Madman urged me to trust him.

Because I look in *this* man's eyes, and all I see is hatred.

8
Pandora

Kit Andromeda is not the looming man of power and punishment his title made me picture him as. Chestnut hair flows in waves just short of his shoulders, slightly damp, as if freshly bathed and slowly drying. Muted green eyes meet my own, and they possess a sort of coldness that makes my posture straighten from where I'm sprawled out on the ground. Looking at him makes me feel brittle, reminding me that I'm only wearing a shirt, and I quickly cross my legs in a way that keeps me modest.

He notes the movement and quickly turns to Andie. "See to it that suitable clothes are provided for our *guest*," he instructs, and the use of the more hospitable term for prisoner does not go overlooked on my end. "And ready her a room on the first floor."

"Of course." Andie stands behind him and retreats without another word, her head down and her steps focused.

Kit wastes no time with introductions. "Dry your tears." He tosses me a handkerchief he kept stashed away in his pockets. "I'm not going to kill you."

"The last guy said the same thing," I quip, but accept the handkerchief, nonetheless. I dab at the underside of my eyes, embarrassed by how puffy and pathetic I probably look. "Thanks," I manage to bid in return.

"I am, however, entitled to ask you a few questions surrounding your arrival."

"Considering you're *housing* me, I'd say my answers are the bare minimum of what you're entitled to."

My reply makes him flinch, but only for a moment, like some unintended insinuation is a slap in the face to his character. "Please, sit," he offers, gesturing once more to my bare cot. I obey, soundless in steps and in words. When I look up at him again, I see that Andie has returned with a dark robe.

"I fetched this from my personal wardrobe," she shares, handing me the garment. The material is plush and comforting to the touch, and as I slip into it, the length of it surpassing my kneecaps to where I feel properly concealed, I shut my eyes and breathe in the scent of it. All it's missing is Mother's perfume for me to convince myself that I'm back in Broadcove, cradled in one of her mending embraces. The thought makes my eyes sting with tears.

"I shall go into town today and gather more," she continues. "What do you require for her?"

"Functional houseware," he replies. "A few pairs of slippers, and anything you think would be suitable to tend to her hair care. That will be all, Andie."

She saunters off without another word, and when the door shuts behind her, I cower deeper within the robe she brought me. "As I was saying," Kit continues, leaning his body against the wall and casually crossing his feet at the ankles. "Your presence here at Andromeda House is rather unexpected. I'd appreciate it if you could tell me a bit about how you got here."

I've never been a convincing liar, but a voice in my head advises me to tell limited truths. Even though I cannot clearly detect if it's my own voice or Madman's, I choose to heed its intrinsic warning.

"I was celebrating Queen's Feast with my family," I begin, knowing the event has been widely gossiped about through all territories. "When I was alone, I encountered a threat against my family, and I chose to try and cut a deal with it rather than fight back. As you can tell, I'm not exactly in fighting shape."

In all actuality, that ending remark may be the biggest lie of the entire statement. I've been extensively trained on how to defend myself from an attacker. I just happen to avoid any instances of harming people until it becomes absolutely unavoidable. But Kit doesn't need to know that.

"Andie told me you mentioned a very peculiar name."

Madman.

"The man I encountered," I try to explain. "I didn't know his name. But he seemed crazed. The name you heard me say was nothing more than an insult."

"I have it on good authority, princess, that your aunt is the reason for a lot of misery. Mine more so than most. And that name you gave her was, indeed, a name. A very distinct, infamous name."

I gulp, hoping the movement isn't too loud or too obvious for him to pick up on.

"But you knew that already, didn't you?"

"Only because he insisted that I address him by the identifier. What's it to you anyways?"

His smile takes on a vicious glint. "I hired him."

The revelation stuns me to my very core.

I came here to kill a queen, Madman had said. And then, he forsook his orders, his *bound duty,* and took me captive instead.

Oh, Kit Andromeda *definitely* hates my guts. He probably wants me dead, too.

"You see," he says, pacing about the room, "Madman's a bit of a legend here on the Isle."

"The Isle?"

Kit catches his mistake too late. "Yes, the Isle. I suppose I can tell you that. After all, it's not like you have any way to signal for help."

He grins at the power he holds, continuing with his pacing. I try not to sneer at him as he does. "As I was saying, most people believe Madman to be the subject of recent, eerie fables. But I know otherwise, because Madman was *unmistakably* real . . . and I experienced him firsthand when he murdered my brother, Cato."

The memory of him firing Whisper brands itself into my mind.

"It was a long time ago," Kit quickly cuts in, not wanting any part of my pity. "You needn't fuss over someone you never knew. Really, I only mention it to help illustrate my fascination with man. I knew he wasn't some scary story, which meant, if I could corner him, he'd do anything I pleased to go free. And I knew exactly what I wanted from his . . . services. I'll spare you the bloody details of how I ensnared him. All that matters is that he owed me a life debt—and the way we'd be even was if he brought back Venus Deragon's head on a spike so not even her lover could hold onto it."

Rage heats my blood, coloring my cheeks. I knew Venus was not well-liked beyond Urovia's borders, and Queen's Feast certainly put a target on her back, but to have this otherwise hospitable man go to such great lengths to have her *killed?*

Something didn't sit right with me.

And yet, my knee-jerk response to the man is to correct him. "Her husband."

Kit's devious smile returns, slowly but surely. "What's that, princess?"

"Her. *Husband*," I enunciate. "Jericho and Venus have been married for twenty years."

Kit's returning expression is laced with disgust. "I meant what I said before, though. I am not going to kill you. I'm just going to use you."

"Charming."

"If Madman has gone back on his word, I'll have to take matters into my own hands. And for now, that means holding you for ransom. Get comfortable, princess, because until your aunt and uncle deem your life more valuable than their own, you're stuck here. With me."

Truth be told, it's not his tone of voice or the satisfied gleam of his eye that makes defeat wash through me like a tidal wave. It's the fact that Kit believes it won't take time for Venus to cave. But I know the wretched truth.

No one is coming for me.

Because as wonderful of an uncle as Jericho has been to me, he would never trade Venus for *anyone*. Not even for his heir.

Kit drinks in my silence, and then, in a sudden change of character, he crouches down to my level where I sit perched on the cot. Nothing threatening remains in his gaze or his stature— only honesty. "Do forgive my temper. You ought to understand, though. After all, I asked for your aunt's severed head, and instead, Madman goes back on his word and brings me you . . . *alive*."

I cross my arms against my chest. "Would my corpse have smoothed things over better?"

Kit laughs, and against all odds, the sound endears him to me. "I suppose we have plenty of time to uncover the answer to that, now. Don't you agree?"

The little voice in my head returns, only this time I know exactly who's speaking to me. Not only does it sound like Madman, but its message is incessant, as if he felt the way my body reacted when Kit chuckled at me.

Don't trust him. Don't trust him. Don't trust him. Don't trust him. Don't trust him. Don't trust him. Don't trust him. Don't trust him.

I spend the next hour, while Andie readies my room on the first floor, wondering whose danger Madman's voice is aiming to ward off: mine or his own.

It could go either way. His self-imposed moniker, the way he slaughtered Ardian without even blinking, and his deviation from orders proves that Madman is inherently selfish. He doesn't make a strong case for himself regarding honor or keeping his word. Or maybe that's just in Kit's case.

I'd almost forgotten about the way Kit conveniently skirted around just *how* he had gotten Madman to agree to his terms in the first place. He'd even used the term *corner.*

It draws my focus to Madman's mask.

I don't get to simmer on the thought long enough, though. Not before Lady Andromeda returns and waves me over to her. "I've got warm stew all set up for you in your room if you're ready."

To settle down somewhere with a window and a mattress? By all means.

As we ascend a short flight of stairs onto the main floor, she gives me a quick run-down of the house. According to Andie, the space I woke up in wasn't a holding cell, but rather a storm shelter.

Being this close to the coastline meant that thunderstorms proved to be more volatile than for those further inland. And when I then follow up by asking why my guest room lies on the first floor as opposed to the second, she quiets for a moment before answering with, "The master suite resides on floor two, and from what he implied, the two of you didn't exactly start off on the right foot."

I don't attempt to rebuttal, but it still gets me to thinking. "I know you can't tell me where the Isle is located in relation to back home, but may I ask where you hail from?"

When the word *Mosacia* leaves her lips, it doesn't surprise me in the least. "Which part?" I run through all I can recall from what Jericho taught me regarding their demographics.

The eastern hemisphere was a melting pot. You could knock on every door of a single neighborhood, and each family unit would have something different going on. Unique occupations, differing family types, varying languages—no doubt due to how many smaller nations were clustered together in one of Mosacia's previous sweeps of ownership. I never told anyone, least of all my aunt and uncle, but I always wanted to know what it was like: living in a place where you'd never run out of things to learn about your next-door neighbor. A castle only feels so big for so long, and after twenty years, no amount of gold on the walls could keep my mind from wondering if I had just been existing in a gilded bird cage.

Towards the center of Mosacia, all of its citizens existed peacefully, circled around an ancient, famed shrine that people would make pilgrimages to. No one ever told me what the shrine held, nor what it honored, but I presumed it had something to do with the deities they placed their faith in. Jericho never educated me on any of them save for the one he first mistook his wife's namesake for. Not much commotion came out of the land-locked nations. They certainly would have raised their fists at Urovia had we stripped them of the sacred shrine, but since we left it untouched, they pretty much complied to the turnover of power in silence.

Out west, a stronghold of Urovian soldiers permanently resettled to keep the continent in line and under Deragon Dynasty regulations. Their written communications to Broadcove Castle were transcriptions I was taught from a young age to digest quickly and comprehend soundly. One dispatch I vividly remember studying from their camp several years back came with the strangest inscription. *Dirtied Water*, it had read. I didn't understand it at the time, given the ledger reported on a Urovian guard and his wife welcoming a newborn son into the world, but I do, now.

His wife was Mosacian, which meant this was the first instance where a bloodline from our home country had been *diluted*. It makes my chest ache at the memory of Madman pointing out the way his nationality never fazed me.

And along the westernmost coastline, the once mighty Sevensberg Palace collected dust. A reminder to all Mosacian inhabitants that even the most powerful had not been immune to Venus and Jericho Deragon.

I'd seen photographs of it before, and in its heyday, the palace was downright otherworldly. Milky-white spires reached towards the sky as if trying to grasp onto their gods. Inside, grand, tiled floors and sweeping windows shed sunlight onto a porcelain dreamscape with endless rooms and finely manicured gardens. I'd have considered the palace to be an almost romantic setting had time not reduced it to a pile of bones.

Andie's somber expression brings me back to the Isle. "I'd prefer not to dwell on the past. Andromeda House is my home now."

"I understand," I say quietly, feeling sorry for offending her. "What about Kit?"

"He's never left Isle," she returns gently. "And neither have I since we came upon this estate. It's a haven for me and my son."

Son, I realize.

Lady Andromeda is Kit's *mother*.

They don't bear too much of a resemblance, though. Then again, it takes two to create new life, so perhaps Kit bears the likeness of his father—who also remains a mystery. The longer I'm here, the more confused I become, and the feeling only grows as we pass over a room I mistake for the one she's prepared for me.

Andie catches my change of pace and turns her head sidelong to look back at me. "I had a daughter once, too," she murmurs. "Her room is likely the nicest one on the first floor, but I cannot bear to stow away her things and empty out her room. Forgive me."

"There's nothing to forgive," I tell her, truly meaning it.

Then, Andie leads me into my guest room. Dull, periwinkle walls with bleak curtains bid me a dismal sort of welcome, but the bed proves to be larger than I expected, dark quilts coating the mattress beneath in layered warmth. Unlike my suites back home, where pillows clutter the surface of my bed, only four rest on the one I'm offered here.

"It's nothing fit for a Urovian Princess," Andie says as a means of an apology. "But I hope it shall suffice."

"Kit has every reason to keep me jailed in the storm cellar," I acknowledge, wondering if he is still debating on doing so from wherever he wandered off to. "This is a kindness. Thank you, Andie."

It truly is. The room may seem cold and hollow in many ways, but along the wall, there's an oval window that overlooks the water. The waves along the Damocles rush against the shoreline and retreat, the moon casting glittering ripples of light over the dark waters, and for a singular moment in time since leaving Broadcove, a calmness settles over me. The sound of the crashing surf soothes something in my aching soul, as does Andie's silent departure as I tuck myself underneath the covers.

But I know, the minute I'm alone, it's not enough to lull me to sleep.

After dozing for Saints knows how long thanks to the tonic I drank, I'm not even remotely tired. The sun's far-away glow against the crescent moon above is keeping me up, along with my stirring heart and sudden homesickness. The things I'd give to go back in time and—if not escape this strange fate—tell my mother I loved her one last time . . .

The memory of her face, of her words as she told me I was the great love of her life—it all threatens to shred me from the inside out.

I've cried myself to sleep before, mostly due to the personal despondency of feeling untouchable, to the stress of lessons with my aunt and uncle, where they would hound me about how I ought to treat any traitors of the crown, or how I ought to garner vital information out of the strongest of war captives.

But now, *I* am the war captive. I'm boarded up in a foreign land I don't know the name of, brought here on the whims of a creature that killed someone I once saw as a grandfather, and am now being held here as bait. There's no other way around it. Here in the darkness of Andromeda House, my every breath is dependent upon Kit's kindness towards me or the timing of Venus and Jericho's ransom. My life is no longer my own.

And the devastation of it is swallowing me whole.

"Oh, angel . . ." a familiar voice whisper-sings in the corners of my mind.

I sit up in bed fast enough to dizzy my head. Stars briefly flicker over my eyes, but once they dissipate, I prepare to set my bare feet onto the cold, paneled floors. But I pause, waiting for another prompting, for the only semblance of optimism I have left to reach me once again.

The last thing I remember him saying to me was a song. A sacred truth.

We are not as different as you think.

I must be downright senseless to seek hope and deeper meaning in Madman's parting phrase. And yet, here I am, searching for his cloaked frame amongst the shadows of my room. Waiting for his pleasing baritone to drift in and guide me towards him—because the minute I heard him sing, I feared the possibility of what exists for certain now.

I don't just *want* to trust him—I *do*.

Because where there is music, there is soul, and I am determined to uncover the man beneath this musical monster.

"Where are you?" I ask in return, the words so quiet I barely feel them in my throat.

"In the forefront of your mind, it seems."

I'm too inconsolable to take offense to the pleasure lingering in his statement.

"Please," I breathe, shutting my eyes in an attempt to keep the tears trapped beneath my eyes. "I need . . ."

"Tell me," he urges, all seriousness, now, and alarmingly closer to me than moments ago.

I open my eyes in time to see him standing at the edge of my bed. Same black cloak, same skeleton mask, same full mouth surrounded by dark stubble. Madman's gaze is brutal and wary, yet I return it with an undiscovered intensity of my own.

"I need something that will keep me from breaking," I finally confess. "I need _you_."

I may as well have ripped his mask off his face and struck him.

"You don't mean that," he insists, straight-faced and stoically still before me.

"I don't know _how_ I mean it. Whether it be your voice or your promises or your presence I need—I'm still not sure. But I want to be, because all I know is that I cannot find peace apart from you," I rasp, realizing how chilling the truth of this conversation really is. "I hear your voice in my head, Madman. You're the only one I trust."

The final phrase of my helpless declaration sounds as desperate aloud as it does in my mind, and I swallow hard hearing it back. It hangs in the air overhead, suffocating me.

But just before I consider turning him away completely— hastily redacting the reality of my current circumstances— Madman extends his hand once more to me. For the first time, his startling exterior and the menacing power in how he carries himself softens, fading into something beautifully human. The gesture is a kindness I know shouldn't be afforded to me.

Knowing that, I accept it in a heartbeat, unafraid of whatever follows.

Madman helps me out of bed. And then, his voice impossibly gritty, he tells me, "Get on your knees."

Panicked exhilaration whirls to life within my core, my brain interpreting the command as a seductive endeavor. But seconds later, I watch as Madman lowers himself at my side, and I follow suit. Privately embarrassed by the trajectory my thoughts took, I wait for what he needs from me next.

"All fours, now," he says.

Saints, my mind is filthy. His instructions do not come across entirely pure of heart, though.

I mirror his movements, braced on the ground before the left side of the bed. Then, he cranes his head to look at me. "Silence is the only way we're making it out of here," he whispers. I nod my compliance, drawing a responding smile across his exposed lips—one that I find myself committing to memory.

And then, Madman draws the bed skirt away from its elevated frame, revealing a hole hollowed out in the floor beneath my bed.

PART II
NOCTURNE

9
Pandora

J ust when Andromeda House couldn't possibly have gotten more peculiar, Madman proves me *very* wrong.

He crawls beneath the bed frame, his torso dragging across the floor, and rather than nosediving into the darkness, he careens backwards so that his feet dangle forward, into the drop-off. Carefully, he lowers himself inside.

"There's a set of stairs underneath," he whispers. "Keep your steps light, or he'll wake up."

It's not that I'm scared of Kit. It's more so that we're about to venture off to Madman's best-kept secret—and Kit might just kill us both if he uncovers it in his own home.

A week ago, I never would have dreamt up a universe where I'd be out of Urovia, let alone clambering towards a hidden vault in enemy territory alongside a man who abducted me. I bet the Saints themselves are shaking their heads at the sight, but it doesn't matter. My gut tells me following Madman into the darkness below is a fate more favorable than staring aimlessly out the window and waiting for sleep . . . somehow.

Sliding along the floor as seamlessly as I can manage, I drape my legs out in front of me and my feet find purchase on a ledge, then another one a few inches lower. I slink into the inky depths behind Madman, the last of the moonlight outside catching on the upper rim of his mask along his forehead. It gets me thinking about what Madman may look like beneath his disguise. Thick brows or thin? Strong nose or narrow? Does he have crease lines from his years of anger? Is his face soft to the touch?

While caught up in the last question, I push past more than one step and begin to tumble. I smack hard against a wall, coming to a stop, and as I try to use the stiff surface as leverage to sit upright, the wall turns out to be Madman himself. He picks me up off the ground despite not being able to see his own hand in front of his face, and files down the final five or so steps needed to get on solid ground.

"This way," he instructs quietly, dutifully.

Together, we hang a right towards what I anticipate being a labyrinthine path, much like the tunnels beneath Broadcove. Instead, I hear him faintly twist the iron knob of a door somewhere in front of us, and at the first crack of light shining through from the other side, my blood thrums with anticipation.

A singular, blue dock light casts a mystical hue over the cave we drift into, and a few yards away, the shadowy path fades down into the sea. Floating on top of the dark waters, however, lies a boat with abstract etchings and a tall, black oar.

"All aboard," Madman says.

"Last time I agreed to get on a boat with you—"

"If you're about to finish that sentence how I think you're going to, let me stop you right now. Why don't we save ourselves the bickering and you just get in."

Had he not cracked a small smile after the fact, I probably would've balked at the statement. But I humor him, letting Madman guide me to the ledge so that I can avoid the splashing waves as I step inside. I only recognize the way his gloved hands warm my fingers after he releases them, and I hide the wince that threatens to show across my face. A plush bench awaits me as I sit down fully, sinking into the cushions, and I watch as Madman sweeps his cloak upwards before dropping into the boat himself. The boat rocks for a moment as it registers our combined weight, and Madman takes up the oar.

"Am I allowed to ask you about the secret passage?"

Madman unfurls the rope that keeps the boat tethered to the cave, then casts a confused look in my direction. "Allowed?"

"Lady Andromeda was a bit protective over what answers she gave to my questions. Then again, I suppose she knows as little about this as Kit does."

He studies my face for a minute, as if noticing a hair out of place that I cannot spot myself. Then, he says, "You have free reign to ask me anything you wish to know, but I will only answer with whatever truth I believe serves a purpose."

"Serves a purpose?" I parrot.

Madman continues to chop at the water with the oar, and I feel the late evening wind bring goosebumps along my skin. The lantern at the front of the ship, which I hadn't caught sight of until now, creaks and swings as we cross into the clearing where the current is stronger. "I don't wish to overwhelm you all at once."

The answer feels surface level, and I bite back. "Considering you killed someone in front of me and stole me from my home without the chance to say goodbye to anyone, I'm not exactly inclined to believe you."

"Yet here you are," Madman says, his voice stern. "Alive. In my boat. *Trusting* me."

My gaze tracks the perimeter of Andromeda House as we coast away towards an unknown location. Ivy crawls up the sides of the building, the reflections of overhead stars speckle across the window panes, and not a single light remains lit on either floor. Normally, I'd be consumed by panic—my fear of the dark as irrational as it is unrelenting—but it's starting to feel as though there is a shield of protection around me when daring to remain with darkness himself.

"Yeah," I say under my breath. "Don't make me come to regret it."

The silence is a blissful reprieve, but the noise inside my head returns the moment Madman fastens our vessel to the mounting posts. Countless questions buzz about like unrelenting gnats, and before I go to swat away their invisible presence, I find enough of a voice to ask him, "How did you know?"

"Know what, angel?" he returns casually.

"Where I was," I say. "What I was feeling."

He hops out of the boat with effortless grace, even as the water rocks us off balance and I nearly tumble overboard. Madman catches me in his firm grip, lifting me over the seawater and setting me securely on the stone-paved deck. I nod my thanks, my gaze falling over the secret, subterranean hideaway guarded by another wrought-iron door. *Not ominous at all.*

"The Isle holds more mysteries than the entire continent of Mosacia," Madman says with a particular twinkle in his eye that would normally unsettle me, but in this case, quietly thrills me. "That sort of wonder, though, has the tendency to intimidate newcomers. That, and I knew that the tonic had likely worn off while I was away, and you'd have questions."

I stumble over uneven ground but catch myself before Madman deems it necessary to throw me over his shoulder and carry me the rest of the way. "How did you cross paths with Kit anyway, let alone agree to do his murderous bidding?"

"You're not going to like my answer."

"We're well past whether or not I'll *like* what comes out of your mouth, Madman," I say bitterly. "Not even an hour ago, I up and told you that you were the only one I can remotely put my trust in, so make good on your word and just *tell me*."

Weaker men would recoil from the force of my tone, but not Madman. His mask hides most of the way his face contorts, but the crooked smile below its border tweaks with subdued pride. "I owe him a life debt."

"He mentioned that." He walks us towards the cave's entrance. "You don't mean to tell me that Kit saved your life, though, do you?"

"*No*," Madman barks, insulted by the idea of ever needing *Kit's* salvation. "I consider it a life debt because the only thing that would fully settle the score between him and I would be a life payment—whether by me or by another. He may be the head of a sizable estate, but I have no interest in playing his indentured servant, nor dying. So he named his price—your aunt's proof of death—and I was well on my way to granting him just that."

"Until you found me," I say dismally.

"Precisely. And now that I have chosen to forsake our deal, he *can't* find me."

I know better than to taunt him about why Kit cannot uncover his secret hiding place, to insult him with the assumption that Madman fears a man like Kit. Instead, knowing the grave consequences for his choices, I dare to ask him, "Was it worth it? Was *I* worth it?"

Madman's smile slackens. "More than you know."

My heart awkwardly stirs at the response, and I thank the Saints Madman looks to the door and fumbles with the lock long enough for me to choke down my surprise and the unfamiliar fluttering that starts low in my gut and bleeds upwards. I hear a faint jingle as Madman pockets a single, silver key and pushes the door inwards.

Scattered flecks of golden light float above cylindrical, cream candlesticks, casting an otherworldly, phantasmal sparkle across the inky expanse. The sight steals my breath away the longer I look at it, the rippling water from behind us toying with the remaining shadows within, and Madman leads us inside. I follow with cautious steps, doing my best to smother the urge to bolt from the darkness. He senses it, and he turns to me with a puzzled expression. "You're afraid of the dark."

Bitterness becomes me. "I'm shocked you're only discovering that now."

Madman shrugs. "Too busy memorizing the structure of your face and the sound of your voice to think twice about the fact that you sleep with exactly six candles lit at night."

Yet *that* he remembers.

If Madman has anything more to say, I tune him out, continuing my initial assessment of his mystical lair. The stone slopes upwards, giving way to a lavish bed with dark quilting and black pillows. Hung in a systematic pattern, the dispersed, padded squares along the walls remind me of an insane asylum, yet it softens the hard interior of the space. I'm not sure what to make of that particular choice in decoration at first, but I finally recognize them as acoustic panels when the lighting sways towards the left side of the den.

A gleaming pianoforte with a matching performance stool graces the ground level. The top casing has been propped up at a slant, revealing polished strings that keep the monstrous beauty tuned and up to date. Beyond that, along a higher level of stone shelving, hordes of sheet music and writing utensils litter whatever open space it is afforded. Canisters of black and blue ink sit in neatly arranged rows, waiting to mark up any of the fresh pages with what I now realize are original opuses.

Madman doesn't just sing. He's a *composer*.

"I got something for you, too," he says when he notices my blatant fascination, his gloved hand gently guiding my head towards the right side of his secret hideaway.

Just as I start to register a newfound warmth stirring inside of me at Madman's touch, my eyes behold an exquisite, silver-coated harp.

"Holy *Saints*," I say breathily, a gravitational pull drawing me towards the masterful craftsmanship.

A soft hum of appreciation trickles out of him. "I heard once that learning the harp is like turning the pianoforte on its side, but I never had the chance to see if the rumors held any truth to them. Even so, when I first came upon the harp, I knew that no one ought to try their hand at it before you got to play it for yourself. Not even me."

I creep towards the beautiful instrument, my finger tracing the curvature of the tinted wood in time for him to say, "Will you do me the honor of a song?"

Something about sitting before the strings at Madman's request makes my heart flutter with newfound nerves, far more than I felt before performing at Queen's Feast.

"Do you have any requests?"

"Anything in a minor key that you can sing to."

Due to the influx of inner excitement and slight terror building beneath the surface, I file through my mental repertoire in search of something simplistic. Something I've played hundreds of times before that requires minimal vocal acrobatics. I'm not here to show off—I'm merely here to please him. I settle in along the bench, scooting my way towards the angled body. My left foot settles near the three pedals, fingers hovering over the coiled strings until, finally, I channel enough serenity to begin playing.

The song that first comes to mind is one that has always been a private favorite of mine. I remember the first time I ever heard it. A musician had been singing in the streets when Mother, both of my aunts, and I visited the Makers District a few years back. His cap had been turned upwards to collect any spare coins onlookers would gift him, and while most had continued onwards amidst his performance, the lyrics of what he was singing had struck a chord within me.

I admired you more than your mirror
Looked longingly after you more than the moon
But now the truth of it couldn't be clearer
Love's bruise won't heal over anytime soon

It was such a lilting, melodic pattern, and the conventional rhyme scheme gave each stanza a bitter tinge of sadness. As he plucked his dilapidated guitar, the stranger sang with such soul that I couldn't tell which emotion ruled over him most: heartbreak or all-consuming love.

Purple demeanor, indigo smile
Eyes so lovely they wound

Beautiful misery I'll embrace for a while
'Cause love's bruise won't heal over anytime soon

Lovely as poison flooding my veins
You were a sickness, and I, far from immune
Surely you'll haunt me for all my days
Love's bruise won't heal over anytime soon

I try not to think about it—how it must feel to love someone so much that suffering is bliss, that sickness is comforting. Especially not when the one person I could potentially fixate that idea on is a man whose face I've never seen and whose secrets aren't mine to know.

You could water your flowers with all my tears
I'd sleep in the snow if you asked me to,
I'm bewitched by your memory, and so I fear
Love's bruise won't heal over anytime soon

When Death hovers close, I'll embrace her the way
I used to cling to you
'Til then this heartbreak with me shall stay
For love's bruise won't heal over anytime soon

Slowly, I diminish the lingering sound of the strings, letting their vibrations faintly rumble against my fingertips until they draw to a close. I wait for Madman's response, but nothing returns. I doubted that he'd applaud, but . . . utter silence?

Turning my body from the harp and spinning along the smooth bench, I prepare for whatever horrible expectations I have churning in my head. Criticism I can handle, but if he doesn't say *something* soon, I think I might wilt—

"I could listen to you sing for hours on end."

Madman looks utterly entranced by my performance, even though his eyes still carry that serious, no-nonsense weight to them. Too caught up in making sure I don't stutter or fumble over the compliment, I find myself asking him, "How did you afford all of this?"

"Aren't there more interesting questions swarming in that pretty little head of yours?"

"Oh, plenty. But I want to know. A criminal nomad like yourself likely doesn't have troves of money on your person. So where does it all sit, and where did you get it from?"

He weighs the consequences of telling me the truth about his visible wealth, and as he does, I try to calm the nerves that course through me.

He's killed people. You've seen it happen once before. But that doesn't mean he's some sort of bounty hunter who kills for the highest bidder. If that were the case, he would've killed Venus and Jericho both before circling back to destroy me too.

"Well?" I ask when my inner thoughts begin to get the better of me.

His lips thin into a line. "Inheritance."

The gravelly sound of Madman's voice at the single word tells me not to push further. He's an orphan. He lost someone dear to him, and if the money was all he had to remember them by, he put it to use. Sheltered himself within the monetary memory of their existence.

"I'm sorry," I say quietly. "For what it's worth, I bet they would have found this place as captivating as I do." It's the truth, and I only hope it neutralizes the defeated look in his storm-ridden eyes.

"It doesn't matter what they would've thought," Madman states.

Something tells me that hanging in the air between us are the missing words, *The only opinion that matters to me is yours.*

"Now, let's hear some of those other burning questions, angel," he whispers, beginning to pace about the room. "Go on."

"Despite your limitations on what you allow yourself to answer, you seem rather eager and open to the idea of me getting to know more about you. Why is that? I mean, wouldn't someone who spends his life hiding beneath a mask and going by *Madman* want to remain hidden in the shadows?"

"Not from you."

I fight to ignore the zing of heat that starts to fizzle deep in my core.

"Pandora, I do all this because I want to establish a line of trust between us. You're an outsider here, and I . . . well, I've allowed myself to wind up alone. We need each other. I knew it even before you confessed to it on your part."

We need each other.

Not just me needing him—but him needing me, too.

Then, something dangerous occurs to me. If he's been studying me for Saints know how long, what exactly does his *needs* imply . . . and why am I dying to find out?

"I do trust you," I tell him.

"In part, yes," Madman nitpicks, "but not completely. I think you *want* to trust me, but you're not all the way there, yet."

All I know is that I cannot find peace apart from you. You're the only one I trust.

The admission had burned me like a live flame, and now, Madman has the gall to tell me that I didn't mean the most painful words I've ever choked out. It makes me want to kick in one of the legs on his pianoforte.

"What makes you think that I'm not fully convinced?"

"Because I don't think you have fully come to terms with the fact that your aunt is alive—*you* are alive—because of me."

"Okay, then," I continue, recalling our brief discussion regarding Kit. "Name your price."

"Pardon?"

I try not to smile all giddy at the way my words surprise him. "I'm alive because of you. You said so yourself. So, considering my very existence is in your clutches, that would mean that I owe you a life debt. Correct?"

His eyes tell me yes, but his words . . . "I'm not looking to cash it in."

"And why not?"

"Because you're already here on the isle, angel. You already have no way to get back to your family or call for help, so all I ask of you is that you not torture yourself over it and try and find some semblance of comfort here. From what I saw back in Broadcove Castle, you were never truly relaxed."

His words nail me to the wall.

"Perhaps, being here could be a good thing."

With me, he doesn't need to say for me to understand.

I risk stepping closer to him, and Madman tracks the step intently. "Tell me what it takes, then, for you to believe otherwise. Tell me what it will cost to convince you of my trust."

I faintly see his Adam's apple bob in his throat, the surrounding shadows nearly hiding the movement altogether. I know with absolute certainty that I'm going to deeply regret giving Madman the chance to speak his mind, but I wait for his reply anyways.

He crosses the distance between us, gloved hands slowly tracing the outline of my arms and settling along my ribs. "Tell me what you desire most in this world, and then, instead of running from me and from your answer, I want you to get in my bed," he whispers, now, pointing to the exact spot in reference, "and sleep."

I feel the color leech out of my face, but not necessarily in dread. "Why?"

"Because back on the boat, I had to drug you for you to finally rest. You want to prove that you feel safe with me? Shut your eyes on your own will and trust that you'll wake up unharmed after laying by my side all night."

Maybe it's the emotions I've been wrestling with as of late, but I haven't pictured sleeping with a man as anything other than being physical. So consumed with the idea of passion and romance and tension, I forgot that the quiet moments with someone also exist in bed. Only now that I begin to dwell on it, I wonder if the act of settling in next to him is far more precarious than letting him put his hands on me.

I seem to be asking for trouble because I dare to whisper, "And the other part?"

Madman chortles. "Mere curiosity."

We stand in silence, my eyes unable to meet his own without the strength in my legs depleting. I don't allow myself to second guess his proposition before I stroll towards Madman's bed. He follows, slowly trailing behind me like I've never had my own shadow—like it's always been him.

Already dressed for bed—so desperate to escape my appointed room in Andromeda House that I fled without shoes on—I peel back the quilted comforter, then the sheet. The candlelight casts rippling shadows over Madman's frame, hiding the bare skin that escapes my nightgown as I drape my legs into his bed. I fight the impulse to retract it, to straighten out the soft material and make sure I'm not revealing too much.

But the look on Madman's face is pained. It sucks all the warmth out of the room, and I'd do anything to restore it—including pat the spot beside me, inviting him to my side.

Madman unfastens his cloak, draping it over the pianoforte before removing his boots. He works the laces in a hurry, setting the heavy footwear far away when his feet finally break free. The mattress shifts towards his side when his full weight sinks onto the bed. Over the covers.

I gather my hair, draping it to cover my exposed shoulders and concealing the goosebumps there that rose just from looking at him. I watch Madman's gaze trace the path of one of my curls beneath his mask, and in the stillness between us, I examine the skeletal outline of it. No string circles around his head to keep it secure, which means it must be some kind of mold. Formed to his exact features. Suctioned to his skin.

I contemplate whether it would hurt him if I pried it away.

"What do you desire, angel?" Madman asks me once more.

I don't have to think long and hard about it, but it takes me a minute to steady my voice. "I feel like it alternates between the same two concepts. Some days, I don't want to be their Princess. I just want to be Pandora . . . even if apart from the crown, I don't exactly know who that is. Other days, however," I say, swallowing in an attempt to loosen the knot in my throat, "I start to believe that I could live with all the pressure that being their heir comes with if I was offered the right outlet to decompress."

Madman elicits a soft groan at the implication, and the sound makes the nerves all throughout my body go haywire.

Stay. Strong.

"Unfortunately, that outlet has a high likelihood of landing me in quite a bit of trouble. I'm pathetically romantic, so if my defenses fall and I give in, I'll dissect every part of the encounter in hope of uncovering even a fragment of love. I know that passion can be a worthwhile distraction, but I've never been able to separate the emotions from it. I probably never will. Deep down, I think it's how I cope with the knowledge that people don't seem to understand how to separate the Crown Princess from Pandora."

Madman's voice is raspy when he tells me, "Waiting for love, for the right person, is not such a bad thing."

"Not for any regular person. But it's never been my choice to deem someone worthy enough to love me." I laugh bitterly at the faraway reality. "The *love* that waits for me in Broadcove, if I ever go back there . . . it may not be cold, but it will certainly contain strategy. Even if I grow to love them, the root of their presence in my life will always stem back to the people that plan to pass me their crown. You'd think Venus and Jericho would've allowed me to figure out my love life without their interference knowing how they found their way to each other, but no. I'll live and die by their decisions, and I'll be forced to love by them, too."

I do not know what's worse: the silence that follows, or the prospect of turning to face Madman and finding pity in his eyes.

I almost think I'm imagining things when I hear Madman whisper, "So which is it today?"

"What?"

His tone is gentle. "Which desire holds dominance?"

"There's no need to ask when you already know the answer," I dare to speak into the dark.

I don't need to look at him to know he's smirking. "I can help with that."

Without saying goodnight, I shut my eyes and feign sleep before Madman gets any ideas or I act on my treacherous urges.

10
Pandora

I wake up expecting the familiar darkness of Madman's lair but lurch up in bed at the sight of a window. The same one back in Andromeda House.

A gasp rips out of me, and not long after, frantic footsteps come padding down the hall.

What time was it? Did I startle Andie? And where is—

"Morning, princess," Kit grunts.

In a rush of realization, I'm reminded of the clothing—or lack thereof—on my body right now, and quickly leap out of bed and tear a knitted shawl off its hanger in my armoire. I weave my arms into it, thanking the Saints for not allowing Kit to see me get stuck in the fabric.

"Forgive me," I say anxiously. "I would never intentionally oversleep, nor would I want to disrespect you by not showing face sooner in the day—"

"I'm not concerned about your sleeping habits. That tonic in your system will probably have you out of sorts for the next week or so anyways."

The moment he says so, the weight of whatever measly hours of sleep I got start to flood my system. My limbs ache, but nowhere near to the extent my eyes do. Daylight or not, if Kit left the room, it would likely take me no more than three minutes to fall back to sleep. But he looks far from finished, inching further into the room. "Can I . . . help you with something?"

He sucks on the inside of his cheek for a moment before settling an internal argument by brandishing a pocketknife. "Yes. I need your blood."

"Come again?" I say as mild-mannered as humanly possible.

Next, Kit reaches for something inside his jacket, revealing a rolled-up piece of parchment tied off by a blue ribbon so dark it looks black. He unfurls the page, and the split-second glimpse I have at the text tells me that its message is no larger than two, brief paragraphs.

"I'm sending your family a message. It seems your captor did an extraordinary job at extracting you to where not a trace of you was left to be discovered. I need to alert them that you're still alive."

I wonder if my mother has already assumed the worst and begun grieving me.

"Give me your hand," he orders.

"Like hell."

Kit exhales in a way that hints at exhaustion. "Princess, I need you to cooperate with me."

"How do I know you won't slit my throat if I step closer?"

The question falls out of me on instinct, and the words may as well have struck Kit Andromeda upside the face.

An expression of clear insult replaces any previous congeniality. "I'm appalled that you assume so low of my character." He extends the knife to me, and in the same second that I transfer it into my full possession, Kit unfurls the note once more. "Have it your way, but if you have any wish to see your family again, you'll *bleed.*"

The way Kit's voice raises doesn't intimidate me like it should. There were times when Jericho spoke softer than that and I felt genuinely sick with dread. Kit thinks that because he owns a nice estate, he owns me. I only decide to play along for the sake of not setting off any alarms.

Angling the pocketknife over the heel of my palm, I look down in time to see the beginnings of the ransom letter, continuing across the page line by line. The text makes my stomach clench, and while I expect Kit to yank the letter away from my sight, he doesn't move. No, he *lets* me trace each traitorous letter—lets me fully assess the vivid threat on my life and the implicit threat on theirs.

I eventually slice the blade across my skin to help dampen the pain in my chest.

My senses burn and tingle as Kit takes up my bleeding hand and squeezes it tight, welling more of it to the surface before smearing the open wound across the page. He dots it in other sporadic spots for good measure, smiling once he is satisfied with his handiwork. "I'll have this sent off momentarily."

Kit turns to leave, and I mouth the word *prick* when his back is turned. Assuming he's left me to my own devices, I check up on the cut I made, smoothing out the reforming drop with the pad of my other fingertips. I look up, however, and see that Kit has paused just shy of the hall, his hand braced against the doorframe.

"All morning," he says, his tone shifting into something tender, something cautious, "I felt as though I was a bit harsh yesterday. You had no control over your presence on the Isle, but I *did* have control over how I could've spoken to you."

No kidding.

Still, I keep my face calm and collected.

"Please accept this as my formal apology. Your family may not be my favorite people in the world, but you deserve the opportunity to prove that you're not like them."

"Alright, then. I appreciate you saying so."

"Suppose we get to know each other a little better over lunch," he says, more of a suggestion than an actual question. I'm about to insist that lunch is not necessary if it's coming from an apologetic standpoint, but he's already rambling on. "Freshen up, dress for the day, and I'll meet you on the back patio."

Lunch, despite my best efforts, was dreadful.

For starters, I felt gummy and greasy and drew my own bath in an attempt to wash off. Once I was fully submerged, though, it dawned on me that Kit probably wasn't the kind of man who waited around. Worried that his offer to keep the peace between us would dwindle, I rushed through my bath and half-heartedly dried myself off before scrambling into a daygown Andie had set aside for me.

By the time I scurried through the kitchen and out the glass, double doors onto the deck, Kit didn't have a plate of food in front of him, and the food on mine looked like the outdoor temperature was stealing its warmth. Andie hastily threw something together from what remained of breakfast, plus whatever meager beginnings of supper she could find around the kitchen. That consisted of lukewarm eggs, sliced fruit, a tin of vegetable soup, and Kit Andromeda practically breathing down my neck as I ate—the latter of which I could have done without.

The air outside nipped at the parts of my skin still fighting to dry off from my bath, and between that and Kit's persistent line of questioning, it took every facet of my will not to shiver and chatter my teeth.

Still, I did get the chance to gather some much-desired information about Kit. Before lunch, all I knew about him was that he owned Andromeda House, his mother still lived with him to provide adequate help, and at one point, he had a sister. I didn't wish to be disrespectful and irreverent bringing up his deceased sibling, so instead, I asked about his interests.

Turns out, Kit loves to read. Specifically, he devours anthologies of natural history and of what *my country*, he noted pointedly, calls the *Myths of Mosacian Past*. "I'm shocked you know nothing of the sort considering your namesake," he had said. But when I asked for further explanation, he avoided my question altogether, insisting I explore the grounds of Andromeda House for myself once the afternoon sun fell in line with the gardens.

Eventually, the atmosphere remained silent apart from my chewing and the scraping of my silverware. At one point, I might have even contemplated jamming the utensils in my eye.

Now, not as hungry anymore and having dried and combed through my curls, I don a shawl and begin a self-guided perusal of the House. My rooms reside on the left-most point of the first floor, conveniently far from the front door. No doubt, Kit believes I'll try and make a break for it, but even if I did, what would I do next? *Swim* my way back to Urovia when I don't even know how many hours away it is by motorized boat? I don't think so.

I start on the ground floor, strolling through the wide halls and examining the art on the wall. The pathways are nowhere near the size of Broadcove's, but for a private estate, the space proves to be rather impressive. Paintings of all styles and subjects litter the space in a way that makes me wonder if there's a cream-toned wall beneath them at all. Creatures of ancient lore, tragic portraits of star-crossed lovers, heavenly landscapes that transport me into another universe. Reality crashes over me in the form of Andie dropping a plate in the sink two rooms away, though, and I continue onward.

Hands clasped behind my back, I stroll past the kitchen and veer towards the sitting room instead. Back home, Calliope convinced Venus and Jericho to let her have a grand piano and a pair of viewing couches put on display. Alongside the palace pianist—another one of her fervent requests—Calliope regularly entertained visitors or members of the King's Guard that cared for a tune before their designated shifts. Andromeda House's sitting room, however, acts as a private library. My fingers dance over the leather spines of what remind me of storybook anthologies, encyclopedias, scattered reference atlases, and perhaps even some fine art catalogs. Three gray-toned chairs in the shape of clamshells christen each of the corners of the room, and I make a mental note to return here when Kit or Andie have the time to tell me more about this nook of their estate.

I skim through most of the downstairs. A butler's pantry, a living room with more couches than guests, a billiards room that smells like previously smoked cigars, a formal dining area, the breezeway that gives way to the other side of the back patio, and two rooms that I don't bother disturbing. One of which has Andie's fresh batch of clean laundry, and the other belonging to Andie's deceased daughter. Once I return to the entryway, the stairs splinter off into sections of six steps each before shifting directions, where an ornate carpet with blue and purple detailing cuts through the middle of its winding path. Afraid of tracking footprints through the textured flooring, I remove my slippers and glide barefoot up to the second floor, hand grazing the smooth, oak railing. At the top lies a sculpture of a woman who I'd otherwise consider beautiful save for the snakes streaming from her scalp, mid-hiss and provoked. The sight of her startles me enough to turn away and continue down the hall.

The second story of Andromeda House carries a different air about it, one of sophistication and intrigue. On my immediate left lies a conservatory—a room I'd expect to find on the ground floor. What would've been walls are windows now, and the early afternoon sunlight from the front of the House streams into the room, illuminating it with a soft green hue. The monochromatic, tiled floor gives the room a vintage touch that feels posh yet heartwarming, but I don't linger long. I've never had much of a green thumb, and every time I wandered my way through North Star back home, I'd get the eerie sense that I might taint the stunning collection of colored blooms.

Hanging a right, I stumble upon the largest space on the second floor, and perhaps even the House itself: a gentlemen's lounge. The room is washed in mahogany browns and sleek couches. As I drift into it fully, my bare feet pad along flooring that reminds me of our grand ballroom back home, and I take note of the massive wine cellar glassed within a crystal cage. Perking up at the presence of alcohol amidst this sobering setting, I dash over to the latticed collection of wines and read the various labels, and after a few minutes of in-depth assessment, I note that not a single Urovian grape is stored here. Figures.

I try to imagine *Kit* of all people throwing a party here. He'd have to have friends to host something, and then, that road of thinking makes me wonder . . . does Kit *have* companions? What would Kit be like in a social setting that doesn't involve his political enemy? I haven't known the man for long, but I struggle to imagine the kind of man he'd be in conversation. Would he surrender the floor if someone interrupted him? Would he be pleasant-mannered, or would he raise his voice, insisting he be heard by everyone?

And that's Kit *sober*. I can only imagine Kit with several drinks under his belt, laughing at something smart aleck I've said . . . a tipsy smile blooming across his mouth—

I shake the thought out of my head and move onward, abandoning the lounge and the cellar as quickly as my two feet can carry me. Along this wall, the rooms face the back of the house, which overlooks the rocky hillside before the choppy Damocles water, which I suppose make complete sense. The lounge has an aura of exclusivity and perhaps even coldness, and the subsequent two rooms—a lavatory and a private study—are similarly inclined. It's only once I approach the final room that I physically feel the temperature drop towards this end of the House.

Just as I poke my head inside, I promptly snake away from it—dodging the sight of Kit sprawled out on his bed.

Saints, did he see me?

I brace myself for him to call after me on an amused yet irritated drawl, but it never comes. In fact, a different sound greets me. Not my name, but . . . a soft rumbling?

I dare a second glance into Kit's suite and find him fast asleep.

Like most people, sleep softens all of Kit's hardened features. His jaw rests lax against his pillow, chest rising and falling in a slow pattern. He *snores*. Nothing obnoxious or overbearingly noisy, but the gesture is oddly human. Though, not enough to keep me from crossing my arms before my chest and rolling my eyes. *Was my conversation over lunch so exhausting that Kit had to take a nap at*—I glance towards the grandfather clock in the neighboring hall—*one in the afternoon?*

Suddenly, a new and slightly dangerous thought occurs to me as I tiptoe away from the scene on silent feet. I pad down the stairs in a hushed hurry, keeping an ear out for any sudden movement from Andie, and when the coast appears clear, I creep back into my room and shut the door. Turn the lock etched into the knob.

As I go to drape my shawl over the edge of my bed, I look down at my feet—having abandoned my slippers back at the base of the stairs—and see half of a page of parchment, the bottom of it appearing torn in haste.

I have some necessary business to attend to, so I trust that you will stay out of trouble for a few days. Do not look for me. I will seek you out when I return.

There's no signature, but the dark blue ink is reminiscent of the jars I beheld in Madman's lair the night before.

Jericho and Venus always taught me to burn secret correspondences, but I don't have a match and my rooms do not have their own hearth. For the time being, I lift my mattress and shove the scrap of paper as far into the center as I can possibly reach. I make a mental note to insist that I wash my own sheets no matter how much Andie may persist.

Then—and only once the coast is clear—I snag a lantern buried in my armoire, clutching it tightly in my grasp, and shimmy beneath the skirts of my bed, descending once more into the dark pit that Madman led me down last night.

11
Geneva

I haven't seen my daughter in seven days. *Seven.*
Every hour with no known update on her is pure torture.
Never in my life has a person's absence plagued me as much as
Pandora's disappearance has. Not the loss of my parents, not
Venus's separation back when Jericho first seized her, not even
Kurt's death. For all I know, Pandora could've stolen a carriage,
gone on a joyride through the continent, and gotten lost, gotten
hurt, or worse—

I drop my face into my hands, unable to fathom a fate for
my daughter that doesn't involve her being whisked back to
Broadcove in one piece. Because that's the worst part of my
pain—the waiting. The not knowing.

No fragments of Pandora were left behind for us to retrace
her steps. All her jewelry stayed on her person, and she didn't shed
her dress and change into something more mobile. Hundreds of
eyes had ogled over her *hours* before someone realized she was
gone, and like smoke on a wind, she simply vanished.

Each day with no sign of uncovering her whereabouts is worse than the last, and the most crippling part about it is that no one properly understands the magnitude of my sorrow, and that's what cuts the deepest. I'm her *mother*. I saw Pandora at every stage of her beautiful, cherished life. Hell, I created and carried that girl inside of me. And now, what? Am I just supposed to sit idly by and wait to see if Venus and Jericho can figure out if she's even still *alive*? Am I supposed to go on watching Calliope hold her three children tighter while the only *one* I had to spare awaits uncertain death—

"Aunt Genny?" A timid voice drifts over to me from down the hall.

My head turns in time to meet my younger nephew's gaze, and Dorian pouts his lip at me. It's a habit I've picked up on over the years, one that typically translates to guilt and his precious inability to keep a secret.

"Hey, kiddo. Something on your mind?"

"Have they found Pandora yet?"

I tell myself that those aren't tears in his wide, brown eyes, but rather that the light from one of the chandeliers is playing tricks on me. "Not yet," I answer.

The welling tears I can make excuses for—the light in the room, the sun outside. Maybe *I* was the one on the verge of crying, not Dorian. The quiver of my nephew's lip, however, is an entirely different beast. "I'm so . . . *scared* for her."

The feeling is mutual, but I see no point in frightening the boy further. "They'll find her."

"Not if he took her away."

My pulse stops beating within my veins, my head slowly inclining towards him. "He?"

Dorian whimpers like a kicked animal, and while I never

enjoy seeing any of the Deragon children upset—least of all at my prompting—I have a horrible feeling that everything Venus and Jericho have been sending out spies to garner could've been solved by a ten-year-old's testimony.

"Sweetie," I say, my hands shaky as I extend them in his direction. "If you saw something, I need to know."

"But Uncle Jericho—"

"Don't you worry about him, love," I interject. "It'll be our little secret."

Dorian stuffs his small hands into the front pockets along his pants, unable to steady them. "I saw Pan leave the ballroom . . ." he whispers, as if the walls have ears to eavesdrop and mouths to tattle with. "With a boy."

"A boy?" I repeat.

"A *guard*," Flora cuts in, her voice at a normal volume and her tone hinting at gossip. "A decently handsome one, too."

I stutter over my initial response, a sudden surge of anger coming over me. Once I find the means to restart, I say to Flora slowly, "And you only care to mention this *now*?"

"I didn't think it mattered much," she returns flatly, picking at her nails like this conversation has become taxing. Saints above, she's *just* like Calliope was at this age. "I waited a few minutes to see if they were up to anything juicy, but I caught the guy retreating from her rooms holding his jacket. Pan probably told him to hit the road."

I try not to let my face reveal anything about what Pandora had opened up to me about. It's perfectly normal for a girl like her to idolize and hope for a romantic encounter. Truthfully, it is a scenario I expected to face with her at an earlier age. But with the demanding role that Venus and Jericho placed her in—I, too, having played a part in it after agreeing to the arrangement—

she's never seemed to have the opportunity. And while I know she will not come right out and say it herself, I know she thinks of it often. That it may not be an issue of someone wanting her, but rather not wanting to stand in her predecessor's warpath.

As dear as Venus and Jericho are to me, the thought makes me resent them on Pandora's behalf.

"Do you know anything about the guard?"

Flora looks at me like my line of questioning ticks her off, and even Dorian seems put off by the sour look on her face. "He's typically stationed along this wing of the castle, but I've seen him stationed in her hallway more times than I can count on two hands."

"Did anything happen afterwards? Do you think he circled back for her? Attempted to apologize for what might have transpired?"

"No," Flora recounts. "The man was out of commission the moment she dismissed him from her room. Rumor has it he downed two goblets of wine and abandoned his post for the remainder of the night."

His post outside *my daughter's room*—the last known location anyone in this Saints-forsaken castle accounted her for.

I want to tear the guard to ribbons, and I don't even know his name.

Suddenly, pounding footsteps tear through the hallway—two sets of them—and I know better than to act surprise when Venus and Jericho emerge. Their hair is askew, like they haven't actually been tearing the kingdom apart to find their heir but doing something else together instead. If that's the case, I try not to begrudge them for it. Grief and fear affect people in different ways. Because my sister and her husband can *confide*—but how do those emotions manifest themselves in *my* case?

Insomnia. That's how.

"Why don't you and Flora see if Samuel is around here somewhere?" I say to Dorian before his aunt and uncle read the look on his face. He nods over and over, darting back the way he came and kicking his feet as he runs off, Flora slinking off after him. Before either of them has the space to make a comment, I bound towards them. Venus, at the very least, has the brains to brace for impact.

"*Tell me* you have an update."

"We do," Venus says stiffly.

"But you won't like it," Jericho finishes.

I steady my breathing, even as I feel fury heat beneath my skin. "I don't care. Out with it."

Venus looks to Jericho, guilt written all over her face, and I realize then just how bad this might be. Because all of Broadcove's security had been focused on protecting *Venus* that night, ensuring that no harm would come to *her*. But as for everyone else . . .

Jericho's eyes darken as he tells me, "Ardian is dead."

Holy Saints.

Ardian Asticova was perhaps single-handedly responsible for keeping Jericho morally sane enough not to kill Venus when they first met. He was a better father figure to Jericho than his real father, Ronan Morgan, ever was. I can only imagine how devastating this loss is for him. For Venus, too.

"How?" I ask.

Sure, the man was old, but the fact that his death is a precursor for Pandora's whereabouts . . . foul play must be a variable. A shiver courses through my spine, and I don't realize how deep I've bitten into the inside of my cheek until I taste blood.

"Bullet wound," he finally says. Then, he opens the palm of his hand, revealing a silver, metallic shelling that's no bigger than the size of my thumb. "Guns have never been permitted for civilian use in Urovia, and when we conquered Mosacia, guns and their ammunition became strictly enforced contraband. We seized them by the *thousands*—"

"What does *his* death have to do with *my* daughter?" I say through my teeth, praying to the Saints that Jericho isn't seconds away from revealing a second shell—one that took the life of my favorite person on earth.

"One of the guards found his body out on perimeter rotation. It seems that Ardian witnessed something suspicious down at Honeycomb Harbor—*someone*—and whoever it was, did not want to get caught."

I close the distance between him and me when he stops short of a full explanation, grabbing him by the collar of his shirt.

"Caught. Doing. *What?*"

Jericho's stare is grave and unrelenting, his jaded way of telling me, mind to mind, that he's here for me.

And then, he hands me a piece of parchment. "Stealing Pandora from Broadcove."

I snatch the parchment from his grasp, anxious sweat beading along my eyebrows.

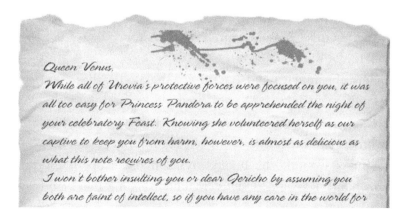

Queen Venus,

While all of Urovia's protective forces were focused on you, it was all too easy for Princess Pandora to be apprehended the night of your celebratory Feast. Knowing she volunteered herself as our captive to keep you from harm, however, is almost as delicious as what this note requires of you.

I won't bother insulting you or dear Jericho by assuming you both are faint of intellect, so if you have any care in the world for *your daughter, you'll show face before Pandora's tribunal is sealed on the first of August. I know it seems far away, but all good things come to those who wait, and I am a patient man. Tell your husband to think long and hard about where we'll be waiting, for if he's wrong, no one will be there to dispute the certain death sentence Pandora faces.*

No direct statement is made, but the dark smear of what must be Pandora's dried blood certainly says enough, and I drop the letter onto the floor.

Dread fills up my stomach. "We have to save her."

"Genny, calm down. Let's think about this for a minute," my sister says, her tone stagnant.

"*Think?* What's there to *think* about aside from how fast we can board a damn boat for the eastern continent?" I rage, shoving my sister with all my bodily strength. "My daughter's *life* is on the line!"

"They didn't assign a rendezvous point," she argues, staggering back towards me.

"I'm not an idiot, Venus. Everyone who called Jericho crazy because they didn't buy into his visions were the ones holding their tongues while you two played couple's conquerors. Two people your age don't just dismantle an entire empire and its royal family from sheer luck. This person *knows* his visions can see into the present and the future."

"I can't dream on a deadline," Jericho tells me softly. "That's not how it works. The Saints show me things on *their* timetable."

"Well then tell them to get it together and show you *something!*" I nearly scream. I try not to descend into madness. "That's my *daughter* out there."

Ever since half of the Holymen Committee was eradicated and Calliope and I invaded the *U. Herald* alongside Nadine Tolcher, the press has dutifully continued the narrative of Pandora being their legitimate-by-birth heir. And I've always complied with Venus and Jericho's request to publicly refer to Pandora as their daughter—but when it comes down to saving her skin or their own, I'm starting to really see how much of a "daughter" Pandora is to Venus.

"I just need some time for the vision to come through," Jericho says, his tone soft as if I'm a horse prone to be spooked. "Time, that it looks like, we're being offered, mind you. We have two months—"

"What will they do to her in those two months?" I start to spiral, eyes pinning Jericho to the spot knowing he may hear my desperation more than Venus will. "Pandora is afraid of the dark. What if they lock her in an underground jail cell? What if they torture her? Worse, what if they try and—"

"They wouldn't," Jericho cuts in before I can say the damning image aloud, tears springing in my eyes faster than I anticipate. My face is wet with them as they streak down my cheeks, and I dare not wipe them away. Let them both see my anguish.

"Yet this person mentioned a tribunal. A *certain death sentence*—"

"They're just trying to ruffle our feathers," Venus says.

But Jericho shakes his head. "Their threat isn't empty. Tribunals are Mosacian court customs," he rasps, his tone foreboding. "And they are typically reserved for their most infamous offenders, which means that while there are numerous places Pandora could be right now, the tribunal takes place in a singular, undisclosed location. We'll send scouts and spies to scope out the continent and find out where it is, so that, worst case scenario, we'll liberate Pandora on the day of her tribunal."

It's not enough.

My daughter could be suffering, starving, shivering in the cold, or anticipating death for wanting to protect rulers—*family members*—that don't seem too inspired to take action against her captors.

"I just need you to know," Jericho resumes, "that I will try my best to find Pandora in a timely manner . . ."

He means to go on, to calm me with the guarantee of her safety despite the ransom note and the markings of her blood. But I refuse to hear another word, refuse to let Jericho console me while his wife—my *sister*—has said nothing close to what could resemble any condolences.

"She gave herself up for you," I say. "Have you nothing to say about that?"

I'm on the verge of lunging for her when she finally breaks her silence to say, "Pandora was trained to protect the crown. Our forces should've been watching everyone, but—"

"Oh, this is rich," I say with a morbid laugh. "I know you're not being serious, Venus. I *know* you're not about to look me in my face and tell me that *my* daughter is *disposable*."

"Not at all!" Jericho tries to offer kindly. "It's only that—"

"We don't negotiate with people who think threatening us earns them anything."

"Yes, we do," I bite back. "Especially when they have *my* daughter—not yours—in their custody."

"Pandora is not mine by birth," Venus shouts. "But she is my *blood*. And while my husband and I didn't train *you* for this sort of instance, we trained Pandora. All we can do now is wait on the Saints and hope Pandora has enough of a spine to endure whatever they put her through and keep her mouth shut."

Fiery wrath consumes my senses. "You're a *monster*," I tell her through tears of rage. "You're *nothing* like the sister I once knew."

"That's because while you were becoming a mother, *I* was becoming a monarch," Venus seethes, and Jericho's grip tugs her backwards in a silent warning when she prepares to get in my face. "Don't act like our roles are even on the same planet, Geneva. I slaughtered the old me to get to where I am, and all you did was lie on your back—"

I strike Venus across the face with all my strength.

The stinging sensation along my palm and the underside of my fingers feels like freedom and divine retribution. It tingles in a way that makes me want to do it again, but Jericho steps between us, his eyebrows diving towards the bridge of his nose and his eyes crazed.

"Venus, you crossed a line. Don't ever speak to your sister like that again after all she and Pandora have done for us."

Deep satisfaction simmers in my stomach at his words, and I watch as embers crackle beneath the darkness in Venus's eyes. She won't apologize, but seeing her own husband scold her reminds me of all the petty fights our father would settle between us girls when we were younger—most of which he'd side with me on.

"And Genny." Jericho turns towards me, his voice low and hauntingly severe. "If you lay your hands on my wife again, I will not be held responsible for what happens next. This is your one warning."

Venus's vainglorious smirk destroys the last of my decency, and so I see myself out of the hallway . . . and out of Broadcove entirely.

12
Venus

J ericho jolts awake in the night, a cold sweat forming along
his brow.

I've become all too familiar with the behavioral patterns his
visions tend to draw out of him—mainly because, sometimes, I
experience them, too.

I've always found our divine connection peculiar, albeit
fascinating. In the beginning, it terrified me to be inside his head
against my will. Then again, nothing scared me more than the way
he lodged his way into the depths of my heart. But throughout
the course of our reign and our marriage, none of my blessing's
other oddities compared to the ability to inherit Jericho's dreams.
Not all of them, of course, as the Saints still afford Jericho *some*
semblance of privacy—but critical ones.

However, there was one vision that I foresaw before Jericho
ever did—*years* in advance. It was vague back then, but it
disturbed me to my very core: Broadcove burning all around,
smoke swallowing me whole. A reaper posed before me in all

black, their face shielded from sight. And Jericho's crown broken down the middle, as if someone sliced it off his head.

I foresaw the doomsday sight the night of our wedding, and was so electrically charged with terror, that I started a path of bloodshed over it. Sure, I would've felt guilty had it escalated to a full-on war, but the Mosacian territories fell like dominoes. I confided in Jericho about it soon after we took control of both continents, and from there, I assumed we'd squashed any potential threat. The dream never came back for me, and it never reared its ugly head at Jericho.

Until, ten years later, it did.

Only when Jericho told me what *he* saw, a few things had changed. First, there was the fact that he saw it from *his* perspective. The fact that he was seeing the scene play out through his eyes assured me he was alive. I hadn't lost him. But the look on his face in this moment tells me that he's uncovered something new, something grimmer.

"What do you see, my love?" I ask, my tone gentle and my hands faintly brushing the skin over Jericho's torso. It's a habit I've done to help lure him back into reality in a less jarring manner, a way to coax him between grave imaginings of the future and the eerie stillness of the present. Sweat gleams along his pectorals, along the dip in his collarbone, and his body temperature runs hotter than usual.

"The attack definitely takes place at sunset. But . . ." he chokes out. His eyes squint against the moonlight pouring into the room. "The concealed figure didn't come alone this time."

My heart gallops within my ribs, the sensation pounding against my stomach in a way that makes me feel queasy. "How many?"

Jericho shivers. "Three of them."

"What about our family? Please tell me Genny was okay," I whisper, remorse for the way I brushed her aside and insulted her earlier today slowly creeping up on me.

"Calliope, yes. Eli and the children, yes. But I didn't—"

Just as he opens his mouth to say more, he promptly shuts it. His eyes expand to a degree that makes me want to leap out of my skin, and before I can stop him, he's sprinting out of bed.

I know better than to chase after him with a robe, even though he stampedes through the halls of Broadcove in nothing but his boxers. He could run through the gardens naked and the staff wouldn't bat an eye, now that everyone believes that the visions that drive him mad are, in fact, real. If anything, they'd rush to his aid. Mine, too.

I take note of the route Jericho courses through—we're headed for the South Wing, where the rest of our family resides. It hits me all at once.

Genny wasn't in his vision at all. He's making sure she's still alive.

Sleek hands on a clock perched at the far end of the hallway point towards 2:57 a.m., just minutes before the rotations of the second-string night guards. Two of them, backs board-straight as they pace the straightened path, catch sight of their relief staff. The incoming guard's polished shoes click across the linoleum floors, screeching to a halt as their faces come alive in recognition of Jericho and I coming at them full speed.

"Your Majesties!" one of them cries out as the other three bow.

"Who last had eyes on Duchess Geneva?" Jericho calls out, unbothered by his volume, despite this unsaintly hour and seeing no sense in wasting one breath on formalities.

The cluster of young, uniformed men stumble over their different versions of what they know about Genny, all of them unfazed by Jericho's state of undress. One has little substance to share, one had just gotten back from temporary leave and knew nothing, and one confessed to having drank alongside some of his comrades earlier that evening.

But the youngest of the group, a strapping blond that reminds me of a young Henry Tolcher grits his teeth before saying, "One of the early evening guards. Word has it he came down with a sudden illness," he says, addressing the both of us with a solemn gaze. "I took over his post at seventeen hundred hours."

"Where was his delegated post?" I ask, my nerves short-circuiting beneath my skin.

"The main slope descending towards the harbor, Your Majesty," he reports.

"Why they hell would Genny be—"

That's when I feel Jericho's hand cover mine, his grasp intentional and firm. I mean to look into his weathered blue eyes for a truth I know I'll dread, but when I do, I find him peering out the window and towards the moonlit expanse of our beloved territory.

No . . . further down.

My husband is studying Honeycomb Harbor.

Where *Crystal Wrath* no longer bobs in its designated docking point.

13
Pandora

My mother always made an effort to remind me what a wise and knowledgeable girl I was. Every time Venus and Jericho would instruct me on foreign policy or nail me on intricate details of Urovia's history, I'd have to pass one of their little tests to ensure I was on track to proving myself. This ranged from written assessments to public recitations when they would hold court with the nobles. But pass or fail, the latter of which was incredibly rare, my mother was always there with an affectionate embrace and a kiss on the forehead afterwards.

"My darling girl," I can still hear her say to me, even now. *"How infinitely fortunate is the one who gets to love a mind as beautiful as yours one day."*

But if Mother saw me now, she'd surely rescind those years of admiration and validation.

Kit and I have kept our respective distances, though Andie insists he's offering me space to settle in, as opposed to outright avoiding me. Either way, I never thought I'd *want* to spend time with Kit Andromeda.

However, Madman hasn't sent word in a week, and my attempts at keeping busy are dwindling by the day. In the meantime, I've resorted to memorizing every square inch of Andromeda House that I could uncover. Mainly, I learned that from the secret passage beneath my bed, instead of hanging a right for the wrought iron door that led to Madman's dispatch boat, a left turn leads me into a subterranean hallway—the same hallway that housed me in the storm shelter until my sleeping tonic wore off. Madman must've dumped me there that way.

Madman . . .

When my thoughts of him sent me into a jittery sense of chaos, I tried busying myself with my other surroundings. The gardens were pretty, but they were nothing compared to the lawns Venus engineered back in Broadcove. I'd have afternoon tea with Andie and ask about the Isle until I wore down her lackluster sense of Kit-imposed secrecy, but even those details didn't hold my attention long.

Tonight's last-ditch effort is to steal a bottle of wine from Kit's cellar and drink myself into sickness so I rot in bed the rest of the day. But having tread towards me on silent footsteps, Kit gruffly seizes the merlot before I can even uncork it. I startle at the sudden yanking motion.

"And just what do you think you're doing with that?"

I shrug through an awkward smile. "Drinking it."

He eyes me funny. "It's two in the afternoon."

Is that a grin creeping along the edge of his mouth?

"And?" I ask, hoping Kit reads into my defiance more so than presuming me a miserable alcoholic.

Kit looks prepared to scold me and return his precious merlot to its proper shelving, but just before he emits a sound, he pauses and looks me in the eye as if to assess the truth of my original intentions.

"Alright, princess," he sighs instead, grabbing a bottle opener and two iridescent glasses. I take the one he offers me with careful steadiness. "I'll bend, but no way am I letting you down one of my best reds alone."

When Kit pours the wine into my goblet, I notice the way the dark liquid swirls in its base, the red gleaming black for a short second. It reminds me too much of home, of my family's coat of arms—dragon's flame licking up the borders and annihilating all enemies in its wake.

"What are we toasting to?" he calls out as he serves himself, pulling me out of my head.

I don't have much to say that likely wouldn't come out moronic in his eyes. I speak my piece anyways. "To disappointing my family. If not for my easy capture, then at least for believing that day-drinking will make me feel better about it."

Kit chuckles—actually *chuckles*—before taking a swig of his drink. I hear him bark out a full laugh, however, when my first sip isn't a sip at all, and I crush my wine like it's nothing. The bitter sucker punch of an aftertaste only hits me once it's all the way down.

"Another," I say.

To his credit, Kit doesn't deny me the drink and pours cautiously, decreasing my second portion as innocently as he can manage. "Care to talk about it?"

"So you can revel in my misery? I'll pass."

I'm surprised that Kit doesn't push back, and asks instead, "Were you this much of a drinker back home?"

"Only when the parties were dreadful."

"And what makes a lavish Urovian party *dreadful*, princess?"

I take another hearty sip of my merlot, the taste stinging the longer I let it sit in my mouth. I swallow with a tinge of internal suffering. "When I'd be forced to perform at them."

Kit appears puzzled at that. "Singing?"

"I sing. I play the harp too. But no, I mean performing in conversations with guests. Those sorts of social gatherings tended to exhaust me."

He nods, taking another drink. "Which do you prefer?"

My face scrunches up at the question for some reason. "Come again?"

"It seems like a simple, non-threatening question to ask," he notes pointedly. "If you enjoy singing and playing your harp, but you were given all day to do one or the other—for yourself, not for an audience—which would you choose?"

The answer is simple. "Definitely singing."

Sure, I craved knowledge all throughout my childhood and still to this day, so when mother and I acquired my first harp, I was smitten. It looked so lovely but proved to be so complex—a challenge presented within beautiful structuring.

But I don't think anything ever beat the feeling of Aunt Calliope and I harmonizing in the sitting room over lines from drinking songs, or how her face would light up with pride and a smidge of envy whenever I'd nail a complicated run in an aria she had idolized all her life.

"Are you any good?"

"You're just trying to bait me into singing for you."

"Even if I am," Kit openly concedes, "I don't see the harm in one song."

"There's no accompaniment here."

"If you're as seasoned of a professional as you're implying, you don't need it." He rolls his eyes. "Come on. One song."

I shake my head, and he groans in a manner that lets me know he isn't truly aggravated just yet. "Not even one *verse?*"

"No can do," I tease, to which Kit reacts in a way like he's about to barrage me with complaints. I settle him with an extended hand. "And before you get all wound up about how I'm depriving you of something simple and unnecessary, or how I should comply to your every whim because I'm graciously being housed under your roof, you should know that I'm only trying to protect you."

Kit nearly guffaws at the statement. "Oh, really?"

"That's right," I say, daring to move closer to him. A playful move, but a calculated, risky one, nonetheless. Then, I peer intently into his green eyes and tell Kit, "Because the minute you hear my voice, Mr. Andromeda, I have no doubt you'll fall in love with me."

Kit visibly halts at my words, eyeing me in a way that makes me wonder whether he believes me to be a downright liar or if he's evaluating my statement's potential actuality. "Is that so?"

I nod, and I don't fight off the blush that floods my cheeks when his stare deepens at the same time his gaze softens.

"We'll see about that," Kit mutters, and even though there's a considerable amount of alcohol in my system, I'm not too far gone to hear the unsteadiness in his voice. It makes me giddy and nervous at the same time, and I begin to sip from my glass again to distract myself from the feeling.

Kit Andromeda and I are ludicrously drunk by the time Andie announces that supper is ready, and we practically mow through our food once we drift into the kitchen on unstable feet, stuffing ourselves senseless.

Andie easily detects our blatant inebriation, but rather than hound us about it, she takes great pleasure in sitting in on our joint conversation. Our chatter gets louder the longer we eat, and it's only once we're all too full to move from our seats that the three of us end up playing cards together. Specifically, we strike up a game that involves two decks intermingled and a jar of green paint—one that Kit and his mother accredit as an Andromeda Family favorite. Every time a person gets caught fibbing about what's in their hand, they inherit the entire discount pile and get to be "decorated" by the person who sniffed out their deceit.

By the time the three of us call it quits—mainly because our sides hurt from laughing—I bear an overgrown green mustache and beard courtesy of Kit. Meanwhile, he wears a painted pair of spectacles and cat whiskers that Andie took great pride in painting on her son's face.

Despite having resided in Andromeda House for more than two weeks at this point, Kit insists on showing me where all the soaps and other bath essentials are in my private bathroom. Now, perched before the doorframe of my room as I pick out a changing robe, he looks to the floor as he says, "I've got to admit, Princess, you're not half as dreadful as I anticipated you to be."

The comment warms a part of my heart that had previously been convinced to remain guarded, and I sense a sliver of ice there beginning to thaw.

"You can call me by my name, you know," I say, hoping Kit registers the fact that I might just want him to call me by it. "It's not poisonous."

But it sure as hell is personable, his temporary silence seems to say.

Still, the alcohol puts a damper on his typical, sober judgment, and Kit nods slowly. "Okay, then. I had . . . quite a day with you, Pandora."

Immediately, there's a voice inside my head groaning, *Dear Saints, don't do it. Don't start to get those ridiculously fluttering feelings for a man who wants your family in ruins, who is actively using you as bait to get what he really wants. You are drunk and already have to make sense of things between you and Madman. Don't add Kit Andromeda to the list.*

But deep down, past all the food and drinks I consumed tonight, something about the sound of my name on Kit's tongue triggers an eerie sensation that I can't quite place. I feel it in my bones, but as for what I feel...

"You look like a scholar," I blurt out, pointing to his painted, round-rimmed glasses.

The words sound idiotic when I hear them back, and it takes great effort to keep from clenching my eyes shut in utter embarrassment. Kit's quiet chuckle certainly doesn't ease my discomfort. "You already know that I am one. Ever since I confessed my interest in history, I've caught you stealing glances at my library at least four times in the last week. Given your curious nature, I can only imagine how many times you've wandered over there and I *haven't* found you."

I shrug, only because I don't want my mouth to further shed light on how drunk I am. Then, in the silence that follows, Kit makes an unspoken decision in his head, his eyes casually grazing mine in a way that feels . . . tender.

"You can borrow a book whenever you'd like, you know."

"I'll believe *that* when you say it to me sober." If he's a stickler about the rest of Andromeda House, there's no way that he doesn't have a death grip on his personal library.

Kit means to argue, but instead, he chooses to be enigmatic and float away from my door. He departs without another sound, and while I've always been skilled at picking fights to get my way, I'm too weighed down by dinner and the day I've had to convince him to come back.

Dizzily, I traipse over to my bed, meaning to lay down sideways just long enough to settle my heart rate before I draw myself a bath. Instead, I fall asleep before the last of the day's light disappears beyond the distant horizon—but it doesn't last long.

No more than two hours later, I wake up on top of the covers with the very distinct feeling that I'm being watched.

I jolt upwards in bed, and sure enough, Madman stands at the foot of my bed. Even in the darkness, his eyes pierce through mine like a blade, but I can't deny the fact that I am pleased to see him. I might go as far as to say that I've missed him. The satisfied smile that spreads across his lips tells me he knows it, too.

"Oh, angel," Madman drawls, amusement dancing in his eyes. "You look . . . terrible."

Suddenly, what would typically be a gas bubble in my throat turns acidic, and both Madman and I look at each other as it happens—me in panic, and him in confirmation of my current state.

Lightning fast, Madman rushes towards me when my feet don't move. My head is so foggy and my body is so full of dead weight that I'm inclined to be sick to my stomach right here in the middle of the floor, but Madman pulls me as firmly, yet delicately, as possible towards the bathroom. I go limp in his hold, so my legs fold beneath me and I'm already kneeling before the latrine when I start to sweat from every pore.

"Don't make me do this," I plead.

"You'll feel better afterwards."

I shake my head, unable to look at him as I fight off the inevitable. "You shouldn't see me like this."

"I'm fairly certain your painted facial hair is more alarming than anything you could conjure up out of your body, angel."

His remark makes me laugh, true and deep, but the motion rattles the sickness in my belly. I only have enough spare moments to mumble the word *please* before Madman sweeps my dark curls out of the way and I spill my guts into the bowl.

14
Pandora

Despite my constant protests—the majority of which consisted of, *"I'm fine. Really, I'm good to go, now"*—Madman had insisted on waiting another night before sailing me into his cave again. Which, granted, was probably smart. The rocking waves and uneven current nearly send the boat hurtling into the moonlit dock. Had I ventured here yesterday, the tides would've made me sick all over again, even after throwing up what felt like my entire *soul*.

He wouldn't come clean about where he was or what he was doing, and while I didn't expect him to, I at least anticipated some sort of conversation. Instead, the boat ride to his inner sanctum is dead silent. When we're finally shut inside the candle-strewn dwelling, the air between us is thick with suspended tension. I know that *something* rages in Madman's mind, I just don't know what.

In my head, however, I'm running out of easy-pitch questions to ask him regarding how he knew to take care of me so well where the answer isn't, *"I observed your life for so long, I'm bound to know everything about you."* I decide to confront my futile wonderings at the root.

"How long, exactly . . . did you watch over me in Broadcove?"

He doesn't miss the strategic use of language—watching *over* me rather than just *watching* me. It pulls a vague smile across his mouth. "How long do you suspect?"

The humor in Madman's voice alerts me to the fact that I may not want to know the answer. If not because it would startle me, then at least because of how torturous an existence living in the darkness of the tunnels must have been.

"Two years," I highball.

"Five."

I audibly gasp, smacking a hand over my mouth. *Saints above.*

"How did you even *survive* down there?" But then an even more dangerous thought comes to mind, one triggered by the memory of days where I'd sneak through the underground pathways to spy on Flora and her male conquests. A lump forms in the base of my throat. "Were there ever times when we'd be in the tunnels together and—"

"I longed to touch you?" he finishes darkly.

Alarms sound in my head.

Danger! Danger! Flee now or—

"I was always so good at keeping quiet when you'd go exploring. I'd walk barefoot to keep my shoes from giving me away. Ensure no rim of clothing would scrape the floor, whether it meant removing my cloak or rolling up the hem of my trousers." He takes pride in his past secrecy, lounging further into his chair. "But on a handful of occasions, I certainly called it close, most of which occurred in the months leading up to Queen's Feast."

Madman's revelation should flood me with terror, but instead, a crazed sense of, dare I say it, *excitement*, takes over. Maybe it's because I've been a rule-follower all my life, but something as close to happiness as it can get without it *being* happiness clouds what remains of my rational judgment at the thought. At the mental image of my back turned to him in the dark, and Madman's trembling hand being mere centimeters from my shoulder, aching to make contact with flesh. Shivers crawl up my bones at the idea of Madman going stir-crazy just to touch me.

My internal alarms start *blaring* as I begin to feel similarly.

"Well, I'm glad you're back," I say when all other meaningless lines of conversation fail.

Madman makes a face that reminds me of a person blushing, but any proof of the possibility remains hidden beneath his mask. Then, in a slow and calculated turn, he angles his body towards the silver harp. "Would you do me the honor?"

Unlike the first time I played for him, I'm not nervous anymore. In fact, settling down before the strings, I feel a sense of total serenity.

I elect to play a tune that's similar to a nursery rhyme my mother and aunts grew up with, but I do not sing. I haven't warmed up, but if I'm being honest with myself, a dull pain still hangs in my throat from all the hilarious shouting Kit and I did last night.

Madman's face shifts in subtle recognition of the tune, and he begins to sing.

In the blooms, a creature looms
With venom in its maw
She picks a rose and sudden blood flows
For beauty comes at a painful cost

The dirge-like song always fascinated me as a young girl. Every four lines told a short, bitter tale that needed little detail to describe its depth. But hearing Madman's baritone carry the dialogue into reality . . . my head spins in newfound awe. His voice is raw magic, unexpected optimism in midnight packaging.

It moves me so much I don't even realize that my fingers have stilled over the strings.

"I didn't mean to interrupt—"

"It's not that," I rush to reassure him, my eyes wide and heart beating frantically fast. "You just have a lovely voice. It's just, well, a bit . . . disarming."

Damn me for saying it aloud, and damn Madman for grinning in response. Because even though I trust him more than anyone else on the Isle, there are too many sounds that should keep me from caving in like I just did. The desperation in Ardian's voice as he registered what was happening to me. The *bang* of the lone bullet leaving Whisper's chamber. The *crunch* of Ardian's body hitting the ground and never rising again.

And yet, Madman's melodic voice traitorously overrides them all.

"You sound classically trained," I add to fill the painful silence.

"You flatter me, angel," he returns, and knowing I do not have the concentration to continue playing, I rise from my bench and pace about the dark room. The scattered candlelight casts speckled, golden bokeh across his relaxed frame. "How are you faring in Andromeda House?" he asks.

There's an iciness laced within the question, as if bracing himself to hear that I've been harmed. No doubt, my drunken stupor didn't ease any of his preconceived worries.

"All right," I mutter quietly. "Andie—Maia—*Lady Andromeda*," I choke out, unsure of how to distinguish her so that Madman doesn't lose tabs on who I'm referencing, "is nice enough."

"No need to feel jumpy," Madman replies calmly. "As long as you are well."

"I am."

"Good," Madman says with a stern nod, and I'm almost inclined to believe that he's going to drop the subject altogether until—

"How long had you been drinking before I found you?"

I cross my arms before my chest uncomfortably. "All afternoon."

I anticipate him scolding me about knowing my limits and pacing myself, considering he found me slathered in paint and sleeping on top of my bed rather than fully inside it. The reminder makes more humiliating color rush into my cheeks. But one of the corners of his mouth tweaks upwards in what almost looks like relief.

"Conversation with Mr. Andromeda is that wretched?"

Kit had barely made eye contact with me this afternoon once I finally emerged from my vicious hangover. Andie had cleaned up our place settings and playing cards, and Kit had eradicated every hint of paint from his face, save for the splotchy, red irritation marks from all the scrubbing he had to do. It saddened me to know his previous disposition was a fluke. But said sadness has now hardened to bitterness.

"The alcohol helped," I mutter dryly.

Madman chuckles. "Until it didn't. Did you try and touch one of his prized textbooks?"

That certainly catches my attention. "How do you know about them?"

"It's my business to know everything about the people I work for," Madman remarks, an eyebrow arched as he looks back at me. "Besides, a blind man could figure out that Kit Andromeda is a pretentious history buff."

"Why is that?" I ask. "I mean, Kit did confess to enjoying the subject, but I never learned why or what his favorite subjects were."

"Mosacian Root History, likely," Madman says. "Customs and lore that descended from a previously fallen empire. As for why, even I'll admit, the knowledge in those books proves to be exceptionally entertaining—particularly the tall tales."

My nose scrunches at the third mention. "Tall tales?"

"Of course," he says, coming out of his seat to move closer. "Especially now that you're in his custody—"

"Oh," I sigh. "Right. My name."

Madman senses the unease in my voice, the lack of understanding in the reference. "I do not know what kind of stories your family wove together about your namesake, but Pandora isn't just some pretty, feminine identifier. The name ties back to the origins of Urovia's greatest rival and of . . . gods, *humanity*," he says emphatically.

"Tell me, then," I say.

I don't realize that I've closed the distance between us, and in my desperation, clasped my hands over his. Immediately, I yank them away, worried that the undetected gesture repulses him.

"I'd much rather see you steal one of Kit's manuscripts to learn the truth than tell you myself," he answers after a long while.

Despite my annoyance, any information Madman omits often proves to be for the better, so I don't push back. I do, however, feel the need to try for a work-around. "Would any of these transcriptions make sense of the sculpture on the second floor?"

A puzzle expression graces what pieces of his face remain visible. "What sculpture?"

"The lady with hair made of snakes."

"Ah, the Medusa," Madman recognizes. "Yes, her history is quite renowned, although often misconstrued. I do notice, though, that you didn't indicate the piece as something scary."

I shrug. "Serpents aside, she appeared somewhat beautiful to me."

"That's a good thing. You don't even know the story, and yet you somehow understand that she wasn't the monster the records portrayed her to be."

I don't bother saying anything about how I tend to view all humans that way. How I view *him* that way. Madman likely already knows.

He gestures for me to take his previous spot, and as I do, he follows me there and sits down at my side. I try not to let my thoughts meditate too long on the warmth his presence seems to carry despite such a cold exterior.

"Before she became what most remember her as, Medusa was a lovely mortal maiden with two sisters. She was the object of great beauty, so much so that she captured the attention of the sea god, Neptune."

When you control the sea, you control everything, I'm reminded again.

"Medusa was intent on being faithful to the goddess of wisdom and warfare, Minerva. However, Medusa's radiant beauty, specifically her hair, rivaled that of the goddess she sought to please, to the point where Minerva resented Medusa for it. All the while, Minerva and the sea god were at odds with each other, so after Neptune learned of Medusa's beauty—and his romantic advances had been continuously rejected by her—he ended up taking Medusa by force to spite his divine rival."

I swallow hard at the sight I picture. "And yet *Medusa* was punished?"

Madman nods. "Essentially yes. As a means to punish Neptune, the goddess turned her into a creature too devastating and hideous to behold directly, with serpents for hair and eyes that could turn mortals to stone. The transcriptions say her disenchanting stare turned hundreds of poor souls to pillars of stone—that is, until a man decapitated her by tracking her movements through the reflection of his shield. Root History always likes to acknowledge mortals as fickle beings, but this story always fascinated me, seeing as a goddess among women proved to be as petty as the rest of us. That, and the mortal man who slew her goes down as the hero when Medusa was merely a misfortunate woman."

Abruptly, an icy chill rushes through my blood, but there's no chance of smothering it—not when I retrace my steps through her tragic story.

Medusa had two sisters, was devoted to wisdom and war, and captured the attention of a god.

Then, I remember how the Medusa statue that silently looms over Andromeda House's second floor possessed that slight flicker of beauty—beauty that, I now recognize, holds a vague likeness to Aunt Venus.

"Madman," I breathe, the sound ragged.

"What is it, angel?"

When I don't respond immediately—unsure of how to form any sort of response—his disposition shifts into something alarming. Madman senses the bleak urgency in my eyes, and he stares into them with the intensity of one of Whisper's bullets. I swear, I see lightning strike in its depths.

My bottom lip quivers as I come to terms with the most bitter reality of them all.

"Kit will destroy me in order to punish Venus and Jericho,

won't he?"

Madman holds my gaze without blinking, without breathing. No sudden movement graces his features. Not even the nervous tick of his strong jaw or the slight adjustment of his teeth beneath the closed doors of his tight-sealed lips. The stillness of the cave and the sudden ceasing of every candle's previous flickering makes my heart stall in my chest.

"Dear Saints," I exhale, the sound coming out strangled as the beginnings of frightful tears sting my eyes.

"Listen to me," he urges, his hand suddenly moving to my left thigh. If he means to steady me, his touch has the opposite effect. "You need to find the means to get your hands on those books. I don't know enough Root History to inform you of everything myself, but it is imperative that you equip yourself with as much knowledge as possible." I start to stumble over some sort of self-deprecating statement—that I may not be able to accomplish this dreaded task in time—but then, Madman's other hand clutches me by the soft flesh along my upper arm. "I've watched you long enough to know how your mind works. You're *brilliant*, Pandora. You crave knowledge, and you retain it better than most scribes know how to record it. Just find a way to collect them, and you'll be safe."

"And if Kit catches me combing through his books?" I squeak, my eyes unable to peel away from the placement of his gloved hands.

I know Madman longs to have a conversation about it—about how I turn flush beneath his hold and how my trust is beginning to transform into outright codependency—but he resists the impulse. He lays down everything he's hinted at before now and tells me with the kind of sincerity that cracks my ribs open, "You charm your way into a clearing. You picture the softer version of him as you do—the one the wine lured out. And then, no matter what, you don't let your actions eat away at your soul afterwards."

15
Geneva

W hile some people put down others to get their way—which I typically don't agree with—I was fully prepared to make it out of Honeycomb Harbor unseen and unreported to my sister and Jericho, even if the plan I came up with felt despicable.

Luckily, the Saints had mercy on me. Rather than presenting me with countless guards I'd have to blackmail in order to buy their silence, they offered me a vacant harbor and a calming sunset. In fact, the only person down by the docks was hull-cleaning *Crystal Wrath* and didn't recognize me as the queen's sister. Poor bloke will likely be fired when the boat gets back to Broadcove, but at least the coins I smuggled from the treasury as his bribe should keep him afloat for the next several months.

The one downside to this spontaneous voyage: not having a sailing crew at hand. The man I talked into taking me across the Damocles essentially steered the ship for a straight twenty-four hours. I felt so bad for the guy that I volunteered to let him sleep an hour or so while I steered through what I believed to be a straightaway.

When we reached the Mosacian shoreline, however, I could tell that the man didn't recognize our location. Still, that didn't stop him from escorting me off *Crystal Wrath* and pointing me towards what appeared to be a small coastal village. "One of 'em locals ought to help you find your way," he blabbed disinterestedly. "I best be going, though. Thank you for the coins, milady."

And just like that, he vanished into the boat.

Since then, I've trekked what feels like twenty miles but has only been five, and the only comfort amidst my aching feet comes from a soothing summer wind, which whisks me towards the town my chauffeur indicated earlier on. The residents here abide in bright painted cottages, with colored flags hanging on thin clothes lines strung from house to house. A foreign sort of happiness abides in the atmosphere here—the kind that makes people want to live their entire lives with the windows open, as if the warm sun shines even in the dark hours of the night. Children I'd imagine would be in primary school were it not the weekend litter the street, kicking a ball around with their neighbors. I veer towards the edge of the pavement in order to give them their space, but I notice a few of them pause to glance my way. I expect a few pursed lips or sour expressions, and yet, every last face lingers with curiosity at worst and quiet excitement at best. Even the adults that observe the children's recreational games from their sitting rooms seem to eye me with faint fascination and are perhaps even . . . welcoming.

While I'm not sure what part of Mosacia I sailed my way into, this place feels *nothing* like the beastly land that Venus and Jericho had described.

In fact, I'm almost inclined to believe that I'm on a completely separate landmass—but then I catch the Deragon crest in the embossing along a clocktower in the center of town square. It's the one, for lack of better verbiage, sore spot amidst an otherwise idyllic scene. Kids fly their kites in the distant open field, families eat sandwiches together along scattered park benches, and the kids playing in the street heckle and laugh at each other until suddenly, the ball shoots through the air and into my unsuspecting shins.

I will myself not to double over, thankful that my tall boots take the brunt of the impact. One of the children in particular looks far more empathetic than the other, and despite speaking a different language, his tone clues me in on the fervent apology he wishes to extend to me. I offer him a warm smile and gently kick the ball back towards him, waving before I depart down a new alleyway.

Here, the cobblestone paths are lined with vendor carts that smell like pastries and an array of breaded wonders I'd love to sink my teeth into. My stomach gurgles in response, and despite feeling guilty knowing my family's face rests on the coins I slip between my fingers, I'm secretly thankful, at this moment, that Urovian currency became universally recognized. At least I'm not stranded *and* broke.

There's a man reading the paper not far from one of the baker's carts, and I dare to approach the stand. Remembering that the young boy didn't speak Urovian dialect, I ask the vendor slowly, pointing to the second tiered tray, "How much for the loaf?"

The worker's eyes brighten as he drinks me in, then traces my finger towards my item of choice. He nods twice, recounting his preferred pricing internally before inquiring, "Whole or . . . half? Slice?"

The gentleman lingering nearby cuts a passing glance in my

direction, right as I look back at the vendor, who is clearly trying his best to bridge our language barrier. My cheeks pinken with the understanding that he is trying to speak my dialect when I'm in *his* homeland. "Whole, please."

"Jericoin?"

I wince at the question, always having found the name of our currency rather narcissistic, but nod in response.

"Three for you," the vendor pronounces congenially.

Truthfully, I think the man is giving me a deal, and the surprised look on the observer's face, who no longer seems to be reading the paper, only proves my theory.

Still, I set the gleaming coins in his extended palm just as he exchanges them for the loaf. The cinnamon scent of it reaches my nose in a loving caress, and with my hunger roiling within me so fiercely, tears of joy nearly well up in my eyes.

Before I can express my gratitude however, the stranger barks an irritated laugh. "A pretty dame bats her eyelashes and gets half the price shaved off her food? Aurelio, you pushover."

Despite the fact that the man uses my native tongue, the word *pushover* seems to ruffle Aurelio's feathers. He grunts back at the man, and I piece together that, at the bare minimum, the two are leisurely acquaintances. What stands out more so amidst their brief exchange, however, are the kind features on the man my attention now rests upon—honeyed hair, soft brown eyes, and the beginnings of a strawberry blond-tinted beard. His wide, curved-lip smile frames his face so well, it's almost laughable.

Yes, he's a bit ordinary looking, but in the way that matters much more than true, or even rugged, handsomeness. The man looks safe to be around. Inviting.

"That's awfully kind of you to imply that I'm pretty," I find enough of a voice to say, the blush that stains my cheeks real and unfabricated.

"I didn't imply," he says simply.

His body appears poised to turn back to his pages, and a voice inside my head begins to protest. *This is your window, Genny. Take it now.*

"I suppose there aren't too many nice men that speak my language around here?" I ask.

His head perks up, looking over me again, as if to assess if my question is targeted towards something specific or merely a means of casual conversation. He settles upon the former, stepping closer to test the invisible boundary between us. "Not here, I'm afraid. Perhaps further inland, or south—"

"That reminds me. Could you tell me . . . where exactly it is I am? My ship's captain was meant to steer me towards Sevensberg, but considering the lack of a castle and the warm welcome," I add, eyeing sweet Aurelio, "I assume I've lost my way."

That sparks his interest. "*Sevensberg?* Why would you ever want to visit that ghost town?"

I don't bother stringing together a lie, so I lay all my cards on the table unashamedly.

"My daughter faces a tribunal the first of August," I pant. "One where her guilty verdict has likely been decided upon already. But she's not . . . she doesn't deserve the fate they're prepared to deal her."

"First of all, the courts don't convene in Sevensberg anymore," he says. "They used to, you're right about that, but ever since the Seagraves left power"—*that's certainly one way to put it*—"these kinds of hearings take place near the sacred migration sight . . . in the *center* of Mosacia."

Saints, I've got a lot more walking in my future.

"Secondly, Tribunals are not petty threats, Miss," the man

argues, albeit politely. "The continent's most notorious criminals face judgment there. If your daughter is to stand trial, it's highly unlikely that her conviction is unmerited."

"Please," I say, not afraid to grovel to the point of laying my face at his sandaled feet. "I'll do anything you ask. Pay any price for you to take me there. If not to stop the sentence, then at least . . . at least to see her face, to reassure her that I'm *there*."

The man weighs on my offer. He could easily turn away without another word, abandoning me here. But he knows I'm alone—and unlike most men, he takes pity on me rather than taking advantage of the situation.

"Alright, then," he concedes.

I nearly sag from the relief my body expels. "Oh, thank you *so much*—"

"But who exactly is your daughter? Maybe I've heard of her offense."

Saints spare me.

Still, I grant him the truth. "Pandora Deragon," I whisper, as if prepared to have my daughter's name be my final words. As if anticipating him to reveal a hidden sword and slice it through my neck.

But the man stands stoically still, examining me intently. No doubt, there are plenty of Mosacians that would snarl at the Deragon name—but this stranger, mercifully, doesn't appear to belong to that demographic. Each breath feels labored the longer he looks my way.

"I can see I've startled you," I say softly, starting to walk onward. I don't wish to let my defeat take over my face, not while he's still studying it. "Forgive me. I'll just be going—"

"You said it's your *daughter* on trial, yet you gave me the name of the Urovian Princess."

"That's correct."

He blinks once. Twice.

Then, after a long while, the gentleman finally sticks out his hand.

"You're too kindhearted to be the queen I've heard about, so I take it you've done her quite the favor in carrying an heir for her. I'm Renatus." Quickly, he shakes his head, correcting himself. "Ren, actually."

He doesn't have all the details, and while his guess is impeccable, that's all it is to him—a guess. For all I know, Ren's assumption may not be for the sake of accuracy, but for self-preservation. The somber notion draws me two steps closer to him, softening the sheepish smile now plastered across my face.

"Your kindness means more to me than you may ever know, Ren. I'm Geneva," I respond, clutching his hand like he's my only remaining lifeline. "But you may call me Genny."

16
Pandora

When I come downstairs for breakfast, I prepare to go about my day without mentioning my birthday. However, the unmistakable sight of the *U. Herald* in Andie's grasp eradicates any of my previous intentions.

"Don't say it," I whisper, to which Andie drops her printed copy onto the table.

"Why didn't you *tell* me—"

"Keep your voice down!" I hiss anxiously, ripping the edition off the table to get a better look at it. I don't bother reading past the headline, which in and of itself makes me nearly retch:

Written by Her Majesty, Venus Deragon	12 JULY

**PRINCESS PANDORA TURNS 21
IN MOSACIAN CAPTIVITY**

Tossing the edition back onto the table, I add for good measure, "Don't let Kit see that."

Andie rises from her seat, eyeing me and then the kitchen. We both listen for footsteps, and when none are detected, her whole body slackens. "I thought you two had a good thing going there."

"Kit never liked me, Andie. Mainly because he doesn't like my family, which, to each their own. His contempt is warranted. But he's *really* had it out for me ever since our night drinking and playing cards. Probably because he hates that he had fun with a *Deragon*."

Bracing myself on the edge of the counter, I dare a glance at the *U. Herald* once more, rolling my eyes at the photograph Venus allowed the staff to publish of me. It's from my Queen's Feast performance, maybe an hour before Madman slipped into my room. Among other thoughts, the main one that overcomes me as I study the image is how old I look in that dress. I'm twenty-one today, but in that getup, I could be mistaken for twenty-eight.

"Look, I know the circumstances aren't ideal, but I'm not trying to be a nuisance." I exhale. "I'm here so that Kit can finally act out on his vendetta against my family. He wanted the queen, sure, but he settled for a princess when he couldn't attain her. I'm the bait to draw Venus or even Jericho in. Until she caves, Kit is forced to shelter me, feed me, tolerate me, and cross paths with me in the halls of his own house. And it *burns* him."

Andie's eyes slightly flare at the notion. "I see."

I wonder if she can hear it in my voice or see it in the reflection of my eyes—that I'm aching for any sentiments of longing and love from my mother after being apart for so long. We've never been separated like this. I should be tearing up over her handwritten birthday cards and eating cake on the terrace with her, not wondering whether she's reached new lows in attempts to cope with my disappearance.

Andie finally breaks eye contact, and I only feel a morsel of relief. "You should at least read the letter your parents wrote you," she says quietly, "before I toss the paper out."

Right, because in this world, Venus and Jericho are my parents. Not Geneva Deragon.

Still, I dare to turn past the front cover and observe the second side where, plastered along the entire page, is a slew of words that I want so desperately to be real.

> To our daughter,
> From the moment you were born, we knew that the fate
> of our dynasty and the livelihood of our great nation
> would be in capable hands when the time came. You've
> grown into such a strong, noble, and graceful young
> lady, always willing to sacrifice your own wants for
> the betterment of Urovia. We just never thought your
> sacrifices would have to reach these extremes.
> We are looking for you and longing for your safe
> return, Pandora. We assure you, if even one hair on
> your head has been harmed, we will make your captors
> pay in blood. Until we can hold you in our arms again,
> we ask the Saints to keep you safe and to steady our
> hearts amidst our sea of grief.
> All our love,
> Mother and Father

The signature is the last straw.

Internally fuming, I crumble up the paper and stuff it in the wastebin and storm out of the kitchen.

Their words weren't even remotely sentimental. How dare they take up space in the paper to stir the pot rather than allow my *real* mother to communicate with me, to say something that would ease the ache in my chest and that wouldn't make me boil over with rage. How dare they call themselves my parents when it benefits their movements as opposed to benefitting *me*, their "child."

I almost wish that I had a staircase to stomp up just to make a scene, but without it, it takes great restraint to keep from shattering a vase in the main corridor. I don't care if my temper makes me seem twelve as opposed to twenty-one. I can practically feel steam blowing out of my ears as I sail into my room—

And nearly crash into Kit, who stands at the foot of my bed with his arms braced across his chest.

I don't know whether to apologize or throw him out—but the jaded look on his face tells me that I have no business speaking to him with any sort of entitlement.

"What are you doing in my room, Mr. Andromeda?" I say with an air of confusion, if only to keep from sneering at him.

"Mr. Andromeda?" he says in a way that should be humorous, but it comes out icy. "Why the sudden formalities, princess?"

Because I'm bait to you and nothing more. Because it's my birthday and I don't have a single loved one to share it with. Because I am Venus and Jericho's pawn in your bitter standoff against them. But mainly, because I need you to feel somewhat respected despite the fact that I've been stealing books from your shelves these past two weeks and then replacing them before you have the chance to notice. In fact, there's a copy of my latest abducted read that I have stashed away in my delicates drawer, and I'd give my all to make sure you don't uncover it.

When I do not utter a response, Kit's half-quirked smile further chills the air around me. "I came to inform you that your parents have yet to send word following the message we delivered to them," he says casually. "It seems as though it may take more than a smear of your blood to get their attention."

"Saints, what's next?" I ask flatly. "A lock of my hair? A severed limb?"

"Spoken like a woman unafraid of pain."

"I'm not the one who should fret," I return, feigning confidence. "For all you know, the king and queen could be forming a mass ground assault, preparing to overpower the Isle and bring me home without adhering to any of your terms and conditions."

To my surprise, Kit seems to consider the possibility. But his quiet second guessing dissipates as rapidly as it first appeared. "All that manpower for a girl they let slip through the cracks of Broadcove? I doubt it."

"If you're done trying to scare me first thing in the morning, you can go now," I bite.

Kit's responding grin turns positively wicked. "Not quite, Princess. I was also wondering if you were behind the disappearance of my collector's copy of *Mosacian Ideologies and Stories of Old*."

Before I have the chance to deny his implied accusations, he pulls that very book out from behind his back, his smile transforming into a full-blown scowl.

A shiver scales each vertebra down my back, but I force the sensation not to show on the surface, containing it beneath my skin. "Nobody likes a snoop."

"Nobody likes a *thief*," he counters, shaking the book in his grasp.

"Au contraire." I raise a finger at him. "You offered to let me *borrow* a book. Then again, perhaps you forgot, considering you were sloppily drunk and practically draped across my door frame that night."

Kit's searching for an insult, and I can see it in his eyes. He hates that he let his composure slip around me, but eventually, he lands on one that makes my insides splinter.

"Who are you wearing those for, by the way?" he whispers,

pure venom coursing through the words. "You're obviously not putting on a late-night lace show for me—"

I laugh in his face to keep from dying inside. "That's your move? Insulting my choice of undergarments? Grow up, Kit. I borrowed a book. No need to throw a temper tantrum."

"You don't touch what's mine," he snarls.

"I'll touch whatever the hell I want," I bite back, yanking the book out of his hand before he can reinforce his grip on it. "That book, your alcohol, the sculptures in the hall. I am very well entitled to touch *you* if I want."

It takes a minute for me to hear the words back, specifically after Kit's voice drops an octave and says in a way that sounds pained, "Do you?"

Panic leads me to stupidly ask him, "Do I what?"

Kit Andromeda leans towards me at a torturously slow pace, a predator memorizing the scent of fear along its prey. His words are a breathy whisper that heats the skin beneath my ear. "Do you want to touch me?"

"You charm your way into a clearing. You picture the softer version of him as you do—the one the wine lured out. And then, no matter what, you don't let your actions eat away at your soul afterwards."

Madman's ominous warning had felt like nonsense, absolute worst-case scenario. I barely let them sink into my conscience, believing I'd never have to heed his words.

But I'm cornered, not just physically. If I take a step backward, I fall onto the bed, and Saints know what Kit might assume considering the current topic of conversation. If I move forward, our bodies will collide, and any accidental movements may be mistaken for an invitation.

There's only one way out of this—through it.

"I can't touch you when you refuse to separate me from my

family," I say, abstaining from an outright denial or confession. "You'd see me as the enemy laying hands on you, not for what it really would be."

I see a lump bob in Kit's throat as he swallows. "And what's that?"

"A woman trying to better understand a man who has shown her unexpected hospitality."

Truth be told, that's exactly what I've been doing while covertly exchanging books from his shelves and reading them cover to cover—trying to know him better. Trying to understand what makes Kit Andromeda tick, and, perhaps more perilously, what sets his jaded heart aflame.

Parched, his words pierce the air around us. "Try, then."

And so, I dare to reach an unsteady hand towards Kit, my fingers delicately stroking the fabric of his shirt. He shuts his eyes, turning rigid and his body flinching at the initial contact. I go to retract my hand at the touch, but find his hand clamping around my wrist before I get the chance.

Kit pulls me flush against him, and I gasp from the sheer force of it, of the sensation of my torso memorizing the outline of his. I drop the book on the floor, my hands circling around his neck.

I know the hell I'll have to pay for this, but I block it out—just for a moment. Long enough for the green of Kit Andromeda's eyes to tear through my defenses. I allow my face to soften under his astute gaze, recalling the sound of his drunken laugh and the way his painted features made him appear comical as opposed to his usual coldness. I accept the heat his hands brand into the skin along my arms, and I stand firm and unrelenting as he allows himself to trace my body further.

My shoulders

My back.

My hips.

"I should have simply asked you for the book," I choke out.

"I shouldn't have combed through your drawers."

Kit drags a gentle hand across the side of my face, and I shiver as he sweeps my curls away. His lingering touch cradles my jaw, and I'm inclined to nestle into it. "And I wish you didn't have to be the pawn in all this. I may go through with it all, but you make it . . . difficult to do so."

Silence looms over us, and just as my mind starts to wonder if kissing Kit wouldn't be so terrible of an idea, he asks me in a feather-light whisper, "You looked upset when you first came in. Would you tell me what troubles you?"

Kit will destroy me in order to punish Venus and Jericho, won't he?

But then, his hold on me slackens, as if to silently assure me that he doesn't mean to corner me into an answer or trap me within his touch.

"I'm trying to convince myself that my family hasn't given up on me," I answer. "But I'm having a hard time holding out hope."

Something about that final word lands an unintended blow, and he steps back. Then, he skirts around me, collecting the copy of *Mosacian Ideologies and Stories of Old* off the ground. Dusting it off, Kit says, "I think that page 213 will change your mind."

He extends the book towards me once more, and as the weight of it shifts into my grasp, Kit dismisses himself without so much as a backwards glance. In efforts to dull the ache his absence leaves me with, I pick through the pages until I see the marker and splay the pages wide.

My eyes bulge at the title:

The Maiden Pandora and her Ill-Fated Box

17
Pandora

I avoid Andie and Kit the rest of the day despite my mind whirring with frantic questions, the main one being why I— Urovia's Crown Princess—would be named after a widely renown and revered story in *Mosacian* root history.

I avoid them because there's only one person I trust to explain it fully for me, likely because he knows all the buried intricacies.

Tonight is particularly prickly weather wise, the heat nosediving once the sun fully sets. My teeth chatter against each other at the base of the dock. Although, as I watch Madman steer his gleaming boat towards me, I don't think it's from the chill in the air.

I haven't seen Madman or visited his alcove since the night he instructed me to start sneaking books and save my skin. Primarily because I've been reading every spare moment I've been granted, but also because there's been the persistent inclination that each night I spend in his inner sanctum, the more my trust in him begins to evolve into a deeper reliance. A physical response to an unspoken, emotional fascination.

Sure enough, as Madman steadies the boat in its mooring, those weeks apart suddenly feel like years. The notion of how lonely I've been hits me like one of the waves splashing onto the jagged shoreline, and when I gear my eyes towards Madman's, the same sentiment mirrors back at me.

The beginnings of a somber smile tug at the corner of my mouth, but it blooms in full when he whispers into the evening wind, "Aren't you a sight for sore eyes."

"It's nice to see you again as well," I say as mild-mannered as I can manage without letting my excitement seep through.

"I didn't expect to see you waiting down here for me," he continues. "You've . . . never done that before."

"Been feeling a bit stir-crazy in my room, that's all."

Madman chuckles under his breath, eyes drifting towards his dark boots. "I figured you'd be celebrating with the rest of the house."

My face heats at the same time my smile deepens. *Of course he remembered.*

"Andie was mad I wouldn't let her bake a cake."

"But you love sweets," he says, concern illuminating his eyes. His mask faintly ticks to one side as the muscles in his face adjust to his outward surprise. "Lady Andromeda is also said to be quite the baker. Why turn her down?"

As he asks me the question, he offers his familiar, onyx-gloved hand in efforts to help me cross over from the wooden ledge into the boat. I ignore the faint sizzle in my blood as we touch. "I didn't want to make a fuss," I say, clunking into the boat and settling into my designated seat as Madman begins to row us out of the bay. "Besides, I spent most of my day reading."

Madman's head tilts in renewed attention. "Oh?"

"*Mosacian Ideologies and Stories of Old*. Kit's collector's edition."

"I can only imagine the trouble you went to in order to swipe it undetected."

I choose not to shed light on the near encounter Kit and I almost shared, even as the gravity of what almost occurred shows all over my face. Instead, I mask my guilt for dread and tell him, "I read the story of Pandora today."

He rows us onward, angling his stance to turn us to the left. "Feeling sentimental?"

"Confused is a better word for what I'm feeling, actually," I say, crossing my legs at the ankle and sinking deeper into the cushion. "I still don't understand why my mother would name me after the story. She knew nothing about Mosacia when she had me, and even after that, all she knew was what Venus and Jericho told her—"

It hits me like a blow, right then and there. The realization physically jolts me, and Madman nearly loses his balance as I *thunk* against the backboard.

My mother didn't name me at all.

After Madman closes us in the darkness, he crosses the space and gestures me over to the divan. I follow in silence, sitting where he offers me respite. "Tell me what you know about my name. How I got it."

"Your mother felt indebted to Venus when she gave birth to you. Because of her relationship with Jericho, she was able to provide their family comfort, security, and wealth. Without Venus, your mother would have raised you in squalor, and to express her gratitude, she asked your aunt to bestow your name upon you."

"And Venus picked *Pandora* of all things?"

Madman shrugs plainly. "Maybe she heard the story from someone and liked the name."

Or its significance.

"I think it suits you. Not because you're destined for a violent takeover or you bring out the worst in everything like the story suggests, but because Pandora is lovely and fiercely curious."

I try not to roll my eyes. "Maybe, but those qualities tend to get me into trouble."

The kind of trouble that had me taking a guard to my rooms just to try and feel known for who I am and not who the Deragon Dynasty paints me to be. The kind of trouble that likely makes my aunt and uncle see me as gullible for following Madman out of Broadcove so easily. The kind of trouble that nearly had me drifting towards Kit Andromeda's mouth and preparing for a kiss that could cause a rift in all my previous beliefs. The kind of trouble that has something inside me reeling the longer Madman looks at me, stoking an unknown fire inside my lungs.

Madman peels his eyes from the floor when he notices I've gone quiet. "But those qualities are what make you one of a kind, Pandora." His tone of voice is grave, an implied warning that I ought to brace for what he says next. "You perpetuate a contrived narrative about yourself to better your family's dynasty, not to better your own agenda. You read books and read people like you're searching for hidden magic rather than their buried weaknesses. But most of all, you look into the eyes of an assassin and willingly offer your hand. Time and time again."

Then, Madman makes a move for one of the shelves, revealing an unwrapped oak box with an indigo bow fastened across all four sides. The deep brown lacquer catches reflections of dispersed candlelight, and he transfers it into my hold. Before I reach for the notch, Madman drapes his hand over mine, the sensation chilling me to the bone just as much as it warms something in my middle.

"Read the note."

That's when I notice the folded piece of parchment with my name scrawled across its plane, tucked under the dark ribbon. The sight of Madman's handwriting—surprisingly meticulous and ornate—stirs something in my chest. I take it into my fingertips and read each word with care.

Dearest Pandora,

Of course, you — my greatest source of captivation — would be named after a story most of us in Mosacia grew up with. Fate seems to have a sense of humor like that: how, in some aspect, I've had your presence in my life from a very young age.

It is fate's kindness, however, that brings me to writing you this. I once told you that your name held great significance, and it does — as does this gift. I thought you should possess your very own Pandora's Box.

I lift my eyes and meet his own. "Madman, you—"

"Keep reading," he presses, recognizing that I have not reached the end of the page.

Considering what this story entails, you might wonder why I gave you something with such ill-omened roots. And perhaps it is not the most cheerful or logical of reasonings, but it's the truest thing I'm allowed to tell you: you deserve better. Everyone you know — both here on the Isle and back in Broadcove — has been lying to you. The full truth of everything I've uncovered lies within this box. Open it alone and when you feel ready to face disaster.

"Disaster?" I say with an uncomfortable laugh. "You boxed up heartache for my birthday?"

"I gave you an option to take your *life* back," Madman clarifies in a slightly firmer tone.

I glance over the written words once more, hovering over a specific sentence.

Everyone you know—both here on the Isle and back in Broadcove—has been lying to you.

"Everyone?"

The beauty in my mother's face burns within my brown eyes, and Madman senses it with a grim expression. "Everyone," he answers.

The polished box seems to scald my hands in affirmation.

No, I'm not ready to uncover everything. Not when it means dismantling everything I know about my mother and her love.

I block the images of my family and the two other residents of Andromeda House out of my mind, bracing myself where I stand before Madman. "You said you kept the necessary things hidden, so what changed? Why give me the chance to know the truth, now?"

"It's not that anything changed, but rather that something was recognized."

"And what's that?" I ask.

Madman releases a long breath. "The depth of my affections for you."

My eyes round out at the words, and I will myself to remain calm, to not be rash. To not entertain the full breadth of my looming thoughts and emotions that have flooded my senses each time I thought about Madman. To not blurt out just how much I found myself missing his presence while he was away, and what the confession of such a notion would mean for my future visits to his private, shadowy haven.

"All those years I spent collecting intel, gaining leverage—it was all just busywork, the labor of the day before turning in for the night and finally finding rest. Because in the silent moments when you'd return to your rooms and go about your routine, when you'd glance out your window even as your mind wandered thousands of miles elsewhere, that's what watching you from afar felt like. It felt like coming home."

I gulp at the sentimentality of what he's saying—that a man forever on the run found a grounding point, a place of refuge . . . in *me*.

"And now that you're here, it's like I'm anchored to the earth again rather than floating above it. Like every symphony I struggled to compose finally came together when you followed me to this place. And each time you come back I worry I'll do something to scare you away." Madman looks down at the box I hold uncomfortably, meaning to go on.

But a sudden surge of uncharacteristic confidence rushes through my bloodstream. "What if the terrible truths inside that box are nothing compared to the terror I experience when I think about my feelings for you?"

He takes a careful, calculated step towards me, but says nothing.

It's a behavioral pattern that I haven't seen from other men I've encountered. Aside from people who have been *taught* not to interrupt—though only in concerns of respecting my Urovian title—most people tend to talk over me or try to finish my sentences before I can get them out. But not Madman. He never assumes things too quickly. He always gives me my space to formulate my thoughts and opinions. To let me clarify myself.

But after what I just spoke into the universe, I feel as though the right words might spoil the moment. "This won't do," I whisper, setting the box on the floor.

Madman's voice is the sound of pure ache. "What do you mean?"

I force the fluttering nerves to settle in my stomach, and I gear my eyes towards Madman's with all the inner strength I can muster. "I don't want the only gift I'm given for my birthday to be ominous. I'd like something else, something . . . happier . . . to neutralize it."

Madman doesn't move a muscle other than the ones it takes for him to form the words, "Is that so?"

I nod, suppressing the lump in my throat.

"A boat tour around the Isle?"

I shake my head, a bashful smile plastered across my lips.

"A song?"

Truthfully, the offer is tempting, but the glimmer in Madman's eyes tells me that he could do better—and I'm inclined to take him up on it.

Before I even realize that he's done so, Madman closes the distance between us, our hands intertwining. "Tell me what it is you desire, Pandora."

Desire.

The word burns through me like a wildfire, eradicating any realization for how rash or impulsive this may be—but I don't care. I tug Madman closer to me, untangling my fingers from his in order to set his hands over my hips. Our torsos brush, then meld together, and I feel his heartbeat pounding against his ribcage like it's trying to break out of prison. Then, I drape my arms around his neck, stretching to meet his height better.

I don't allow myself to think about how crazy I am for finally saying, "You know exactly what it is I desire."

To know that my faith is not misguided.

To prove that there's more to Madman and me than mere trust.

His smile dips, saddening a touch. "I'll show you when I'm ready," he murmurs.

I shake my head faintly before bringing my forehead to his own, to the surface of his mask. It's not as cold as I anticipated it to be against my flesh. My words are barely audible, even in my own ears.

"I know you will . . . but that's not what I mean."

My fingers graze through the dark waves along his scalp, and it untethers something in the both of us. His eyes sparkle. And then, Madman softly laughs at the gasp that escapes me as he pulls me impossibly closer and, just this once, surrenders his mouth to mine.

18
Geneva

I missed my daughter's birthday.
I've *never* missed one of her birthdays.

And yet, here I am, riding a clunky Mosacian railroader from the northern coast towards the plains. It's transcontinental, and far larger than any train system I'd seen in Urovia, even in Broadcove. But according to Ren, who has been accustomed to transports far more upscale than this one, the railroader up north tends to move at a snail's pace.

"Innovation always improves the closer you travel to the center of the continent," Ren told me yesterday as I tried not to let my anxiety show about missing the chance to celebrate Pandora, or at least hold her in my arms for a minute.

But as I watched the sun set on my daughter's first day of a new year, my soul ached in the darkness. I broke down the minute I woke up this morning, consumed with despair and self-loathing, feeling like a wretched mother for not having ripped the world apart to find Pandora by now. And I haven't stopped crying since.

The only kindness has been the fact that no one deigned to fill the two apportioned vacancies in our private cabin—likely because I *reek* of hopelessness. The divider that closes us off from the public, free-moving aisle is a glass sliding door that is only slightly frosted for privacy, and poor Ren has spent the last hour assuring other passengers and railroad attendants that I just received devastating news about a relative and to kindly give the two of us space.

The two of us—like we're together, or something.

When I feel a brief reprieve from my sobbing, I blubber out the words, "I'm sorry," while trying not to wipe my tears in a way that smears the kohl along my eyes. It's bad enough that I'm an ugly crier. There's no need to make myself look like I've crawled my way out of my gravesite. "I don't mean to be a bother, which I know I have been, but—"

"I'm not sure why you're apologizing for the grief you feel," Ren says softly, but with full enunciation. His eyes drift to mine with endless compassion, having stomached the sounds of my smothered sobs as I brokenly went on and on about missing her big day. Missing *her.* "It's clear that the love you have for your daughter knows no bounds."

"But I can't *stop*—"

"You will when you're able," he soothes, laying a hand on my shoulder. "But there's no rush. Your pain is no imposition to me."

Stunned by the words, the last of my sobs die in my throat. For now, at least.

I sniff, the movement a hard jerk. "Why are you being so kind to me?"

Truthfully, I'd been wanting to know the answer since the moment Ren agreed to my terms and introduced himself back on the coast. A man with his charm and his looks should've kept him far from available to catering to my whims, yet Ren appeared to have no conflicts to mitigate before insisting we head for the train station twenty miles eastward. It also didn't hurt that he was the nicest man I'd ever met, both inside and outside of Broadcove.

Talking to Ren felt like talking to a friend. A real one—the kind I would have had to make on my own if our family never made it out of the marshes all those years ago. Whether in the market, at my old job, over dinner at one of the dingy pubs, wherever I could. The normalcy of truly knowing one another, despite our limited time, made it all too easy to share the intricate details of my circumstance—my status as Duchess, what I knew about Pandora's disappearance, the relationship with my sister and her husband, the king. Whether Venus and Jericho would hound me for being too trusting, if they ever found out somehow, I don't care anymore. I'm a mother on the edge.

"You want the short answer or the long one?"

I shrug. "Both."

Ren cracks a smile that sends warmth skittering about our cabin. "Long answer, after the Seagraves fell, my friends and I had this epiphany that we shouldn't waste our time living in one place—that we ought to see the world before it turned into something devastating. So we ended up traveling the continent, which was fun and all, until my friends started meeting women who'd become their wives and they decided to settle down wherever we were at the time. I eventually got sick of traveling to see all of them and tried to plant roots along the northern coast. I was wading through life there for the last few years . . . until you."

I try not to let the blush that those last few words summon to the surface overtake me. I picture it then: Ren watching his companions dwindling over time, growing weary to the beauty of the world when he lost out on his friends to women they'd never known beforehand. It reminds me of how, in some senses, I lost parts of Venus and Calliope when they chose to get married and start their families. Perhaps they felt the same when Pandora entered into existence as well.

"And the short answer?" I ask, almost as an afterthought.

Ren tilts his head at me, his gaze deepening. "I thought you were the most gorgeous woman I'd ever laid eyes on. To refuse your request, no matter how complicated the conditions were, would have been irrevocably stupid."

I remember then that his first words to me back in the street, both directly and indirectly, were compliments of my appearance. The depth of his attention towards me, however, rattles my nerves more than I expected it to.

"Are you going to make it a habit of flirting with me, Ren?"

"I'll flirt with you until I'm blue in the face if it keeps those tears from staining your pretty face," he says.

He's right. My tears haven't just *stopped*. They've dried up, now replaced by a childlike smile that has my cheeks pinching the sides of my face. I'm so flustered by the realization of it that I nearly swat at myself to stop. I laugh as I tell him, "Sorry, it's just been . . . a long time since anyone's made me feel this way."

"Feel what way?" he asks innocently.

A tender smile blooms across my mouth, like a flower emerging from a long, harsh winter. "Young."

We both quiet within our cabin, my gaze drifting to the sweeping hills beyond the glass of our window. I shut my eyes for a moment, imagining how the summer air likely turns colder the further north one may climb. Snow dusts the peaks of faraway mountains, even in July, and a herd of humped animals I can't place graze the valleys below without a care in the world—

"Young, as in, before Pandora?" Ren's voice softly pulls me

back into the train car.

I swallow, hoping the sound isn't as visible as it feels. "Not that I resent her in any way, but yes. Before I became a mother."

"Tell me about it," he whispers, crossing his legs in his cushioned seat and positioning his body to face me fully. To let me know that I have his full, undivided attention.

Tongue stumbling over half-formed words, I try and spit out, "Well, I was the youngest of three sisters. I'd heard that in wealthier families, the baby tends to get spoiled compared to their older siblings, but my family . . ." I try not to dwell too long on the horrors of poverty, which I had only grasped in its totality the longer we lived in Broadcove. "I don't think I was supposed to happen. We were so poor, but my parents had loved one another so deeply, so they made it work for a while. When Mother died though, things really took a plunge."

"I'm so sorry," Ren offers up, his eyes as empathetic as a hand on my shoulder would be.

I don't allow myself to linger on the sadness of that time in my life. "Her death brought out the worst in Father. His devastation turned into rage, and, to make a long story short, brought about his demise, too. That left my older sisters to play parents for me, and the only thing they could afford to spoil me with was security. They never said it aloud, but when we were fighting for scraps, or trying to keep out of trouble, I could sense their unified agreement—that they would take the brunt of whatever suffering we'd face before they'd let it touch me. And maybe, knowing that, I started to look for a way to alleviate their problems."

The railroader jostles a bit, likely converting from one set of tracks to another. I catch Ren surveying the aisle beyond our cabin, waiting to see if the sound had arisen from a stumbled passenger or two. No one draws near, and he settles deeper into his seat.

"Kurt Prokium was a boy I'd seen a few times at the Trading Block," I tell him, casually observing the way the rising sun spotlights Ren's golden features through the window. "It was the marshes' bartering hotspot since most residents didn't have enough coins to outright *buy* anything. My sister, Venus, was going toe to toe with some sleazy baker, trying desperately to get our oldest sister ingredients for some semblance of a birthday cake, and I just remember being so furious at the way the men of the town thought they could walk all over her. Over *us*. But Venus never balked. She was the strongest of all of us. I just stupidly stood there and watched in awe as she haggled the price down to a tolerable amount."

"A family trait, I see," Ren comments casually.

If he weren't sitting across from me, I'd have swat Ren across the shoulder. Instead, I flash him a dimly humored glance and roll my eyes, to which he smiles and further reclines in his seat.

"And then, Kurt came up by my side, asked if Venus was going easy on the baker, and if I was the true muscle of the operation. I told him I wouldn't hurt a fly." I feel warmth in my cheeks, the wind from that autumn day nearly twenty years ago coursing through my hair somehow. Ren senses it, too, eyes on fire with silent ponderings.

"I wasn't looking to fall in love if that's what you are wondering. Your eyes have a way about them that makes them all too readable, Ren." I don't know why the second statement is phrased aloud, but I let it hang there for a moment. "But I was looking for a way out. Out of my family's house and into the arms of someone that could provide for me without feeling like my existence was a burden to them."

"You're not a burden, Genny," he says so sadly it pierces deep.

"I'm not anymore," I say, knowing the sentiment he's trying to reassure me of. "But I was, then. They loved me despite it, but that doesn't change the fact that I was. And I clung to Kurt because of it. I think, without going into the nitty-gritty of it, I went along with his insistence for privacy as we navigated us—what we were to each other—because of the guilt I felt. Even after I fell for Kurt, I couldn't escape the fact that I had allowed him to pursue me out of an opportunistic mindset."

I shut my eyes so that I can choke out the words, "He died before he could tell me he loved me, if that was even on his mind. And he never got to know—I didn't know, then—that I was . . ."

Ren's hand rests upon my knee, and the touch unfurls the knot that was beginning to tighten in my chest, my stomach. "You don't have to keep going if it hurts too much," he murmurs. "Not for my sake."

I shake my head, opening my eyes despite knowing they've gone glassy again. "The worst part about it all is that it's not his permanent absence that eats away at me, and it wasn't even that way when Pandora was born. It's that I'll never know what his intentions would've been. For me. For our daughter. Kurt was already so on guard about keeping our relationship private—sneaking me in and out of his house, insisting I burn every note that he ever wrote me and slipped in my pockets before I'd dash home—that had I come forward about the baby, who knows if he'd have stayed with me or scorned the both of us."

Ren's expression saddens, his tone gentle. "That's such a harmful way of thinking, Genny."

My name on his lips wounds me, the responding ache so insufferable that I lash out. "Well, it felt better to assume the worst in him rather than grieve the only man who ever considered loving me."

I hear the snap in my tone once it's too late to rein it in, and while I begin to form an apology, Ren merely holds out a hand. "Not for my sake," he repeats. Still, a question reflects in the depth of his warm eyes. "You never thought about . . . trying again?"

With someone else.

"There's a very slim margin of men interested in pursuing a woman who has already been so clearly shared with another," I say, the laugh in my throat bitter. "Besides, Jericho became the center of Venus's universe, and Calliope's husband hers. But my little girl . . . she's *everything* to me. I had created something that brought me enough joy to last me the rest of my lifetime, and that was enough."

The cabin goes quiet for a series of moments, silent and serene.

Then, Ren asks, "And what now?"

I look at him sidelong, a silent demand for clarification.

"Now that she's gone—if she stays gone—what joy will carry you through the rest of your life?"

The only thing that keeps me from gaping at his question is the sound of an unanticipated knocking of a fist on the cabin door. The sound jolts us upright, Ren nearly stumbling over his own feet.

A steward pulls open our door and flashes me, in particular, a bright smile. "Care for some refreshments, Miss?"

"She's not thirsty," Ren pipes in, not even a whisper of his genteel demeanor to be found as he stares down the uniformed gentleman. "You have plenty of water left, don't you, sweetheart?"

"*Ren,*" I snarl, embarrassed by his territorial outburst. Then again, maybe going along with whatever makeshift relationship ploy he's pulling out of his ass might serve me well. "Be nice—"

"The conductor would like to lay eyes on you," the steward

explains, undeterred by Ren's unwarranted distaste. "He wants to know that you're doing well, now."

Part of me wishes to go with him to get a free pass from where my and Ren's conversation was swiftly heading, but the look on Ren's face . . . that's panic. True, utter panic.

I then see that the steward isn't looking at me anymore, but at Ren.

As if to keep him in line. Silent.

It's while his neck remains craned Ren's way that I see a nasty bruise that dips below his neck, a surface-level gash wound slowly staining his shirt crimson—his shirt that, I realize, isn't buttoned in the right spots, the collar of it drooping on one side.

"I'll come with you, then," Ren insists, rising to his feet.

Even before I'm able to play along, the steward bristles. "That won't be necessary. Only the *lady* is required up front." His Mosacian accent deepens in irritation before he evens it out, looking at me once more. "I can assure you, Miss, your husband will not be kept waiting long."

Ren says my name, the sound of it uncharacteristically harsh. Desperate, even.

That's when I catch a passing glimpse of the menacing blade in the steward's pocket, blood speckling its jagged edge when it catches light from beyond the window.

"Let's go," the steward demands, and with a piercing clamp, he grabs me by the wrist and begins to pull me out of the cabin.

I'm not my daughter. I haven't been brought up with proper self-defense training, and I don't wish to bet my survival odds on the mere *guess* that sweet-as-sugar Ren Setare knows anything about fending off an attacker.

Though, maybe I'm selling Ren short—because he bares his teeth at the man before freeing my wrist.

"*Nobody* puts their hands on my *wife.*"

And then, Ren drives his foot right between the steward's legs with all the force he can muster and yanks me from the cabin.

19
Geneva

The male howl of agony follows us down the narrow aisle as we zoom through the connecting train cars. Past the elegant, upper-class cab, with its shimmering bar cart and the startled passengers sipping midmorning cocktails. Past the staff quarters and the restocking stations. Past another eight sectors of segregated cabins and a series of startled faces.

"He either won't be down long, or there will be more like him coming," I pant, darting through the narrow aisle, my hand clasped within Ren's. I will myself to make longer strides. "Where are the emergency exits?"

Ren mentally recalls the safety demonstration the attendants had prepped us with before embarking, the one that I couldn't hear over the sound of my incessant crying. "Aisle fifteen has the largest door, but we're likely closest to the back quarters—"

"*They went this way!*" a gruff voice shouts from the car behind us.

Ren calculates our best odds, and the morbid expression tells me all I need to know before he says it aloud.

"We need to jump." He points his free hand towards the next connection. "I'll get the door."

I don't have time to think about how fast the train is moving or whether the ground outside is going to make for a painful landing. "Okay," I breathe, albeit shakily.

Ren's shock at my lack of a rebuttal, even for fear's sake, radiates in his eyes. Still, he doesn't let the feeling linger, inclining his head towards the metal door and making a mad dash after me.

Harsh, pounding footsteps sound from behind me and Ren, and I don't care to look and see how many people are gaining on us. Ren does, though. I feel his body shift directions slightly, and a strangled yelp escapes his throat. "*MOVE*, GENNY!"

We reach the connecting sector, and Ren finally releases my hand in order to get a strong grip on the iron latch keeping the door to the outside world shut. He has to descend two of the steps to get close enough, to establish a comfortable stance and keep from flying out when the door finally gives way.

Dust and wind bite at both of our faces, the summer sun momentarily blinding him. With eyes pinched shut, Ren offers his arms out to me. "Hold onto me!" he calls over the roaring wind.

I reach for him, and with no shred of regret or second guessing, Ren pulls me tight to his chest before throwing us both into the daylight. The scent of his clothes on my face calms me down as we go airborne.

And as if the Saints mean to cover us in their favor, the breeze swings the metal door shut, concealing our desperate escape route.

The crunch of our impact rattles through our bones, but Ren still hisses the words, "Stay. Down."

Our feet touched down on the uneven, grassy path moments ago, but as the rest of us hurtled towards the ground, Ren had torqued his body to where his back would take the brunt of our fall, me landing over top of him. My head knocked into his teeth and his jaw collided with my own.

But now, even with parts of me numb to the shock of coming to such a drastic halt after throwing myself out of a moving railroader, all my muddled brain can focus on is Ren. The rise and fall of his chest beneath me, moving me with him. The malicious tone in his voice as he sprang into action.

"Wife, huh?" I ask, hoping to make light of the ache in our bodies.

Ren coughs out a laugh, and I try to hide my horror at the blood it summons across his teeth and tongue. His nose is bleeding, too. He says in panting breaths, "What an ass of me. I didn't even get you a ring."

I laugh, and the movement hurts my ribs. I reach for the spot, but touching it only makes the pain deepen. I shut my eyes. "You've already outdone yourself in the chivalry department. I mean, if I'm in this kind of shape, I can only imagine how banged up you are."

"I'd never complain about being *banged up* by you, Genny."

I bite my tongue to keep from snickering. "Real mature, Ren."

"You married me," he retorts, his smile grand and utterly infectious.

Slowly, Ren helps me to my feet, even though both of us feel as though we've split a lung. It takes me two tries to find the proper footing, and Ren allows me to drape most of my weight towards his front as I rise. Once securely settled, and despite the un-ladylikeness of it, I spit out what I think is saliva that has begun to pool in my mouth onto the grass but discover that I accidentally douse a budding wildflower in fresh blood.

"News must have broken about you being here, out in the wild," Ren theorizes. "And considering the grudge a decent portion of the Mosacian Empire holds towards Jericho and Venus, you're not safe unaccounted for. Then again, if Mosacians know you're here, your family's forces are likely scouring the continent for you, too."

There's no need to tell him what he can already deduct himself: that falling into the possession of either camp is less than ideal if I'm apprehended before I can get to my daughter.

"But I won't let that happen," Ren vows, his eyes intense and unwavering as they hold my stare. "I will not let them, *any* of them, take you from me. Even if keeping that promise ends up breaking all my bones."

Ren voices the words with such authority that my legs nearly tremble, threatening to send me tumbling back to the ground.

It won't be too hard to play your wife if you say things like that, I want to tell him.

"Come on," Ren urges, wrapping my arm around his shoulder to provide me better support. His smile widens beneath his slight, golden scruff—although, it may be another slight grimace of pain. "There will be another train in a couple hours. We'll be able to flag it down if we keep to the tracks."

20
Pandora

Madman hasn't kissed me since the night he gifted me my Pandora's Box, likely because I've expressed no interest in opening the dreaded container—and I'm inclined to pick a fight about it.

At first, Madman appeared well and fine with my choice to avoid the box and the horrors within. "You deserve the necessary time to brace for the emotional impact. It's a lot to handle, so I wouldn't want you jumping into its contents unprepared," he had told me, generosity and patience practically dripping from his mouth. It was all so swoon worthy . . .

Until I realized that any chance for a romantic reprise was contingent on forward progress towards opening the box.

Madman hadn't outright told me that, though—that he would pull away in the hopes that I'd focus my attention on strengthening my heart rather than strengthening our connection. But had I known his coy act of pretending we never kissed would go on this long, I would've made a stink about it sooner. Because nearly two weeks later, I'm not sure what's worse. Replaying the moment in my sleep and waking up in Andromeda House out of his reach, longing to make it real, or going along with the fake normalcy that Madman silently insists on upholding. I've only kept going back to his lair every night in the hopes that we can at least *discuss* it.

The way the universe halted at the first press of our lips.

How Madman devoured me until my body, my very *soul*, trembled.

The silken softness of his hair between my fingers, and the way our hands frantically clutched for more of one another.

The taste of his tongue brushing over mine, and the way his breathless sounds of uncaged joy nearly made me set the cavern ablaze.

How my body felt electrically supercharged—even after Madman released his grip on me and said through gritted teeth, "It's late. You should get some rest." Madman may as well have doused me in ice-cold water and then spit on me. Shame put me to sleep out of self-preservation.

The only thing that's gotten me through it, oddly enough, has been Kit's gradual change of heart regarding sharing his collection. Once he granted me permission to read his copy of *Mosacian Ideologies and Stories of Old*, he started making conversation over breakfast about what I'd read. Sure, it felt somewhat akin to the literature comprehension assessments my Broadcove tutors used to put me through, but rather than receiving a test score at the end, Kit Andromeda would stew on what parts of the stories intrigued me most and recommend me something in a similar subject field. Even Andie seemed keen on asking me about how I felt regarding their territory's history, to which I'd always ensured a polite response.

Andie's been a surprising delight as well. She never mentioned anything about my birthday or the *U. Herald* to Kit, and whenever he decides to leave on temporary business, she makes for surprisingly good company. She sits right around Aunt Calliope's age, if I had to guess, but speaks in a manner that drops her age by a few years. It makes her more approachable, to the point where, a week ago, I asked her to teach me how to cook a few basic meals. Andie never pestered me about why, deducting that Broadcove Castle had troves of chefs that made everything for us, and made it enjoyable. Even on the nights when Kit was away, Andie and I had no trouble entertaining ourselves, swept up in the fun of messing up a simple recipe or kicking each other's asses in board games.

But tonight, Kit is still away doing . . . whatever he slips off the Isle for, and Andie's been particularly quiet all evening, retiring to her rooms the moment we finished cleaning our dishes. As if Madman anticipated it, too, I find him waiting for me just beyond the dark depths of Andromeda House's underbelly.

"Good to see you again, angel."

I try to grant him a congenial smile, but it doesn't meet my eyes. "Yeah. You, too."

I don't take his hand tonight. I see myself into his boat without so much as a passing glance.

Madman blows out a breath as he steps into the boat and rows us away from the rock-laden berth. "Did I do something to offend you?"

His cluelessness does me in this time, and I decide to hell with it. I'm picking a fight.

"You've been ignoring me."

Madman's brows crinkle in bemused disagreement. "I didn't realize spending nearly every night with you for the past month was considered ignoring you."

"You know what I mean, Madman."

"Why don't you spell it out for me, just in case I'm mistaken?" he challenges.

I cross my arms over my chest, knowing damn well Madman could see the movement as defiant and childish. I don't care. "We kissed, and rather than acknowledge how it felt for either of us, you've *insisted* on avoiding it. Talking about anything else as opposed to owning up to all those beautiful, moving things you said."

Madman appears genuinely thrown that I chose to speak out about it. "Pandora."

"Do you know how *stupid* I felt this last week, singing harmonies at the pianoforte with you when there were several other things I wanted our mouths to do? How silly I feel now just thinking about it, about how badly I *still* want to—"

"*Pandora.*"

The breath I loosen then is near guttural. "Is there something wrong with me? Or did something in that kiss make you realize that, maybe, all that time you spent watching me from afar was overhyped. That I was more fun to look at than to finally connect with. To touch—"

"That's *enough*," he growls.

"Hardly," I sneer, standing up with a rush of jilted rage, unphased as the boat rocks on the indigo waves. "You *embarrassed* me, Madman, and you know it. Are you at least going to take accountability for that?"

He's as stubborn as I am. "I don't know what you're talking about."

"You kissed me like *that*, and then told me to go to *sleep*?"

Hands curled into fists around the boat's oar, Madman finally comes loose. "Because had you not, I would've gotten carried away—"

"I *wanted* you to," I cry out in a moment of personal boldness. I dare not let any timidity overtake me. Not this time. "Don't you get it? I was already in your bed. Every night. What difference would it have made if I was sleeping in it or *sleeping* in it?"

"*So many things, Pandora!*" he roars, dropping the oar entirely, now. He rises to his feet in a rush of fiery movement, face contorting in such anger that his mask moves against the muscles below. "I've known you for *years*, but you've only known me for what? A month?"

"And you get to decide when and how I act on the feelings I have for you?"

"I wasn't finished," he cuts in, eyes darkening with fury and tone dripping with unexpected venom. Storm clouds roll in the depths of eyes I'd once considered soothing. "You don't know me, Pandora. Not the way that I know you."

"*Then let me the hell in!*"

Rage curdles my blood like sour milk, and the intensity of my voice shocks us both.

"You know what? You're right," I say, wrath quieting my overall demeanor. "I don't know you. All I know about you are the scraps you're willing to give me. You sing. You compose music. You hunt your prey. You hide from the light. But did you ever consider the depth of my understanding about each of those things? Because when you sing, something in my heart soars. Because when you spend hours at the pianoforte, you're not just creating something, you're casting a spell. Because even with that gun on you at all times," I say, pointing to the inky depths of his cloak, "you don't have the stomach to take life as flippantly as you pretend to. And when you spend years in the dark, altering your very way of life to become some sort of nocturnal being . . ." I say, and the realization of it all is so sad. "You convince yourself that even a morsel of light will ruin you forever."

Madman looks at me as if I had just ripped his mask off his face and stared into his very soul.

"Of course, that's not enough for me to truly understand you, right? Let alone *be* with you. Seeing the best in you doesn't cut it. I get it. But don't punish *me* because you refuse to be *honest* with me, or with yourself."

He goes ghastly still, and I'm half inclined to end my tirade there . . . for all of five seconds.

"Tell me, like a man, that you're too scared to let yourself give in to me," I seethe, my anger making me feel ten inches taller than him, even as I must raise my chin to meet his glowering stare.

Madman does nothing of the sort.

"*Tell me*," I repeat, sharper this time. "Or you can forget about me."

It's a threat. A blatant one. And I think, for the sole sake of seeing if I mean the words, Madman merely crosses his arms across his strong chest and waits. Waits for me to redact my statement.

Like hell I will.

"Fine, then," I stiffen. "You'll be sorry."

I take two careful steps backwards, with the last dregs of hope that Madman will reach out for me and pull me close—capture my mouth in his own. But he remains fixed to his current spot, eyes cold and devoid of any kindness.

"I hope that kiss curdles your blood and rots your very bones," I tell him on a whisper that is barely audible over the night breeze. "I hope my voice haunts you for the rest of your days, and that you never find another pretty dame who can sing their way into your soul like I did."

I don't bother waiting for Madman to steer me back to shore, I simply dive into the water.

The currents sense my presence, though, and before I can scramble to the surface, the water pulls me toward its icy depths.

I'm going to drown, but at least my last words were fiercely spoken. Venus and Jericho would be proud.

Even as I prepare for the high likelihood of my watery demise, I kick my feet, trying to propel myself away from the vicious current that threatens to tear me away from any chance of oxygen. Out of pure spite and rage, though, I fight my way *further* from the direction of Madman's boat. Closer to shore, yes, but further from him.

It only takes another few seconds for the burning in my lungs to begin, pain unlike I've ever known starting to bloom beneath my sternum and in my throat. Panic forms along with it, and for the first time in my life, I must decide what will hurt worse: holding my breath longer or breathing in the sea.

My body makes the choice for me, lungs desperately sucking in any chance of fresh air—but the Damocles water feels like unending misery in my lungs, and as my system tries to eject the water by force, it only draws more in.

I'd heard stories about how death by water feels peaceful at the very end—that the world and all sound and all of one's being goes completely still—and knowing that, I choose to cherish the agony of my present circumstances. It means there's still time. Not much, but enough to keep my body moving. My hands slash through the water, pounding towards higher ground.

There's no sense in wasting breath forming the words aloud

for only the sea to hear, so I shut my eyes in surrender. My heart weeps knowing I'll die like this—in the darkness I've always been so fearful of, whether below the surface or behind my closed eyes—and I pray to whatever Saints care to listen.

Tell my mother I love her.

The bleak serenity I'd been warned about falls over me, and I sense what's left of my weary existence floating through the dark blue water. I must've fought my way past the current after all, but with all the seawater in my lungs, I'm just . . . so . . . tired . . .

A strong hand wraps around my wrist, pulling me skyward, but it's not enough to wake me from what must be death's eternal slumber.

21
Pandora

Tangy seawater spews from my mouth when the earth rips me back to reality, and it feels like days before I finally stop heaving. Wiping my mouth with my drenched sleeve, I prepare to give my all into berating Madman, insisting he stay the hell away from me, no matter if he just saved me from the brink of death.

But when I crane my neck to meet his eyes, empathy that I've only ever seen in Lady Andromeda's gaze greets me instead.

"Andie?" I shiver, spastically clutching at my soaked clothes. "What are you . . . *how* did you find this place?"

"I'd ask you the same thing," she says firmly.

Aware that it may blow any kind of cover story I could improvise, I throw an assessing glance over my shoulder—towards the route Madman and I sail each night to reach his private alcove—but no sign of his boat remains.

He fled the scene.

"I should be dead," I whisper, even though it's not the answer that Andie's looking for.

"But you're not. You're alive, and you're going to come clean about what you're doing so close to a certain someone's hidden property."

I scan Andie's face for any signs of guesswork, any chance she's merely reaching for the truth rather than calling it out with unwavering clarity. Andie raises a brow, and my lips thin into a line to keep my teeth from chattering. "You know, then."

"We all have our secrets, and it's my business as Lady of the House to know them. *All* of them," she adds pointedly. "But don't worry. I'll keep this one to myself. And to prove to you that my word is trustworthy, I'll let you in on a little secret of my own."

A chill races down my spine, my blood cooling beneath skin that nearly lost its color from my time underwater. I've never heard her speak to me like this—like she might just be more diabolical than Kit or even Madman. That she holds more uncovered mystery than them. In my dazed recognition of the fact, Andie provides me the assistance needed to stand, unbothered by the damp press of my clothes against hers when I nearly lose my balance.

"Your mother escaped Broadcove Castle, stole a ship in Honeycomb Harbor, and sailed for the continent."

My surprise is insuppressible. "Venus and Jericho are actually making the trade for me?"

Andie's glower only intensifies. "You think I don't know that either? That Duchess Geneva is your real mother, not Venus."

Bloody Saints. That means—

"Who told you that?" I ask, my voice thick with dread.

"The same person you came down here to see."

My eyes bulge and my heart stalls. I don't care to know the gory details of how Andie crossed paths with Madman of all people—not yet anyway—and ask instead, "And why not rat me, or the both of us, out to Kit? Why keep this valuable information from your son, especially for the likes of *me*? His enemy."

"Perhaps it might serve you well to start characterizing yourself not as Kit's enemy, but as something of great value to him," she says, the sentiment ominous. "The sooner the better."

It's not an outright answer, but it sure is something.

It's a warning.

"Come on," Andie instructs, not allowing my mind to start stirring with frantic questions. She leads me back into the darkness, to the concealed stairs beneath my bed. "Let's get you cleaned up and into bed."

I lie when Andie asks if I'm comfortable in bed, and I shudder from the sheer weight of the last two hours once she retreats to her rooms for the night.

I will myself not to cry, not to cower. I had nearly *drowned*, for Saints' sakes, and yet, this moment overwhelms me more. The absence of the sun. The curtains drawn shut. The inability to see my own hand in front of my face—all while trying to viciously dissect Andie's omen about proving my value to Kit.

I'd always loathed myself for being afraid of the dark, for having to explain to Broadcove staff and family members why I insisted on keeping the mantle lamps burning in my rooms. It just always felt so childish, so humiliating.

The only person who hadn't chastised me about it was Madman.

That's what our secret rendezvous started as, after all— Madman's gentle offer to guard me from whatever lurked in the darkness so that I could sleep. Why he kept scattered candlelight spread throughout his cave.

But after what I had said on his boat and seeing me jump into the inky waters without resurfacing . . . would he blow them all out? Would he subject himself to the darkness he'd grown accustomed to in the tunnels?

Does he feel *any* remorse?

I flip on one of the lamps at my bedside, grateful for the golden glow it disperses through the room. Kicking my feet out of the sheets, I set out for my armoire, to the back corner where I stashed my Pandora's Box. The wood glistens in the lamplight, warm in my touch.

I should open it.

After all, what's a little more hurt? If I beat death, surely I can face what's in this box.

Like a child trying to make sense of their holiday gifts, I shake the box, curious to find out if anything rustles or clatters within. The sound is muffled, indistinguishable, as if nothing resides in it at all. Is the box some test of self-control? Perhaps I'm no better than the original Pandora, chomping at the bit to know what horrors or splendors lie within. Infinitely curious, and so close to unlatching its lid . . .

My fingers halt on the mechanism.

Everyone, Madman told me. *Everyone* bears a devastating secret that will reach the limelight if I open the box. Kit, Andie, Venus, Jericho, Mother . . .

Dear Saints, how could I be so blind?

Of *course* Madman let me withdraw from him, insisted that I don't truly know him. Because there's something about *him* in there, something he believes is so corrupt, I would scorn him forever. Refute any of the affections he has for me—that I have for him.

I'm going to open the box. I'm going to prove Madman wrong. I'm going to show him that I can handle—

The distant sound of an engine thrums beyond the House, my heartbeat going quiet so my ears can scope out the scene.

A car door shuts, but the engine . . . the engine keeps rumbling.

Suddenly, Andie's ominous words echo in my mind like a menacing, phantom wind.

Perhaps it might serve you well to start characterizing yourself not as Kit's enemy, but as something of great value to him. The sooner the better.

I've been so consumed by the number of days I've spent pointlessly pining after Madman that I haven't kept track of what day it was now. Her warning wasn't just about how I can sway Kit to tolerate me. It was to warn me—warn me that time was no longer on my side.

My tribunal.

It's *tomorrow*.

I make a mad dash across the hall, knowing my Pandora's Box is no longer safe in my room—especially not if I'm to pretend to be asleep when Kit gets here. In a surge of panic, I throw open the door to the well-preserved room that belonged to Andie's now-deceased daughter, mindful of all the toys, trinkets, and pillows that are better left untouched. In the span of five seconds, I scan through the pink-purple shrine, hoping for a clever hiding spot.

The minute the inside door to the backyard unlatches, I notice a gap in the back of the dusty bookcase and tuck the box into its barely visible pocket and sprint for my rooms on feather-light feet. I turn off the lamp right before footsteps sound in the main entryway, working their way to my side of the House.

Sure enough, Kit Andromeda strides in moments later, a no-nonsense expression plastered across his face and a drink in hand. He doesn't bother to be quiet about it, either, but I pretend to jostle awake anyways, as if breaking past the last layer of an unhappy dream.

"Kit?" I say hoarsely. "What's wrong? Are you all right?"

He stops in his tracks, studying the concern in my face. Not for me, but for *him*.

He dismisses it like a waved hand through thin mist. "Pack a bag, princess. We're leaving."

22
Kit

Pandora Deragon snagged a knitted sling bag from the hook in her armoire and wasted no time gathering her meager choice of belongings.

First, she shuffled into her bathroom and fished out a handful of feminine cycle necessities, an embroidered handkerchief, and a canister of unmarked medications. I didn't care to ask what kind, but the red rings around her otherwise doe eyes suggested it might be something to help her sleep through the night. She returned soon after, swiping her hairbrush off her nightstand before combing through her drawers. Wordlessly, Pandora stuffed lightweight shirts and linen shorts into her bag, and while I was inclined to tell the princess that she won't be allowed to keep it where we're headed, I decided not to deny her what will likely be the last of her simple luxuries.

I previously arranged for a speedboat to be waiting along the eastern coast of the Isle. But with Andromeda House stationed on the westernmost edge—Pandora's room in particular looking out towards the wide-open Damocles, towards her faraway, unreachable home—that meant I'd have to drive the two of us to port.

I expected Pandora to go out kicking and screaming, given she likely remembered what day her scheduled tribunal was to occur. And yet, when I barged into her rooms, Pandora looked me over as if I had just outrun unspeakable trouble. She looked restless . . . like she was worried about me.

An hour into our drive, almost an hour past midnight, the memory of that look on her face still threatens to disorient me.

That, and her dark hair catching in the wind as we drive. She'd tied it back before we took off, but in an effort to cut down the drive time, the speed in which I sent us flying down the paved streets worked against the temporary strength of her ribbon. A sick, twisted part of me doesn't seem to mind it, though. Pandora doesn't fuss with it and tips her head back, counting the stars to herself. All the while, the scent of her curls drift into my nose— freshly washed, but not with product. No, her hair smells like the sea.

She looks so at peace with the world, even as we drive towards what is sure to be her ruin.

"Kit," she sighs, eyes closed now.

"Yes, princess."

I don't know what to prepare myself for. Sobbing? Groveling? Hatred? A mix of all three?

Instead, Pandora says, "Do you remember the day you came into my room looking for your copy of that book I'd stolen?"

The surprise of not being verbally assaulted after enough pent-up silence draws an unexpected laugh from deep in my stomach. "Yes."

Never mind that most of my memory surrounding that day pertained to the uncanny thrill I felt holding her—the feel of our bodies fused together.

"What about it?" I ask.

Her returning smile is tinged with defeat. "It was my birthday . . . and I was too scared to tell you."

I'm not sure what to offer her in response, mainly because I feel pretty terrible that I hadn't done enough basic research on her to know that. But before I get the chance to form even a half-hearted apology, Pandora opens her eyes again and readjusts herself to a normal posture. "I don't say that to garner any pity, I just mean that . . . I know what day it is, Kit." Neither disdain nor dread lie in her voice. Only acceptance. "So you don't have to find ways to avoid telling me the truth. That we're heading for the coast and riding in your car to reach the court on time. You can be honest with me."

Damn her.

Damn her for saying what she does and then looking away from me like she's hiding tears of bitter recognition. Damn her for exiting the car and approaching the speedboat with no signs of resentment. Damn her for being *nothing* like her hellish bloodline, and for always approaching me in whatever way removes any burden from my conscience.

Gods, if only she knew. Knew that I had been waiting for Venus and Jericho to prove themselves noble enough to trade their lives for hers. Knew that, when no word was sent regarding Pandora's ransom note, I was enduring the torture of readying the arrangements for her trial. Knew that I had been fighting the fire in my blood that sparked to life thinking about how I touched her that day, how she had *let* me . . . and how I craved *more*.

Pandora looks at me expectantly, and I try to shake myself awake. "What's that?"

"I said is there anywhere I can lay down and get some sleep?"

"Oh, right," I sputter, only slightly hating myself for sounding so taken off guard. I look around the boat, which is a meager, curved line of a sitting bench and a mat-lined floorboard. And then, I catch myself saying, "Lie down. You can rest your head in my lap."

Her surprise matches that of my own beneath the surface. "Are you sure?"

"The waves will throw you around if you're sitting upright, and you deserve a full night's rest. Yes, I'm sure."

I'm surprised at just how agreeable the words sound out loud, and mercifully, Pandora doesn't argue further. Instead, she tucks her sling bag into one of the side compartments, twisting the lock shut once it's completely concealed, and waits for me to secure my desired seat.

I pick the spot furthest from the side of the boat, knowing one rogue wave could drench us both. Once I'm settled in, Pandora crawls into position. She drops her knees along the cushion, her back mirroring the curve of the bench until her head nuzzles against my lower torso, the tops of my thighs.

I wonder if Pandora can sense every nerve in my body going haywire with simultaneous confusion and delight.

After a deep sigh, she mutters the words, "I'm sorry,"

My throat tightens. "For what?"

Her eyes glide shut, exhaustion quickly getting the best of her. She yawns, shoulders slumping. "That your assassin brought me instead of my aunt, and that it had to come to this since they wouldn't come for me. Such a shame . . ."

I almost assume she's fallen asleep until she adds, the words gutting me, "That I likely matter more to you more than I do to my own blood."

It's torture. Pure and utter *torture*.

Pandora's head draped over my lap. Her full lips parted in sleep, gently pressed against the exposed skin of my thigh. Her hair spilling onto the leather seat at my side, conveniently where my hand rests. Her brokenhearted words replaying in my head like a harrowing echo.

"Such a shame . . . that I likely matter more to you more than I do to my own blood."

It's been like this for hours, and while I expected to drift off into sleep eventually, I'm anything but relaxed. Or tired. Rather, I'm hyperaware of any movement or dialogue that could wake her, I've kept to myself. The captain I hired to navigate us across the southern strip of the Damocles seems to bode well with the silence, at least.

In the end, I'm only able to nod off for a few ten-minute intervals, but it doesn't matter. I'll finally rest once Pandora's out of my custody.

Right?

Gods, I missed her birthday. The one day of the year when someone's allowed to feel joy, to take pride in themselves. She'd made it another year around the sun, and yet, she dwelled in Andromeda House believing it'd be her last—and it's *my* fault.

Pandora is already so young. So full of potential and grace and beauty. But in sleep, innocence becomes her. I look at Pandora like this, and all I see is the little girl she once was. The girl that loved to read to distract herself from growing up in a castle under the instruction of such disgusting people. Being raised as one of *them*, yet turning out to be so . . . herself.

She doesn't deserve the fate I'm about to deal her.

A bump against an undercut wave jolts us upward, and

Pandora stirs awake. Stretching out her limbs, she lets out a sustained grunt as she works the tiredness out of her bones. She rubs at her eyes. Yawns. Then, Pandora registers where she is, where her head has been resting for the last four and half hours.

My lap is still warm when she scoots away from me, and I choose to ignore her flustered apology. The sunless summer morning will soon give way to the dawn, painting the sky the loveliest shades of orange and pink. Mosacian sunrises always bring me a deep sense of grounding—peace amidst turmoil. But today, I dread the sight of the sun. The minute the atmosphere goldens, I turn her over to the court authorities waiting for us to reach the port.

"How bad is it going to be?" Pandora asks, her voice a gut-wrenching rasp. "Is it quick?"

"The tribunal?"

Pandora goes deathly quiet. "No."

I twist my head away from hers, unable to stomach that look on her face. The somber preparation in her eyes. I can only imagine the kind of pulse-easing statements she's having to coax herself into, to keep from hurling herself off this boat and swimming for shelter. Swimming away from me.

Because the truth is, I didn't ask at all. When I made the deal with the courts to take the payout for her life, it didn't matter to me then what would happen to her, *how* it would happen to her. Not when the only remaining traces of Princess Pandora would be the coins I'd receive for her bounty—coins that bore her father's face. *He* would get to live with that shame, and so would Venus.

And yet, the guilt I feel now is near debilitating.

"I'm so . . . so sorry."

"Don't waste your breath on apologies, Kit. Not when we

both knew that we would always end up here."

Disappointment churns in my gut. "You're not surprised that I followed through?"

"Not at all," she says solemnly. "Just because I don't appreciate what you're about to do doesn't mean that your integrity was ever in question. You held true to your word, and frankly, I expected you to be rid of me sooner. To do so in worse manners than this."

"Why are you doing this? Why are you being so *good* about this?"

"Because *nothing's changed*, Kit!" she cries out. "Don't you understand that? I went along with Madman's offer because I thought it would spare my aunt—my queen—from harm." I grit my teeth at the sound of that poisonous name on her lips. *Madman.* I'd heard her say it once before, then banning her from her vocabulary, or so I thought. "And even though no one will be there to bail me out, I will go to that courtroom still protecting them. It's what our culture does. People die for Venus and Jericho every day."

But it's not just a guilty verdict that lies ahead of Pandora Deragon.

No—before the tribunal announces her sentence, she'll have to face more than just the court. She'll also endure the *crowds*, the brutal condemnation from strangers who know her only by her bloodline as opposed to how I've begun to recognize her. They will see nothing of the young woman with a thirst for knowledge; who sneaks books like most people her age sneak booze. Nothing of the playful girl with an outrageously painted face, howling in laughter over a drunken game of cards. Nothing of the lonely, regretful soul standing before me now, facing charges that killers deserve when she's only ever brought me joy, not death.

They will only see her name—*Pandora Violet Deragon*—on a

tribunal ballot. And they will choose to sentence her to death.

"Stop the boat," I finally say.

"What?" Pandora squeaks at the same time the captain calls out, "Come again?"

"I said, stop the boat." I stiffen, turning to the captain's chair. "Kill the engine. You're dismissed."

The gentleman's eyes go wide, assessing our surroundings, estimating how far we are from the shoreline. "Sir? You wish me to—"

"Get the *hell* off this boat!" I shout, eyes ablaze with clarity and indignation. "Swim to shore, sink to the seafloor, I don't care. Just *go*."

I had paid him prior to embarking across the water, so I don't feel a shred of remorse when he quickly scrambles to the back of the speedboat and dives into the Damocles. His captain's hat fills with water before sinking into the depths below, and he's smart enough not to swim for it.

"Saints, Kit," Pandora says, rushing forward. "He didn't *do* anything—"

And that's when I decide to be selfish.

I pull Pandora towards me in a swift jerk, one hand splaying across her lower back and the other cradling the nape of her neck, beneath her hair. The curls seem to spool into my grasp on their own accord, and as my eyes descend towards her full mouth, I watch as a softened, startled gasp leaves her lips. Pandora's eyes pierce through mine, and she stares at me, not with fear, but with a tenderness that is borderline erotic.

Holy gods, I am in so much trouble.

"Tell me that you don't think about what almost happened between us," I rasp, laying all my cards on the table. I don't bother explaining what I'm referring to, not when the glimmer in her brown eyes tells me she already knows.

"That," she whispers, "would be a lie."

"Then tell me something true. Something real."

Pandora gulps, but finds the strength to reach out her hand, resting it along my jaw. Her fingers slide across my face in a delicate caress, fingernails grazing the slope of my ear. Chills scatter across my arms, my neck. She bites her lip, shaking her head.

"Please," I beg.

Pandora looks to the shore, where the first signs of court authorities begin to assemble at the edge. Then, she meets my gaze again, determination locking into place across her lovely face.

"You touched me that day, and it's been wreaking havoc on my soul ever since."

Suddenly, I'm leaning in.

She's *letting* me.

"But I thought you hated me," she whispers, the last of her defenses sneaking out into the open air.

"No, Pandora," I say weakly. "I hate what you've become to me."

Our kiss is catastrophic. It undermines every move and countermove I've made to punish the Deragons. As her body loosens against my own, all remaining instinct to protect herself from danger, from *me*, crumbles like the fallen cities her parents stole for themselves. My own do the same.

Electricity hums in my blood as I grapple for more of her, her hands digging into my scalp like I'm the only thing keeping her from splintering into a million pieces. Her lips are so soft, even as they scrape over mine, pleading—my control nearly snaps as I swallow a desperate sound from her.

"I'm going to miss you," she says against my mouth, letting my tongue move in tandem with hers.

I deepen the kiss for a moment, then frame her face with my hands, forcing her to look into the depths of my eyes. My soul.

"You're not going anywhere."

Her lip quivers. "What?"

Distant shouting from the shoreline echoes through the atmosphere. The sun finally peeks over the horizon line, showering us in its golden rays and warmth. But there's nothing warm and welcoming about the voices coming from the edge of Mosacia Proper, so despite my longing to keep kissing Pandora until we're both sweaty and breathless, I tear myself away from her and race for the captain's seat. I flick on the engine and grip the wheel with whitening knuckles.

"Hold on to something, princess. We're going rogue."

PART III
BALLAD

23
Ren

If I ever get the chance to have kids, I will spend what's left of my lifetime telling them about the crazy days their old man lived out—and how every escapade brought him closer to the day he'd cross paths with Duchess Geneva Deragon and jumpstart his wildest adventure yet.

Outrunning two groups hellbent on Genny's capture—let alone the fact that those two "groups" are the angry Mosacian public and the bloody Deragon Family themselves—has far surpassed all my previous undertakings. It beats riding boards down snow-covered mountainsides, hijacking horses and racing them through open fields, or even spending two nights in jail for pissing in one of the fountains outside the sacred shrine's gate. I take pride in telling people I toughed it out in a cell for more than one night, but always omit the part where my friends made me kiss their asses over the jail's dial line so they'd post my bail.

Another railroader hadn't come around like I'd thought it would, but the hours passed by like minutes as Genny and I strolled down the tracks, talking about life before all of this. I spilled my guts out about all the stupid stunts my friends and I pulled over the years—Genny's favorite anecdote being the one where I climbed onto the roof of an abandoned villa to look out at the stars, only to have it cave in on me. I told her how I can still feel the hard *splat* and the crack in my arm as it broke on impact, and the sound of Genny's roaring laughter unfurled a long-suppressed anxiety in me.

Once I ran out of tomfoolery to revisit, Genny shared everything that came to her mind. The dynamic with her sisters, then and now. But mostly, she gushed about Pandora, about how wonderful she was at nearly all stages of her life. How she slept through most nights as a babe, proved to be the most well-behaved among all her cousins and the other kids that lived in Broadcove Castle, and grew into immense musical talent.

"She sings and the world goes quiet to watch her. She plucks the strings of her harp and even the most esteemed nobles and royals pause to hear her play. That's the kind of power she has," Genny said, reverence in her every word. "And to know that, somehow, the enchantment she casts through people might have come from a part of *me*?" She shook her head, unable to process the possibility of it.

But I could—I could absolutely see it.

Because Geneva Deragon spoke in a way that told me she loved others more than she paid attention to herself. I had asked about *her*, and she'd spent hours boasting about the joys of being Pandora's mother, or basking in the presence of her family in Broadcove Castle. I wouldn't dare interrupt her, not when she spoke about the world she knew with such optimism and delight— but that wasn't what I wished to know.

I wanted to know her favorite foods, her favorite phase of the moon. I wanted to learn how she takes her tea—if she drinks it at all—and what color of the sky makes her feel most at home. I wanted to cater to her favorite kind of humor if only to memorize the sound of her laughter. To know every desire of her heart, and find a way to fulfill them all.

She deserves that much.

She's the *only* person I've ever crossed paths with that deserves it.

We stumbled upon a herd of cattle as night fell—the stock sensing her gentleness and approaching her with no reservations. Genny let them come over, allowed them to take their time and stride across the grass at whatever pace they felt most comfortable, then embraced them all with a devotion that was almost heartbreaking. "Beautiful creatures," she hummed to herself more than to me. "I haven't seen any free roamers like these since my days in the marsh."

She was nuzzling the thick nose of one of the brown speckled cows when a few independent travelers passed by, not deigning to stop. Even so, Geneva had marveled at the two cars that passed, sputtering on and on about how Urovia had only just *started* manufacturing the baseline models for personal vehicles within the last ten years, nothing to the fashionable degree of what those strangers drove. When the third car drove up, however—two women coasting through the vast plains with the kind of free-spirited glee I hadn't felt since my twenties—they had quickly offered us a lift and graciously answered all of Genny's fascinating questions about their car. If the girls had any suspicions about Genny's nationality and upbringing, they didn't mention it.

They had stopped driving ten miles short of our destination, and we arrived at their villa late in the night after our third full day of traveling. Genny insisted they accept the money she wished to extend to them as a gesture of their gratitude, and after two full minutes of bickering, they conceded, wishing us the best of luck on the rest of the way.

After so long sitting in one spot, Genny and I were glad to be back on our feet. Her cheery, courteous disposition had vanished entirely, however, when a nearby clocktower chimed the first hour of a new day . . . the first of August.

We walked through the night, her energy renewing in her sheer desperation of making it to the courthouse before a sentence could be carried out against her daughter. She trusted every vague recollection I could scrounge up of where the tribunals are held, just beyond the walls of the Sacred City, and despite the audible nervousness in her voice, she talked with me all night, as if worrying I'd turn back and lead her astray out of boredom.

Only when her feet began to swell in her shoes—when I could physically make out the blisters forming there—did she sit and let her eyes fall shut, insisting she only needed a minute.

A minute turned into twenty, though. Ten of which I beheld firsthand until exhaustion overcame me, too.

Now, jostled awake by Genny's grip and her devastating, horrified realization of how much time flew by, I jump awake and assess my surroundings. A bustling crowd sounds from distantly down the road, and given the slope of the rising hills . . .

"We're a mile and a half shy."

"I'm not missing my daughter." She grits her teeth. "Even if I have to run the rest of the way there."

"But your feet—"

"They're fine," she says sharply.

I don't bother disagreeing with her. Not when we've come this far—not when we're this close. We both look around for any sign of the time, and without the presence of a clock, we make guesswork of the sun's position peeking over the Mosacian horizon. My guess is that it's nearly eight in the morning, and when I turn back to communicate my observation, I watch as Genny takes her shoes off, abandoning them on the side of the paved road.

A laugh gets the best of me. "When's the last time you've run more than a mile?"

"Too long," she admits with a wry smile.

And then spearheads down the street, her mother's fury carrying her through the morning glow.

The courtroom is full by the time we get there—its doors shut to the general public once the seating fills up—and according to the whispers, all that remains on this morning's docket is Pandora's sentencing.

Few observers can see past the two rectangular windows that peer into the dreadful scene, and despite feeling guilty for falling asleep and barring us from being there to look at Pandora directly, I count it a small mercy. Because even as Geneva Deragon trembles in my arms, her tears returning and splintering something in my soul all the while, she doesn't have to see whatever state her daughter's captivity has reduced her to.

That, and it's likely the High Judge or members of the jury would recognize a Deragon Duchess if she casually waltzed into a courtroom set to convict a member of her family.

"They're announcing it now," one of the clustered bodies in front of us hisses before secretly cracking the door open, allowing the High Judge's bellow to float past the courtroom and into the crowded, expectant hallway.

I clutch Genny tighter to me, albeit for unspoken, selfish

reasons.

"The court's verdict is as follows: Pandora Violet Deragon, in a ninety-seven over three evaluation, has been found guilty of treason, for knowingly carrying out the agenda of Venus and Jericho Deragon—the perpetrators behind the Seagrave Slaughter."

I watch as Genny's face visibly contorts at the ruling—how only three people saw her life worth saving.

Three.

"She will be detained in the tribunal penitentiary until the method of her final sentencing is established." *Meaning, they're still debating how they'll actually kill her.* "And there will be no bond."

"Like *hell* there won't—"

I slam my hand over Geneva's mouth, the heel of my palm landing harder than I intend it to, and I whisper-hiss a genuine apology when a short cry of pain comes in response. I don't even want to think about what I'll find when I peel my hand away. A busted lip? Bloody nose? Chipped tooth? *Gods above.* Our only saving grace is that her outburst wasn't in the courtroom itself— the throng of people still blocking our view of the action.

But then, the High Judge releases a weighted, reluctant sigh.

"As for the princess's *handler*," he drawls, irritation that simmers near fury taking root in his voice. "Kit Andromeda faces the same sentencing, seeing as he failed to meet his arranged appointment with the court to transfer custody of Miss Deragon. Should he and the Urovian Princess be apprehended and brought into court custody by a member of the Mosacian public, we will make it worth your while."

I feel Genny's breathing halt, her pulse flickering.

Our eyes tear their way back to each other in unsuspecting relief.

Either Pandora escaped the person who was prepared to turn her in, or her keeper had a sudden and costly change of heart.

"This court will not stomach the weak-willed, just as we will not tolerate traitors. Let it hereby be declared that any citizens able to accomplish the task of apprehending Pandora Deragon and anyone of her ilk—whether by blood or sympathies—will be offered one million Jericoin. Dead or alive."

Holy gods. One million *Jericoin—*

"Ren . . ." Genny shudders.

It hits me then—the implied threat to her own existence.

Whether by blood or sympathies.

Mosacia knows that there are more Deragons on the continent, meaning there's a bounty on Genny's head, too. A massive one.

There's one on mine, now, as well. But that comes more as an afterthought. Right now, my mind swirls with the dreaded possibilities in play. If we don't get somewhere safe, and get there soon, anyone could get their hands on Genny. On Pandora. If the reward for their lives is not determined by whether they bring her in breathing, they'll kill both of them before they can set foot in court.

"*Husband,*" she says, her fear punctuated by our placated endearment towards one another.

Slowly, I trace her eyes towards whatever seems to haunt her, only to find a man studying her face with subtle yet vicious intent. He might be beginning to recognize her, but I refuse to let his eyes linger longer.

"Come along, sweetheart," I say, the ruse all too easy for me to resume. I weave my fingers against hers, and the knitted feel of our hands stirs something inside of me that I don't have the proper time to unpack. "Let's go home."

Never mind that we have no home. No plan. No refuge.

Nowhere to run.

All that remains is this silent, unwavering notion within me: one million Jericoin is a laughable fraction of what Geneva Deragon is truly worth, and I'll be dead before I allow anyone to collect her or that pathetic sum.

24
Pandora

Kit and I haven't spoken much since he veered the speedboat away from the coastline—since his kiss nearly knocked the wind out of me. Mostly, it's been brief exchanges and emotionally charged eye contact, but I learn to take Kit's cues, to let him make the first push towards any and all conversation.

After all, the man just defied the most radical sector of his government to save me from certain death, and there's a good chance that the kiss is what convinced him to do so.

I'd kissed him . . . or maybe Kit kissed me. However it happened, it's sure to haunt me. I know it for certain as Kit steers the boat like a maniac, tearing through the choppy waters like they don't nearly throw him from his captain's chair. I sense it in the way time moves at a glacial pace, even at the rapid speed we soar at. And worst of all, I feel the notion in my bones like the death toll I would've faced in the tribunal.

It doesn't matter that the kiss was desperate, or that the high I rode in the midst of it has since trickled out of my bloodstream.

If I want Kit to keep me alive, I need to pretend like that kiss was *everything*.

Even though it didn't hold a candle to the spark I felt when Madman kissed me in his lair.

Kit found a river path wide enough to still maintain our speed, though the wake we leave behind drenches the side streets and footpaths that the morning city-life treads. It takes every instinct in me not to apologize to alert passersby of my presence. Eventually, Kit finds a vacant mooring to dock the boat at before urging me to lay completely flat against the boat's flooring, shielding my body from sight by leaning against the sitting bench. He's gone all of ten minutes, having disappeared down an alley of merchant carts and mortar storefronts before returning with a sky-blue shawl, a thick overcoat, and a small capsule of red ink.

"What's this for?" I say, forming my first full sentence since our…moment.

"There's a good chance your absence is being reported to the court. Drape this around your hair so that it casts a shadow over your face," he says quickly, standing by to help if need be. I do as he bids without aid, and when Kit feels confident enough in my capabilities, he dons the coat and ruffles his hair through his fingers.

Then, dipping a finger in the ink, Kit draws a symbol that reminds me of an infinity broken before the two loops can connect in the middle across his forehead. Before I can shy away, he lifts the edge of my shawl to repeat the marking along my head, too.

"What does it mean?" I ask.

"It's the refugee mark," he says, his voice lowering to where I can barely understand him. "If we can make it to the Sacred City, which should only be two miles from this intersection, we will be offered shelter without question.

"Even if they recognize us?"

Kit smiles vaguely, helping me out of the boat. The gesture proves to be eerily reminiscent of Madman's mannerisms. "Even then."

"How?"

"By law, the Sacred City of Vesta—named after the goddess of hearth and hospitality—is required to take in any refugees that present themselves for asylum. People all across the Mosacian continent travel to visit the shrine, which rests in its center, but the city itself is reserved as a haven for those with no place to go. Even better, no one can legally bring any violence against us once we're past the walls, or they'll face their own tribunal for it."

Dear Saints.

"Which is why you and I need to get to the entry point before the court announces the massive bounty on our heads," he whispers, increasing the pacing of our steps.

"*Our* heads?"

"Tribunals don't take lightly to broken promises. I told them I'd bring them the heir to the Deragon Dynasty, but by not showing up, not even to report that I had lost you somehow . . . it means my dissention is equally as damnable as your sentence would have been."

I gulp at the weight of his words—the realization that by choosing to spare me, he might not be able to go home to Andromeda House. And Andie . . .

"I'm so sorry, Kit," I choke out.

I hate what you've become to me.

He should. He *should* hate me for it, because if he could read my mind right now and see that despite the insane risk that he just brought on himself by bringing me here, I'm still thinking about someone else . . .

I thought it was the end. My family hadn't come, my mother was Saints knows where on the continent looking for me, and Madman . . . well, that's what seemed to burn me the most. I'd die for them—for a bloodline that hadn't cared to negotiate my release in any form—but I would have left things with Madman on bad terms. My final interaction with him would have been a fight, and it broke me.

The uttered words were a disastrous slip of restraint.

"I'm going to miss you."

Not parting words for the man I presumed was ready to turn me in, but a silent prayer that by some supernatural force, Madman would hear me. That even if he couldn't bail me out at the last second, he'd know that if I was given the chance, I'd have reconciled with him.

But then, Kit Andromeda took the words to heart, which left me with no choice but to do as Madman had once instructed me.

So as Kit twines his fingers with mine, more so to drag me behind him than to be endearing, I will myself to cling tighter to him. The increased closeness in the touch makes him glance at me over his shoulder, and he halts for a moment before he steps towards me to conceal my face from two onlookers across the street. I let my eyes fall shut, breathing in his scent.

And then, Kit says, "I couldn't let you die for them."

"I know that, now," I wince. "I wasn't sure before, but I—"

"And I get that it may feel like an insult, to mean more to me than to your family." His nose draws a tender line down the bridge of my own, a soothing sensation against the gut-twisting reminder of what I had murmured inches shy of what I believed was oblivion on the boat. "But what if, in time, I can give you that sense of family you need?" His voice is a devastating whisper. "What if we find a way . . . some way to get back to Andromeda

House, and wipe the slate clean. What if I promise you years of daylight and stocked shelves of books and card games with Andie?"

My eyes turn misty at the idea, at the sight of Kit piecing together a future for us.

"Would a makeshift life with me be enough to outweigh the world you once knew?"

Even though Kit's heart has shifted, mine lingers elsewhere. Lingers in a place that I never would've wandered to on my free will two months ago, with a man who found a way to make the dwelling of my deepest fears feel like a sacred space. A man who would've offered me a life of blissful darkness, beautiful music, and unwavering devotion if only given the chance.

Still, I nod through the lump in my throat, if only because I would loathe myself anew by saying the word *yes* aloud. To vocally lie. I allow the tears to spill over for Kit's sake, even as I silently wonder whether I'll ever lay eyes on Madman again—and then, I let Kit Andromeda whisk me up the street and towards the Sacred City.

Had Kit not cut through the riverbend, we would've been swarmed by the general population the minute the tribunal declared the monetary value of my arrest reward, not to mention Kit's. Thankfully, fate or the Saints or the gods—I'm still trying to understand how the culture operates here—remains on our side, because with minimal resistance, Kit and I manage to complete the trek to the walls encasing the Sacred City.

The walls span at least twelve feet high—likely a nod to the amount of deities represented in the shrine, Kit had explained on the walk over. Polished stone with illustrative etchings of people and settings I recognize from reading *Mosacian Ideologies and Stories of Old* separate the town from what lies within, but the images are not carved deep enough to provide anyone the ability to wedge their feet there and attempt climbing over. This close to the gate, which Kit insists is down one more winding pathway, I can't see what treasures Vesta waits to grant us. But earlier on, I could see a porcelain building gleaming in the daylight atop the steepest hill, Corinthian columns striped across its perimeter beneath a gray-gleaming roof. Surely, that must be the shrine.

"Let me do the talking," Kit instructs.

The moment I behold the silver gates, sharp tips pointing up towards the clouds, my blood runs cold. A booth rests perched on the right side of the gate's yawning mouth. As we approach, however, I find that the gatekeeper starkly defies my fearful expectations.

A girl, no older than Flora if I had to guess, leans at the base of the security booth with fair skin, a lighthearted disposition, and the purest, river-blue eyes that seem to pop against her braided, chestnut hair.

Before Kit can make the first interaction, the girl carefully steps towards us, as if worrying we'll spook easily. "I see that you both bear the refugee's mark," she says, her voice wrought with a gentleness I wouldn't anticipate from a city gatekeeper. "I only hope your journey here has not been too perilous."

Kit's brows scrunch in confusion, as if the girl's kindness flies completely over his head.

"Adventurous, yes," I reply in his stead. "But not dangerous."

The somewhat lie hangs in the air for a moment before the gatekeeper smiles, as if sensing it. Still, she replies, "Well then, welcome to the Sacred City. May Vesta grant you all that you seek."

"Thank you," I say, looping my arm through Kit's to further imply that we're together. Only once we're a few steps past the girl do I dare to whisper, "Nice *talking* you did back there."

"How come you understood her?" Kit says through his teeth, arm locking mine into place.

"What do you mean?"

"The girl greeted us in Mosaith, and you *answered* her."

The dominant language of the continent. I had gone through a series of tutors over the years in order to be able to carry casual conversation—mainly if the instance of possible capture ever arrived. I had prepared to speak that way when Madman first stole me away, but he spoke the Urovian tongue. Kit, too.

But I *know* the girl at the gate spoke Urovian to the two of us—and I *know* I responded in the same language.

"You're probably sleep deprived," I say passively.

"Then what's that?" he asks snidely, pointing towards the entrance again.

My steps come screeching to a halt as I hear her honey-sweet voice speaking to a new passerby—this time, her words manifesting in a dialect I've never heard. My eyes flare at how seamlessly the two strangers converse together, and even Kit seems taken aback. "She's speaking Kionan, now," he marvels. "That's a language way out eastward."

Kit shakes his head, beginning to walk us both deeper into the city, but before I turn my attention fully towards our unknown fate, I catch the girl looking my way again. Studying me. There's a gleam in her eye that tells me this won't be the last time we talk, but I don't get to react before Kit tugs me towards the Sacred City by the arm.

Vesta teems with life from all across the continent.

Everywhere we turn, navigating through the route of hostels and stone-lined inns, there are herds of people that look nothing like the people that now act as their next door neighbors. Every culture, every conquered tribe, every skin tone and dialect—they're all here.

Convening with one another.

It almost feels like I'm intruding on a party. The entire community seeking shelter lines the streets of the city, passing food to their families or playing games on the shaded pavements. Not everyone in the city bears the refugee mark—the ones without them likely venturing towards the shrine situated skyward—but the ones that do offer smiles towards Kit and I as we coast through the crowds. Those that don't are already wrapped up in conversations, and something swells in my soul as I watch people from different parts of the world speaking in different dialects attempt to tell each other about themselves. Their stories.

It's the most beautiful display of humanity I've seen in all my life.

It fills me with such hope that I drift aimlessly through the masses until Kit guides us into a hostel lined with uneven stone and indicated by a green flag posted above the door frame. "This will be our home base," he exhales, hand already on the knob of the door and twisting it open.

I take note of the stairs on the immediate right of the door, which leads up to two higher floors, those demarcated flags colored red. Occupied. No doubt Kit will probably complain about hearing footsteps at whatever hours of the night our new neighbors might move around at. Meanwhile, I just hope they're kind people. Gearing my eyes back to the door, which now gives way to a humble living room, I step inside and instantly feel the air in the room turn cold.

The temperature only seems to drop as I assess the rest of the space we're to share this next . . . however long.

A small kitchenette rounds off the corner of the living room, the black hearth and matching stove sticking out amidst the otherwise beige suite. A wicker basket of woven blankets and a gray-stitched couch rests not far away from the fireplace's steel grate. But the entire suite is one room save for a closeted toilet, which likely leaves little mystery and privacy to be had. Specifically, it's the sight of what constitutes our bedroom that does me in.

I don't bark out any sort of protest at the single bed, even though my gut churns at the lack of pillows. One for each of us—but with my tendency to clutch a pillow while resting my head on another, I'm worried I may try to cling to *Kit*.

To his credit, Kit doesn't outright smile at the sight, but his disposition tells me he's weighing the prospects of sleeping together, too.

My eyes snag on vacant shelves along the back wall, and I point it out to him. Kit turns to the shelves, and his smile crushes a piece of my soul. "Maybe we can find some books for you in the city," I say.

But it's a new voice that remarks in answer, "Oh, I think we can manage that."

Kit and I both jolt at the young gatekeeper's sudden presence, not having heard her pad into our hostel.

"I wanted to introduce myself earlier, but you seemed to be in a hurry to find lodging," she says, eyes flicking towards Kit with quiet amusement. "I'm Marzipan."

I recall the detail Kit mentioned about being safe within the city's walls, and feel inclined enough to trust her with our real identities. "It is nice to meet you, Marzipan. This is my partner, Kit." I'm almost surprised by how easy the words come, not to mention the fabricated, smitten blush that floods my cheeks. "And I'm—"

"Pandora Deragon," Marzipan says with a broad smile, dipping in a short curtsy and bowing her head. "You're a long way from home, aren't you, princess?"

"This is our home, now," Kit speaks up, his voice earnest and soft despite his rigid stance.

"That's the spirit!" she chimes happily. "I'm a permanent resident here in the city. Actually, I'm on the third floor." She points up at the ceiling. "So if you ever want company or have questions about—"

"How many languages do you speak, Marzipan?" Kit asks before letting her finish her statement.

Marzipan giggles. "A few."

It's not a clear answer and we both know it.

"I can assure you there are far more interesting things in the Sacred City than little old me," she insists. "Speaking of which, I'll track down a few books for your shelves. Do you have a genre of choice?"

When Kit doesn't immediately respond, still suspicious of the girl, I answer on his behalf. "Historical accounts, perhaps. Anything that covers the origins and legends of the land is right up our alley. Isn't that right, Kit?"

I look to Kit just in time to catch him grinding his teeth before schooling his face back into neutrality. "Indeed," he murmurs, and I try not to let the notion of his silent yet evident distrust in Marzipan shake me.

"Should be easy enough," Marzipan says as she begins her departure. On the way, she accidentally bumps into me, briefly apologizing, and then stops before the door. "See you around, neighbors," she grins, then vanishes without a trace.

Kit *harumphs* before leaving my side to assess each of our appliances. "We'll have to pinpoint different food spots within Vesta's walls. I'm not particularly hungry yet, but we can——"

He drones on, but his voice turns muffled as my attention focuses elsewhere.

To where Marzipan had bumped into me and conveniently slipped a secret message in my pocket.

25
Jericho

When the Saints first showed me Pandora's whereabouts, I didn't believe them. I'd never had any *reason* to doubt them—they'd never lied or shown me false events before—but I just couldn't wrap my mind around what I was seeing.

Underground, but not chained or gagged.

She wasn't a prisoner at all. In fact, she looked like . . . someone's guest of honor.

That was a week ago, and against my better judgment, I said nothing. Not even to Venus. She'd have questions about who Pandora's not-jailer was, and I didn't have enough answers. Only the vague depictions the Saints provided. Which was another thing that threw me—the fact that all the variables in place were neither outright explained nor perceived. All I saw in that vision was Pandora alive, sitting in a cavern lit by sprinkled candlelight.

Singing with someone.

The tribunal met this morning, but with the time difference and with us having to wait on confirmed sources for messages, the evening sun is nearing the lip of Honeycomb Harbor's horizon by the time we hear anything. In Ardian's absence, I assigned Henry Tolcher the task of temporarily filling his post—more so to keep my mind at bay from the truth of him never coming back than for organization's sake. So when he comes striding into the throne room, eliciting a hushed silence over the room, his presence comes as a worthy distraction.

"Status report." My hands grip the arms of my throne.

"Rumors say that Duchess Geneva may have been spotted at the tribunal."

"*May* have?"

"The few locals that picked her out were unsure, but our eyes in the field caught sight of the person in question." Then, he reaches into his uniform pocket and hands Venus the object first: a faded, folded photograph. She stiffens to my right at the sight as Tolcher informs us, "It's her."

"Holy Saints," I swear when the proof finally meets my grasp.

Genny's not just near the scene of her daughter's sentencing. She's *there*. Just beyond the sight of the jury and High Judge. The under part of her eyes gleam with tears already shed, but the look on her face here . . . pure anger. A mother's vehemence.

"*How?*" Venus barks, pointing fingers at the guards stationed throughout the room. She comes rearing off her throne, disposition ablaze with righteous fury. "How does *Geneva Deragon* not only escape to Mosacia *unsupervised*, but navigate her way to the center of the bloody continent?"

I don't have the heart, nor the gall, to tell her that underestimating Genny is what got us into this mess in the first place. Not when she's this wound up.

"It's embarrassing enough that Pandora's capture was an oversight. But to have *two* Deragon girls running amuck in

Mosacia unchecked by our security? Pure and utter *humiliation!*"

"Venus," I murmur.

"Beyond this castle, she's your Duchess. But *here*," she bellows, " in these walls, you know who she really is. *She* kept this bloodline, this dynasty, alive—and if we lose her, we may very well lose *everything.*"

"Darling," I say calmly, eyes still hung up on the photograph.

"*What?*" she snarls.

Her anger takes over her entire posture, her entire, lovely face. But it's only then that I realize Venus's hazel eyes are glazed with tears that threaten to pour over. Still, I find enough of a voice to say, "Genny's not alone out there."

With years of practice, I've learned to let my visions unfold without knocking my corporal form fully unconscious. Instead of falling prey to passing out, I feel the Saints' intuitions like a subtle spike and temperature and revert to a prayer-like posture. Ready to receive.

No sound from reality interrupts my current circumstance—where I find myself in the streets just outside of the Mosacian tribunal. Despite the dust kicked up underneath people's feet, the climate isn't as arid as it appears. But it's certainly warm. I know so because the sun sears deep into the dark fabric along my back. Citizens are retreating from the scene of the sentencing, their whisperings filling the atmosphere every direction I turn.

One person bristles, "That coward."

"You think the princess slipped past him?" wonders another.

"Doubtful," the first one returns. "She likely seduced her way out. That serpent."

I try not to feel utter repulsion at the thought, at the way he reduces the Crown Princess of their ruling nation to a snake—

"She must be quite the charmer if she can change the mind of Kit

Andromeda."

The mention of that strange name signals another passerby's attention before I can utter some sort of reaction. "The rich gentleman whose house lies on the edge of the Lonely Isle? How did he come across Pandora Deragon of all people?"

"He has a . . . habit," the first one says snidely, "of acquiring things of great interest."

Even though I get the feeling that I'm missing out on an inside joke, the mention of the Lonely Isle strikes me like a blow. I've never done any official business there, let alone with some wealthy aristocrat bearing such a gaudy name. Still, something eerie festers inside of me the longer I think about that place, or the fact that people other than myself know about its existence enough to converse casually about it.

A flash of gold catches my attention from the corner of my eye, and as I turn away from the gossip session to my left, I squint against the way the sun catches on the shimmering object.

No, not object—a person. A man with a scalp full of golden, furling hair that matches the scruff starting to form along his jaw. His white shirt, likely dirtied from wrestling his way through the crowds, billows in the breeze. And when it finally falls flat against his strong arms—

"What's our strategy now?" a familiar face asks from the man's side. Geneva.

Just as the photograph showed, there she stands. Dark hair pulled away from her face to let the sunbeams kiss her soft, brown skin. Like Pandora, she appears completely unharmed, which manages to settle the secret anxiety I've harbored since she first fled Broadcove. At best, Genny reaches shoulder-height to the man I figure must be her companion, the only plausible reason she's made it as far across the continent as she has.

He smiles at her question, like there's no need to panic and this is all just some puzzle they must solve. "If Pandora really did escape her captor, she'll likely have done it on foot, which means we need to stay local should she be returned to the tribunal."

"But people are looking for me, too," Genny protests quietly, and as both this gentleman and I take in the look on her face, I realize this truly may be the first time she's thought about herself. Her wellbeing. Her discovery. "I can't help her if they find me—"

The man shushes her in a slow drawl, embracing her. He pulls back enough to look at her and cradles the side of her face with a dove's gentleness that feels borderline romantic. His next words sound soaked in honey.

"Trust me, Genny, I won't let them take you from me."

Seeing the way Genny swallows against his touch, I start to think I'm not just imagining things. Saints, Venus will have an absolute conniption.

"Besides," he says, pulling away slowly once Genny's smile has returned. "Where we're going, you won't need to be on guard about people recognizing you."

I keep the details brief as I report them to Tolcher, instructing him to meet the other foot soldier scouts across the Damocles. He concedes, requesting he leave in the morning to spend one more night with his wife, Nadine, and their two boys. Venus relents, though I see the battle in her eyes.

Once Venus and I clear the throne room and escort ourselves down towards our private hall, however, she halts me with a hand to my chest. "You're not telling me everything."

You don't need to know all the ins and outs if it will only make you upset.

Venus crosses her arms, the fabric along her sleeves creasing. "Talk."

"You'll get caught up on everything in a matter of days anyways," I groan, trying not to make the impression that, sometimes, it stings to know that there's little privacy I have left from her. Even if it's true. "Why bother?"

"Because I'm—" she blurts, the first word firm but the second . . . weak. Choked. Venus shuts her eyes tight to keep from shattering. "I'm to blame for all this."

"Venus."

"*No*, I am!" she shouts, and in that moment, the dam breaks. "I reprimanded our guards, but had I not been so fixated on my safekeeping during Queen's Feast, Pandora would still be here— *Genny* would still be here. They wouldn't be being hunted down by lands I insisted we conquer, and I wouldn't have to pretend that the guilt and agony isn't eating away at my soul."

It's been a long while since I've seen Venus cry like this, internal brokenness contorting the lovely features in her face. Tears dilute the brightness in her eyes, and as they cascade down her cheek, they leave a faint line along her skin. It vaguely reminds me of a cat scratch, and the pain overcoming her likely bears the same physical manifestation.

"First of all," I say, pulling her hands free from her defensive stance and taking them within mine. I squeeze her fingers to remind her I'm here. Listening. "We conquered those lands together. Sure, you set it into motion, but I've been behind you every step of the way. They nearly dismantled everything the Morgan Dynasty built, and it was time for retribution. You have *nothing* to be ashamed of."

Perhaps the last statement goes too far, but I do not retract. Not when I know the heavy burden and shame Venus has harbored in her heart all these years, and I with her.

Venus went off the deep end for me, devised this insane scheme to lure Slater Seagrave into her heart, her bed, and into the jaws of death. All according to plan, she stole his power and his kingdom like it was nothing.

But the cost took her life in more ways than one. Yes, she

had lived to tell the tale, but Greer had perished. Harriet and Emmaline—the only other soft spot in the Seagrave Dynasty—gone. Her only shred of hope was that she could spare the remaining children from the fate she dealt the others. The unique little girl and the twins, they didn't deserve the slaughter the rest of them faced.

But no one sent word of their survival. Not even the Saints, and as I watched the realization of it sink in fully, I witnessed Venus experience the kind of personal devastation that I know well. The moral consequences, the *soul wound* one ought to feel after every kill. Venus hadn't been able to stop the Seagrave Slaughter once she set it into motion, and I couldn't rewind time and give Pandora the father she looked for in me.

We were equals in our despair, our self-disgrace.

"And second," I press on, "your sister is resourceful because I firmly believe that mindset is hereditary. Pandora is resourceful because we spent our lives training her to be. They're both as smart as you are stubborn, so I have faith that they both will fare just fine until our soldiers can get to them."

"Do you?" Venus chokes out, the look in her bleary eyes telling me she doesn't buy it for a second. "Yes, Pandora is intelligent, but she isn't like us, Jericho. You know this. She's never killed. She *wouldn't*—"

"You said the same thing about Calliope once."

The memory of it takes her by such surprise that Venus keeps walking down the hall. I trail her, waiting until she feels ready to speak again. Her hand pauses over the knob on our bedroom door before she whispers, "I just. . . I worry that it's too late to help her. Either of them."

"It's a human thing to worry, Venus. Being human is appropriate, even when you wear a crown and bear the responsibilities of a nation. It's perhaps *most* appropriate to feel how you are when you have all that going on."

"Don't do that," she begs, her voice ragged. "Don't console me. Not when the way I'm feeling is my own fault. Not when I pushed them both away, but this time, they're too far for me to reach them again." She sputters over her words again, biting down on her lip to keep whatever remains of her stony composure. "I left my sister no choice. All those years she let the world believe Pandora was mine, and I repay her like *this*— by abandoning her daughter. Of course she'd leave!" she says, holding the photograph up again and shaking it in my face. "Of course she'd trust some *stranger* more than she'll ever trust me!"

"It's not that Genny doesn't understand. She just doesn't have the full picture."

The prophecy. Yet another liability we took on in secret—one that, most recently, excluded Genny from the equation.

But then, another thought comes crashing over me.

Pandora was never in that vision either.

Not when Venus first beheld it when Pandora was a newborn. Not when the Saints first revealed it to me when Pandora was ten. Not even in its newest development.

I even out my expression before Venus starts asking questions, and I press a kiss upon her brow. Her skin runs hot against my lips, and I make a note to draw her a bath before she can insist otherwise. "We're going to find them, Venus. We're going to find them and bring them home safely. Then, we'll explain everything. We'll make amends. All will be better than it was before, I promise."

She's hesitant at first, but eventually surrenders. A rarity.

There's no need to make things worse by telling her where Genny is headed, and how her sister's eyes had glimmered with an emotion for the man accompanying her that I remembered fighting so valiantly against as Venus and I first grew closer.

26
Pandora

So long as I am in Kit Andromeda's line of sight, I do not dare open Marzipan's note, even though the urge to do so nearly eats me alive.

The only thing that takes my mind off the piece of paper burning a hole in my pocket is the matter of my physical proximity to Kit. As the first day drags on, I don't know which is worse—the silence when we run out of things to say, or the way our new closeness makes everything feel so *loud*.

The two of us can practically hear a pin drop as we eat supper, but after the pork and rice from one of the sacred city's food banks begins to disagree with both of our stomachs, falling asleep this first night becomes nearly impossible with all the noise.

All day, I have dreaded using the bathroom more than anything else, even the prospects of what could happen while we sleep beside each other. Kit doesn't mind—mainly because he can't afford *not* to frequent it with how our supper sits with us—but out of courtesy, I plug my ears every time he gets up to use it. I, however, remain stubborn, and certainly don't want to imagine Kit listening in from our bed. Instead, I try to control my breathing and distract my brain from the roiling in my stomach. Waves of nausea sometimes crash over Kit and I at the same time, and just as I'd be about to cave, Kit would rise from the bed again and occupy it. In the end, I wait until Kit finally dozes off to excuse myself out the front door and vomit into the hedges.

Relief sweeps over me like a warm cloak in wintertime the moment it passes, and after wiping my heated brow, I step back inside the hostel—

Kit sits board-straight in our bed, the covers tousled like he was about to bolt from the room had I not caught him. "Are you alright?" he asks, his voice entirely awake.

"I'll be fine—"

"You've been suffering in silence all night," he says.

My smile downturns. "Yeah, well . . . you don't need to see me like this, Kit."

"All I need, Princess," Kit murmurs, "is you."

As my eyes flare at the gravity of what he's saying, Kit quickly adds, ". . . to feel better."

He fetches an empty bowl from the kitchen and sets it on the floor on my side of the bed. "In case you don't make it in time," he says quietly, not wanting embarrassment to swallow me whole but understanding my predicament. My throat is hoarse as I thank him for his generosity, to which Kit merely waves me off. Before I can climb back into bed, however, he stops me with a hand. "You need to change."

"What?"

"You shouldn't be sleeping in clothes you've gotten sick in," he explains.

I want to argue that *he* shouldn't be either, but then remember that Kit's not wearing a shirt. Or his slacks. I ought to act like it stirs me somehow, but I've been too busy forcing acid to stay in my stomach to notice.

I gulp, a new wave of queasiness dawning on me that has nothing to do with my previous sickness. "But I don't have anything else to wear."

"Then at least take those off," he points directly at me.

My pulse and heartbeat are jackhammers beneath my skin. "Kit—"

"If they have food banks here, they likely have clothing depots, too. I'll go stock up for the both of us and bring you back something clean. Until then . . ." He doesn't want to say it. He doesn't want to voice the words *take off your clothes*, because despite the feelings that won him over and ultimately betrayed his agreement with the tribunal, my eyes give me away.

I'm nervous.

"I'll be going now," he says briskly, turning on a heel and leaving me to my business.

Despite anticipating Kit will barge back in claiming he forgot something he needs, I peel myself out of my clothes, tossing my shirt onto the floor and shucking off my bottoms, I try not to resent the fact that Kit was right: I do feel better. Within seconds, cool air dries the sweat accumulating down the center of my back. I feel like I can *breathe*—

"I forgot to ask what size you—"

And then, Kit and I are staring at each other.

He's just as he was a minute ago, and yet . . . the intensity with which Kit looks at me defies gravity. In a way I don't want to admit to myself, this heated moment plays a mean trick on my mind. Reminding me, somehow, of the masked man I left in the past. The man who, come to think of it, *also* happened to insist I

225

abandon my old clothes and battle oncoming sickness with sleep once before.

I manage to drag the covers over my nearly naked body before I outright flash him, the hem of the quilt lining up just before my cleavage dips. Fighting the urge to look at my clothes on the floor, I watch, instead, as Kit chews on the inside of his cheek.

"I'm sorry, I should've . . . I mean, I . . ." he stumbles, and for the first time, a full spread of pink colors his face.

He's nervous, too.

Kit clears his throat. "What size do you wear? I want to make sure I get you clothes that fit you comfortably. Do you prefer something loose or . . . form-fitting?"

There's an audible struggle in the last phrase, and against my better judgment, a girlish laugh escapes me. I don't bother skirting around it. "Worried the men here will gawk?"

"No," he says dryly. "I'm worried about myself."

And *that* is a can of worms I do *not* wish to open, especially not when my clothes are on the floor and I'm in a bed I share with him.

"I don't know my exact measurements," I mumble. "If you're getting pants, though, try and find something with laces I can tie or sinch, in case they're too big."

"Of course." Kit nearly trips over his own feet backpedaling to the door. "Of course," he says again.

"Kit?" I say, even though I have nothing to ask him in response.

It's like he can read it all over my face, so he doesn't prompt me further. Instead, without needing me to ask, he lights the lone candle previously discarded on the kitchen table, as if knowing the darkness deters me from slumber. Rather than say goodnight, Kit tells me, already retreating out the door, "I'll be back as soon as I can."

Kit insisted on fetching our meals from the food banks for the next four days, likely so that he could *personally* chew out the cooks responsible for the spout of food poisoning we underwent.

Even though the both of us made a full recovery after two days of conserving our strength, he refused to let me break his mandated schedule: rest through breakfast and drink lots of water, stew and non-acidic fruits at lunch, and gradually increased portions of white meat for supper. This morning, however, I stir from my morning daze to find Kit leaving the hostel to go on a walk. The door barely makes a sound as he delicately feeds the lock into the plate, and once his form passes the view from our window, I surge from the bed.

I'd been careless and forgot that I left Marzipan's note in the pockets of my old clothes, the ones I'd worn when we first arrived. Fishing it out in a mad dash, as if Kit hadn't just made the effort to secretly slip away, I fumble with the scrap of paper and read her concise message:

Mosacia needs you.
Find me when you can.

Needs me? Mosacia *hates* me, as proof by the bounty on my head.

How could a territory my family has conquered *need* me in any facet?

The laughable concept is enough to draw me out of bed, into fresh clothes, and up to the third floor. I'm mid-knock when

Marzipan swings open the door to her home, as if anticipating my arrival. "Ah, Pandora! I was wondering when you'd—"

"I don't have much time." The words fall out in a frantic blurt. "Kit's on a walk, but I don't know when he'll be back. Does this conversation require privacy?" I hold out the scrap of paper to her.

Marzipan's eyes glimmer at the sight of her slipped correspondence. "Don't worry. I've memorized that man's routine over the past few days. We've got an hour. But . . . yes, you should probably come inside."

"What's this about, anyways? Why would a nation out to sentence me to death need me?"

"Oh, right." She giggles. "That *may* have been a stretch. You see, they don't *know* they need you. Maybe not yet, at least, but they do. They need someone on the other side to see the truth, and *I* need to know if you're the kind of person I'm hoping you are—all curious and kind and compassionate—so that you won't bury it."

"Bury what—"

"*Marzi!*" the elderly downstairs neighbor heckles. And then, she yaps something in a dialect I've never heard before. My eyes go wide at the intensity at which she verbally flings it at Marzipan.

Still, Marzipan laughs, unaffected by her berating. She leans in and whispers, "To put it nicely, she said something along the likes of, *what have I said about having your conversations on your front porch this early?*—and the answer is not to. Anya's not a morning person."

Then, she cups her hands and loudly responds in the woman's native language. And while I can't understand what Marzipan means in return, her childlike smile seeps through every foreign word, lightening the tension. I hear the woman scoff but retreat into her hostel, and only once she's gone do I have the strength to ask her what Kit had wondered from the start.

"How many languages do you know, Marzipan?"

She gestures me into her place so sweetly that I almost mishear her as I walk through the door. "All of them."

I chuckle. "No seriously, how many."

"All of them," she repeats candidly.

Finally, I gear my eyes back to her in horrified shock. "How's that even possible?"

She must be joking, I tell myself. *That is both statistically and physiologically not possible.*

Yet, the way Marzipan stares me down with that carefree, pleased smile . . . she's serious. There is no mistaking it, not as she carefully shuts us inside and leans against the door, as if to trap any sound from slinking out.

"I'm like them," she whispers. "Venus and Jericho."

The warmth in my blood chills in an instant. My veins crackle against the ice forming there, and Marzipan bares her teeth in an uncomfortable smile. "Surprise."

27
Pandora

"What do you *mean* you're like them?"

"Come on, Pandora," Marzipan says with another chuckle. "We both know there's no need to resort to silly questions. You know exactly what I mean. But if you want me to just come right out and say it, fine. I'm—"

I slam a hand over her mouth, fearing that the walls will catch wind of our conversation.

Marzipan still mutters out a slightly smothered *"Blessed"* against my palm.

"But it doesn't make *sense*," I hiss. "You're so *young*. From what I've studied, blessings don't manifest early in life. My uncle didn't uncover his until his early twenties. Same with Aunt Venus. Age aside, though, you're also not—"

"Urovian?"

I stop to study her face at the recognition of it, shaking my head. "This isn't normal."

"Right, because speaking every world language would be

totally customary if I were across the Damocles instead."

There it is. There's her spark. There's her spunky attitude that finally reminds me just how grown she feels despite being so young.

"I just . . . don't see how it's possible," I finally articulate.

"It's pretty neat, actually. My brain digests a person's native tongue and translates it in real time to what language I speak most dominantly. And then, while it makes it *feel* as though I'm responding in Kionan—the language I converse most dominantly in—I'm *actually* speaking the language of whomever I'm conversing with. For instance, you communicate in Urovia's most dominant linguistic, but in my head, it's like I'm talking to someone from back home."

"No," I say softly, enthralled by the concept of her blessing despite not intending to ask quite *literally* how it works. "I mean how can you, a *Mosacian*, be blessed? History clearly stated that Mosacia had been so strict about the ways people could worship, not to mention *what* they worshiped, that they had to migrate . . ."

Marzipan sighs. "Look, I'm not going to assume you're clueless, given a Crown Princess would likely be well educated regarding her homeland's religion and roots. Still, I know this is all a shock, so I'll try and explain everything without bombarding you. Maybe you should . . . uh . . . sit?" she says, the last word coming out on a question.

"Good point," I mutter, situating myself on the edge of her bed.

"Okay. So, as you know, a blessing can be passed down through appointments. If there's only one Blessed individual with that particular talent, upon entering the Beyond, they are able to select a successor—someone to take on their blessing after they're gone. However, history has shown that if a *woman* is bestowed the blessing and she has children, her offspring—male or female—are statistically shown to inherit those gifts also. The only outlier among these recordings, of course, is Venus Deragon."

I try not to feel a tinge of guilt, or fury for that matter, when Marzipan says her name.

"We know now that the late Queen Merrie had clairvoyance, but seeing as her son already possessed the gift, she decided to bequeath her blessing in a way that granted Venus divine connection, an entirely new trait. There's almost never been anything like it, and there will likely never be anything like it again," she says with the sort of finality I'd expect out of the revered Holymen in the Royal Domain, not a teenage girl.

But then, the addition of a single word slowly registers.

"Almost?" I whisper.

To her credit, Marzipan smiles before she releases a steadying breath. "You've likely read the documented accounts. Eight patriarchs experienced the supernatural after praying with enough reverence to woo the divine beings into bestowing each of them with a unique blessing. But did history ever record *why* they were praying, or what they were praying *for*?"

"I was taught, like most scholars, that they wanted deliverance from Mosacia's constricting rule—how they prohibited religious expression. So they cried out to the forces above and—"

"Can you cite that?" Marzipan inquires.

"What?"

"Can you *cite* that? Can you clearly cite a piece of history that lays out, in perfect detail, that *that's* what they were praying for? That they *specifically* wanted deliverance from Mosacia's oppression."

I dwell on the thought for a moment . . . but come up short.

Uncle Jericho always stated it as if it were fact, but I'd never seen anything. Still . . . there has *to be*—

"There's not," Marzipan says, reading the look in my eyes like she can translate my inner thoughts, too. "I know, because my mother and I scoured every library in Urovia for documentation on it, and we found nothing. We began to grow suspicious, as we didn't know Mosacia's side of the story. Of course, living in Urovia at the time, we knew it would be nearly impossible to understand the Mosacian perspective, not with the barrage of *U. Herald* editions and the surge of public nationalism since the re-conquering of the Empire. Still, Jericho and Venus didn't live across the Damocles, which meant that we had a better shot of uncovering the truth if we could find the means to leave in secrecy."

Marzipan doesn't have to say the rest aloud for me to understand where this story's headed. There are no secrets with Jericho and the Saints, no ways to slip through the cracks. His visions always find those that might stir up trouble—even if the trouble they're starting is for a just cause.

I glance around the room, and the state of her house says it all. Marzipan is an orphan. No adult belongings. No mixed scents of bodies that could occupy the space with her. I fight the wince overtaking my bones as I dare to say to her, "Tell me everything."

"Pandora—"

"No, Marzipan. I need to know. I'm not in Broadcove anymore, and I don't think I'll ever go back, not even if I wanted to. Just because I share blood with them doesn't mean whatever you've endured and the things they've done are justified. So, please, just *tell me*."

I don't wish to pry—especially not in a harsh way—but I cannot fight the internal nudge to acknowledge the long-gone presence of her family like a divine conviction. That, and I *want* to be the person Marzipan hopes I am. Truly.

And so, Marzipan, for the first time in what little amount I've known her, begins to wilt.

"Mama passed me the blessing, but she died of an infection two . . . no, three years ago, now. It was Daddy, however, that died in our efforts to relocate. I was thirteen. I don't dwell on it often but, between me and you, I miss them in a way that no language seems to be able to describe fully. Every day."

My stomach twists at the similarities between us—only I cannot fathom a world where I had to go at things *entirely* alone . . . without Mother.

Saints, who would I even *be* without Geneva Deragon?

"My voracious appetite for literature came from Mama, but my heart for communicating with new people was all Daddy. He always instilled the importance of not overlooking even the lowest of life forms at first glance. It didn't hit me until a squirrel bid me good morning once that I realized he meant the notion *literally*."

Marzipan laughs at the memory. Meanwhile, I marvel at the fact that she can translate the language of animals on top of every human dialect. Then again, Venus idolized a tiger she domesticated as a castle pet in my early childhood. Sometimes, I *swore* that they understood each other, somehow.

"Daddy had such deep compassion for people, one that really rubbed off on Mama and me over the years. So when Mama started noticing the missing pieces of Urovia's origin story that she'd been studying, Daddy was the first one to suggest we migrate, go learn more from the source. He made plans for one of the cargo ships to smuggle us across the Damocles late one night. Mama and I made it on the ship, but Daddy . . ."

I can't go back in time and change her reality, yet my very marrow wails *no, no, no.*

"No one came after Mama and I, which means he likely confessed to being the last in his family line to bear the blessing of Many Tongues. He died for a lie. For *us*. And while Mama and I could've hardened our hearts in response, we knew that Jericho's violence meant we were on the heels of something big. Something important."

My heart stalls and my stomach drops. "*Jericho's* violence."

It's not a question—just a shock. Jericho hadn't killed a Urovian citizen in years, not when Venus had replaced his dirtied hands with her own. But to kill a Urovian after all that time . . . and a *Blessed* one, at that?

What the hell were they hiding?

"That's why I live here, in the Sacred City. Not out of fear, but in efforts to right a wrong without any chance of being silenced," she says carefully. "Because of the laws, no one can cause me harm until I settle down and start a family outside of Vesta, passing my blessing onto the next generation. Until then, it's my sole responsibility to tell as many people as possible the truth about this city. This continent. This *gift* that I have."

I can hardly bear the weight of what I fear is coming.

"The deities commemorated here in the Temple of the Shine . . . they're Mosacia's attempt at searching for the divine. Not because they are devout, but because they are *desperate*," Marzipan explains. "They look to these beings recorded in history as their masters because they don't *remember* that the Saints were true. That they loved humanity enough to bless them with a divine thread back to them."

My voice breaks. "The blessings existed to prove to the world that they were real?"

"Yes, Pandora. *That* was why the patriarchs were praying so fervently that day," Marzipan says, her eyes grave and wild. "They and the rest of Mosacia had believed that there was no hope beyond the natural course of human life—nothing beyond the grave worth believing in. Not even the deities they still worship now felt enough to them. And from their desperation, the Saints had answered their pleas . . . and the patriarchs responded by hiding what they granted them from the rest of the world. By building a new world and rooting it in their selfishness."

I think I might be sick. Might heave up whatever meager amount of food still rests in my body right onto her floor.

"Tomes on Mosacian Root History, along with countless personal journals, had been preserved here in the Sacred City. And after Mama and I spent the better part of a year dissecting them all in their various translations, we discovered that the blessing of Many Tongues came nearly two centuries *after* the patriarchs received their initial gifts. Bestowed specifically on a Urovian family of meager wealth and boundless curiosity. It was clear to Mama and I why the Saints had picked them— my grandparents several times over. Because just as the Saints' blessings had wandered across the Damocles once before, they expected this new gift to do the same. And knowing how Jericho nearly kept it from doing just that, it was *vital* that it did."

So much anger and resentment and confusion thrums to life, heating the blood in my veins.

But Marzipan merely sets a steady hand over my own, looking into my eyes with such warmth and peace. A sensation I haven't felt in so long. It washes over me like a rolling tide.

"Our gift wasn't bestowed on us to strengthen their arsenal." Marzipan smiles. "It was created to help restore the divided lands. To remind the world that there is life after death, joy after an early end. And I intend to devote my life to sharing that with anyone who will listen."

28
Geneva

No one batted an eye two weeks ago when Ren and I first walked through the gates of Vesta and set up camp—and no one does so now as he and I careen through the Sacred City's streets, greeting several of the locals we've recognized on our daily walks together.

It seems like the vast majority of people here recognize me as the younger Urovian Duchess. My pictures have been printed in editions of the *U. Herald* plenty of times. Every birthday and holiday portrait, at minimum, has been distributed for public consumption. But whether my presence here disturbs or offends anyone around us, nobody lets on.

Least of all Ren, who looks at me like I am the source of his unending enthusiasm.

That much is obvious—the thrill. The excitement in this arrangement. The knowledge that I'd go anywhere Ren leads, not because I'm naïve, but because I trust him. And he trusts himself to lead us well, to keep me safe.

But Saints, the signals are really starting to blur. I'm starting to not distinguish clearly between Ren's eagerness and the fact that . . . well, a man hasn't looked at me like this in a *very* long time. And the frantic fluttering feeling I have in my chest each time he does is one I haven't felt since I was a teenager.

Since Kurt.

The reminder of his name, his death, and his absence in Pandora and my life makes me sober up instantly. Makes me forget how the twinkle in Ren's eyes stops me in my tracks and replaces it with a guilt I deserve to live with. Guilt for going along with this husband-and-wife coverup when we're in public, and guilt for not minding it one bit when we naturally allowed it to permeate our private life. Guilt for sleeping at Ren's side without hesitation and waiting until he's deep in sleep to trace my fingers through his hair and breathe in his honey-kissed scent. Guilt for savoring it, committing it to memory while I still can.

Because when I get my hands on my daughter again, when I get to hold her and ensure that she's safe—and I swear to myself I will, and so does Ren—what then?

I'll have no choice but to return to Broadcove. To the sister that saw no merits to rescuing my baby girl and the husband I'm starting to see as spineless for backing her. But if Pandora and I return, will Ren stay behind? Or will he—

I don't allow myself to picture it, to picture anything more than a friendship.

Face it, Geneva. He's kind and protective, but he's been running around his whole life, and he doesn't look like he's going to get tired of it anytime soon. Don't start convincing yourself that Ren would settle down with you, let alone while knowing you have a daughter. A grown one. A royal *one.*

I sigh, not wanting to pity myself. Still, I never thought it would come to this: wondering if poverty in the marshes would've been more survivable than the secrecy and lies I've been honor-bound to.

Suddenly, I feel Ren's hand along the side of my face. I twitch at the contact, and in a rapid glance, I see a little girl standing before the both of us, bright flowers picked from one of the overgrown, grass medians. She must've handed Ren one, and when I finally stand still, Ren weaves the stem through my hair. He tucks it along the curve of my ear and whispers, "And I thought you couldn't be more lovely."

As the child skips off, pleased with her floral offering and giddy over the way I blush in response to Ren's words, I take it all back. I'd go through it all—the loss, the grief, the hunger, the deceit, the guilt.

I'd do everything all over again just to have this time with Ren Satare, however fleeting.

Before I know it, we've made it to our dinner spot. Not to one of the food banks, I realize—which is contrary to our typical routine—but to a bistro with a quaint little patio. It reminds me so much of the street I first met Ren on. I wonder if he picks the spot solely because of the fact, and I try not to meditate on what that could mean in a deeper sense.

There's an open table settled along the edge of the wrought iron gate that separates dining patrons from the public footpath, and as Ren approaches it, I hold out a hand. "Wait, I forgot my coins back at the—"

"It's on me, dear," Ren says in a manner that feels almost melodic. He doesn't avert his gaze as he says it, either—as if wanting to capture my reaction fully.

I don't have enough restraint to school my face into neutrality, not after how persistently I've buried my feelings ever since I've known him. If he looks hard enough, I bet Ren would be able to see the truth there. That every *dear* and *darling* and *sweetheart* has turned into something I wish were real, not just for show and security.

Ren pulls out my chair, scooting me in once I'm settled. I can feel the warmth of his skin radiating onto mine without even touching, and I shift in my seat from the brief distress it floods me with, what it might indicate. I push it away but still etch out a congenial smile at Ren. He mirrors the look on his own face, and I swallow.

I know better than to ask if this is a date, because the question would conflict with the role of the married couple we're playing. I also know better than to let my mind spiral down a path of questions that are sure to leave me hurting later on—like whether this is his attempt at really dating me, displaying romantic interest that would finally, wondrously, be deemed mutual.

Instead, I ask him, "Have your eye on anything in particular?"

Ren chuckles under his breath. "You. In that dress."

I resist the urge to cross my arms over my chest, even though the neckline is completely innocent. Ren had gone out earlier today to the clothing depot and fetched us some nicer garments for dinner. The technicolor pattern likely traces back to one of the smaller Mosacian lands bordering Vesta, and the oranges and golds pair well with the richness of my brown skin. The silk ties together at the base of my throat before looping around my neck, and I try to banish any thoughts of having Ren's fingers replace the fabric's touch. My hair flows faintly through the evening breeze, and I tell myself that I'm tucking a strand behind my ear because of that, not because of my sudden self-consciousness.

It's just for show, I remind myself. *It's just for safekeeping in case someone listens in on us, or thinks twice about my identity.*

Quirking the menu at him in clarification, I say, "I mean to eat."

"Ah," he sighs with a quiet sense of happiness. "Well, I've eaten my way across the world plenty of times before, so I'd be fine with anything you want to try. I will, however, need a glass of wine."

"Careful, now. Too much, and you might get carried away when we get back home."

I hear the unintended flirt in my words, and I fumble for some semblance of clarification in the hopes that I don't sound like a complete lunatic.

But Ren merely leans in, his golden stubble brushing my jaw. "Is that a warning or a request?"

No part of me balks from his closeness this time—not when I've been starving for it. Not after I've started preserving every passing glance and casual graze these past weeks. I shiver from the thrill of it all, and Ren catches me in my trance, eyes hazy as they glance beyond him at nothing at all. He pulls back. "Where's your mind running off to, Geneva?" he murmurs.

I try not to make my gulp so obvious as I bring my gaze back to his own. Saints, looking at him and willing myself not to combust is like staring at the sun. "Nobody's looking at us."

"Do you *want* people to look at us?" His tone is almost comedic.

"It's not that, I just—" I groan at how desperately the words are flying out of me. "The comment about my outfit. The wine. There's no need for it, not if no one can hear you flirt with me when you're this close."

"They don't need to hear me," Ren teases, inching across the table, "when I tell you this."

The blood in my face darkens in anticipation. He was already so near without crossing a line, our faces already touching . . . and yet, Ren's here. Impossibly close. One hand crooks my jaw so that I'm forced to stare straight into his eyes, while the other traces the neckline of the dress he picked out for me.

"I look at you every day, Genny, and my senses feel so brilliantly warped. Like I can't remember how to keep my eyes on the road in front of me rather than on you. *Always* on you. But looking at you now, with that flower behind your ear and the adorable blush on your cheeks every time I tell you how pretty you are," Ren says, his smile hinting at something filthy. "Everything about you outright *brainwashes* me."

I'm damn near ready to turn my head half an inch and consume Ren in a vicious kiss, when suddenly, a male server approaches us, brandishing a polished bottle of an unidentified alcohol. We both pull away, more for his sake than for ours, and I instantly feel his warmth retreat from me.

"Pardon my intrusion, and good evening. Our staff wished to gift you a bottle of our best mulberry."

Despite his warm tone, I note the way his eye contact skims over Ren entirely, speaking directly to me. "It's not every day a Urovian royal wishes to dine in Mosacia Proper."

I try not to squirm in my seat at his blatant recognition of me.

Ren registers the look on my face, but our server is already in motion before Ren can say anything. "I understand your presence in the city may be out of necessity, but it truly is an honor, Miss Deragon—"

"Satare."

Only now does he give Ren a proper glance-over. "I'm sorry?"

"It's *Mrs. Satare*. Not Miss Deragon," Ren hisses possessively.

His outburst is a bombshell—one that I fear might get leaked to the *U. Herald* if our server doesn't maintain discretion—but more than that, it's firm. Territorial, even. Worst of all, it makes me cross my legs tighter under the table to keep calm. The sensation sends an electric current through my whole body.

Our server's assessment concludes with a wide, knowing smile. "My mistake. Would the two of you prefer champagne, then? I take it you're celebrating away from home."

"The mulberry sounds lovely, still," I chime in, knowing that champagne has resulted in me becoming sloppily drunk a few times before. And I want full control of my faculties when Ren elaborates on what he was saying earlier . . . once we get back to our place.

"Of course. I'll give you both a few minutes to look over the menu. In the meantime—"

Our server goes on his spiel about house specialties, recommended dishes, and that he'll return with two glasses for our mulberry. We both bid him a warm smile as he departs, and before I can prepare myself, Ren's hands return to cradle my face. His hair glimmers like gemstones in the light of the setting sun, to the point where it's almost hard to keep eye contact with him.

"You look like you're about to jump out of your skin," Ren starts again.

"What's happening here?" I blurt. "With us? What is this?"

His responding smile shaves off ten or so years. "This is a date."

"As what, Ren? Pretend spouses? Friends—"

"Don't insult me with that word," he interjects. His tone is serious, but his smile remains, gentling the sentiment. "You and I both know what this is becoming."

I bite my lip on instinct. "Yeah, but I want to hear you say it."

It's not just a request. It's a prayer—a fervent one. I *need* this verbal confirmation to keep my head from spinning so relentlessly, to know that this isn't some crackpot disillusion I've created in my brain.

There's a dark gleam in Ren's soulful, brown eyes. "How long have you wanted me?"

"What?" I squeak, sounding like a small creature that just got stepped on.

Where the hell is our server with those glasses? I need a drink to hide behind, to drown within.

"How long," he repeats undeterred, "have you fought against this phantom pull towards me? How long have I been clueless to the fact that you might see even a *fraction* of worthiness in me the way I've been aching for you?"

"Ren—"

My voice gives away the hidden desires of my heart, how I'm dying for him to take what he wants from me—even when that's nothing like his character. Ren has been nothing but a perfect gentleman. But even with it out in the open like this, Ren tells me, his tone pleading, "How long have you felt this way?"

"Too long," I rasp. "Long enough to make me feel restless when I'm near you, and borderline senseless apart from you. I don't know which is worse."

"Apart," he whispers, his face deathly serious, now. "Apart from you is *infinitely* worse."

I barely manage to choke out the word, "You?"

"I know you touch me when you think I'm asleep."

The sheer force of my terrified realization is enough to knock the wind out of me.

"I never allowed myself to wonder why, not when my mind could get carried away. I wrote it off as a reminder to myself that you're a mother. It's your instinct to nurture, nevermind that you were damn good at it and each touch made my insides writhe. Truth is, though, I can't find sleep anymore until you do it, Genny—not until you touch me."

I shiver as Ren's hands courses through my hair in time with the words *touch me*, and suddenly, my blood is fire and my veins are smoldering wood. Everything curls inward and charrs beneath my skin. I might just explode.

"But last night, you got careless," Ren says, a playfulness in his slight admonishing. "I felt you kiss my spine, and that simple touch you thought would go undetected kicked open the gates of my restraint. And now that I know for certain the way you feel about me, it's time I return the favor."

My eyes bulge just in time for our server to cut the tension and come around with two wine goblets. I thank him graciously, though my voice comes out hollow. Dry. He scurries off, sensing he's interrupted something again, and when he's gone, Ren leans back in his chair, eyeing me with an intensity that is all man and no amusement.

"We're going to drink wine and enjoy the sunset. You're going to tell me all the desires of your heart until you're blue in the face and worried that I'm not listening, even though you've always had my undivided attention. And as you do, I'm going to will myself to stay in my chair, to keep from clambering across this table and doing something *very* indecent in such a public setting. But after we've had our food and the sky turns dark, you should know that I have every intention of taking you home, tearing off your dress, and kissing you everywhere you'll let me. And I won't be shy about it. Nor will I let you be."

We haven't even kissed *once*, and yet the mental image of what we'll be up to later . . .

"It's just been . . . a long time for me," I say quietly. Physically and emotionally.

"You're not alone in that," Ren returns sincerely. "And that doesn't hinder me."

Wildly, that was my only holdup—the one, frantic condition that I wanted reassurance on. I don't need to worry about the years that have passed, or how I may not know what to do with my hands, or that this is the best kind of nervousness I've ever experienced.

I just need to trust him. And given the way his pupils dilate, I know in my gut that there's no way that Ren fakes the tension simmering here.

"All you have to do," Ren says on what sounds like a groan, like his soul may very well splinter from his bones, "is say yes."

And then, my breath stalls in my chest.

Only it's not because of Ren.

No, all my thoughts bottom out as I lay eyes on her—*my daughter*—roaming the street with a young girl I've never seen before.

I almost convince myself I'm seeing things, but then, I hear her laughter clear as day and *know* it's her, the sound of it undeniable. Their heads are dipped, attention focused on what looks like two translations of identical textbooks, and while I don't understand the context of their interaction, it doesn't matter.

Somehow, Pandora escaped.

She's here in the sacred city. No one can harm her here, even if she's recognized.

She's *safe*.

Frankly, she's even more beautiful than she was when I last laid eyes on her. Pandora's always been lovely, but something about the Mosacian sunset coasting over her skin—skin that appears untouched, unharmed—suits her well. It soothes the ache in my heart.

It wills me to still in my chair, to let Pandora round the corner and disappear.

I will find you again, Pandora. I swear it. You just stay in this city and stay alive until I can get to you again.

I don't allow myself to feel any shame for the choice I make. I'll have time to wallow over it and feel selfish when I'm back in Urovia. All I know is . . . my time with Ren is borrowed, and if I just let my daughter slip out of my grasp with no guarantee of her returning to me, I'm going to make it worth my while.

"Yes, Ren," I answer, and the sense of confidence in this choice—in *us*—is one I haven't felt in decades.

29
Pandora

I've been tiptoeing around Kit regarding Marzipan since the moment I snuck away from our hostel and learned the truth about Urovia's origins. I had played off my horror as lingering nausea, which Kit tried to treat in kind—and while the ruse has been simple enough, it all started to crumble when Marzipan showed up to our front door and invited me on an evening walk.

To his credit, Kit doesn't fight her on it. Instead, he gives Marzipan another investigative glance over—the same eerie assessment he sported when I first arrived at Andromeda House nearly three months ago. In return, Marzipan reveals two, cloth-bound editions of old texts. "As requested, Mr. Andromeda," she says wryly, extending the books to him. "These should keep you occupied until I bring her back here."

Kit's fortified exterior lifts for a moment, and against what looks to be his better nature, he simply instructs me to be careful and not to roam too far.

"He's scared that I'll take you past the gates," Marzipan

explains, waiting to create a four-block berth before piping up about him again.

I rub at a crick in my neck. "Not sure why. I'm totally capable of taking you in a physical altercation if you tried."

Marzipan *oohs* at that, as if happily uncovering a different side to me. "I forget sometimes that you're still a Deragon."

I don't let the negative, unspoken implication of what all *being a Deragon* means in this hypothetical instance. "It's not even that. It's just you're . . . well . . ."

"What?" she asks stubbornly, crossing her arms in defiance.

My grin is taunting. "Tiny."

Marzipan glares at me, but her ferocious expression doesn't hold out long before we're both laughing far too unladylike for our own good. When we finally start to calm down, I find myself saying through bated breaths, "I still don't understand why Kit thinks you're some sort of bad influence on me."

"He just doesn't like when his girl has her eyes on anyone else."

I nearly lurch at the response. It's said so nonchalantly, like there's no denying it.

His girl.

"And not to be nosy," Marzipan adds with almost comedic timing, "but you don't seem too fond of the association. Care to talk about it?"

I toss a look at her over my shoulder that clues her in on the fact that it's complicated, but Marzipan doesn't balk. She makes a slashing movement with her hands, crossing her heart. "You can tell me. I'm a vault."

"I don't think you'll believe me if I do."

Marzipan grins at that, accepting my remark as a challenge. She raises her brows as if to say *go on.* And so, releasing a breathy sigh, I put words to what I haven't let Kit uncover, and what I haven't let myself stew on much since arriving in Vesta.

"Kit may have brought me here, but somebody else brought me to him . . . and I can't stop thinking about him."

Marzipan's face stretches in surprise, but not in a horrified way. No, her mouth puckers, as if trying to bottle up an elated smile or even a laugh. "No way!"

"It gets worse."

The responding look on her face is pure exhilaration.

"I don't know his true name. He goes by Madman." It takes all my strength to choke out the words, "And was hired by Kit to kill Venus."

"*Pandora*—"

"Only he didn't. Obviously. Instead, Madman defied orders and brought *me* as his live consolation captive instead." The words tumble out of me in a panicked frenzy. It only registers now how desperately I've been meaning to talk to someone about this rather than keeping it locked up tight. "To say that Kit was displeased is a royal understatement. In fact, there were times when I half expected him to finish me off while I slept over how miffed this new arrangement made him—and when the thought of Kit doing just that kept me from sleeping . . . it's like Madman knew. He'd come and find me at night and let me sleep in his secret abode beneath one of the Isle's cliffs."

Marzipan isn't smiling anymore. "Oh?"

I dare not mention the intimacy Madman and I experience when we sing together, nor do I mention the kiss that transformed mere curiosity into a soul-hunger that I struggle to fully stomach in his absence. It all feels too hallowed to comment on publicly. So I tuck it away, deep into my heart, as we round a corner and stroll towards the culinary district. Boutique eateries and bake shoppes line the streets and fill the air with sweetness, but when I shut my eyes for a moment, attempting to reset the pace of my quickening heartbeat, the memory of Madman leers in the darkness there.

"I left him on bad terms, and before I could make amends, Kit . . ." I swallow hard. "He boarded me up and prepared to take me to the tribunal."

Truth be told, I don't enjoy holding it over on him—that he had full intentions to sell me out to the highest bidder—but he did.

And maybe, there's a part of me that's still hung up on that. Maybe, twistedly, *that* is the real reason I haven't fully been able to transition my romantic focus from Madman to him. Even after he tended to me when I was sick, after he took control of our spiraling situation. The guilt I feel over it has become inescapable.

"I said some things in haste," I resume, not proud of what I say next. "I thought I'd be long gone before I could see another sunset, and he . . . he thought those words were for him. But they weren't."

Marzipan's expression saddens, and it leeches color from the once vibrant, evening sun. "They were for your Madman."

Your Madman.

This distinction doesn't carry the phantom burn that *his girl* did, and I damn myself for it.

I barely manage a nod. "And now, in concealing me here, Kit's put his life on the line, too. The minute we leave this city, anyone can come after us. They could drag us *both* to the courts and have us killed. He endangered himself for a woman who wants someone else, someone who undermined him. And . . . oh Saints . . . if he figures it out—"

"Well, what's a worse fate to endure?" she asks so matter-of-factly. "A life masquerading as a lovesick fool for a man who wants to butcher your family, or a death knowing you won't waste your days unable to be with the man you want most in the world?"

The question stuns me, even though the answer is so simple.

I see him in my dreams, I think, as if the very words might corrupt the sacred aura of the city engulfing us. I wonder if Marzipan's blessing can make out the silent, internal confession. *I hear his voice in the back of my mind when the world goes quiet. I don't know his name or even his face—but I know his heart. And I know mine, too.*

My throat is on fire. "I don't want to live a lie . . . but to die without having the chance—"

"Stop," Marzipan snaps. "I shouldn't have asked you that. Saints, the look on your face is excruciating, Pan."

Something in my chest unfurls at the familiar nickname, sounding far better in Marzipan's voice than it ever did in Flora's. Even so, I tell her, "Lies of omission are still lies, and I don't know how much longer I can live like that."

"Then tell the truth somewhere Kit can't find."

I almost think Marzipan is trying to blow me off, but then, an idea sparks in her crystal blue eyes. She's moving in an instant, rummaging through the messenger bag she has slung across her body, the one that drapes over her left hip. She pulls out two textbooks—translation manuals, I realize—and distributes one to me before tucking one for herself underneath her arm. Then, she offers me a small, leatherbound journal.

"The book is yours to keep. Every word in your language is arranged alphabetically, and there are several translations for each word you want to look up. Forewarning, it doesn't include conjugations, so if you try conversing with strangers solely on whatever words you strand together, you might come across bizarrely at first, but they'll understand. I can help with that, though, if you're ever interested."

I study the weight of the book in my hand. *Saints, Marzipan was just casually toting two copies of this cinder block around town?*

"And the journal?"

Marzipan smiles at that. "To pen your soul into words. Write what you feel in your language, and if it interests you at all, I can translate it into any dialect you wish. We'd tear out the original pages before Kit gets his hands on it. A coded collection of letters to your Madman."

"You'd . . ." I swallow, overwhelmed with sudden emotion. "You'd do that for me?"

"Of course I would. It may feel like you're fawning over someone," Marzipan says. "But to me, your feelings are the first Urovian story I'll get to record for history. This is way bigger than you and me, Pandora."

I nod as we turn a few more street corners, and we approach a food and beverage cart manned by a vendor who reminds me so much of Ardian it stings. Weathered face, wrinkled forehead that creases deeper as he smiles at us in greeting. He hasn't spoken aloud, but he radiates kindness.

Marzipan approaches the cart and indicates her two preferred options. "Sweet or savory?"

Assuming Kit will forage for supper without me, I decide, "Savory."

In turn, Marzipan greets the worker and says, *"Kebabo por la sinjorino kaj torteto por mi, mi petas."* The language I cannot identify sails off her tongue in a smooth, seamless glide, and before I get the chance to fetch the coins from my pocket, the vendor is already passing our choices over the counter. Four kinds of meat samples skewered vertically are paired with varying peppers between them—reminding me vaguely of the homemade beaded bracelets I'd make with Mother in my early childhood—while Marzipan accepts a small, take-away dish with three miniature tarts, each adorned with blackberries.

We park ourselves on one of the street curbs and eat in silence. In a matter of minutes, all that remains of my kebab is a chunk of glazed pork, and as I bite into it, I trace the ascending path to the historic, sacred temple. "What's it like there, in the shrine?"

Marzipan stares out towards the high sloping hill with equal enchantment. "Something rather close to magic."

"Really?"

"Oh yeah." She chuckles. "Even though I know the Saints are real and every one of those deities don't compare, there's something . . . supernatural about that place. It's hard for me to stay away for too long."

"What do you see?"

"Something new every time. Although, each deity specializes in different domains."

Marzipan cracks open her volume of historical accounts straight down the middle, as if she's read the book thousands of times over and knows exactly where her intended subject matter is located. A photo spreads across the two, open pages. Mosacian deities immortalized in stone stand in a proud lineup, and Marzipan poises her finger over a statute of a lovely woman. Her body, bare save for a sash lazily draped across one arm, is soft in a way that one might right off as maternal, but I see as rather sensual. Delicate yet alluring. "Who is that?"

"That's Venus," Marzipan says.

I nearly lurch at the name, but then, I cast my gaze down to her finger where Marzipan points at the woman's descriptor.

Goddess of Love, Beauty, Desire, Sex, Fertility, Prosperity, and Victory.

"You know what I think?" Marzipan proposes. "You should

go to her."

"To *Venus*?"

"To her shrine, yes," she specifies. "I don't know what you'll perceive versus what *I've* seen before——"

"What *have* you seen in there?"

Marzipan's smile turns sinister, even as her laughter remains childlike. "Each person who enters Venus's shrine experiences a different pillar each time. I've only been in there once, but that's because I doubt *anything* could top waltzing in there and being seduced by a devastatingly handsome ghost."

"*Marzipan*," I bark out.

She shrugs like it's nothing, even though she likely thinks about the encounter more than she'll admit to verbally. "All I'm saying is, maybe you'll find some clarity on all things Kit and Madman in there."

I gnaw at the last of my kebab, suddenly not hungry anymore. My mouth dries out.

I might see Madman in there.

When I arrive back at my hostel, the journal Marzipan gave me is hidden behind the translation manual I clutch to me like a flotation device that might save me from the Damocles waves. Kit sits upright in bed, reading one of the volumes Marzipan gifted him that did, in fact, keep him busy. He doesn't stir at my presence.

"Glad you're back."

Safe is the word Kit doesn't need to add. His tone articulates it enough.

"Did you eat?" I say, side-stepping any discussion about Marzipan, or what we discussed.

"At the hall, yes."

"I see."

We're both silent for a beat before Kit shuts his book with a *thunk.* "I'm sorry."

"For what?"

He drapes his legs over the side of the bed and finally makes his way towards me. "I don't know, for being . . . untrusting? I don't *actually* think that girl would hurt you, and I know that you need someone here in the city besides me to bond with. But when you walked out that door, I knew I couldn't protect you if something happened—"

I don't realize that he's trembling until my hands grip him by both of his shoulders. "Kit," I rasp, suddenly flooded with the same frantic energy he's fighting to keep at bay. "Marzipan would never—*Saints*," I almost snarl. My hands finally register the fact that his skin is clammy and cold. "Are you feeling okay?"

"*No*, I'm not okay," he bursts out. "I feel like we've been here in Vesta for almost a month, and we haven't had a proper discussion about what's going on between us. You were sick for a spell, so that's excused. But the rest? I'm racked with all this guilt and confusion and *longing* . . . and I just need you to talk to me. *Please*—"

"Longing?" The word sounds almost accusatory when I say it aloud.

Kit scrunches his eyes shut. "Yes, princess. Longing."

"But you told me that you *hated* what I've become, Kit. Why would you long for something you loathe so deeply?"

"Because they're one in the same for me. Don't you get it? I'm *fucked in the head* for you!" he shouts, and somewhere amidst the outburst, my hands drop to my sides and Kit's got me pinned against the door. "I risk my neck for you, and I don't ask for anything in return. I sleep at your side every night; I take care of you. I'm so treacherously *close* to you, and yet, there's still this invisible wall you have up. Like you're afraid to let me in. I don't want to pry, but I'm . . . I'm *dying* in here without you," Kit moans, removing one hand to point to his head. His mind.

Why does it strike me so deeply that he's not pointing to his heart?

"What's keeping you away from me, princess?"

I stiffen under his smoldering gaze—like I, too, might catch fire. But I offer Kit the truth, just this once, and say on a horse breath, "*That* is."

"What is?"

"The fact that you can't call me by my name."

Kit blanches, preparing to say more, only I hold out a hand to him. "I know, no doubt, that it's hard to differentiate me from the sins of my family, but you need to figure it out, Kit. Because when I look at you, I don't see your hatred for them. I just see *you*. And maybe that's another thing that scares me—that every day we're here, I'm *really* starting to look at you. Meanwhile, you still can't seem to stomach the sound of any part of my name on your lips. Which is a real slap in the face, considering—"

I wince recalling the memory—the same one that Madman pointed out so vividly when he came to collect me. I force it out all the same.

". . . Considering that was the *exact* issue I left behind in Urovia. Anytime I ever tried to be with someone, they couldn't see past my bloodline, my role in society. Everything about our interactions—their words, their mannerisms, their touches— all of it was catered to curry favor rather than bestow any true affections towards me. And I did *not* get dragged across the Damocles just for those same issues to chase me down such a great distance."

Kit looks at me as if my words physically struck him, but he stands still. Unflinching. He's waiting for me to tell him that I'm done, not wanting to interject—and despite the decency of it, it reminds me all too well of a Urovian subject staying silent out of forced respect.

"I know I've yet to perform for you," I tell him weakly, and I hear just how mousy my voice has become. It sickens me. "For a long time, I've told myself that it was because I've seen the kind of sway my musical talent has on people—the way my voice and my harp can pluck at one's corresponding heartstrings—and I didn't want to maliciously garner control of you. But I think I realize now, I haven't shown you that side of me because it's the most sacred aspect of myself. If you can't say my name, why should I even consider giving that to you?"

"Pandora," Kit grates, attempting to make the effort. "*Please.*"

But it's not enough, not when I can hear the hurt that he can't quite push past.

"On stage, people's expectations of me are what I'm most skilled at, most prepared for. The challenge of maintaining my renown excites me. It's *off* that stage, however, when the real performance begins. When I am forced to play the part of Venus and Jericho's cutthroat circus monkey heir. When I am quizzed on old war correspondents and active military tactics as opposed to spending my mornings reading something for the sole purpose of leisure. When I'm not allowed to be *myself*—"

Kit's words are soaked in despair. "I'm sorry—"

"You look at me, and you see a burden," I say, and I taste a salty tear falling into the corner of my mouth before I realize I've begun crying. My words burn in my throat like liquor. "And as indebted as I am to you for bringing me here and sparing me from that tribunal, I will not settle for someone who says my name only when he feels cornered."

It's a low blow, and I force the guilt I feel because of it to stay back until I can be alone again.

"I deserve someone who looks at me with the kind of reverence that has nothing to do with where I come from. I *need* that. I need someone who sees me and doesn't get hung up on the fact that I'm a Deragon. Someone who looks at me and just . . . just . . ."

Kit reaches out a hand, but I can't bring myself to accept it. The choice wounds us both.

"Someone who looks at me and understands their fate is sealed," I finish. "And that the realization of it fills them with assurance, not dread."

I don't mean to bash Kit over the head with his misgivings, but it's time I stop pretending. If I can't give him true affection, he deserves my honesty. I just wish it didn't sting like this—for him and me both.

"I'm going to stay with Marzipan for the night."

He's already moving for me, eyes dewy and remorseful. "But—"

"Just for tonight," I explain. "I promise, we'll face this conversation head-on tomorrow. But I don't . . . I don't feel comfortable sleeping beside you tonight, and I want to be alone."

I expect him to retaliate, to talk me out of the things I want at this moment—but he gives in before I have to ask him to respect this boundary.

"Okay then," he says stiffly, like there's an inkling in him that wants to blurt out so much more beneath his calm exterior. Still, he nods again and steps back, worried that his previous steps made me feel unsafe. "I'll be waiting for you, whenever you're ready to come back to me."

I don't take anything with me aside from my journal, because

I'm not going to sleep. Not here nor at Marzipan's.

I'm going to the shrine of Venus, praying to the Saints that, by some miracle, I find Madman there.

30
Pandora

The Temple of the Shrine—the sacred pilgrimage site that nearly every Mosacian citizen visits at least once in their life—sits atop the crest of a mighty cliff, overlooking a glittering lake full of what looks more like starlight than water. The crescent moon hanging in the dark sky smiles down on me as I soar up the footpath, and I barge through the gilded doors with minimal resistance.

I don't outright ignore the temple's cavernous atrium, but I do make a mental note to come back here in the daylight to better observe its glory. Seeing what I can of the carved statues and the sprawling inscriptions, I can only fathom how magnificent this space is with the sun streaming through the glass windows high above me. Perhaps I ought to bring Kit here when we both have our heads on straight.

Still, with most of its splendor diluted by the ever-present darkness, I'm able to veer straight for where I need to go with absolutely no detection from those still perusing. Very few visitors frequent the space, and the only person that bothers to speak to me is someone I realize is required to. A short, veiled acolyte approaches on soft feet. "Might you need guidance toward one of the deities, miss?"

"The temple of Venus," I reply, casting my eyes downwards in hopes that she doesn't make the connection.

"Just this way," she whispers, and while she doesn't touch me, I feel the phantom presence of her arm pushing me forward. Mosacia's depiction of Venus the goddess stands high above the yawning mouth of her temple's entrance, her beauty radiating through cold stone somehow. The sculpture is a clear match to the image Marzipan showed me in the book earlier today, and for once, it's heartwarming to think of *Venus* without the association to my aunt overruling other opinions I can form. If I had to guess, I'd imagine the goddess to be fair skinned with rose-gold hair, an air of innocence about her that my aunt certainly lacks. Then, between the archway and where her crafted feet stand on a pedestal, the goddess's listed domains etch their way across the cold stone in countless languages. The Urovian translation rests at the very bottom.

Love, Beauty, Desire, Sex, Fertility, Prosperity, and Victory.

"Miss?"

I suddenly realize the temple acolyte has likely been trying to get my attention. "Yes?"

She silently extends what I perceive to be a slip of thin, translucent paper. I look for crease lines of some sort to help open it wider and recoil sharply at the sandpaper texture. Purple powder stains my fingertips. "What is—"

"Set it upon the surface of your tongue."

My eyes go wide as we stand before the door. "What?"

"Don't immediately consume," she warns. "The dosage is

meant to unfurl gradually. Let it sit and dissolve on its own."

Dear Saints, am I about to do drugs?

"Thank you," I force out without looking at the acolyte directly, attention still fixated on the slip.

"Of course. May the goddess meet your needs," she says as she departs with a curt bow of her head. She's off to assist another visitor within seconds.

My awareness of this moment is unwavering. As tense as the prospect of her instructions are, I don't allow myself to be afraid. There are seven attributes about the goddess before me, and I'm prepared to encounter one of them. If that means ingesting this substance and subjecting myself to a mysterious fate, I'll do so. If it means shutting myself inside whatever dreamscape or hellhole this place really is for the small *chance* of reuniting with Madman, the choice is simple.

So simple, that I don't let the idea of seeing anyone but him infiltrate my brain.

Not before I set the coated tab along my tongue and march inside.

The vast darkness engulfing me is almost enough to make my hair stand on end, were it not for the single teardrop of orange flame flickering in midair. A candle.

"Madman?"

I almost swear the darkness smiles back at me in answer, and I bound towards the light—towards him—my arms pumping ferociously. *"Madman—"*

An invisible force extinguishes the flame, and my heart falls into my stomach not because of the darkness, but because a dim, overhead light suddenly casts the atmosphere in an amber glow.

Revealing Venus Deragon standing before me.

"What are you doing here?" I sneer, months of pent-up anger and resentment bubbling out of me.

"You've got some nerve to ask me that when *my* name is carved into the stone, Pandora."

"This land doesn't revere *you*, nor do I have interest in speaking with you. So I suggest you get out of my way."

Venus lets out a low whistle, impressed yet vividly irritated. "I will . . . once you tell me who Madman is."

"He's none of your business."

"Defensive, are we?" she croons, striding closer. "And rather . . . *possessive*."

Her smile is serpentine, and I almost want to reach for her throat in retaliation.

But Venus stops me short. "There are two doors behind me. One red, one blue."

My eyes dart beyond her to confirm she's telling the truth. The red one has a fiery glow around its frame, while the blue looks to be coated in an otherworldly frost.

"Since you seem awfully frantic to reunite with this *Madman*," she drawls, "I'll just go ahead and tell you that he's here. Behind that door," she says blandly, gesturing to the icy, cerulean door. I ought to keep my eagerness in check but knowing that Madman is who I came here for, I start moving, my speed increasing with each step—

"A word of caution, however," Venus hums, her tone with oozing amusement.

The frenzied sensation in my chest only aches further.

"Should you open his door, there are no guarantees that Madman will even want to see you, let alone speak with you."

I grit my teeth, recalling the last words I'd flung at him.

"I hope that kiss curdles your blood and rots your very bones. I hope my voice haunts you for the rest of your days, and that you never find another pretty dame who can sing their way into your soul like I did."

"But I know, beyond a shadow of a doubt, that should you open the red door," Venus resumes with such blatant slyness, "the person there will be *dying* to see you. She might even let it slip where she's been hiding out."

The image of my mother burns across my eyes. "You're lying."

"Open a door and find out," Venus taunts back.

I cross my arms like a petulant child, and Venus finds the movement amusing. "Too bad you're not blessed. Our kind can visit any door, any time. The temple doors will always open for those with a divine touch."

She means to make me feel worse about being ordinary, but she's mistaken. Because being *unlike* her is a far more rewarding option than being like her. Still, the temptation and boasting in her words rears its ugly head at me, and I force myself to straighten out.

"This is just some drug-induced state." I make the desperate attempt to convince myself that my words are true. "This place . . . it's not *real*—"

"The drugs only bring out what your soul is keeping locked away, but they'll wear off if you don't act soon. Open a door, Pandora." It's a command from my queen rather than sage advice from my aunt. "And decide what it is you desire more."

Then, without another word, Venus disappears into thin air.

Desire—*that's* the domain I've been brought face to face with.

Only it's not the way I imagined it would be. It's a million times worse—mainly because I am not offered enough time to dissect her words and whether she's telling the truth.

But she's right about one thing: I can feel the powder dissolving swiftly.

So I send a silent apology up to the Saints for whatever they're about to see and run like hell towards the winter-blue doorway.

Madman's alcove is torn to shreds and trashed so thoroughly that I feel the urge to weep.

Every candle is snuffed out and spilling old wax onto the rock flooring. Sheet music with furious scribbles and denotations litter the place in parchment, and even the gleaming piano is a pile of carnage and keys. The alcove is now lit by flame so hot it burns blue, licking across shelves of records and writings and literature. I feel the heat on my skin, but like the door I stumbled in from, everything looks . . . cold. Devoid of life. Even the harp didn't survive the slaughter.

"Madman!" I scream, the ache insuppressible. "*Madman*! It's me! Where are you?"

And then, I hear his voice moaning my name in a way that hints at disbelief, hidden somewhere amidst the destruction.

"Pan . . ." He can barely form the other syllables. "Pandora?"

"Yes! It's me! Where—"

Madman's hands sharply yank me into him, and I stumble backwards for only a second or so before our bodies collide. He must've been lingering behind me, slinking through the shadows somewhere, but I don't mind the surprise. Because even as being held into him feels like cradling steel, I find an unshakable comfort here. I catch myself taking a deep inhale of his scent, grounding me to this moment before it has the chance to wash away, and Madman chokes on tears I never expected him to shed.

"I thought you were dead."

"Andie found me in time," I tell him, turning in his grasp so that I face him.

He still wears his mask, hiding himself from me despite knowing I see far beyond it. He's still heaving and fighting to catch his breath, but he doesn't go to adjust himself. If he cries hard enough, though, his mask will slip.

Then, Madman shakes his head. "No. After. When I went to your room to apologize."

My heart stalls beneath my ribs. "You came back?"

"And you were gone," he croaks.

My knees go weak, and we crumple to the ground together. He secures me by both wrists and we kneel before one another with a sadness that is painfully reverent. My head falls against his collarbone, and he rests his chin on the top of my head. It feels more soothing than the promise of a crown ever has.

"I thought I'd never see you again."

It's a cry, and I'm not sure who says it. It doesn't matter, not when both of our souls are so clearly sobbing the sentence back to each other.

"What happened here?" I ask, unable to look at the mess of this place.

"It all reminded me of you, and I couldn't stand the sight of it," he rasps, his voice seething. "I couldn't *live* with seeing these objects outlive you, not when your expert hand and angelic voice were what brought them to life to begin with. What brought *me* to life."

"Madman—"

"My soul fell asleep in your absence." His voice is mournful, tortured. "My worst nightmares became my reality. But seeing you alive right now . . . it erases all the sorrow that nearly drowned me these past weeks apart. Holding you like this, every fractured piece of me feels mended. Whole again."

I bury my face in Madman's neck, if only because my snot and tears are mingling together too disastrously to capture his mouth in a spell-binding kiss. But there's a secret solace in hiding my face from his full gaze—much like it must feel for him when he bears his mask. And so, feeling equally concealed as I am vulnerable, I find the will to say the words, "I chose you over her, Madman. I chose to see you again . . . over the chance to reunite with my mother."

The amount of honor in that choice is not lost on him. I sense it in the way the pace of his heartbeat skyrockets, then stalls altogether.

"How long did you wrestle with your choice?"

"Not long enough."

Madman laughs, and the sound of it solidifies itself as my new favorite melody.

"When I see you again, angel," he whispers, his mouth brushing my ear, "I won't hold back from you any longer. I won't restrict myself from you in any way. No secrets. No evasions. No mask." I gasp, and the sound unleashes something in him. His words turn guttural, hands grappling me in a manner that I'm certain will leave bruises. "I *swear* it, Pandora. The minute I lay eyes on you, I'm getting you the hell out of wherever it is you are and taking you *home*—"

"Home?" I almost hiccup.

Madman finally notches my chin upwards so that I face him fully, a hair's breadth away from a cataclysmic kiss that I'm starting to drift towards. My eyes are still glassy, but his come back clear. Steady.

"Tell me where you are, Pandora."

"The Temple of the Shrine in the Sacred City," I whisper, as if the admission is a betrayal somehow. "I'm in Venus's sanctuary."

The corner of his mouth ticks in a knowing smile. "Which pillar brought me to you?"

I sometimes forget that Madman, like Kit, is also Mosacian—meaning he's likely made the pilgrimage before. "Desire," I confess.

I prepare to give way to the gravitational pull between our mouths, but Madman presses a finger to the seam of my lips. Then, his voice drips with the kind of heat that racks through my whole body. "Patience. When I find you again, I'll make sure that the real thing is worth it."

And then, I succumb to my substance-induced stupor.

31
Pandora

Journal in hand, I race back to Marzipan's hostel and knock on the door until she grants me refuge. She passes out cold minutes after letting me through the door, but in the undisturbed hours glancing out at the stars, my mind runs wild.

By the time Marzipan wakes up and brews a pot of herbal tea, I've filled thirty pages, front and back, with my crazed handwriting and one-sided desires to see Madman again.

"Bloody Saints, Pan," she barks, nearly choking on her drink. "Did you even sleep?"

"Not a wink."

Marzipan shakes her head in disbelief and takes another long sip before catching sight of the Temple of the Shrine branding on the inside of my right wrist. Her grin of recognition pins me to the spot, evidence of yesterday's wanderings and the foolproof prevention from visiting until the same time this evening. "It was the phantom fornication that sold you, wasn't it?"

"Don't say things like that," I gag, shutting my eyes as if I just tasted something sour.

Marzipan glides across the room, fetches a long-sleeved wrap, and tosses it to me. "You're going to need to hide that mark from Kit. Otherwise, he'll blow a gasket."

"Right," I say, fumbling my arms through the inserts. "Thanks."

"What are friends for?" She sighs, then returns her gaze upon my discarded journal. "Which reminds me, it may take me a while for me to translate . . . well, *everything*—"

"Only translate what you think holds significance," I say, throwing Marzipan the book, and thank Saints I do, because she's right next to her bookshelf, giving her the perfect cover to stash it away just as Kit erupts through her front door.

Marzipan screeches in surprise, and the gasp that leaves my body nearly sends me into a choking fit. I'm half inclined to believe Kit brought out some sort of battering ram to break in with, but sure enough, he's empty-handed, as indicated by the balled-up fists at his side. His skin burns red with indignation.

"We need to talk," he bristles.

"And that's my cue," I say feebly to Marzipan. "Thanks again for letting me crash."

"Anytime," she replies. But the word makes Kit tense up even further, as if worried there might be a *next time* that he'll make me uncomfortable enough to run right back to her. Without having to touch me, his glowering demeanor yanks me out into the mid-morning air, and I close us off from Marzipan's view.

I wait for Kit's verbal barrage, but nothing comes. No, he waits for *me* to start blurting out something. An apology? An icebreaker? I don't know.

"What do you want to talk about?" I ask, putting the ball back in his court.

"The fact that you look like death," he huffs, and I outright scoff at the remark. The sound does little to deter him. "Were you too busy telling Marzipan how unfeeling of a bastard I am to get even an hour of sleep?"

"Is that what you think of me? That I spend my free time spewing filth about someone who, despite our complications, has been nothing but kind to me? Wow, Kit, you really do see me as a Deragon and nothing more, don't you?"

My temper seems to throttle him. "Princess, please. It's not like—"

I point at him, my finger jabbing the center of his sternum. "Have you learned *nothing*? My name is *Pandora Violet*—"

I want to burst into spontaneous flame, to scorch him with my momentary wrath.

But the fact of the matter is, no matter how desperately I search for separation, Deragon *is* part of my identity.

For the sake of gathering my bearings and appeasing the crotchety neighbor between our floor and Marzipan's, I take a steadying, cleansing breath. "You know what? Let's not do this. I don't want to fight with you. I just . . . gods, I just want to get *past* this."

Kit blanches, and only then do I hear my words back.

Gods.

Not Saints.

"I've been reading about them in Marzipan's books," I lie, pulling the sleeves of my wrap up towards my fingertips on instinct.

"I've been thinking things over all night," he says calmly. We descend the steps and pause before the threshold of our hostel, unsure if we should turn in until lunch or meander through the city streets. "And your hesitations are merited. I feel my actions speak louder than words, but maybe you need those words . . . and maybe, I need a sign."

"A sign?" I squeak.

"I have a hard time trusting others . . . and myself," Kit explains. "In the ways that matter most, I need all of someone's cards on the table before I'll even show parts of my hand. I will not, no, I *cannot* give someone the full picture of myself until I know they are a sure thing. And for you and I . . . I think there's only one way to find out the truth."

The gulp in my throat is painfully audible.

"I have to go to Venus's temple," he declares. "It's the only way to know for certain—"

My heart hammers nervously in my body, my neurons spiraling and my pulse skyrocketing.

Kit can't go there—not when I just resurfaced from there and saw . . . well, not him.

Worse, he could visit her temple and see just that: me and Madman reuniting in the other realm. If he did, he'd be mad enough to—

I try not to let the grave realization show on my face.

He'd kill me.

He'd *actually* kill me once he realized the pursuit of me to begin with was a hopeless one, merely a survival act on my end.

He'd drag me to the tribunal, off me in my sleep—impale me with a knife he could smuggle from one of the food banks. I don't know how, but I *know* he would. It's inevitable, especially when Kit was already on the brink of doing so when I first met him, when my track record was spotless.

I crawl out of my panicked headspace in time to hear him say, "I want you to be there." He leans towards me, the positioning strategic and romantic were it not for the apprehension I'm battling within myself. "I want you waiting for me when I come out on the other side. That's all I ask."

I offer him a weak nod and pretend all is well in the world. "Anything, Kit."

He dares to press a tender kiss to my temple, and at the contact, I send up a silent prayer to both the Saints and the long-gone gods and goddesses, if they're even listening, that Madman gets here before Kit reduces me to a corpse.

32
Geneva

R en gave me the official rundown on what to expect from the Temple of the Shrine as we walked here this morning. Individual chambers for each deity—all of which are uniquely experienced by every individual visitor—and only one room can be visited in a twenty-four-hour period. To ensure it, I'd leave with a mark across my hand. It wouldn't hurt, but it would bear the look of a scalded, white-hot brand.

"It encourages travelers to stay longer," Ren explained over breakfast. "To experience every sanctuary before returning home."

What he hadn't quite prepared me for, however, was how *massive* the space was.

In many ways, it emulates the same glory and splendor that Urovia's throne room does, only instead of it being extensively wide, it towers high. The floor we enter upon stands at the temple's summit, and as the building drops down from the edge of the great hill, winding stairs help direct patrons to different sanctuaries. Like standing inside a colossal silo. Signs indicate who occupies the top deck and how the deities progress the lower you descend—Pluto residing in a subterranean space that even Ren, a seasoned veteran here, doesn't wish to explore.

Sunlight streams through the overhead windows, warming the skin along my neck. The rays draw Ren's attention there, and in its wake, we both remember Ren's lips and what they were doing in that exact spot last night . . .

Ren clears his throat. "I know where I'm going," he says plainly. "Do you?"

"Minerva," I answer, the blush in my cheeks negating the solemnity in my tone. "Maybe she'll have answers on Pandora's whereabouts."

He nods. "Good choice. Meet on the front steps when you're done? The weather's lovely, so if one of us takes longer, it shouldn't be too—"

I shut him up with a kiss, sparing him the need to scramble for an explanation.

Ren frames me instantly, his kiss soft and exploratory all at once. No dramatics or flare or heat—as I certainly wouldn't hold enough composure in such a sacred space if he started down that road. Just a gentle reminder of how much we enjoy one another. *Care* about each other. I try not to think about how I'll miss him, even though I'll see him again in a few hours.

And then, Ren strolls down the first set of descending stairs without a care. Only once he's gone do I realize I hadn't asked him which deity *he* was off to confront.

I stand among a bustling crowd of travelers, my eyes tracing the signages of which deities lie where. Minerva's name appears etched into an emblem instructing me to descend two levels, which shouldn't be too daunting. But if that's the case, why am I so conflicted?

I came here to visit Minerva, to clear my conscience about letting Pandora slip past me in the streets yesterday. Any guidance she could bring me to keep my suppressed culpability from overcoming me is *vital*, and likely only something she could grant me.

And yet . . .

My traitorous heart begins to race, my skin heating as every instinct drifts towards the statue of Venus. The shape of her body reminds me that my own body is beautiful, even after an early motherhood and years of healing from malnourishment. But the statue's eyes . . . that's what really bewitches me. I look into eyes of stone and somehow see an otherworldly persuasion. A dreamlike temptation forever frozen in her molding.

The words *Love, Beauty, Desire, Sex, Fertility, Prosperity, and Victory* in various translations grace the stone wall overhead, and as I approach the arched doorway, a veiled attendant closes her small hands over mine. I don't know how to interpret the kind gesture until I feel the touch of something thin graze my palm.

"Set this along the surface of your tongue," she prompts, her voice light, like the first warm wind on a winter's day. Then, she cracks open the temple door and nudges me inside. "And may the goddess meet your needs," she adds, and just as quickly as she appeared, she departs, shutting the door with a resounding *clang*.

I stand motionless in a room of silence and stone. No inscriptions or decorations line the walls here, but the very architecture seems to slope towards the smaller door in front of me—porcelain and teeming with mystery.

Peering down at the contents in my hands, I immediately make note of its texture: one side smooth, one side sandpaper. Like a square piece of tape without the sticky side. Stamped into its lavender center, a heart in darker purple seems to glimmer back at me, even with the minimal lamplight.

I turn from the shrinking side of the room and place my hand upon the door I entered from. It faintly creaks—and I realize that the acolyte didn't trap me here. I don't *have* to face what lies within this chamber if I truly don't wish to.

But Ren's already been traipsing through whichever sanctuary he wandered off to for long enough. He's done this likely *several* times before. So I do not allow myself to dwell on any more possibilities or apprehensions, setting the patch along my tongue, turning from the exit, and entering Venus's sanctuary.

The room is pitch dark until the first orb of violet light burns in the faraway distance.

I almost presume it to be a torch set aflame by enchanted firelight, but the light begins to flit around the space, drawing close. Soon, the orb takes shape, a circle stretching into an oval, and the oval adopting symmetrical, sloping lines near its base. Almost like—

A human jawbone.

I don't bother asking who approaches, not when I know that bone structure. I *made* that bone structure. More light drips towards the floor, forming limbs, a torso, and a head full of curls I'd recognize anywhere.

"Pandora?"

"Mother!" she calls out, no hint of surprise in her voice. Only delight. She rushes towards me, her features detailing the closer she becomes. Her light surges in a glow. "We've been waiting for you!"

"We?" I ask.

At the same moment the word leaves my lips, another beacon of light emerges. Brighter—not in intensity, but in hue. Pandora's purple light has a coldness about it, but there's only heat in the red flames that burn in the distance. The very essence of it tells me it's my sister, and its magenta twin sprinkles into existence beside her. I watch as Venus and Calliope float towards my daughter. In a defensive movement, I reach for Pandora's hand, attempting to shelter her from Venus's wrath, and yelp at the heat that sizzles my palm.

Real fire—Pandora and the rest of them. They're made of *real fire* here.

But at the spark of that touch, I see a haze of light wrap around my limbs, too. Suddenly, my hands poised before me glow like liquid gold, igniting a bright aura from within me. I reach for Pandora again, and this time, there's no pain.

I clutch her tightly before turning to look at Venus again, braced for another altercation—

"There's no animosity, sister," Venus explains as she draws closer, the full dimensions of her visible now.

Doubt trickles in. "There's not?"

"Not here, at least." Calliope laughs, the sound like a bell. "This space, it's for you."

I mean to ask further questions, but the smiles on each of their faces wrecks something in me, and I'm unable to find the right words.

Then, Pandora cradles my face in her hands—the gesture so motherly it threatens to sideswipe any composure I have left.

She whispers, "Everyone that you've ever loved is here to visit you."

Instantly, I gasp out the words, "Does that mean Mother—"

"My lovely girls," her voice chimes from a few paces away.

Violet Deragon sounds exactly as I remember her last, and I thank the Saints with all my soul for allowing me to preserve her memory so well. Chills scatter across my arm at the realization that she's here—that I'm encountering my mother again for the first time in thirty years. And as she fully materializes into being, I weep at the sight of every woman I've loved in my lifetime standing all in one place.

I smile at the gradient of color, despite feeling oddly out of place among them. My presence glows like sunshine, but across the four of them, hues of near blue all the way to fiery red bleed together in a slow blur. Pandora's aura is purple, yet on the verge of indigo—more blue-tinged now that she's standing beside her grandmother. Violet is, well, pure violet. Calliope—the closest portrait of our mother—shimmers with a pink flame that heats whenever her smile deepens. And furthest on the right, Venus's bloodred fire dances with a subdued sort of happiness.

Mother steps towards me and kisses my brow. Purple flame mingles with yellow at the touch. "You gave her my name," she says, such human inflection in her voice as it breaks with honor and joy and sadness having been gone all these years. "But oh, how she carries *your* beauty, my dear Geneva."

I think I could drown in the tears I shed in this moment.

"How lucky am I," Violet Deragon sighs like a song—awed disbelief and love abounding. "To see my baby with *her* baby, and they're both all grown up now."

To keep from breaking down, I look around the room and ask, "Where's Father?"

Venus visibly flinches. "What do you mean where is he?" she hisses.

"I mean exactly that," I say, not backing down. "I loved him too."

Despite what was later discovered about him.

How he resented Venus so deeply for Mother's death—even with it being her choice, her sacrifice—that he was willing to let her die in Jericho's penitentiary for his conspiracies. How Venus's wrath still burned for the man, if not because of those choices, then because he thought so poorly of the man she grew to love with such unwavering intensity.

"He may take some time to come around," Mother answers softly, grief for the man she adored so evidently coasting in the depths of her eyes. "I have a feeling that even a realm after death could not spare him from the shame he feels now."

Perhaps his temporary absence is for the better, then. At least I have my ladies. The truest loves I've ever known. My mother, my sisters, my daughter . . .

"What about Kurt?" I ask no one at all.

There's a suspended span of silence before Calliope of all people asks, "What about him?"

The question seems to trigger a landslide's worth of panic.

No, he has to be here. I loved him. Even though we were each other's best kept secret, our hearts belonged to each other. There was no one else. There were no hesitations. I had given him a daughter despite him not being around to meet her, and although I had forgiven Jericho, I had never forgotten the short stretch of time I had with Kurt . . . and how I would've given anything for another year. Another month. Another day—

Would've.

The word catches in my throat, forming a knot.

I *would've* given anything.

But now . . . did my heart deceive my head? *Did* I love Kurt like I believed I did at nineteen?

Then, bright as the midday sun, a golden sprinkle of light tinged with orange drifts into view. The warmth of its presence beats into me. It grows more sweltering by the minute, but I don't mind. Not when this means that in this liminal space, even if it's only for a heartbeat, Kurt will have the chance to behold the beautiful girl we made together. The orb of sunshine delays on taking form, but I find relief knowing I hadn't forgotten him like I feared. That forgiving Jericho's sins hadn't rid Kurt from the most sacred part of my heart.

"There you are," I say, heaving a breath of immense relief. The whole room feels the complex array of emotions seeping into the sound of the words—the sadness. "I was worried you wouldn't come."

More sunlight shimmers as the entity laughs. "Of course I'd be here. My heart has always called to yours."

My face wrinkles with misunderstanding. Not at his response, but at the sound of his voice. I silently loathe myself for not being able to remember the way he spoke while he was alive—not like I could with Mother—no matter the years apart.

My lips tremble. "I've missed you so dearly."

Another confused laugh. "I find that hard to believe."

Does he doubt me that much? My stomach lurches at the thought, at the guilt that slowly creeps into my system—even here, in this otherworld. "How could you think that? Of course I did," I reply unsteadily.

In my trepidation, I didn't realize he had crossed the remaining distance to reach me, and it's his golden touch pouring into me that wakes me up to the notion. Our hands intertwine, and the sensation courses through me like trying to contain a shooting star in our shared grasp. Daylight explodes throughout the darkness, banishing it altogether where we stand united. It's undeniable, now—that something supernatural exists between us. As if no time or distance can taint the bond we have.

"But Genny," he says so calmly that I'm inclined to shiver. "I've never left you."

Finally, the detailing in his face comes into view, and I look upon the man who captured my heart.

Only it's not Kurt.

It's Ren.

33
Kit

The walk to the Temple of the Shrine is quiet, and my only attempt at casual conversation finally comes out when we get to the base of the temple's steps. "You really don't have any interest in seeing one of the deities?"

Pandora hadn't voiced the fact aloud, but the discomfort on her face was evident enough.

"It feels a bit . . . sacrilegious, considering my upbringing. My beliefs."

Guilt permeates her every word, and I don't push further. Of course she doesn't want to step in there. Her heritage runs deep, and maybe it's not entirely imposed upon her. Maybe it *means* something to her.

"I'm sorry if the culture here has not been to your liking or offensive—"

"I enjoy the culture here, actually," Pandora tells me with an excitement that feels faintly forced, but the core of it is real. I know so, because whenever she's unable to look at me, she can't tear her eyes away from the world around her. It's like this part of Mosacia exists in technicolor, while the life she led before was utterly monochromatic. "Marzipan says that Vesta is the crowning jewel of the continent, and each day I wake up here, I realize just how right she was."

I hate to leave her here while I go inside, but Pandora squeezes my hand reassuringly. "I'll wait for you here on the steps."

Nodding in understanding, I pull her hand to my lips and brave the act of placing a kiss atop the soft skin there. But just as my lips brush the spot, Pandora stoops lower and captures my mouth like it's been hers all along. As if she masked her true ownership over me so that I'd feel in control.

I do not shy away from her touch in response, not when this feels like explicit permission. Instead, I choose to be greedy. I slide my hands along as much of her back as I can roam in one go. The muscles there contract and stretch as she decides what feels best, and the hand that trails towards her waistline casually glides lower. I take my fill of Pandora with my hands, my mouth. I commit the scent of her to memory as if I could bottle it for personal use, and for once, she doesn't pull away first. She waits for me to feel satiated enough to retreat a step, and it feels like a blissful eternity before I finally garner the willpower to do so.

I should tell her what she means to me—the depth of my growing affections.

But I'm a coward at heart and tell her instead, "I won't be long."

It's true. Knowing all the times I've frequented the Temple of the Shrine, I expect to be back to Pandora before the hour is up.

What's *not* true, however, is that Pandora believes I'm visiting the goddess of love—when Venus is the only deity I've outright scorned and sworn to myself never to visit.

I don't care if it's cheap or petty, because *anything* bearing that Deragon monster's name, even coincidentally, is out of the question. It does not matter how badly I want things with Pandora and I to work out, I will *never* give Venus an ounce of my honor. I'd rather face death.

And so, I prepare to do just that.

It's the middle of the week, and people typically wait until the sun is at its peak before visiting the god of the underworld. Sure, they make the journey to visit their beloved dead, but they need that extra reassurance to fully commit to entering Pluto's sanctuary. I'm a man of little fears and plenty of structure, however. Coming here is almost second nature, and knowing who awaits me on the other side of the door, I have no trouble sinking deeper into the temple's depths. A group of patrons even offer to let me enter first, fearful of what lies in waiting beyond the chamber's shadowy exterior.

My last thought before accepting a chalky chewing tablet from one of the temple attendants and tiptoeing into the darkest part of the Mosacian continent is selfish.

What lies can I spin to have Pandora surrender to this attraction once and for all?

People would assume that convening with death would take the wind out of one's sails entirely, but for me, it's quite the opposite. Death is a constant I can rely on. I don't fear the end or the fact that, one day, it will come for me too. Instead, I choose to use pieces of my life, provided by this temple, to reacquaint myself with it.

And with my late sister.

She never ages—frozen in the state of being she was when she passed. But each time I visit her, her voice possesses such a mature *soul*. There's no other way to describe it, perhaps because that's all she is in the aftermath of death's dominion, merely a soul. She isn't the mortal body or her personal conditions that so many people felt the need to comment on. She's simply *her*.

When the tablet I consumed loses its potency and my sister fades into the fatal gloom, I walk out of Pluto's chamber feeling refreshed. Still, the burst of adrenaline and optimism doesn't get me higher than the third flight of stairs before my lungs start to blaze in my chest. For the sake of pragmaticism, I use the uphill trek to come up with something to say, something convincing. Something that isn't outright tacky but affectionate enough to keep Pandora from stewing on it too deeply.

The goddess of beauty showed me every version of you that I've become entranced by.

The goddess of sex filled my head with the filthiest realities I want to replicate with you.

The goddess of prosperity showed me a luminous future for us, one wholly separate from the damage of your past.

The goddess of love—

All ability to compose a decent story abandons me the moment I step outside.

Because the steps are empty, and Pandora is nowhere to be found.

34
Pandora

"Calm down, catch your breath, and say all of that again. *Slowly.*"

I'm so painfully out of shape that I nearly heave my guts into the potted plant in Marzipan's living room, but I do as she says to the best of my ability. First, I let my sprinting heart rate settle down with the rest of my body. I slump over in the chair that Marzipan yanked from her flimsy kitchen table and try not to collapse in on myself as I relay all my frantic updates one more time. All of which boil down to the fact that I *left* Kit.

And now, I can't take it back.

"He's going to come looking for me here—"

"Not yet, he won't."

Her words bring me no sense of comfort. "I need to get out of here. Out of Vesta. But the minute I do . . ." The tribunal. People hunting me. All of it swarms my vision like stars do after a head injury.

And then, an even more grim realization dawns on me.

"What is it?" Marzipan asks, tracking the terror in my gaze.

"I told Madman I was at the temple last night. I have to go back. But knowing Kit, if he's not at the hostel, he'll be waiting me out there—"

"No," Marzipan mumbles, her eyes teeming with realization. "He won't be. He'll have the mark, which means he can't loiter there past a certain time. Otherwise, the mark will start to burn him. And your mark dissolves in . . ." she glances at the clock, then at the brand on my skin. "A little less than two hours."

The tears that leak from my eyes are a result of too many emotions to name at once. "I know that the law says that no one can harm me here, Marzi, but Kit might think that his retribution for what I've just done goes *above* the law." She doesn't argue or try to chime in, but still I find myself babbling, "You don't get it. For one reason or another, the man *loathes* my bloodline, and by proxy, loathes *me*. Even though he wants me, there's a great chance that when Kit visits the goddess, she shows him his greatest desire and he realizes my death will satisfy him far more than a future together will."

My anxiety consumes me like a meal, and but Marzipan, undeterred by the complete and utter mess I've been reduced to, clutches me to her with an intensity that transcends understanding. I've known her for such a brief span of time, and yet Marzipan comforts me with a tenderness that reminds me of Aunt Calliope.

Marzipan kisses the crown of my head in an attempt to soothe me. "I know this has nothing to do with the fear you're facing right now, but you write so beautifully."

I don't bother looking up or asking about how much of my journal she read. Rather, I burrow deeper into her warmth.

"You write the way you speak, and Pandora, the way you speak is . . ." She shakes her head, unable to find the words. "The way you wrote about your mom, about Madman . . . even about the people who have *wronged* you. If someone wrote about me like you wrote about them, I'd—"

I feel a sob crack out of her before I hear it, but once it's out in the open, she comes unglued.

"The world is so vast, and I'm just . . . so *small*," she cries out. "I'm one person, Pandora, and sometimes, I get so exhausted trying to continue my family's legacy. Trying not to get bogged down by the weight of my insignificance. Trying to find the same fulfillment my family gave me, even though I now live alone, amongst a pile of books. Trying not to forget my purpose. But after reading the way you bled your soul on paper, after becoming your *friend* . . ."

A wave of sadness and adoration crests in my chest, and we cling tighter to one another.

"After all of it," Marzipan sighs, restoring the rhythm of her breathing, "I feel as though the spark of hope I carry with me has caught fire. Mosacia *needs* a voice like yours. They need to hear your heartbreak, witness your empathy, feel your grace. They need to know how you—an *outsider*—have come to see the beauty of a territory you were taught to scorn."

Then, Marzipan forces me to look at her, our eyes equally red and watery. For the first time, I witness wrath in their depths.

"And I'll be *damned* if Kit Andromeda interferes or poses any harm to you."

There's a promise in her words that chills my blood. "What are you going to do?"

Her voice is low and authoritative. It reminds me of one of Jericho's threats. "All you need to worry about," she says, finally breaking our embrace, "is getting back to that temple."

"Marzi—"

"Take the long way there," she instructs, rushing to her shelves to fish something out from the row of manuals and sacred texts. "The one we walked last night. Don't get too close to the perimeter to avoid being cornered, but don't drift too far inward, as it might cause you to run into Kit should he start making his way back here."

"And if he's waiting on the steps—"

"He won't be," Marzipan says with an unnatural sense of certainty. "Whether for the sake of recovering lost love or apprehending a stowaway, Kit will go on the offensive. The moment he finds out you've bolted, if he hasn't already, he will check to see if you're here first."

I try not to shiver at the fact that Marzipan doesn't specify *here* as the hostel I've shared with him these last few weeks. In her own way, she fears Kit's wrath, too.

"I know that in your uneasiness, you might start to walk faster. But if you get to the temple before your time is up, your mark will burn you the closer you get to any of the sanctuaries. Do *not* force your way into a sanctuary, or the mark will poison you."

I look at the clock, then at the mark on my wrist.

Under two hours to go.

"And when the mark vanishes," she finishes, her voice raw and eyes stone cold, "seek out Apollo."

"Apollo?"

"You said that you play the harp, right? That you're a performer? He's the god of music. The happenings in his sanctuary shouldn't frighten you, which would result in a shorter visit. You'll be safe there, and it should buy you a few hours."

"And after that? What—"

"You need to get going, Pan," is barely out of her mouth before she's outright dragging me to the door, slinging a cross-body bag stocked with meager necessities, including a sandwich she somehow had prepped and ready before I barged in earlier and a mystery sum of Jericoin. She shoves my journal in there, too.

"Promise me that when you get to the temple, you'll go to him. To Apollo."

"But what if I don't make it—"

"You *will*," she snarls, accepting nothing less for me. "Now, *promise* me."

A tear trickles down my cheek, the skin there still warm from our tight embrace. "Okay."

"Okay," she says back to me, swallowing hard.

And then, before Marzipan can fill the silence with some half-assed attempt at pushing me out the door, I take both of her hands in mine and give them a squeeze, hard enough to bruise her bones. "The world is vast, but in many ways, it's small too. The world cannot possibly be so large if it couldn't keep me from knowing you."

We've never told one another *I love you*, and I don't know why. Maybe it's because of the short time we've truly known each other, or maybe it's something else entirely. Either way, Marzipan knows every language, which means she must be able to deduct what those words really mean. Her pearly smile makes my heart constrict in my chest, and for a moment, it's too hard to breathe.

I want more time with Marzipan . . . and I have more stories to tell.

I will come back for you.

The moment I reenter the atrium of the Temple of the Shrine, my wrist begins to burn my skin.

I could've sworn I kept a slow pace. A watchful one, but still *slow*. It felt like I was inching through the Sacred City like a worm, and yet, I still beat my time by four minutes.

I wish I could say that the sensation only affects me mildly, but the closer I step into the center of the atrium, the more that the burning begins to feel like being absolutely scorched. As if the sun itself takes its anger out on me. I keel over in agony—

"Your time has not come yet," a mousy voice says from behind me. Another temple maiden.

You don't say, I gripe internally.

"Please, can I just . . ." I grit my teeth against the pain. "Can you give me directions to Apollo's temple? My waiting period concludes in three minutes, and I—" I fight the urge to swear, clamping my free hand over the writhing spot. "I *need* to see him."

"I'm afraid you'll have to wait until—"

Damn the pain and consequences. I can't let these last three minutes be what costs me my neck.

I take off in a run, sprinting past the attendant, and it almost unsettles me how calm she is about the scene I'm causing. Then again, she's likely seen hundreds of visitors bring themselves harm for the chance to convene with the deities again. She probably pities me, or maybe, she's wagering with herself as to how far I'll get before the pain makes me pass out and she has to scrape me off the floor.

Making a beeline for the stairs, not seeing Apollo's name or his attributes scrawled along smooth stone, I try and read the temple directory through my eyes, which are now starting to tear up from the scalding in my wrist. All details indicate Apollo's chamber being three levels down, but in order to get there, I'm required to pass through level two's vestibule, with the continuing flight on the opposite end.

I dash there without hesitation, my hair catching the breeze as my speed cuts through the air. Thankfully, I don't start tripping over myself until the last step before floor two, so my fall from grace is more like a stumble. I recover well though, only stopping twice through the vestibule. Once to try and soothe the unrelenting pain in my wrist by clutching at the spot just below it—cutting off further blood flow—which, to my astonishment, dulls the sensation just enough for me to slow my legs.

And another to read the name of the only deity that graces this ghost town of a floor.

Diana.

Hunting. Archery. Animals.

Suddenly, the hurt subsides. Whether because my duration has ended or because my unyielding terror supersedes anything my pain receptors could pick up on, I'm not sure. Nor does it matter.

Much like with the temple of Venus, staring at the statue of Diana, I see a different depiction—muscular physique, bow and arrow drawn and ready—but it never quite erases the image my mind conjures up at the name. Perhaps in the events of Root History, Diana was exactly as she appears to be: an indomitable warrior, a *champion*.

But to me, the only Diana I've ever known is none of those things.

She's a traitor—the second child of the late Seagrave monarchs, with a soul as dark as the ink one would write letters with. Worse, she's the one member of that dreaded family we collectively refuse to speak of, and for good reason. To mention Diana in Broadcove Castle is to openly insult the Deragon name.

The soul-consuming disgust should be enough to escort me across the rest of the vestibule and lead me down the stairs. And yet, I'm still here. Staring. Succumbing to the realization that the wrath that should be moving me along doesn't outweigh the dreadful wonder that floods me, that keeps me planted in place.

What would even be in Diana's sanctuary?

This is a mistake, this is a mistake, this is a mistake.

My subconscious shrieks it continually, its voice desperate. Pleading. The words begin to turn hoarse, and invisible hands seem to claw at its nonexistent throat. The statement rattles me like a death cry as I step towards the doorway without fully sensing myself do it.

THIS IS A MISTAKE!

It's the Deragon in me that begs me to turn and run—and she can go to hell for all I care.

Without looking at the person that extends it to me, I pop in whatever substance the temple requires me to consume, chewing it hard enough that I cut open an old wound in my cheek. Then, I push past the fact that I broke my promise to Marzipan and bear myself fully to whatever Diana's sanctuary wishes to show me.

35
Pandora

I had a vague assortment of ideas on what the goddess's chamber would be like—a green-shrouded forest, an archery range, or even a wild animal terrarium. I pictured scenarios where I held a sword while people ran from me, and I pictured realities where those same people brandished weapons of their own and charged after me.

But instead, I'm in a nursery.

One with gilded walls accentuated by familiar scarlet curtains. A woven bassinet rests in the center of the space, a stitched blanket draped over its yawning mouth.

"Isn't this rich?" a feminine voice muses haughtily from behind me. The closeness of her snide voice sends goosebumps up my arms.

As I pivot to face her fully, her presence halts my breathing. The expression on her alluring face nails me to the floor, her aura threateningly familiar despite no memory I have of encountering her before this moment. Still, I look at her, and I feel the bizarre instinct . . . to weep. Not with misery, but with pure, bone-chilling terror. Like something in my DNA *wills* me to remain utterly petrified.

Diana Seagrave looks just as I would've imagined her. Angular face, piercing eyes, elegant posture. What does *not* match the description my family fed me long ago, however, is the way she carries herself. Proud, yet . . . diminished.

"Why am I here?" I ask, refusing to balk from the wicked grin deepening along her lips.

She ignores the question for now. "You have defied your own blood by speaking with me, *Pandora Deragon*." I cannot tell which part of my name comes out in more of a sneer. "And I'd like to know why. I'd like to know *exactly* what prompted you to enter *this* chamber."

"I wanted to go somewhere that Venus would never dare," I say through chattering teeth, as if all warmth in the room has been sucked out. It's the truth. "I came . . . to try and uncover the truth."

Her gaze poses a challenge. "The truth of what?"

"Whatever I'm missing," I respond, the answer vague. Then, I shut my eyes, trying to grasp the circumstances I'm standing amidst. "So, wait . . . are *you* the deity of Diana? But how would that work with all the historical recordings and accounts—"

"You've been reading about our culture?" she asks, but her tone sounds posh, offended.

"I think the culture here is fascinating," I tell her. "Beautiful, even."

Her eyes flare, brows furrowing at the improbable concept of her political enemy—even through a new generation—finding admiration in a land she ought to abhor. I can tell she wants to say something snide in response, but she holds her tongue and reroutes her wording.

"Alright, princess. I'll grant you the truth you seek. But you must ask for it outright . . . and tell me the secrets of your soul as well."

I don't waste another breath. "Did your brother Slater truly love my aunt?"

There's no point in playing coy about my real parentage—not when all truths are likely known to those in the Beyond. Still, any hint of Diana's previous grin disappears at the inquiry.

"In his own way, it's possible. Infatuation is a better word I'd use, though. He always was a glutton for pleasure—and this time, he got caught between her legs and couldn't claw his way out."

Forcing myself to stay mild-mannered and not let the obvious insult rattle me, I stand tall, waiting for my first trade-off.

"What's the most . . ."—she ponders for a moment, and then her eyes flare—"*depraved* thing you've ever done?"

"I'm afraid I'm rather cookie cutter," I say flatly.

"You have to at least *thought* of doing something debauched before, then," Diana amends.

"Nothing crazier than imagining a steamy encounter in order to go to sleep."

Diana smiles at that, the expression feline. "Details."

Choosing to give her what she wants before I become self-conscious, I find the will to tell her, "I've never been with anyone like that. And yet my mind illustrates it all in vivid detail, all the things that haven't happened yet. The way a heated glance, no words required, could have him undoing my corset, or how his hands in my hair would make me want to scream."

"Still sounds boring," Diana drawls.

I grind my teeth together, fists balling up at my sides. "He's the only person, aside from Mother, that I feel truly cares for me, that sees me as something entirely unconnected from my bloodline. I resent them beyond measure for leaving me in the care of a Mosacian loyalist and an *assassin*, but . . ." I shut my eyes to keep from seeing the growing joy on her face. "Some nights—*most* nights—when my loathing matches the intensity of my attraction for Madman, I imagine a scenario where he worships me in a manner that feels like punishment. And that they hear it as it's happening. They hear him *defile* me, body and soul, and realize that I let him. That I *begged* him to do it."

There's a beat of silence.

And then, her amusement barrels into me like one of Whisper's bullets. "I'll be damned," Diana says through dark, mocking laughter. "The Deragon Heir ensnared by the man who killed her king's advisor. *Aching* to expose yourself entirely to someone who won't even show you his face. How dreadfully *hilarious!*"

The sound of Diana Seagrave's cackling will likely haunt me the rest of my days.

"Why this room?" I sneer, ready to move forward. "Why show me a nursery?"

Diana's smile deepens again, and the sight is absolutely unnerving. "You don't remember because you were only days old, if not hours," she answers. "But this is where we first met."

No.

It can't be.

"You were the last person I spoke to before the end, princess," she says almost sadly, though bitterness coasts in the depths of her voice. "It was only for a moment, but rest assured, I made sure to use the time I had with you wisely."

I grit my teeth. "Doing what?"

"Ensuring that you'd atone for the sins of your family. You

see, your aunt, through her scheming and her betrayal," Diana seethes now, inching towards me, "forced my hand into an act that would've damned my soul had I survived what happened that dreaded day in Broadcove Castle. She had turned my sister, Greer, against our family—convinced my sister that her side was the righteous one. My brother overpowered her, but I was the one to plunge my sword into her. To silence her once and for all.

"Slater had wanted to seek Venus out, still believing in her partial innocence, but I saw through all the lies. My father was gone. My mother and her baby. My—" She halts and swallows hard. "Delta was dead. I knew we were outsmarted, and likely outnumbered, so after gutting my insolent sister, I found you in your crib, stooped over the sides . . . and cursed you."

Run, a voice urges, the sound breathless and frantic. *Get out of there. RUN, PANDORA—*

"I voiced a declaration in the name of the Saints your lot believed in so deep-heartedly and cursed you to carry out the same vile will that Venus left me no choice but to follow." She grins, the expression so spider-like I feel it crawl across my bones. "To murder a member of your own family. And considering those Saints turned out to be the real deal . . ." She laughs in a way that almost sounds like a scoff. Like even in death, Diana still cannot fathom it. "I'd say it was worth it."

From my first experience in the Temple of the Shrine, I learned that I'm supposed to let the substances ebb out on their own time before exiting a sanctuary. But I'm so aghast over what Diana Seagrave just shared with me—albeit to intentionally terrify me—that I come tearing out of the room and into the level two vestibule.

It can't be true.

I will not be destined to kill a member of my family.

Just because I do not measure up does not mean I'll resort to the despicable violence that took hold of the Seagraves. Never.

I don't know how long I stand there, but eventually, one of the temple maidens approaches me, profound worry in her narrowed eyes. She tries speaking to me, but no sound comes out—at least none my ears can detect. *Have I gone deaf to anything beyond the hysterical beating of my heart?*

And then, faintly above my rocky breathing patterns, I hear it.

Music.

Sad guitars, lilting flutes, the soothing bleed between saxophones and clarinets. Full-bodied bases and cellos accompanied by the singing of violas and one operatic violin. And underneath it all, two finely tuned pianos that play such complex, compelling melodies with supernatural unity.

They call to me from beyond the grasp of Apollo's sanctuary.

I sail through the air and move at a snail's pace all at once, but the hard crash of tumbling down the temple stairs and splatting on the mezzanine knocks me awake. I scramble for my footing, unbothered by the stairs, or the fact that the attendant from moments ago comes chasing after me—though slowed down by the need to pick up her skirts in her hurry.

Time moves in slow motion, but this time, my feet don't. The wind rips past my skin as I pump my arms and haul ass for the door. The attendant guarding Apollo's door possesses enough intelligence not to stand in my way, but I realize why as my hand makes purchase on the sanctuary's gilded handle.

The brand hasn't set in yet.

Without hesitation, I throw myself at the mercy of Apollo,

the god of music, healing, poetry, and truth—and while there's always been a spell of silence as the scene in each sanctuary formed, this time, it's different.

The scene before me lies untouched by supernatural intervention or any human participants before me. I merely stand on a stage so shrouded in shadows that I cannot clearly make out the material of the floor—but in its center, a singular spotlight settles upon a lonely, silver object.

Madman's harp.

Feeling helpless and sad and yet so *connected* to the means of playing music again after so long apart, I dash forward. I nearly crash into the stool but find my bearings enough to slow my heart rate and sit before the familiar instrument. The calluses on my fingers practically sigh as they reunite with the finely adjusted strings.

For an audience of none, I pluck my favorite series of chords and melodies across the harp. I let my performance act as a prayer to a deity I don't formally believe—wishing Madman were somehow here again. And as I let myself get lost in my music, to the point of losing my way from reality entirely, I don't feel the mark on my hand fully materialize. I simply let the poison sink in.

36
Ren

I mull over what I saw in my chosen sanctuary while I wait for Geneva to resurface.

Nothing in my life ever mattered like traveling the world did, so each time I found my way back to the Sacred City, I always paid a visit to Mercury. The god of travelers and tradesmen always welcomed me with a warm embrace and never sent me on my way without pointed guidance towards my next adventure.

But this time, the sanctuary lay vacant. I stepped into a stone-walled room, the same statuesque depiction of the god from the main mezzanine resting in the center of the otherwise empty room. I waited a minute. Then two. Then *ten*. I almost wondered if one of the attendants had given me a defective dosage before a small voice in my head said *You've already found it.*

When Geneva fades into view, I finally understand why Mercury's sanctuary stood barren.

Because *she* is my sanctuary. There's nowhere left I need to traverse to feel satisfied. I've seen the world by land and by sea, seen the sun rise and set on so many glorious places, but I always knew how to leave them behind and move forward.

Genny is different.

The thought of parting ways with her twists my stomach into knots. The idea of having to relearn life without her feels no better than torture. As she gets closer to me, I feel a supernatural sense of calm and excitement all at once—and if I thought I was spellbound by her before last night . . . the here and now won't let me brush aside the truth.

I am so off the deep end for her, and she doesn't even know it.

Genny walks towards me on an uneven rhythm, her eyes darting between the steps and literally anywhere else but my eyes. My pulse begins to hammer against the tender point in my neck.

Oh gods, did I do something wrong? Or wait, what if Minerva relayed bad news? What if there's no way to recover her daughter after coming all this way? Is Genny starting to see all this time we spent together as a pointless distraction? What if—

"Did I keep you waiting long?" she calls out a bit breathlessly.

The question takes me by surprise. "Not at all. How did everything go?"

"Just fine," she says, not elaborating further.

"Any worthwhile answers?"

I don't know if it's my wording or my tone or something else entirely, but Genny dons the expression of someone deeply nauseous. "To an extent. Perhaps we should—"

Suddenly, a slight commotion from the temple atrium sounds off. Gasps, hurried steps, hushed conversations. Genny and I both study our hands—the brands slowly materializing but not completely stamped in yet—and we make the simultaneous decision to investigate further.

I knit our fingers together and lead us back inside, following a small herd of bystanders down to the second floor. I'm used to the resistance the mark gives off when I'm meant to exit the temple, but Genny isn't, and she squeezes my hand tighter as her mark develops fully. Just this once, I'm grateful to something that brings her pain, if only because it brings her closer to me.

Suddenly, the crowd goes still, halting our steps when we're barely halfway down the stairs to the third deck. Two deities grace this floor, and while Neptune's side is otherwise empty, it feels like the temple's entire nightly congregation stands enthralled before the closed door of Apollo's sanctuary.

Where enchanting music pours out from the crack beneath the door.

No one moves nor breathes, listening with undivided attention as they come to recognize the same thing I do within mere seconds.

"The Lover's Grand Lyre."

Genny peers up at me from her lower step. "The what?"

"It's a well-known story I learned about when I was young, one of the most famous recordings in Mosacian History," I murmur as to not disturb the others entranced by the blissful music. "The lyre was rumored to be crafted by Apollo himself, and somehow in the transit of time, it fell into the possession of a man named Orpheus. His talents in music already went beyond the extraordinary, but with the lyre in tow, he *captivated* the world. His music warded off malicious sea creatures, wooed a lovely maiden into marriage, and in the overwhelming grief of losing her tragically young, it even moved the god of the underworld into bringing her back to the land of the living."

The wonder in Geneva's eyes radiate like faraway stars before sharply retreating. "A love that surpasses even death," she mumbles with the most somber of smiles. Like she almost knows the feeling.

I don't bother telling her how sourly the story ends, not when I know she's thinking about Kurt.

I don't know every detail about Pandora's father—only the pieces that Genny has given me on her preferred timetable—but the way her demeanor takes a nosedive, I know enough to try and gear her attention back to the music.

"I don't think anyone's been able to hear what's happened inside a sanctuary before. Not even the acolytes," I add, pointing to the stunned expressions on the veiled ladies poised at the base of the stairs.

Geneva's whole body has turned towards the door, now, just as the occupant begins to sing.

A feminine voice as sweet as sugar cane permeates the air, and people around us part down the middle to let Geneva walk through. I drift after her, and a part of my soul that I haven't been in tune with in so long starts to stir the closer we get. The woman's tone exhibits grief and adoration at the same time, and as the sound crescendos, my lungs forget to draw breath. My heart forgets to pump blood.

Only hoping the tune is as transfixing for Geneva as it is for me, I squeeze her hand again—and when she turns back to me, I study the way silent, streaking tears faintly sparkle in the light of distant moon. "What's wrong, Genny?"

"Nothing," she whispers. "That's my daughter's voice."

My jaw slackens.

"We found her, Ren."

She's crying, throwing her arms around my neck and trying desperately to muffle the shaky sounds coming out of her. Then *I'm* crying.

Just not for the same reasons.

For she gained back her missing daughter, but I'm about to lose the very woman my life was missing. She finally found her lost love, and I'm about to forfeit mine to a nation that failed them both. It's so cruel and unfair that I consider burning the temple to the ground—

My thoughts stop me dead in my tracks, and I carefully retrace them until I confirm what I thought let slip past my defenses.

Yes . . . I do.

I love her.

I *love* Geneva Deragon.

The thought of her walking out on me in favor of her daughter doesn't wound me. But the thought of not *telling* her before she slips through my fingers? That is a fate worse than loneliness—than death.

"Geneva?"

She's still fused to me, and I feel her jaw move as she whispers, "Yes, Ren?"

Before I speak up, a devastating sob breaks out again—but this time, it's not from Genny, nor from anyone in the crowd. No, it comes from within Apollo's sanctuary. From *Pandora*.

The sharp sound is warning enough to get most of the masses to scram, but Genny does the opposite. In fact, she storms towards the door, and she's just out of reach as it swings open with the force to send it sailing off its hinges. In a manner that almost feels possessive, I yank her back into my hold, fearing she may be trampled underfoot somehow.

But the only thing that emerges from the sanctuary is a tall, ominous man in dark cloaks and a skeletal mask that conceals most of his face. In his arms, he carries Pandora within a death grip, who nestles herself firmly against him, as if searching for enough warmth to survive a fatal frost.

"It's all right, angel," he murmurs, though his voice proves to be just as icy as his exterior. He strides out from beneath the doorframe. "I've got you. Just hold tight to me—"

"Put my daughter down, *right now!*"

Geneva Deragon faces off against the formidable stranger with more gall than I've ever mustered in my entire life combined. Even after the statement—no, the *command*—hangs in the air between them, she doesn't rescind her words—her steps. Fearlessly, her eyes barrel into his, as if forcing him to obey.

Slowly, Pandora cranes her neck out from her liberator's broad chest. "Mother—"

"No, angel. It's the poison spreading from your brand," he insists, helping her situate her head back into its original position. I watch as true anger casts a shadow over Genny's eyes as he strokes her hair with his gloved hands. "You're not in your right mind."

"Pandora is *not* your property," I sneer. "She belongs to—"

Holding her limp body with one arm, the man uses the other to brandish a gun and point it directly at the center of my head.

Geneva shrieks my name.

"You can't hurt me here," I counter quickly, not bothering to raise my hands to ease his temper. "The laws here state—"

"Tribunals can't prosecute someone they can't catch." The figure flashes me a vicious smirk. "And no, Pandora isn't property. But she *belongs* to *me*."

Suddenly, the masked man kicks out his leg, making harsh contact with my stomach and sending me stumbling backwards. I end up taking Geneva down with me when I hit the ground, and despite the crack I feel in my hip on landing, no physical pain amounts to the sound of Genny's vocal cords shredding as she screams *come back, come back, come back, come back*—

37
Pandora

I pour my soul into the silver harp—my calluses threatening to reopen and scar—when all at once, my soul pours onto the floor instead. My weary eyes momentarily make out Madman's awed expression from below the stage, and then a sob cracks my chest wide open.

He's here.

Madman is *here*.

With reckless abandon, I leap off the stage, knowing with absolute surety that he'll catch me. The instant strength of his arms sweeps me away from reality, and I slip in and out of knowing what's truly happening around me. It's dark, then light floods my senses, which I duck away from instinctively. The darkness doesn't let up as I cling tighter to Madman, so maybe the light was merely in my head. But when I breathe deep, his scent fills my nose, and he presses a fierce kiss to my brow in response, I know *he* is real.

But then, slicing through the haze of my relief and euphoria,

I hear my mother's voice.

It's distinctive, undeniable to the point where I almost leap out of my skin. But my body is so worn and weary, rendering me useless—and somehow, Madman doesn't seem to tense at what sounds to be a severe reprimand.

"Mother?" I barely manage to exhale.

"No, angel," Madman answers. "It's the poison spreading from your brand. You're not in your right mind."

Just before my head lolls backward and I begin to succumb to the approaching darkness, I remember that I entered a second temple in twenty-four hours. I lingered there too long, despite Marzipan's warnings.

And now, death has come to collect me as payment.

When I come to, I know instantly that I have not reached the Beyond, because the realm after my earthly existence would not have let me take Madman with him—not unless Madman begged to see me into death himself.

That, and I can hear his heartbeat from where my ear remains pressed to his broad chest. I don't suppose the body still functions after . . . well, organ failure.

Stars lay sprinkled across a deep blue skyscape, and aside from an abnormal chill in the otherwise airy midsummer night, all seems well. I don't know how the poison didn't pull me completely under, but I choose to ask questions later—after I regain enough control to soothe Madman, whose hands grip me like a precious childhood toy he'd lost ages ago and finally reclaimed.

"Oh gods," his voice breaks, eyes grave and devastating from beneath his mask. "Oh *gods*, I thought you were leaving me."

"I could never," I tell him. "Besides, I doubt I'll be able to walk straight when I manage to get onto my feet."

Madman's eyes fill with mirth in a way that makes me think he's got a few ideas on how to further solidify my trouble walking, and my pulse pounds faster against my skin as if it were a jail cell. Like it might hammer its way to destructive freedom.

And then, we're both moving. I peel my back from the ground just as Madman lowers himself to me, and we kiss as though we've been starved, like we've been *dying* for each other. Madman roamed continents to experience this moment with me, and the thought makes my throat bob with emotion. I don't know what street we're on, nor who's watching, but I'm indifferent to it all. We fuse our bodies together in an equal effort to pull each other into our very essences.

"I don't know how you're not dead right now," Madman admits through a confused yet relieved chuckle against my mouth.

"Me neither, but I'll definitely die if you stop now," I rasp on a dark smile and kiss him harder, letting my body tell Madman everything at once, which is far too much to make sense of aloud. He absorbs it all, humming against my mouth before sheltering my body beneath his and sliding his tongue against mine.

The sheer perfection of this reunion makes a sweat break out all over my body, but I push the frightening part of the thrill away, giving over to the way I feel *everything* of his on me. The strength beneath his clothes, the scent of the Damocles in his pores, the groan of pleasure filling my ears in ways that coordinate with the development of such depraved thoughts . . .

"Did you mean what you told me?" I gasp and his lips move to the column of my throat, his teeth grazing there. "When I saw you in Venus's temple?"

I won't hold back from you any longer. I won't restrict myself from you in any way. No secrets. No evasions. No mask.

"Yes." Just as his head bows towards my collarbone, he stops, panting. "But not . . . here."

"Where, then?" I want to tell him that I'll be patient—that I'll be good—but I know better than to lie. Patience and goodness are virtues I extinguished long ago. All on my mind right now is *him*.

"Home," he purrs.

"But your cave—"

"We'll mend it together," he tells me steadily. And honestly, there's nothing I want more than that. The chance to rebuild a place of isolation into a home. *Our* home.

"Together," I whisper, as if I'm having to relearn the word in my native language.

Madman's expression appears puzzled for all of two seconds before he dons his typical glower. "It's late enough, now. We should leave the city before—"

"We have to go back for Marzipan."

"You know she won't leave the city, Pandora."

"And *you* do?"

Madman grins at my backtalk, but his knowing smile is short-lived. "Why else would she have directed you to Apollo's temple?"

His question floors me, and I put all the loose pieces together as Madman explains it fully. "I got to your hostel this morning, apparently right after Kit escorted you to the temple. Marzipan was keeping watch from her balcony when I showed up."

"But you—" I stop, doing a few mental calculations. "You never operate during the day."

"I barely slept when Kit first took you," Madman says through his teeth. "And the minute your mind found mine in the temple, I haven't slept since."

I shouldn't be surprised by his devotion—the profound

insanity of it—and yet it never fails to stun me. It never gets easier to accept; to know that there truly is someone out there that would tear apart the world to get to me.

"I'm shocked that she, or the whole city of Vesta for that matter, didn't have a conniption when you showed up," I try and joke, pointing to his mask for emphasis.

"She didn't," he says so matter-of-factly that it breaks my heart. "Because I wasn't wearing it."

He showed Marzipan his face. Showed *strangers* his face. But he won't show me. *Me*, the woman he would tear apart the world for. I try not to let my internal devastation consume me.

"I have to tell her goodbye at least."

Madman says nothing, offering a hand to help me find my initial footing. When my head clears, I take note of the alley we ended up in, the sloped curb having supported my posture while Madman waited for me to yield to the ineffective poison. I recognize this street.

"We're only two blocks away," I state, increasing my pace.

Despite Madman's long limbs, my feet carry me fast enough down the pavement to always stay two strides in front of him. By the time we round the final corner, he's caught up, though—a vicious determination marring what little of his face the mask gives away. I never intended it to be a race, but considering the confession about paying Marzipan a visit undisguised, he might be worrying that I'll beg Marzipan to divulge details and descriptions before he can show me himself.

However, just as I turn into the hostel's door frame, Madman yanks me behind him.

The whooshing of his cloak sounds off before the click of his gun loading stills my heart.

I try and swallow my scream.

"*Don't move, angel,*" his tone is fiercely unflinching. Almost cruel.

"What's happening——"

"Do *not* look past me."

And then, a familiar voice with a stony sense of calm orders Madman sternly, "Give us the princess, and we'll spare your life."

My stomach lurches.

If who I'm hearing hasn't come alone, they won't spare him, not even if he complies. They'll butcher him and make a show of it, a repayment for what he did to Ardian.

Madman doesn't move an inch, even as my bones yell at me to take Madman and run miles away from here. "You're in no position to make demands."

"This is *Jericho's* territory, so I think I do, actually," the voice barks. It confirms exactly who I feared to be speaking with Madman so gruffly.

Henry Tolcher, Captain of Jericho's indomitable King's Guard.

While the man always proved to be friendly beyond his post or at family gatherings, Jericho had instilled enough sense in me to fear him. Henry was pleasant——a friend to Venus long before her Deragon name made people tremble in their shoes——but over the years spent in my uncle's service, Henry adopted the unnerving skills of a huntsman. His capability of tracking down missing or hiding persons became almost instinctive, rivaling Jericho's supernatural blessing.

But Madman seems undeterred by Henry's words or his company of soldiers. "Not here, you Urovian mutt. Not on *sacred ground.* And certainly not after you just broke this city's most hallowed, unbending law."

That certainly shuts Henry up, and while I know I shouldn't,

I silently revel in—

Wait.

The world goes quiet save for the building roar that reverberates within my skull.

Vesta's most hallowed law is that anyone, no matter their culture or tongue or heritage, is *safe* here. They cannot be harmed, or the perpetrators face a tribunal's prosecution.

I hear the hyperventilation in my words as I choke out from behind Madman's back, "What have you done?"

I start to move—

"*Don't*," Madman urges, his tone pleading rather than forceful.

But I want to see it for myself. Tolcher's face, the size of his company . . .

Marzipan.

The atmosphere shifts when my eyes peer out from behind Madman's shield and meet Marzipan's, the baby blues there frozen in time and unblinking—glassy, as if tears do not possess the means to spill out. Then, her lips are crusted in blood that looks fresh. But it's the sight of her small hands—dark ink still stained to her fingertips from writing—curled in towards her ribs that sucks the breath from my lungs. There's no blood, but two jagged points puncture a hole through the fabric of her shirt.

They broke her ribs.

They *killed* her.

My family's forces killed my only friend on *sacred ground*.

When I start to weep, lantern lights from inside different hostels start to flicker to life. Windows open and people peer out onto the scene. But when Madman moves, it's not to usher us out of attention, but rather to shelter me in his arms. He holds me as if he could take on the soul-splintering grief for me, as if he could conceal me from this devastation.

All the while, the cross expressions on the faces of soldiers I grew up seeing in Broadcove's halls do not soften, not even for my sake at the loss of who is obviously a friend. And all that Henry dares to say is to Madman. "Let's not up the casualties. Release the girl."

Princess.

The girl.

Even Madman knows the irrevocable error Henry made not once, but twice now—and I unleash my wrath on him for it.

As pure, undiluted hatred spews from my mouth, I don't even register exactly what words they are, only that they taste vile. Spit flies from my mouth as I shout and curse and rebuke, and I don't care about the risk I run when I step between Madman and Henry. Even as I position myself in the line of fire should Madman's gun go off, all that stays with me is the pain. The loss.

Because it's not just her life they took. They took her *purpose*, too—her attempts at salvaging a severed land. Marzipan's dreams died the same painful death she did, so it no longer matters that I knew all these men growing up. They're dead to me now.

I don't catalog the sadness in Henry's voice when he says, "What has he done to you?" Not when the implication of his words puts the blame for this—the butchering of an innocent girl—on *Madman*. As if *he* forced their hand to kill Marzipan.

Sickness spreads through my stomach the longer I dwell on it, but I shove it down, refusing to let them render me weak. Venom courses through my bloodstream, and my sneer in response is downright poisonous.

"He's saved me from being honor-bound to cowards. That's what."

One of Henry's seconds roars at that. "How *dare* you—"

Madman sharply yanks me backwards before his gun goes off.

Bullets spray through the courtyard and in the sudden absence of sound—seared out of me from the shooting—I see red *everywhere*. The tarnished sashes indicating their Urovian affiliation. The blood pouring from their bodies.

The wrath that swallows me whole as Madman resorts to throwing my stunned body over his broad shoulder and taking off in a sprint away from the hostel.

I want to look at Marzipan one last time, but Madman jolts my focus away from her with a sharp turn, likely to keep me from committing the sight of her in death to memory. It sends tears springing from my eyes, nonetheless. It doesn't matter that her corpse wouldn't hear any sputtered apology I could offer her—not when my soul aches to go back and give her whatever words I could muster. To bury her properly. To *mourn* her.

People are shouting in the streets and from inside their homes as Madman and I make our escape, but I'm surprised to see them all pointing towards the scene of the original crime rather than in our direction. It seems the city knew Marzipan quite well, and they are choosing to rally for her support one final time.

It buys us the time we so desperately need.

At some point during the mad dash for the coast, I force Madman to set me back on my feet, insisting he not waste his energy. Even so, it takes me at least three minutes to fully convince him, and I understand why the moment I force myself to maintain his pace; the shock starts to wear off, fading into grave understanding. It's not just rabid anger filling me anymore, it's sorrow so dense it makes my shoes feel full of lead. Grief so numbing and heady that my brain seems to melt inside my skull.

A getaway boat bobs in the harbor, and I don't let myself ponder on the potential methods Madman took up to keep his arrival and docking here unseen. Rather, I let him escort me onto the vessel, careful not to slip when the waves make the surface underneath me dip ever so slightly. Madman crosses over with ease, quickly getting to work at the rope keeping the boat in place.

There's two ties left for Madman to attend to—one at the stern and the other along the starboard—and it's as he fusses with the latter that I hear it again.

My mother's voice.

Only this time, I *see* her, too—bounding towards the shore in a crazed tumble of limbs.

"Mother?" I whisper to myself in disbelief. When I swipe at my eyes, making sure the tears haven't created some sort of mirage, my heart soars. "MOTHER!"

"PANDORA!" she calls after me.

I wave about spastically, leaving no doubt in her mind that I'm just as real to her as she is to me, but the movement starts to wither when I take note of who follows her. Closer to her, a man I'd only describe as a sunbeam running beneath the moonlight pursues her with an intensity I realize isn't threatening. It's protective. He calls out to her, over and over, "Keep going, Genny! I'm right behind you!"

But then, quickly gaining on him, Henry surfaces from the last of the brush, blood coating one side of his face and fury engulfing the rest of it.

Madman frees the last of the boat's bindings, and gradually, the boat drifts forward. Before I can cry out for him to stop the boat, though, Mother's feet pound onto the wooden boardwalk at a pace I'm impressed she maintained after the distance she's already traveled. Madman shoves me aside to extend a gloved hand beyond the side of the ship.

In milliseconds, he heaves Mother into his arms and onto the boat, and I'm a heap of tears and emotions and unyielding *love* as she transfers from his grasp into mine. Her embrace feels more like a collision, comforting and bruising me all the same. But I don't complain—not when her touch feels more in tune with the divine than anything in any of the temples ever did.

Rivers flow down each of our faces.

"I missed you," we say over top of one another.

And then, the hard *thunk* of a body hitting the dock echoes through the night.

The man who encouraged my mother to keep running curls into a ball, shielding his vital organs, as Henry towers over him and violently swings—wailing on him with the weighted baton he keeps stashed along his uniform belt.

And I've never heard Mother scream like she does now, the sound strangled and ear-splitting and *raw*. She screams for this stranger like one would under gruesome torture—louder than him as he takes an *actual* beating.

Mother releases herself from me, and an all-out war breaks out across her brown eyes. Her final line of defense breaks down as she looks at me.

No . . . beyond me. Directly at Madman.

The words are guttural in her throat. "Protect my daughter."

Madman pieces it together before I do, clamping down onto my shoulders as Mother leaps overboard and back onto the boardwalk. I hear her kneecap crack on impact, but the blatant injury doesn't deter her.

I recognize that struggle, then. That *fight* in her. It spells itself out clear as day as she damns the consequences and throws her body over top of the man's broken frame, taking one of Henry's swings in the process.

She loves him.

She loves him.

I don't notice when Madman releases me again, nor do I stir once our boat reaches open water. I simply stare at the sight of Henry restraining them both before ordering them onto *Crystal Wrath* and into Urovian custody.

38
Pandora

I don't wonder about Kit once. Whether he's roaming Mosacia alone and under the cover of nightfall, evading tribunal scouts and fanatics hellbent on collecting his monetary reward, or actively making his way back to Andromeda House—it doesn't matter.

Kit Andromeda is the *least* of my concerns.

Instead, I think about Marzipan. How she recorded each of my heart's lamentations, and in my terror of what transpired, I didn't think to grab any of her other transcriptions. How, at best, they will collect dust in her hostel back in Vesta. At worse, they'll be cleaned out and discarded to make room for future travelers. I think about the man that fought tooth and nail to bring Mother and I together—the one whose name I don't know but the one whose heart so clearly captured Geneva Deragon's that he was prepared to take a beating to let her escape with me.

And then, I think about Mother—about how close I was to finally having her back, and how hollow I felt as the boat sailed away from her.

How will I survive this? How are all these atrocities supposed to settle into place with enough time? How long will it take for this gaping soul-wound to heal over?

Being back under the same roof with Andie is a start. Madman takes some time to clean up the rubble of his lair before designating some space for me, and I understand why the second Andie opens the door and cages me in her arms. Her embrace isn't quite like my mother's, but it's close.

I come apart right there on the doorstep, spewing out every terrible heartbreak I've endured since I left. Every loss of life, trust, and hope all spills out on the floor, and Andie just . . . lets me unpack it all. My tears taste like acid and fall like unforgiving sleet, but amidst it all, Andie's arms hold firm. No bout of despair sways her—and that, too, makes me break down.

When my hyperventilating spell starts to ease, Andie leads me to one of the couches in the sitting room. She boils a pot of tea and offers me something to wipe my face with, and when I regain full control of my faculties, I start to apologize for the scene I caused, which bleeds into a confession that, "I'm in hot water with Kit. Deep enough that, should he come back and find me on my own—"

"You listen to me," she says, pointing a stern finger at me. She clearly doesn't care to entertain any of my apprehensions. "My son made his own choices, and rest assured, he will answer to *me* for them before he gets the chance to even *look* your way. But do not start telling yourself that his choices translate in any way to you deserving this fate. None of what you have experienced is on your head."

"Not even—"

"*None* of it," Andie stammers, her hands crashing down on

the side table. "I know you're hurting, and you might feel fragile because of it, but you are *strong*. I'm not here to tell you that your pain will pass, nor do I know how long it'll take, if it ever does, but you've fought your way to this point, Pandora. Keep pushing forward. I'm here for you every step of the way."

I note the silent implication of why she adds that last statement. She knows that my return here is a result of no one coming to claim me, and this is her way of doing just that.

"Why?" I croak, my body too weak to summon more tears.

"Because the minute I got a look at you, dear," Andie returns, "I stared into the mirror of a pain I felt firsthand, one that I tried to put to rest a long time ago. Knowing what it's like, I won't let you endure it alone."

And she doesn't.

For the rest of the day, Andie and I find new diversions to keep the horrors at bay. We read our way through the House's bookshelves. We play lewd card games over uncorked bottles of white wine. And when the alcohol finally catches up with me, she lets me tell endless stories about my shiny life in Broadcove, when I wasn't studying or training or being told to behave like the future monarch I was destined to become. I recall the days when Flora and I were more like friends than cousins, how we'd play practical jokes on Samuel and gossip about noblewomen. I tell her about all the times I snuck into Queen Merrie's revered greenhouse in search of the same divinity Venus found there. Then, I come clean to her about why I don't call Venus "Mother," and oddly enough, it eases something in Andie's mind.

We eat sweets for dinner because we're too tipsy to properly cook, and by the time our conversations run out of steam, it's nine o'clock. Andie retreats into her room for the night, and for a moment, I consider letting the sugar coma take my body hostage and lure me to sleep. The dull throb in my chest lies buried beneath all the food and wine Andie and I stuffed our faces with, enough to where I don't feel its vicious intensity. I cannot cope like this forever, but for tonight, maybe it's enough.

Then, as I close my bedroom door behind me, I find Madman hiding in the corner, waiting for me.

A brief curse escapes me in surprise, and I draw a hand through my hair to calm down. "Sorry. You scared me," I explain quickly. "What are you doing here? I figured I would meet you down by the——"

"Pandora."

His *voice* . . . there's a quality about it that deeply unnerves me. "Yes, Madman?"

"I've changed my mind."

I can't remember how to breathe.

"About what?" I squeak.

But I know what.

Still, Madman says, "Everything."

Suddenly, I feel the weight of everything I ate, and I feel it rising in my throat. My brow begins to bead with sweat. Every happy memory I've ever made escapes my head, leaving me with the dregs of my depleting sanity.

This can't be happening.

"I can't see you anymore," Madman tells me, but his voice sounds muffled, like I'm hearing it from underwater. I blink, and he repeats himself, firmly this time.

"You're lying to me," I say.

"I've never lied to you."

"Then you're lying to *yourself*," I snarl, feeling like I could spit fire.

"Don't make this harder than——"

"*No*. Don't *you* make this harder than it needs to be. Nothing needs to change here, aside from figuring out what has you so *scared*. What changed between last night and now, Madman?" My voice sounds like an entirely different woman, one under such great duress that she comes off completely warped. "Are you feeling bad about all those soldiers you gunned down? Bogged down by the prospect of having to help me gather up all the broken pieces of myself until further notice?"

Madman says nothing, his lip curling with frustration below the rim of his mask.

"Or was it seeing my mother in the flesh that did it to you?" I take a guess, and I realize instantly that I strike a nerve. The recognition of it makes my throat tighten. "Oh, I understand, now. You saw the way I was with her, and in the wake of her picking that man over me, you thought I wouldn't make the same choice, didn't you? Even though you know I have before. I picked you over her once, but it wasn't enough to convince you, was it?"

"Stop. Talking." He grits his teeth. "You aren't helping."

"And what about what she told you, huh? What about taking care of her daughter? You think leaving me here to collect dust until Kit comes back is *taking care of me*, Madman?"

"That's enough!" he hisses. The only thing keeping him from outright yelling at me is the fact that he doesn't want to alert Andie's attention, and he barely maintains that control.

Madman turns his head to look away from me, as if the movement helps him catch his breath. His dark hair remains gelled against the slope of his neck like always, and just when I think he's going to say something else, he moves. He prepares to walk out on me.

I set aside my anger to beg him, this one, final time. "Don't go."

"We both know I'm not good for you," he whispers.

"And since when has that ever stopped you?"

And then, before the spontaneous rush of courage and clarity fizzles out, I tell him on a shaky exhale, "I love you."

I don't expect him to say it in return. Knowing how volatile this situation has become, he might believe that I'm saying the words just to rile him. And yet, it wounds me even more than I anticipated when his first words in response are, "You don't mean that."

"You think I'd waste such words on someone I don't truly feel them for? You think that just because you memorized my routine from the Broadcove tunnels, you're headstrong enough to believe you know how my heart works, too? Well, I've got news for you Madman. I fell in love with you without you even being around for it! My soul sought yours across cities, across seas. It hunted you down in my dreams and *twice* in sacred temples. My love for you defies reason just as it does duty—both of which are unimaginable standards for someone like me. And even so, you want to look me in the face and tell me it's not enough?"

Again, he says nothing.

Hurt crawls its way up my throat, and I dig into the feeling rather than run away from it. "I thought that you wanted me at least half as badly as I wanted you, but perhaps I was only ever pouring my heart out into a corpse."

Madman grimaces at the final word, and in a last-ditch effort to keep him here with me, I shut my eyes and confess. "I love you with no reservations, even though parts of you remain a mystery to me. I don't care if I never get to lay eyes on the face beneath your mask, if I never get to know all your secrets—I love you. Even if you disappear forever like you're threatening to, I love you. I'll love you my whole, miserable life. And when Kit comes crawling back here and kills me for all the lies I told him, I'll die knowing I didn't go to my grave scared. But you? You'll live with regrets. You'll come to realize that you were too afraid to let me love you, and by the time you do, I'll be gone . . . and the memory of what could have been will haunt you for the rest of your days."

Sadness, true and undiluted, pierces through me like a knife as I will myself not to look away from him. I memorize the structure of his mask, the strength of the muscles usually covered by his dark cloaks, the full mouth no longer surrounded by stubble—expecting him to turn on a heel and abandon me forever.

Instead, he strides closer. His anger magnified.

"I would never—" he chokes out, unsure of how to form the remainder of his phrasing. He starts over. "I would never harm you like that, Pandora."

"I didn't say *you*. I said Kit."

There's a long pause before he says, "I know."

And then, with one fluid movement, Madman removes his skeleton mask to reveal his true face beneath—a face I've seen many times before. The face I ran like hell from.

Kit's face.

The silence that descends over the room grips us both like a vice, and my knees nearly buckle in the wake of it.

Kit waits for me to make the next move, his mask still in his hand. I take note of the white-knuckled grip he has on it, though, and I relish in the fact that he's just as scared as I am with how things may proceed.

"*You*," I say in a tone I cannot distinguish between hurt, wrath, and . . . I don't even know.

"Me," Kit sighs in confirmation. "Gods, the look on your face is killing me. I knew I should've told you sooner."

Saints, this is . . . what, exactly? A nightmare? The most awestruck I've ever been? A relief?

My mind catapults into a dangerous thought pattern as I restlessly try to compartmentalize everything I *thought* I knew about my life since the night of Queen's Feast. Immediately, things eerily begin to align.

For starters, Kit and Madman were never in the same room together. Then, there's the fact that I only ever saw Madman at night—and most mornings, Kit slept in.

It only gets worse the deeper I dig. They stand at roughly the same height, they relatively carry the same muscle mass, at least when Madman didn't don his protective gear, and they both have dark hair. Kit never wore his tight like Madman did, though—never smoothed it down his scalp like Madman's always was. The sleekness always made his hair appear black, while Kit's was more chestnut.

The minute I find a discrepancy, I blurt out in challenge, "Your eyes. The Kit I knew had green eyes, not gray."

A heartbeat later, he's reaching into his eyes, as if to pry them out—

"Colored lenses," he says so matter-of-factly, his tone gentle as I squirm at the way his fingers invaded his sockets so casually.

My pulse thrums anxiously as I look for something else to deny what's happening here. But there's no way Madman would have a secret passageway connected through a bedroom in a house he wasn't a resident in. It makes no sense. *Kit* would, though. The owner of Andromeda House would *absolutely* know about it, especially considering part of that passage connects to the room he first found me in. Or, rather, first dropped me in, before dropping his masquerade.

Most devastatingly, however, lies the fact that from our very first encounter, a seed of discovery was planted for me to trace my way back to him. Because even as he reached for my hand to whisk me into this mess, his hands were gloved . . .

And Kit bears a distinct scar that cuts across his palm.

"Being a monster is what I'm best at," Kit says remorsefully. "I just didn't think that's the version of me you'd fall for. I thought the darker side of me would scare you into my arms, and instead, it had the opposite effect."

"But Madman . . . he *cared* for me. But *you* told me yourself that you loathed what I was becoming to you. What am I supposed to believe, Kit?"

"That I'm rotten and confused about so many things, but not about you. That there are demons I still need to work through, but that so many of them have dissolved over the time I've had with you. That I still hold resentment for your bloodline, but knowing who your mother *really* is, I'm able to finally make sense of why you're you and not *them*—and that I have no words for just how sorry I am for how long it took me to get here."

I have yet to fully grasp *why* being Venus's daughter was ever such an abomination, but I set it aside. I've had enough of the heaviness for one evening, and I steady my breathing before extending a hand to him. The symbolic gesture is far from lost on him.

"You're not . . . rescinding the things you said?"

I swallow hard. "No, I'm not."

"You still love me?" he asks, dropping his mask on the ground, forsaking it forever to take my hand in his own.

The sound of it hitting the wood panels in the floor along with the feel of his bare skin untethers something in me, and my brain bobbles in my head from how hard I nod in return. "Painstakingly so."

His smile is radiant, but his words ignite a wildfire within me.

"Then come here."

All doubt disappears as I step into him, setting my hands upon Kit's chest, and let his kiss consume me. It's apologetic and reverent and disastrous—a storm that sweeps me off the ground and sends me sailing into dream. It disorients me so thoroughly that when Kit reaches for more of me, I let him have it all.

Every piece of me he asks for with shaky hands and murmured adorations, I give over to him willingly. I let him heft me into his arms and press me against the wall. I fuss at his shirt and sink my teeth into his shoulder as his hands teach me how a woman ought to be touched. I shut out the secret sadness I know I'll face in the morning as I learn to let go of the Madman I thought lay beneath that mask—whatever it might have been—and trust that Kit won't let me go.

39
Madman

Pandora isn't waiting for me down by the water when I steer my boat into its usual spot.

She's never stood me up, and even with the grief she's undergoing, she had told me herself she'd meet me here tonight. *Sworn* she would.

We didn't settle on a time, so I wait on her for an hour. Two. Frankly, after staying holed up in Broadcove's tunnels for five years, a couple of hours is certainly no skin off my back. Or, at least, it shouldn't be. But each minute that passes, my internal alarms are blaring—screaming at me that something is wrong.

Very wrong.

Blood thrumming in my veins, I don't bother going up to my old rooms. Instead, I put my vehemence to good use and scale the rock-lined wall onto the ground floor. The leather of my gloves takes the brunt of the brutal texture, not cutting up the skin there, and I stand on my feet before the manicured lawn.

With long strides, I finally saunter through the darkness and towards the front porch light that illuminates Andromeda House. I bang my fist on the door like I might just break it down, over and over, until it finally opens inwards.

"*Where is she?*" I roar.

A serpent's smile paired with pinstripe pajamas greets me in return. "Where's *whom?*"

I strike *Kit* across the face, throwing my entire body weight into the movement. He recoils with a sharp hiss, and I see the flush fill his cheeks before he can cover it with his hand.

Good.

"Don't play dumb with me," I snarl. "This is business."

"The same *business* as you bringing Pandora to the Isle after we struck up a deal to kill Venus Deragon? Whatever happened to what we talked about, one grave in exchange for another?"

My blood now boils for more reasons than the one that originally brought me to this doorstep. I haven't dared come through the front entrance in . . . gods, more than half a decade, at least, and *this* is what gets handed to me.

"I don't know where you buried her, but wherever it is, I'll find it myself. Our deal's off," I sneer, getting up in his face.

We're the same height when we face off like this, when he's too caught off guard to stand a step higher than me.

He's always done that—looked down on me. When we were young, he took advantage of every instant he could to make himself look better or embarrass me in front of an audience. Even now, it is clear that he clings to those four minutes of life before I arrived like a weapon, one that he always points towards me, sharp side out.

"You *deserted* us," he seethes. "Any hurt I felt by what you did was eclipsed by how much it tore Anna apart, and when her heartbreak killed her, I knew you were to blame. Her blood was on *your* hands, so I only thought it fair that you get your hands dirtier to make up for it. I buried her *alone*, and for what? So you could play your precious little instruments for whatever Urovian scraps the nobles would toss your way?"

The words strike my soul like a barbed whip, and he knows it. But I won't stand for this sort of abuse. I came here for Pandora, and I'm not leaving here until I get some answers. Until I get *her*.

"Although," he drawls as I'm drawn closer. "Perhaps I should be thanking you, given the present circumstances."

"What's that supposed to mean?"

"It means that I was more than displeased to play host to Pandora's whims when she first arrived," he explains casually. "Had I not thought of using her absence from Broadcove as potential leverage, I might have slaughtered her just to prove a point. But even now, *knowing* that Venus would rather leave her niece to rot than risk her neck to save her—smart as she may be to do so—I find myself oddly indebted to you. To your failure. Had you not diverted from the original plan, I would never have gotten the chance to throw it in your face."

I stand there, heart hammering in my chest to where I fear my ribs may crack. "To throw *what* in my face?"

My brother's grin resembles that of our father from what memory serves me, and I'm consumed with disgust at the sight of it. "Use your imagination, Madden."

Brothers bicker and brothers fight, but unless some outside force miraculously steps in and stops me, I might just kill mine.

The first swing of my fist against Kellan Seagrave's jaw feels like pure joy, but the longer I wail on him, taking a few blows of my own in the process, the more rage creeps in. My vision darkens; our mingled blood fills my senses. I go *feral* for this, letting each swing stoke the fire of my hatred.

Kellan finds a gap between punches to shut the front door, herding us outside. I make contact with his shoulder once more, hearing a crack deep in his bones, before he chokes out the word *stop*.

"Princes don't act this way," he reminds me pointedly. "Besides, we wouldn't want to wake up Pandora, now, would we? Not when she's sleeping so soundly."

The smug look on Kellan's face and the implication of *why* Pandora's getting such restful sleep . . . I could start a bloody war over it. And he reads the look on my face like one of his prized books.

"*Pathetic*. You're mad at *me* when all I did was seize my opportunity when the window appeared. You wasted, what, four months? Gods, *years* more if we're counting how long you had to stalk your prey—"

I swing on him so hard that, had I missed, I would've shattered the bones in my fingers along the brick wall. Luckily, my braced fist slams into the ridge of his jaw, and he yelps at the forceful contact. Kellan spits fresh blood onto the floor.

"Fine. Maybe I deserve that for how stupid I was to think you wouldn't be lurking around my property, waiting for her each night."

"*Your* property?"

"Yes, *my* property. You up and left this place years ago, which left *me* to tend to the House. Anna certainly couldn't, and Andie needed the help." There's a roughness in his voice that turns his next words venomous. "I've been trained to keep this House and its occupants a secret, so when *Pandora Deragon* of all people just *showed up* here, I didn't think about you once outside of my anger.

I was focused on how the Urovian Princess could spoil *everything* I have been working towards on a complete and utter *accident!*"

Kellan charges at me, and for once, I let him get in a hard shove. I scramble backwards, grunting as I fail to find my footing and smack onto the gravel lot.

"So I learned to play nice. Got to know her a bit. Turns out, she's not like their lot, and it *kills* me. When I'm with her, it's like I'm dying a slow, tortuous death. I kiss her, and I taste my own treachery. If only I could've searched past my own headspace to get a proper read on hers, to discover that she had grown feelings for her captor . . . it just wasn't *me.*"

The satisfaction his admission gives me spreads across my face in a cruel smile—but it doesn't last. Not when he smiles back and taunts, "What did you even do together once I fell asleep? Have fireside chats and look at the stars?"

I go to open my mouth in rebuttal, but Kellan holds up a single finger, that demonic grin further curving along his bloodied mouth. "Don't worry, brother. I'm not *that* naïve. I know you want to brag all about it—I can see it in your eyes. You're just *aching* to tell me what she's like in bed. How her hips bow when your fingers—"

"Be *very* careful what you say next."

Even if he stops there, I'm already making silent plans on killing him in my head.

How dare he touch what's mine.

"But that's not even the best part," Kellan adds. "No, the best part is the way Pandora insists that you take off her clothes. Slowly, to where it tortures her, builds up her anticipation. And then, when she's naked, she *trembles*—"

Kellan's smart enough to catch my fist within his readied hands this time, but he has to throw my fist away from the heat that burns within my blood. "Oh, I see, now," he dares to drawl. "You wouldn't know."

I dive for him, wishing I had longer nails to tear open his skin and longer arms so that I could reach into his sockets and gouge out his eyes. But Kellan's always been a bit faster than me, more on the slender side and quick to dodge my movements every time I'd lash out.

"For what it's worth," Kellan says, "I do like her. She's got a good personality, and she's a decent lay."

"*Watch your mouth*—"

"But she's the runt of her bloodline. Worse, she's the *daughter* of the runt. I knew those Urovian assholes carried heavy influence over their mass media, but to convince the world that Pandora Deragon is their direct heir when she was really the bastard child they made their heir because they couldn't conceive? It's *rich*," he guffaws.

If Pandora were here to hear the words fly out of his mouth so flippantly, let alone learn the magnitude of how he's been lying to her, *using* her, she'd be heartbroken. Infinitely more than she already is.

"Suppose those Saints ran out of blessings when it came time for them to procreate?" Kellan quips, hammering the nail into his coffin.

"That's *enough*," I say, my tone vicious, and the words acidic in my throat.

"Fine, I've had my fun. Just remember, that mask you wear; you don't wear it for Pandora's sake. You wear it for *yours*— because you've always feared that when you shed your disguise, she'll think it's me at first, and it *destroys* you."

There's something deep in my gut that roars at the accusation, at the accuracy of it. Then, Kellan steps back into the House.

"But don't worry, Madden. No need to find the balls to show yourself to her anymore. I'm taking care of it."

There is nothing in that statement that makes me feel better or even remotely at peace.

"Why'd you think I asked you to keep your voice down?" he asks, ever the twisted showman. "This way, the princess doesn't go down struggling. Her last memory will be a happy one, even if it's a lie."

With that, Kellan slams the front door in my face, locking it tight.

And I shred my vocal cords as I beg Pandora to run for her life.

PART IV
RHAPSODY

40
Pandora

A hard banging sound wakes me, but I fight the urge to stir, to even flinch in response.

It's an instinct Venus taught me to respond with—to go absolutely motionless in the face of potential danger in the event that Broadcove were ever broken into. Lie still, breathe in silent, shallow doses, and slow my heart rate.

In contrast, Kit is the portrait of paranoia. The relentless pounding throws him out of bed, and he jostles me as he works to get out from underneath the covers. I hear him swear through his teeth shortly after brushing me, but two blinks later, he's blowing out a steadying breath and darting out of the room. Just this once, I can admit to myself that Venus taught me well.

I refuse to move, mentally assessing how many seconds it takes Kit to reach the front door and appease the unseen force. Whoever it is, though, must be angry, because it's an unsaintly hour in the morning, and—

The door slams again, and I close my eyes and count down

the seconds before Kit might come striding back in. Only he doesn't appear. Not even the ghost of his footsteps sounds from the other end of the House—which means he's stepped out to handle whoever it is directly.

It's the final confirmation I need to drag myself out of bed, throw on my robe, and think things through.

The moment the soft fabric of my robe graces my bare skin, I can't help but recall the way Kit's fingers and lips had been there hours before. Hungry rather than reverent. Rough rather than gentle. There was an eagerness about it all that almost made him feel *entitled* to me, and right before the point of no return, I realized that . . . things didn't feel right.

Which made *no* sense at all.

I felt so embarrassed and confused when all I've ever wanted was to be his—when all I ever felt in Madman's presence was confidence.

Why was putting two and two together like this so unsettling? Why couldn't it have just clicked right away? Why did I have to go and ask him to stop, to let me sort things out in my head for a little longer before we crossed that bridge? The hurt in Kit's face was evident, but he managed to work through it enough to lie in bed with me until I fell asleep. Holding me tenderly, as if realizing that the harshness of his touch before may have scared me off—but it shouldn't have. The Madman I knew never shied away from his intensity. He gave it to me on full display, a major piece of what had me falling for him to begin with.

Things should be picturesque. Perfect, even.

And then, I remember my Pandora's Box.

Nausea roils through my stomach as I tiptoe out of my room and across the hall, disturbing the peace within the immortalized room for Andie's daughter.

Even in the haste of hiding it originally, I almost glance over its secret spot, my eyes just barely snagging on the gleaming, dark wood of the latched box Madman—*Kit*—gave me for my birthday. I remember the way its texture glided across my fingertips the first time I held it, and when my touch reunites with the object once more, it suddenly feels heavier in my hands.

I give it a shake, remembering how no sound had emitted from the gesture. This time, however, there's an obvious clunking buried within. My grip tightens on the box's rim to keep from dropping it as the weight shifts around. An intrusive thought deduces that there could be some kind of explosive in there, but rationality tells me that, somehow, it's worse.

Suddenly, I hear the harsh sounds of male grunting and shoving.

Oh Saints, Kit—

My heart races, terrified that something bad is happening out there, and thankfully, unlike my rooms here in the House, this one looks out onto the front drive, towards the open expanse of the rest of the Isle. Not wanting to draw too much attention to myself, I squint in hopes of seeing well enough through the blinds.

A deeper voice, hidden by my limited vantage point, snarls out some sort of muffled allegation. To which I clearly hear Kit state, "Yes, *my* property. You up and left this place years ago, which left me to tend to the House. Anna certainly couldn't, and Andie needed the help."

Kit and the other figure drift closer, just enough so that I can see who he's talking to—

And that's when I see him. Same dark cloak. Same gelled hair. Same unyielding disguise and storm cloud eyes.

Madman . . .

And Kit.

Separately.

"I've been trained to keep this House and its occupants a secret," Kit growls. "So when *Pandora Deragon* of all people just *showed up* here, I didn't think about you once outside of my anger. I was focused on how the Urovian Princess could spoil *everything* I have been working towards on complete and utter *accident*!"

When Kit lashes out, seemingly through with what he wants to say, I watch as Madman—the *true* Madman—falls into the gravel with an intensity I imagine would fracture bone. He gnashes his teeth, but not because of the pain. The pain is nothing compared to the absolute vitriol that leaks out of him.

"So I learned to play nice. Got to know her a bit. Turns out, she's nothing like their lot, and it *kills* me. When I'm with her, it's like I'm dying a slow, tortuous death. I kiss her, and I taste my own treachery."

The haunting omen I tucked away for safe keeping all those moons ago finally returns to my senses, as if trying to shake me awake to what is unfolding before me.

Everyone you know—both here on the Isle and back in Broadcove—has been lying to you.

I go deaf to all that happens outside, my eyes homed in on my Pandora's Box as if it carries a supernatural, hypnotic aura. Maybe the history behind it has gone straight to my head. Maybe I'm too paranoid for my own good. But my fingers tremble over the metal latch, shivering on their own accord.

My gut was right about Kit—about what lengths he would go to seek revenge on me for scorning him. For deserting him at the temple, for evading his longing, and for sneaking around with the man he hired to destroy my family.

If I was right about that . . . it must be right about this.

So I shut my eyes and throw open the lid of the box before I can take it back.

Delicate, plinking chords softly chime through the room, shrinking the space in a way and pouring out above the sound of the altercation happening outside. A supernatural sense of solace washes out the dread.

Is that . . . a music box?

I dare a glance at the container, decently confident in the fact that no monstrous claws will stagger out and grab me by the throat. Sure enough, harmless and lovely, a porcelain ballerina spins clockwise en pointe, arms raised in fifth. It turns to a haunting melody—one that, come to think of it, I've caught Madman humming beneath his breath when he thought I'd fallen asleep.

Beneath the ballerina, however, lies the object that made the box heavier in my hands.

The journal Marzipan gifted me back in the Sacred City.

Why would this be in here?

How had it gotten here?

I tear it open regardless, my bruised soul aching to see any living piece of her, even if it's only her handwriting. Even if I can't make out the transcriptions in whatever language she desired to ink into the pages. I nearly cut my thumb open on the edges as I flip to the pages I hadn't gotten to, and when I see her handwriting—

I understand everything.

I didn't memorize the passages I'd poured out onto the pages, not in the slightest. In fact, writing what I had felt like the exorcism of a demonic entity, and by the time I gave Marzipan the book, I remembered little to nothing of the pain before. But there's no denying what is clearly right in front of me.

I read the words with ease, *her* words. Words written in Mosacian languages I've never studied or even knew the names of until now. I comprehend all of it. Every conjugation, every inscription, every dialect . . .

Everything.

"Pandora?"

Andie's voice takes me by complete surprise, but it also keeps me composed enough to lock in the sob that wants to break free. Mainly because her tone is accusatory and heartsick at the fact that she's caught me disturbing her deceased daughter's space.

"Oh Saints . . . Andie, I promise, I meant no disrespect—"

"Do you know?" she cuts in, her voice brittle.

I say nothing, shutting the music box and tucking the journal deeper into my robe.

"Do you *know*?" she punctuates in a way that turns my stomach.

"That they're two different people?"

Andie means to say more, but suddenly, the front door closes. I hear the deadbolt hinge into the front door, the chain *clink* from down the hall.

And Madman screams bloody murder from outside.

"*PANDORAAAAA!*"

Madman wails loud enough to irrevocably damage his voice.

"*RUN* PANDORA! RUN FOR YOUR LIFE! GET OUT OF THE HOUSE—"

Andie pulls me close, her hands shaky as she grips me by the neckline of my robe and hisses almost too softly to hear, "When I tell you to, you run out the front door and after Madman. You hear me?"

Andie doesn't wait for me to confirm my understanding before putting her other hand to my mouth, insisting I stay quiet. I obey, and we both wait anxiously for Kit to trail back through the hallway. At the sight of his nearing shadow, everything inside of me screams at me to flee. Pure and utter terror replaces every sweet or nostalgic moment I have of Kit in my mind. How his face softened after our drunken night of playing cards, the way he took care of me while I was sick in the Sacred City, the kiss on his boat that made him change the course of my fate—all of it is wiped away by the way he stalks into my room.

Even after he turns into the space fully, the sheer force of his murderous intent creeps up my skin like unseen insects, and I'm on the verge of spilling my guts onto the floor because of it when Andie bursts into movement.

The Saints kindly spare me the sight of Kit's reaction to seeing that I'm awake and out of bed, and Andie yanks the door shut behind him, channeling her entire body weight into keeping it closed.

"*Now!*" she mouths.

The first jerk of Kit fighting back launches me into motion, and I bolt down the hall faster than my legs have ever carried me. It helps that they're carrying me to Madman and away from the jaws of certain death. My trembling hands manage to make quick work of the lock and chain, and I slip out of the front door in such a mad dash, I forget to close it behind me.

Madman's still screaming when his eyes capture mine, but the sight of me alive eases them ever so slightly into sobs. He's hyperventilating, down on his knees and torso bent towards the ground like he was begging, praying that by some miracle, Kit wouldn't get to me. Madman knew better than to waste his breath on pleading for another change of heart.

In silence, I reveal Marzipan's journal, and Madman sobs harder.

"You opened the box?" he chokes.

I nod, still running for him. Aching for him to rise to his

full height again. He senses my desperation and does just that, realizing that we're running out of time to make a clean getaway. "Then we need to go."

"Go where?"

"You'll see."

Hand in hand, he tears us towards the other end of the house, toward where the sharp, jutting rocks on the edge of the Isle give way to a steep, makeshift footpath. One that leads right to where his familiar, onyx boat bobs on the shoreline.

A little over halfway down to sea level, I dare to whisper his name on the wind.

"Yes, angel?" he replies instantly.

"Did you read any of the journal?"

"No," he answers. Then amends, "Well, I tried to. But it was a lot of foreign scribblings. Marzipan was quite the scholar."

My pulse beats hard enough to break out of my skin as I pull out the journal again and splay the pages wide. I see the uneven threads from where Marzipan must've torn out my original writings, swallowing hard, and hold it out towards Madman.

"You can't read any of it?"

"I only know one of the passages," he says calmly, even though he knows we're too short on time to be talking about this right now. "Fourth page. Third paragraph. I know what it says because it's written in my second most dominant language."

I flip to the page and question and let my eyes rove over the page. At the same time I read her translation with unfathomable ease, Madman speaks it back to me, having memorized it like a proverb.

I'd thought my fate was cruel before, but I'd rather live a thousand, unbearable lifetimes never measuring up to my family's legacy just so that I wouldn't have to die in this one with unfinished business. I'd tear heaven apart just to crash back to earth and tell Madman he's the song of my heart. If hell called me home instead, I'd plead with the devil for one last look into his eyes. And it would be enough, because I never needed to see beyond them to see into his soul—to see into myself and know how in love with him I've become.

I'm crying again—for more reasons than one.

Of course Marzipan would translate this passage into a language Madman could read. And of course I love him, even as the disbelief of hearing back those recited words takes over his entire body.

But as I descend the last of the rock-lined path, I don't feel the sting that comes from cutting open the side of my leg on one of the jagged edges. I let the blood seep into my house slippers and sputter out what will surely plague me for the rest of my life.

"Marzipan . . . she passed me her blessing."

41
Pandora

We sail through the night in silence, something I ought to be grateful for. Madman surely can sense how volatile everything is now, and there's a thickness in the air that threatens to crawl beneath my skin and suffocate me. Each new thing to process cuts deeper than the last, to the point where I regret saving Venus's words that ricochet off the walls of my mind for last.

"Too bad you're not blessed. Our kind can visit any door, any time. The temple doors will always open for those with a divine touch."

The brand's poison should've plunged me into death the moment I forced my way into Apollo's sanctuary. Were it not for getting swept up in seeing Madman again, I would've been able to take my uncanny survival for the clear sign it was—the proof that Marzipan had slipped away instead, and had chosen to bestow her gift of Many Tongues upon me.

The fact of the matter doesn't let up in my dreams, either. If anything, her voice and her familiar words grow louder.

"I'm one person, Pandora, and sometimes, I get so exhausted. Trying to continue my family's legacy.

"But after reading the way you bled your soul on paper, after becoming your friend . . . *I feel as though the spark of hope I carry with me has caught fire. Mosacia needs a voice like yours."*

Fear, inadequacy, and leftover sorrow gnaws at my gut like a crippling sense of starvation. I nearly double over at the feel of it, but my eyes briefly catch something tall and looming sticking out from the fog. A heartbeat later, I straighten, watching as the thinning fog gives way to—

Holy Saints.

The Damocles water turns bluer the closer we get to the Sevensberg docks.

Figures. Uncle Jericho *detested* blue. Even in mixed colors, if blue dominated the resulting hue, he couldn't bear the sight of it. The only exception were any instances where Venus or the other ladies in Broadcove would wear violet. Otherwise, to don blue was to threaten the king in his own home.

I wonder what Jericho would say if he knew where I was right now. Maybe he already knows—and if so, I hope it curdles his blood.

Sevensberg Palace, at least from the outside, remains a pinnacle of unmatched intensity, the photographs I've seen not doing justice to its physical majesty. Its iconic, seven spires protrude from the grand, metallic roof. A fountain in the centermost point of the property appears dried out, like the faraway sun sucked out all its contents, but the swirled tiling around its base remains magnificent.

It is, however, the only part of the Mosacian palace that remains untouched by the hand of war.

Drawing closer, I notice how the paint and stone along the

front walls have chipped away, if not with time and disuse, then as a result of its initial conquering. The roof is marred with craters from where they've either caved in or have been broken through, and should Madman dare to lead me inside, I can only imagine the rubble waiting within.

The thought only makes my heart race further, and not in a way that has me feeling hopeful or explorative. Madman ties off the ship and kicks down the gangway so that he doesn't have to lift me over the divide. He steps off first, ensuring that it won't cave beneath our weight, and like every time we've taken a fateful step forward, Madman extends a gloved hand towards me.

Only this time, I hesitate to accept.

"Why have you brought me here? How are we even able to *be* here right now?"

His silence indicates that whatever his answer is, it should come with a precursor. A statement along the likes of, *Promise me you won't get upset,* or *This may be a lot to take in at once, but try and push through.*

Then, he asks me, "Have I ever lied to you?"

"Not once." My answer is so immediate, unwavering.

"You opened your Pandora's Box."

"I did."

"Are you're prepared to accept the consequences that come with that?"

"Yes, Madman."

"And you trust that everything I'm going to tell you, show you . . . all that I've seen, is real?"

An invisible force gently shoves me closer to him, as if knowing he needs this proximity to fully accept my consent. Rather than simply say *yes,* I tell him, my eyes burning into his own beneath his mask, "My hope in finding you again kept me alive back there.

There is nothing, *nothing* that you could bring into the light that will pry me away from you."

Madman flinches at the declaration, his gaze narrowing in attempts to sift out any distrust. But he finds nothing, just like I knew he would.

"Okay," he says, his voice dropping an octave. "But first . . . did you give yourself to Kit last night?"

The shame and embarrassment that engulfs me feels a lot like drowning.

"Oh gods," he interjects. "I shouldn't have asked, not like that—"

"Did he tell you that?"

Madman goes ghostly pale from what little of his skin I can see. "It was implied."

I think his response only scratches the surface of whatever monstrosities Kit likely spewed about me, and I try not to dwell on it.

"I thought it was you," I say, my voice breaking. But I choose not to hide from him. "I don't know how he got your mask, but I was so convinced that I got carried away—"

"You don't need to say anything else," he cuts in pleadingly. "It doesn't matter—"

"*Look* at me," I grit out. And in a surge of courage, I grip him by the clasp of his coat and pull him impossibly closer. "I let him kiss me, yes. Touch me, too . . . but I stopped him."

I know that somewhere beneath his calm exterior, he's beaming. "Why?"

"Intuition."

Madman grins at that, the softer kind as opposed to something sensual. He doesn't pry for any specifics, and before long, I'm allowing myself these last moments knowing him before the mask comes off.

"Is it unfair to say that I might just miss you like this?"

Madman shakes his head, eyes downcast and gloomier than I've ever witnessed. "Your love wounds me like nothing else in this world. How dare I deserve you? How dare I accept your devotion when I've hidden the most fundamental parts of myself from you?"

My heart threatens to shut off completely, to drop from beneath my ribs and fly right out of my ass. It's not the only piece within me that breaks. It's my bones, too. The strongest parts of me turn to rubble from the sheer force of his will insisting on being unlovable. I feel like screaming my lungs out, crying until my eyes dry up forever, kicking through every single window of Sevensberg Palace and shattering glass.

"Pandora," Madman murmurs, sensing my internal distress.

There's an air to his voice just then that fascinates me as deeply as it terrifies me. A quality that he's never carried in full, but one that I've been taught to uphold my whole life—to hold my ground and assert my dominance in society.

Suddenly, Sevensberg Palace doesn't feel like some looming, dreadful surprise that I don't have the in on.

It feels like facing my deepest, darkest fears.

"Say it, then."

Madman knows what I mean, but still has the nerve to whisper, "Say what?"

"Your name."

No hidden identities. No monikers. His real, *birth* name.

Every time I've tried to get Madman to tell me his name—first, middle, last, whatever he'd be willing to give me—he's refused. Denied me even a letter.

But now, it seems he wants to make amends, because before

he forms the truth in his mouth, he unfastens the mask from the front of his face, shedding it completely.

Kit truly had played an evil trick on me—because for a brief moment, Madman *does* bear Kit's face.

I blink, however, and I start to see what truly sets these two men apart.

The man who stands before me has hair slightly darker, a raven's feathers as opposed to Kit's coffee tone. Slight, but still distinguishable. His nose is stern, and his jaw cuts at a sharper angle towards his ears than Kit's does. Undeniably, though, his cold eyes shroud me in shivers just as they had that fateful night I let him lure me through the trick door. His eyes are real. *He* is real. Every emotion and affection I developed for him was real . . . but so were all the things I established with Kit.

Brothers, I realize. *Twins.*

"You're the only one," Madman sighs painfully, his eyes tearing up in a manner that matches my own. "The only one to ever come close to calling me by my true name. And I intended it to be that way. You're all that ever mattered to me after I lost this place," he finishes, eyes dazed as they drink in the palace once more.

No.

No, no, *no* . . .

Madman was never an insult like I first believed it was. It was a part of him—the *real* him.

Madden Seagrave.

The last son of Victor and Harriet Seagrave, who the world believed had died long ago.

"I—" my sentence fragments the moment I start it. I reach for my throat, wanting some sort of voice to come out, but it's stifled beneath the increasing weight of everything else his revelation has me uncovering.

What this means about Kit—

No, not Kit. *Kellan.*

Their sister, Anna. *Princess Annabelle.* She'd survived, too.

Saints, their existences . . . *they* are the mercy Venus loathes herself for showing long ago.

And I see, now, why Venus and Jericho never searched for me after I disappeared. They saw my empathy, my *mercy*, and were reminded not of Mother's goodness, but of their regret. Their failure in fully wiping out a rival bloodline. It wouldn't matter if I found my way back there and told them how I'd been passed a blessing.

Nothing would deter them from the resentment they've built towards the Seagraves and all those who associate with them.

"I need a minute," I get out.

Madden nods like he expected nothing less. "Pick any room in the palace. I won't bother you."

I turn from Madden's true face and head for the massive front doors. My organs start to shut down from the pressure that builds up inside of me. My steps are heavy as I trudge towards the massive entrance, and each one further emphasizes the same, horrible understanding from before: I won't survive the pain that's prepared to swallow me whole.

42
Jericho

Henry Tolcher enters my room after performing our coded knock pattern on the door, conveniently as Venus finishes up her morning shower on the other side of the wall.

"Prisoners await you in the interrogation chamber," he briefs me curtly before dismissing himself.

Prisoners. No mention of recovering Genny and her daughter, only that of multiple captives—whose fate now becomes contingent on the state that my family is in.

An old, electric feeling courses through my veins at the thought, the kind that kept me company before Venus entered my life. Even when she despised me, when her hate held me down to the earth more than my dreams ever did, she never outright asked me to change my ways. I did so as a token of my affections, just as Venus, too, had changed for love.

The darkness only made her more magnificent.

It's no small thing to discover that a woman would live for me, but it was another to watch one *take* life for me, too—to see Venus coat her arms elbow-deep in blood just to intimately know my pain. Killing is different between her and I. I spill blood because the Saints impart orders to do so. But Venus doesn't need a sign from above to know when to strike. Her tether to me is reason enough.

So when Venus strides out of the bathroom, silk dressing robe clinging to the wet skin along her arms and legs, she only arches a brow at me in interest. "Souvenirs from Mosacia?"

The causality of her tone gives her a fearsome edge. The years have certainly aged us, but it's moments like these that play mind games with me. For a moment, it almost feels like I'm talking to the Venus Deragon I first married—the one who woke up on our wedding night and decided, with no prompting from me, to squash our rivals once and for all.

"It would seem so."

"There's nothing quite like a good interrogation to start the day," she hums in approval.

I clasp her hand in mine, leading us down the necessary corridors. "It's not every day we get to lay eyes on captives that managed to outsmart the King's Guard," I add, my tone turning bitter mid-sentence.

I worked hard to keep my temper in check after we laid waste to the Mosacian Empire and took claim of the Seagrave war spoils. I thought that returning to normalcy, or at least channeling my anger into the fervor of which I could love Venus with, would be a healthy endeavor. Truth is, though, my anger never left. It simply holed itself away for safekeeping.

For this—a failed extraction mission by my King's Guard.

Pandora and Geneva both missing in action.

I consider it a mercy that the guards that had been incapable of bringing either of them back to Broadcove had died trying, because if I were to see them now, I'd tear them each limb from limb. Urovian soldiers do not fail. Maybe struggle, but *never* fail.

This isn't just a defeat. It's a bloody *joke*.

Venus senses my frustration reaching a pinnacle and lays a hand over my thundering heart. "The tribunals would be flooding our intel passages if the princess or the duchess had been apprehended, which means they're alive. That ought to count for something—"

"If they're not *here*," I snarl, pointing straight down into Broadcove soil, "they're as good as dead, Venus."

"Do not speak things into existence that might not be true, Jericho," she urges, her voice wobbling on my name. There's no additional counter argument that follows.

"My King," a guard cuts in from across the final hallway, his voice awkward and trembling. He races over to us, bowing before me, then before Venus. "Queen Inherit. You must proceed wisely. We are dealing with traitors to the crown. Particularly *volatile* ones."

"Traitors?" Venus drawls with the kind of delight that drives me wild for her.

The guard slides open the observation window in response.

The mirrored walls within cast the unforgiving image multiple times over, and I study the different angles of how the two traitors in question lay on the floor, chained down and knees bruised from kneeling for Saints knows how long.

The man I don't recognize, and not just because he's beaten to a pulp and making a slow recovery. Golden hair, ordinary face, tattered clothes—the kind of man anyone would easily pass over in a crowd. His eyes track every movement his cellmate makes, and I, in turn, direct my gaze there, too.

A woman braces herself on her hands and knees, the look

in her bloodshot eyes bordering on feral. So fearsome I cannot look away. Her bottom lip appears split from whatever previous struggle landed her here, and as the observation window fully clicks into place, her head turns towards the sound, revealing her face fully.

When Venus and I get a clear look at her, we freeze.

The gag in Genny's mouth does little to smother the hatred she spews towards the both of us. A threat—no, a promise.

"I will *never* forgive you."

43
Pandora

The moment I burst through the doors of Sevensberg Palace, all hell breaks loose.

I'm crying and cursing and clawing at an invisible, gripping vice. I'm stumbling blindly through a palace that's starting to feel like a massive, porcelain tomb. Beheaded statues of gods Madden grew up revering litter the floor with stone and dust, except for one left strategically unharmed. I recognize her from her shrine, and it sickens me what she represents here.

Victory. The vanquishing of her enemies, and the pleasure she takes in it.

I'm climbing a set of stairs onto the second floor, contemplating the idea of leaping from one of the windows just to put myself out of this briskly escalating misery—only when I look through the glass, assessing if the height could do any real damage, Madden stares after me through its vantage point.

Darting into a hallway and hiding myself from his view, I take off in a run until my lungs burn. I cough out my broken sobs, my back sliding down one of the walls when I finally resort to sprawling onto the ground and wailing. I don't care how loud I am, don't care that Madden may enter the building and hear me. A part of me *hopes* he sees the price of his secrecy and feels the weight of my agony.

My friend is dead. Kit—*Kellan*—turned on me. I'm a lost cause to my family, save for my mother, although my mother chose to run after some *guy* instead of boarding the ship out of Mosacia with me. To the people that should matter most—the people who birthed me or raised me or set a crown upon my head—I'm none of their first priorities.

By some twist of fate, however, I'm Madman's—no, *Madden Seagrave's* top priority.

To him, I'm the easiest ask, a steadfast choice he's been making five years over.

The reminder of that only makes me sob harder. That somehow, in the midst of so many lies and hurts and treacheries, his love remained unfaltering for me. All this time, he knew the sort of betrayal loving me, a Deragon, would be to his Seagrave lineage. The *ultimate* betrayal.

And it never swayed him.

I peel myself off the floor to glance out the window I passed by, and while Madden still lingers on the front lawn, he's no longer standing. Instead, he's sitting in the grass, his face bowed into the shelter of his hands—and it shatters me anew.

I retrace my steps to him in a full sprint, no longer concerned with how withered my heartbreak makes me look—not when he's only ever looked at me with devotion. Yes, I accepted him amid his self-imposed mystery. But now, he *needs* me more than I have ever needed him. Needs me to accept every truth he's been burying away.

To accept him as Madden despite loving him as Madman.

Madden must hear me coming back for him, because I barely make it to the palace's threshold before he crashes into me. His arms bind me to him, holding me tight enough to crack my spine. "I thought you needed—"

"Withholding truths is still lying," I stammer, a jittery, furious, brokenhearted mess. "And I don't want to be in the dark. Not with you. So I want you to tell me all of it."

After a long, suspended while, Madden nods once. Then again, slowly. "Okay."

"And I swear to every god you pray to, if I figure out that you're hiding pieces of what you know from me, I'll make you suffer."

Madden stiffens, and knowing how his temper takes the wheel in hostile situations, I'm impressed to see him keep himself reined in. "Okay," he says again. "But . . . let's go somewhere."

His eyes cast a passing glance at the Venus statue, and I realize just how deeply it must offend him knowing the history there. I give him my hand in acknowledgement, and as he weaves our fingers together, he tugs us down the hall opposite of where I first ran off towards. The only sound between us is that of our footsteps, which gradually goes in and out of sync the longer we coast through the looming space. Madden doesn't look back at me once, and a wounded part of me wonders if it's because he needs his full concentration to remember his way around this place. The thought guts me like a spear.

After rounding one more corner, we turn into a room that makes my eyes bulge in my skull. If this is what the space looks like *trashed*, I cannot even begin to imagine the kind of splendor this room held in its heyday. High ceilings, marble floors, and a larger-than-life bed that couldn't possibly have belonged to a young child. Although, being a member of the richest family in Mosacia, I suppose nothing is off limits.

"This was . . . your room?"

"My parents'," he corrects, then closes his eyes. "Well, more so Mother's. Father would sleep in a room two wings over whenever he was angry."

The revelation makes my heart squeeze.

Madden closes the door behind us as if this moment weren't private enough already. Then he sheds his signature, black cloak, breaking the loop around his neck by the center clasp. The movement is minimal, and yet, I feel like I'm watching a soldier remove his armor after a bloody, costly battle. There's a deeper weight to it when he takes his gloves off, too. I note the absence of the scar that Kit bore.

One last time, Madden stares me down. "Everything?"

"Everything."

Obediently, Madden sucks in a deep breath as I awkwardly settle onto the foot of his parents' old bed. He begins with, "I thought that your aunt was one of the most beautiful women I'd ever laid eyes on."

"Nice start," I scoff, the disgust in my voice palpable.

"Notice how I said *one of* the most beautiful, though. Not *the* most."

"Like that makes any difference at all."

"It does," Madden snarls, one fist slamming into the dilapidated bedside table. "Because since I was seven years old, I was enamored with a woman named after the goddess of beauty, and yet, one look at you . . ."

My palms turn clammy. All words are lost in my mouth, in my mind.

"I was enchanted by you from the moment I first laid eyes

on you. Then, I heard you sing, and I became utterly *infatuated*. Whatever attention I once had for anyone on this planet, or could ever conjure up for another woman dropped dead the moment you opened your mouth."

My heart wails its fists against the inside of my chest, begging to break out just to intertwine with his own. My eyes burn with the ghost of tears I shouldn't be shedding yet, and so help me, I'm scared that Madden isn't going to stop his declarations there. I fear, more than anything in the world, that he won't give me the truth I'm longing for—that he'll profess his love and go to his knees for forgiveness—and I'll be too lovestruck to say no.

The Saints must hear my silent distress, though, because Madden straightens himself out again. "But maybe I'm getting ahead of myself. I mention Venus first because the moment she walked into my life, my days in Sevensberg were numbered, and I didn't see it coming."

The reality of who *Madman* really is still feels fresh, and his words wake me up in a manner that feels more like a sharp, static shock rather than a firm nudge. Venus may have raised me and taught me everything I know about how to rule a kingdom, but to Madden—to Kellan, too—she did the unspeakable. She destroyed their family from within, like a fatal virus. She ended one story just to start another. *This* one.

"Mother had gone home to the gods," Madden tells me. "We had already said our goodbyes, to her and to the little sister I had for all of maybe . . . three days?" Madden shakes his head, a tortured expression on his face. "Her name was Emmaline, and she was—"

I see the words drifting in the glassy ocean deep beneath his gray eyes.

Beautiful. Innocent. Too young.

He doesn't finish his earlier sentence. "Kellan and I thought that the worst was over. Father had gone to Urovia to discuss business, specifically the arrangements for Slater and Venus now that they were married."

My uncle had told me how horrible of a man King Victor was. That he neglected his wife during her latter pregnancies. Worse, that he abused one of his daughters when she found out the truth of his deplorable character. But now, I have an eerie inclination that despite his reputation, Madden may have seen Victor Seagrave as a decent man, whose nastiest qualities were magnified because of Jericho's very existence.

"Before he crossed the Damocles, Father broke the news to us in total honesty. Venus had bested King Jericho in a long-willed battle of wits, killing him in a moment of farced romance. Then, to rub salt into the wound, she married my oldest brother. Father was practically smitten with Venus's ingenious, and to reward her for her valor, he announced that the line of power would be transferred upon her and Slater. Anna was never in line anyway with the challenges she faced developmentally, and Kellan and I were boys. If we cared at all about Father's crown, the desire was always dampened by the existence of our three oldest siblings, so his plan never felt like an insult. Truthfully, as the baby of the family, I loved the idea of growing up without the responsibility of being all my brothers' and sisters' failsafes. And after the loss of Mother, I don't think that Father felt inspired to keep ruling."

Madden's throat bobs. "I got to say goodbye to my mother. *Really* say it, as in I knew that our parting would be final. The same, however, could not be said for how I last interacted with my father. I think my version of goodbye included something along the lines of, *"Tell Slater to share his bride when you bring them home,"* which, knowing what ultimately happened, still turns my stomach."

My own reaction has my muscles tightening, and I bite down on the inside of my cheek to redirect the pain.

"Had I known what would become of him and the rest of my family, I would've held onto him with all my strength. I would've forced him to break the bones in my fingers to pry me off him."

I'm too antsy to sit still for much longer, so I shift my weight a bit. The closer my body drifts to the bedpost, however, the heavier I must feel to the abandoned furniture. I try not to grimace as the old thing creaks beneath my weight.

"You already know the story," Madden continues bitterly. "Your aunt and uncle have probably *raved* about it countless times over dinner—how the once mighty Victor Seagrave and his entire security league fell prey to poisoned goblets, and how his eldest son became a meal for the tiger Slater quite literally gifted her. But what you may not know is that before Diana was slaughtered, too, Venus called the palace. Andie had picked up the Dial Line, and to her utmost surprise, the new Queen of Mosacia was ordering her to get Anna, Kellan, and me out of the palace as quickly as possible. She knew how to steer a ship, but in her haste, she forgot to grab an updated map. We landed on the Isle by accident."

The mention of Diana's name pricks my conscience like a needle, and for a split second in time, I'm back inside her sanctuary hearing her reveal the curse she cast over me.

I shove the thought away, choosing to empathize with him rather than retreat into my memories. As fearful and disoriented as I was when Madden first took me to the Isle, I could not imagine being seven years old, deserting my home with no preparation, and sailing blindly towards what they could only *hope* was safety.

"The Isle was no more than camping grounds when we first

arrived, populated by nomads or Mosacian architects keen on testing their newest builds on unoccupied land. It was a lonely existence for the next few months, one plagued with unanswered questions on what happened to the rest of our family. Even at our age, we knew death had come to collect, but it was the brutal fixation on *how* that ate my younger self alive. Eventually, all our questions were answered in the form of several cases stuffed with money—*Urovian* money—which had now become the primary source of currency in Mosacia as well as their home territory, compliments of the Deragons. Not the Seagraves or even the Morgans. The *Deragons.*"

Madden seethes my family name as if the very sound of it is poisonous, and in the silence that follows, I try not to focus on how much worse it sounds on his lips than it ever did on Kellan's.

"The cash value was the equivalent of our inheritances alongside enough money for Andie to build an estate for the four of us—a way to buy our compliance and anonymity. It came with a note, too, but Andie never let us read it for ourselves. All she revealed before burning it in the fire was that it came directly from Venus herself, and for the sake of our *safety*," he snarls, "we had to create new identities for ourselves, that way our *enemies* couldn't find us."

The fact that their true enemy was the very author of that letter makes my blood run cold.

"Maia Andromeda was a scullery maid when we lived here, so no one knew her personal history or that she was ever affiliated with Sevensberg. However, just to be safe, she started asking those she met to call her Andie, a nod to the fact that she was the primary tenant of the estate. Annabelle, stubborn as she was in addition to her inability to understand this significant change, simply became Anna, and Kellan became Kit. *My* chosen identity took longer to formulate, however. Grief seemed to consume me the deepest, which made me exceedingly indignant when it came time to disguise my true self. After all I had experienced, all I had lost in Venus and Jericho Deragon's wake, I didn't understand why my *name* had to die, too.

"Everyone grieves in different ways, but my coping method of choice came through music. Listening to it. Making it myself. Learning my way across any instrument I could find. Singing myself hoarse. And as the gods would have it, we soon discovered I had become quite the virtuoso. Andie decided that my name would be Marcato—a musical term that, translated, means *played with emphasis*—but I would go by Cato for short, the hard consonant sound of the name matching my twin brother's.

"For nearly a decade, my life as the reimagined Cato Andromeda consisted of my brother, my sister, my makeshift mother, our estate, and my music. Mainly the latter. There were days—*weeks*—that I wouldn't see anyone aside from passing through the kitchen for meals because I was so consumed in crafting a ballad that expressed my emotions. Even if no one spoke, Andromeda House was never silent. My hours at the pianoforte in the sitting room, or my restless nights spent at my desk etching notes into empty sheet music as I sang aloud never left any room for it. I liked it that way, and in time, the rest of Andromeda House did, too. Anna would ask me to sing her something before bed every night. Kellan, despite insisting that my supper serenades proved to be bothersome, would always be caught tapping his foot along to the rhythm my playing provided. But Andie resonated with my music far beyond mere enjoyment, and for my seventeenth birthday, she surprised me with an acceptance letter to the premiere music and arts academy . . . in Urovia."

Madden swallows hard at the memory, one side of his mouth crooking upward in a defeated smile. "She broke the news to me that morning without telling the others. It was the first time any of us had dared to think about Urovia again, let alone consider *going* there. But she had done careful research on the program. Apparently, the academy had existed as more of a trade school for poorer citizens in the continent, a way to take up an artistic skill to find employment. But as a wedding gift when your Aunt Calliope got married, the Queen Inherit made a sizeable donation to the institution, elevating its price and overall prestige. Fortunately, I possessed the skills to be admitted, and the funds from our estate and my remaining inheritance easily covered the cost."

"That's wonderful," I sigh.

"Except I couldn't tell Kellan where I was going, not unless I wanted to be smothered in my sleep before I could make the trip. So Andie crafted my cover story; I would be making the citizen's pilgrimage into the center of the Mosacian continent, and after that, I'd settle in somewhere over there to study their music and culture. Kellan didn't even bat an eye, and neither did I as I boarded a boat and embarked on my future, just hoping that no one would grow suspicious of the identity I prepared to don like a second skin."

I never got to attend any sort of formal, public schooling, no university or international travel-based education. I can only imagine the sort of fun Madden must've had. The friends he made. The knowledge he gleaned and the joy he experienced around my current age.

He chooses not to dwell on it. "I graduated from the academy a few months after I turned twenty-three. I had set aside a month to return home and reconnect with my family before venturing back out at the start of the new year to pursue performance full-time, and while I missed Andie and my siblings, Urovian winters were the bane of my existence. I couldn't get out of there fast enough. The Isle always provided its residents with an uncanny sort of warmth, and I had grown to miss it after six years of studies."

Madden's eyes cast a traitorous glance towards the door. He means to look down the hall he's closed us off from, and I brace myself for the worst of what's to come.

"The minute I set foot back on the Isle, the very atmosphere felt . . . off. Like all the joy in being home with my family had been leached out of the air, and I felt it like the first chill of winter in an autumn wind. I staggered into Andromeda House, and all I had to do was look at Andie to know things were very, *very* wrong. That, and with how long I'd been gone, I found it hard to believe that Annabelle wouldn't have ambushed me at the door."

I extend a hand, silently assuring him that I don't need the details if it'll only hurt him. But he tells me anyways, "People with her condition don't live longer than thirty-five years on average. It was just . . . her time. The unforgivable part of it, though, was that Kellan hadn't alerted me to when, exactly, her time came."

"What?"

Anger mars his beautiful face. "When Annabelle passed, Andie panicked about sending correspondence to me at school, and when Kellan realized that I wasn't where she'd told him I was, he . . . lashed out at her. Not physically, well, not entirely at least. My guess is that the moment he found out I was in Urovia, he threatened violence against her should she reach out to me. Instead, they buried my sister without me. I lived four months of my life not knowing she was gone, and to this day, I want to tear Kellan limb from limb for it."

So do I.

"He confronted me about it just as kindly as I did last night," he says, drawing my attention back towards frustration as opposed to deep grief. "Andie had to beg me not to put Kellan six feet under for his manipulation, but I complied for her. She was the only mother I had left. What other choice did I have? Of course, that question would rear its ugly head at me when I eventually asked them to tell me where she was buried. Andie looked at Kellan with such contempt, and that's when he told me that I'd never learn unless I made up for my betrayal."

"Betrayal?" The word tastes bitter in my mouth.

"Yes, angel. The same way your family likely writhes at the thought of you even remotely enjoying your time in Mosacia Proper, the same can be said about Kellan in concerns of me being in Urovia. So he came up with a proposition: prove that I haven't entirely disgraced my heritage, and he'll tell me where they buried Annabelle. One grave in exchange for another. I think his exact words were 'You were a traitor the minute you boarded that boat without telling me. What's a little blood on your hands going to do in the long run? Unless, of course, you've come to empathize with the people who *killed our family.*'"

I shudder at the corruption Kellan believed was appropriate for his brother to take on—and then it dawns on me just how long ago that was. I do the math, discovering that Madden didn't hesitate before preparing to give his brother what he demanded of him. Heartbroken to the point of compliance.

"You likely don't remember, considering it was five years ago, but a few months after I returned to Urovia, I was invited to perform at that year's Queen's Feast. All my classmates from the academy had nearly clobbered me with congratulations, but their words meant nothing to me. Their praise never rose above the noise in my head, the buzzing of anticipation and dread and disgust for what I knew was in store. My performance was a success, but I made sure not to turn too many heads. I didn't want anyone to remember me from it, to risk that someone might try and trace my voice or my face back to a person that didn't really exist. And then, as the party slowly dissipated, I began roaming through Broadcove.

"I connected the different wings in my mind, stalked through the shadow-lined halls on silent feet, and watched as young couples crept down corridors stealing lewd touches. I realized then, as I watched it all unfold, how skilled I was at remaining concealed, and I used that to my advantage once I found my way into the kitchens. One of the pastry chefs accidentally opened a trick door, mistaking it for the pantry, and in the split second she turned her back, I slipped into the tunnels undetected."

A tear slips past my defenses, and we both dare to meet each other's gazes. I find his own sorrow starting back at me.

"I learned my way through the Broadcove's underbelly, and nobody ever came looking for me. But I knew it was better that way, because if I could pull this off—if I could kill Venus Deragon and take back my birthright, my homeland—there'd be no need to explain what happened to Cato Andromeda. I'd finally get to go back to being *me*, and the rest would sort itself out. It took about a month for me to master the underground passages and secret entryways, mainly because I started out by homing in on what routes took me directly to Venus. Of course, I quickly learned that if I wanted to be successful in my deadly endeavors, I needed to understand Jericho's routine, too.

"One day, however, there was an opening where they both had separate matters to attend to. Jericho got word from the King's Guard about something, and I wasn't quite sure where Venus was headed. All that mattered was that their room was left unattended, which bought me the perfect amount of time to steal a weapon and slip back into the darkness. I ran through the tunnels, desperate to get Venus alone and dole out my family's retribution, because who knew how long I'd be stranded there if I didn't act right then and there. Kellan insisted the kill be *Venus*, not Jericho—but when I found her holed up in a private office, she wasn't alone anymore."

Before I get the chance to turn my head in hopes of warding off the tears that spring into my eyes again, Madman's ungloved hand ticks my chin towards him. The feel of his bare skin breaks down the last of my defenses.

"You were so young. Sixteen if I had to guess. And you looked at Venus with such devotion. But I could sense that beneath your calm exterior, there burned a lonely fire of resentment. You were too composed to be the Deragon heir Kellan and I presumed you'd be, because despite sharing a vague resemblance to Venus, I couldn't trace any of your attributes back to Jericho. And that fascinated me."

"You could tell," I whimper. "From one glance?"

"Not for certain, but I had a hunch," Madden says. "The feeling only grew as I watched her reprimand you for whatever it was that day. I was so fixated on the way your face became a blank slate of understanding, but the minute Venus turned her back, your chin lowered. The look of defeat in your eyes struck me dumb, Pandora. I didn't know anything about you, and yet I *ached* for you. I wanted to tear Venus to shreds for making you feel like that . . . but I *needed* to ensure you weren't going to curl up in your room and break down because of it. So I followed you as best as I could through the tunnels, eventually tracking you down not to your personal suites, but to a private room with a harp in its center. And that's when you started singing."

We're both crying, his voice breaking on nearly every syllable. "Watching you was one thing, because your grace and beauty doomed me. I thought it couldn't get worse for me, but your voice?" He marvels, stroking my cheek with his thumb. "It poisoned the last of my goodness in the greatest way imaginable."

A fat tear falls from the corner of my eye, and Madden kisses it away.

"I never found another opening to target Venus again. Not until Queen's Feast—and it was worth it. Abandoning my plans and picking you was well worth it. Even now, I'd gladly repeat those five years going mad in the darkness of Broadcove's labyrinths and sleeping on the stony ground, because *you* were there. Waiting for *someone* to see you for who you were, not for the way everyone wanted you to be. And I wanted to be that for you more than *anything*, Pandora."

I shake my head in quiet disbelief, fighting the subtle sickness in my stomach as the dread slowly fizzles out. "That doesn't make sense to me," I whisper. "How could I, a stranger to you, anchor you in the midst of such . . . nothingness?"

"When you spend long enough in the dark, you go mad for even a sliver of light. And watching you all those years, it felt like the sun shone only for me. Like I had found a lifetime of warmth in the freezing cold just from all those stolen glances. You weren't a stranger, nor were you my enemy. You and I were kindred spirits—you just didn't know it yet. Despite coming from the two most opposite sides and viewpoints of the world, we shared in each other's pain without even realizing it. You had no idea that I even walked the earth, and yet, it felt like you *saw* me, angel. The same way I saw you."

He cradles my right hand within both of his own, and I savor the feel of his unguarded skin. "The moment I first took your hand in mine, I finally understood why so many people fled to Urovia centuries ago. They wanted to be where divinity dwelled. And in that moment, even wearing my gloves, I knew I had grasped a fragment of something holy."

Saints spare me.

"And I'm sorry I didn't tell you all this sooner, that I waited this long to come forward with the truth. The *full* truth. But I was selfish, too consumed by the fear that telling you everything would scare you away from me—that you might judge me like the other Deragons would. I cannot bear how awful it sounds now that I'm hearing it aloud, but I did it. I'd take it back if I could. I'd tell you everything just to keep your heart from breaking like it is right now, but I can't. And I'm just so, inexplicably sorry."

The word strikes a nerve. "You're sorry?"

A thousand different apologies flood his eyes in the form of brewing tears. "More than I can express."

Every ugly truth he's given me feels like nothing more than a scratch in comparison to the way *sorry* guts me like a harpoon.

"Don't start with that. It's not fair. You don't get to ask for forgiveness . . . not when you've been the only one that's ever tried to offer me the truth."

My words fail me at the confused expression on his face, and I draw closer towards the intensity of his gaze—a howling storm stirring within the gray of his eyes.

He's scared, I realize, and something bobs in my throat at the thought.

As my lips part to form invisible words of assurance, my fingers grasp his own. Twining them together.

"I'm hurting and heartbroken and drained. I'm coming to terms with so many things at once. My mother's unknown fate and the fact that there's someone out there that she might love on the same plane as me. That the Seagrave line didn't die off all those years ago like I was led to believe. Trying not to crumble under the pressure of Marzipan's death and what I've inherited from it."

Saying it aloud helps reassure me that it's okay to bend beneath the weight of it . . . so long as I remember I'm not bearing it alone.

I brush my nose against Madden's, grateful and emotional that I finally get to feel the exposed skin there. "But even amidst the mess of it all, if there's one thing I am more than anything else, it's *yours*, Madden. I am yours."

44
Pandora

A small whimper escapes Madden at the sound of his true name on my lips.

"You must know the spell you've cast on me," I say, teaching myself to be unafraid of these feelings or the prospect of laying my heart out on the line. "You must know how I began allowing you to lure me in a long time ago, and how I'm aching for the moment you'll ensnare me forever."

"Pandora," he trembles, his lips brushing mine as he says my name. "Please——"

"And maybe it was all a game. A masterful, calculated way to get me to see all the atrocities of those I trusted with my life. If so, you've won—because after what I've seen and everything you've told me, I am furious enough to learn how the hilt of a knife may feel in my hand as I drive it into someone I once looked up to. I hurt for you so fervently that I could forsake my own *family*."

The storm in his eyes settles, as if holding his stare equates to standing in the eye of a hurricane. And a stillness falls over me, a foreign sense of peace—one that tells me that he never played me. Never lied.

Madden Seagrave lost *everything*—his siblings, his parents, the security and power of his bloodline—and sacrificed his one, potential shot at retribution. He traded vengeance . . . for *me*.

"But that doesn't even seem to scratch the surface of what you deserve, and it overwhelms me. How is there *anything* I can offer you that would be worthy enough to honor what you've done for me, my love?"

"That," Madden tells me tenderly. "Your love. *Yourself.* That's all I will ever need in this lifetime. So long as you love me, my world will not carry on in vain."

My bottom lip trembles.

"It never did," I say.

And in a surge of reckless adoration, I throw myself onto him.

The kiss we collapse into is frantic, wild, and thrilling all at once. More than that, it's healing. It mends the wounds in my soul to the point where I feel an invisible force stitching me back together—or maybe that's just Madden grappling at me. His touch is hungry. His eyes are ablaze with heat before they dip down as he lowers his lips to my neck.

In my bones, I know the kiss isn't stopping here.

"Say it," I whisper as I dare to guide Madden's hands towards the hem of my dress.

His eyes go wide at my silent permission, and I hear his heart thundering beneath his chest. "I'm yours, Pandora," he says, rounding the fabric up my thighs. His eyes follow the path of his hands in a manner that makes him look like he's come undone. "I've been yours since the moment you opened your mouth and sang your way into my soul."

"Tell me that I belong to you," I plead, shifting to let the fabric move up past my waistline.

He smiles darkly at that, but his words remain gentle. "You're mine, angel. You always have been." The certainty of his statement summons shivers across my skin. "You belong to me."

The sheer possession in his voice seals my fate, and Madden guides my arms above my head to remove my dress. Before any sort of anxiety gets the chance to creep in, I kiss him deeply, fiercely. I busy my hands by fumbling with his clothes, unsure of how best to remove them—

"Slow down, angel," Madden croons in my ear, laying me out on the bed so fluidly it feels like the wind carried me there. "We've both been waiting for this for a long time, and I intend on getting it right."

My eyes burn as I drink in his handsome face for as long as he'll let me, memorizing every feature like I would lyrics to my favorite songs. I think I forget how to breathe as Madden scans me over again, the brazen eye contact setting my body aflame.

"Let me be the first and only one to ever tell you," Madden murmurs, lips peppering my collarbone with kisses before descending lower. "You look perfect like this. Skin flushed, bashful smile, no fear."

"Madden."

The desperation in my voice has his name coming out on a sigh, and the depraved sound makes an accidental reprisal as he dips to press a kiss onto the inside of my thigh. I writhe in his hold. "That's it, angel," he urges, his touch turning savage. "Sing for me."

Everything beyond this room melts away as I give myself over to him. The anxieties of learning the truth about everything, the dangers waiting for us back at Andromeda House, the years of feeling so isolated in who I was. None of it matters anymore when, in its place, our adoration abounds. And as Madden decides neither of us can hold out any longer, he vanquishes our long-standing loneliness in a blistering kiss that has him shedding the last of his barriers.

Madden leads us out of the palace for some fresh air, insisting that we cannot embrace the mid-September sun from behind the panes of the windows. And while I'm content with staying burrowed up in the sheets with him, I must admit, the warm rays casting light onto the gardens easily lure me further from the back courtyard. The trees are overgrown and the topiaries that once bore designs of grandeur have given way to nature in the absence of permanent staff. Still, I can imagine what the space would look like with the right amount of love. I shut my eyes against the warm breeze and picture public festivals, solstice parties, or even family picnics—the images deepening as Madden drapes an arm around me.

"My mother loved to host," he mumbles. "That much I know, even if I wasn't old enough to attend most of her parties."

"I like that—picturing your mother in her element."

"Did you picture her differently?"

"Not really. I mean, I've seen *actual* pictures of her before, but—"

"You have pictures of her?"

His voice comes out tortured, and only then do I think about the fact that in their haste to leave the palace, no one might've thought to grab one. "Back in Broadcove, there are troves of them. Harriet and Jericho's mother were loyal pen pals, and your mother would send photographs with every letter. I'll be sure to steal them away for you when I get the chance."

We both drink in the implication of me having to go back there sometime, but he doesn't press me about it. He merely says, "That would be wonderful."

"Seriously, though. I don't ever think about your family operating . . . normally. All I know about your family is the slander Venus and Jericho always spouted about them, the stories they told me. Is there any truth behind what I already know?"

"Well, it depends on what exactly it is you know."

"Now that I think about it," I say, chuckling at the vague memory, "they did mention you. Once. You were just a boy, you and your brother." *That* information will certainly take some getting used to. I already want to tear Kit—*Kellan*—limb from limb for deceiving me. But to think about him being mentioned to me before we ever met, and I never knew . . . I choose to focus on the here and now with Madden instead.

"Because of how young you were, the two of you were more of an afterthought in my uncle's mind. My aunt's, too. Despite my reaction earlier, Venus did mention once that you may have fancied her upon first sight."

Madden doesn't deflect, even though color rushes into his cheeks. The fact that I'm finally offered the privilege of seeing his skin blush without a mask hiding the human gesture fills me with warmth. "Old habits die hard, I suppose."

"And the Deragon genes prevail for an additional generation."

Madden presses a fleeting kiss to my temple. "What can I say? I recognize beauty when I see it."

"*Anyway*," I rein him in. "I also know that, despite the bad blood between families, the Seagraves gave Venus her tiger, Roxie. She was the most loyal friend I knew growing up, carnivorous beast aside. I'll never forget the look on Venus's face when she realized Roxie was getting too old to function properly. It was like she had lost a child."

I try not to be jealous of a dead tiger—to envy how loved she was by Venus—and Madden notices the shift in my demeanor. He promptly reverts to our earlier tangent.

"Slater was as gullible as he was headstrong. Venus just happened to be the first woman to capitalize on that part of him. Honestly, if any other objectively attractive woman would've walked into his life first and batted her lashes in his direction, he would've fallen for their whims, too. Greer . . . well, she never had much to say."

That's a light way of putting it. Greer Seagrave, Madden's middle sister, had gone mute in response to her father's abuse and retaliation for uncovering their family's dark secrets. I wonder if Madden ever knew, or if he merely thought something was wrong with her—

His fingers tip my chin towards him. "I spied on your family for five years, angel. I might know more than you do on certain matters—I just don't care to voice some of them aloud."

Understood.

He gently releases me, setting that same hand on the small of my back. "Annabelle loved animals. Learning about their behaviors, identifying their different breeds, playing with them. Our parents were frequent donors to Mosacia's wildlife conservation efforts. I only hope, for Anna's sake, that those causes managed to stay afloat after . . . everything. And Diana—"

Her face immediately brands itself behind my eyes. Were Madden touching me along bare skin, he would feel the goosebumps cropping up along my arms, my legs. I force the shiver climbing up the column of my spine to dissipate.

"She was the sibling that cared for Kellan and me the most.

Mother doted on us, sure, but in regards to our siblings, Diana loved us. *Empowered* us. She made sure we knew that our roles were just as vital as Slater's, even if our position in the bloodline made it highly improbable that we'd ever rule." He smiles solemnly at the memory of her and stares out at the horizon. "Diana saw us as people instead of princes."

Madden doesn't need to ask me if I understand the feeling. If anyone on this planet understands, it's me.

"Was she your favorite?"

"From what memory serves me, yes."

The forlorn in Madden's eyes tells me that I ought to tread towards something new, because the longer we fixate on Diana, the queasier I feel.

"Do you think," I start, testing the waters a bit, "that everything between our families had to unfold so tragically in order for us to find our way to one another?"

Madden's eyes glimmer with quiet interest at the question. "I'd like to think that in another world, where you and I weren't descendants of rival bloodlines, we would've hit it off on our first encounter."

"Is that so?"

"Absolutely, had I really been Cato Andromeda and you Pandora Prokium."

His final word jolts me, the name foreign and damning in the same breath.

"What did you just say?"

Prokium.

The sensation that courses through me then feels otherworldly, like someone in the Beyond breaches through realities and flashes me a knowing, somber smile.

"You didn't know?"

"I only ever knew my father by his first name," I stutter, the echo of his family name—my *true* family name—reverberating in my ears. "Kurt."

Kurt *Prokium*.

I spied on your family for five years, angel. I might know more than you do on certain matters.

I try to divert my attention away from the new, heart-halting piece of knowledge about the father I never got to form a relationship with. "Do you truly think we'd get along?"

"More than *get along*. It likely would've been love at first sight."

"Quite presumptuous of you to think so."

"Imagine you first saw me in the Noble Lands. Imagine that I sang a ballad before an audience of hundreds, and yet, your presence was all that tethered me to the earth. Imagine that my eyes befell you in a stunning gown that *you* wanted to wear—not something your family stuffed you into—and in one glance, I wanted to know everything about you."

My heart gallops in my chest, threatening to break open the front of my body as I picture it for myself. In the universe behind my eyes, my caddy friends grab fresh flutes of bubbly when our eyes first connect. Stars explode around him like obliterated diamonds, as if the Saints are crying out, *"It's him, Pandora! The search is over!"* I make up a song for him to sing in my head, his soothing voice and dapper suit drawing chills up the length of my spine. I let the finality of this first meeting and what it means for the rest of my days course through my entire being.

"It's a beautiful concept," I say, the words turning sad.

"Imagine it takes only that one look to know that there's no one else for us," Madden continues, painting the picture in vivid, tormenting detail. "No deception, no games, and no going back. Imagine that I court you in front of our entire community, and your loved ones and all of those around us come to accept the inevitable just as we did. Imagine, when the timing feels right, I work up the courage to ask your father for your hand, and he relents for a moment, if only because he wasn't prepared to let go of his little girl so soon in life."

My eyes fly open when I sense Madden draw impossibly closer to me. Tears scorch my eyes and fall like the first signs of afternoon rain, sudden and surprising.

How could I so deeply mourn a man I never knew firsthand? How can I mourn a reality I never got to live out with him the minute Madden brings it up? I try to fight off the sorrow, but it persists with a vengeance.

Madden delicately wipes away each tear that falls. "I would have loved you in every lifetime that fate allowed me to spend with you. Even if they weren't at your side or in your bed—even if each and every one of them forced me back into the shadows of isolation—I would consider myself eternally grateful just to exist at the same time and place as you."

I might just die if he says anything else. "Madden—"

"But the fact of the matter is, that life, that *fantasy* . . . it could've been real for us. I know it could've. And instead, Jericho took that away from you."

"What are you talking about?"

"It all leads back to him, Pandora. The root of every evil and every tragedy can all be traced back to him. Think about it. Venus never would've sideswiped the Mosacian Empire if she didn't love him, if he hadn't pursued her in the first place. If his dreams hadn't *insisted* he do so. My family would still be alive, and your father might be, too."

A horrified sob breaks in my throat, and I struggle to hold my ground.

"My father?"

"Yes, angel," he confirms bleakly. Somehow, his gaze is both apologetic and stone cold. "Jericho murdered your father."

45
Ren

The soldiers guarding Broadcove Castle treat Geneva Deragon like she isn't, in fact, a Duchess of the continent—and I know it's in efforts to further torture me.

The ruthless beatings I undergo right as my wounds begin to mend are tolerable, or at least they would be if, just once, they wouldn't force her to watch. The depth of Genny's worry hurts more than it does when they crack another one of my ribs, and every last scream she emits as they do haunts my sleep.

The only forgiving sentiment is that while they keep Genny locked in here with me, they feed her well. Three full meals as opposed to my meager one—though Geneva always makes a point of apportioning most of her servings onto my tray. "To keep you strong for when they come back," she told me the first time. Every morsel she gave me managed to keep me alive. I know that. But it doesn't quell the rage I feel when her growling stomach returns.

I don't know what day it is, only that the main door

unexpectedly flies open, casting the first beams of daylight Genny and I have seen in a long time. She shields her eyes from the sudden harshness of it, and three uniformed men appear, two of them flanking the guard that had taken me down back on the docks of Mosacia Proper.

"Get up, Setare," he barks.

"Watch your tone when you speak to him," Genny sneers.

The look in his eyes at her reproach reminds me that Genny *knows* him. Had likely grown up in the same circles of influence. And now, they both stare each other down, feeling as though they each betrayed one another in the worst possible manner.

"I don't take orders from you," he counters. "Even if you were still Duchess."

Were. The implication sinks in immediately—she's been stripped of her royal title.

I expect Genny to appear dumbstruck. Heartbroken, even. But man, am I dead wrong.

"Nadine would be embarrassed to see the person you've become," she comments without hesitation, and the casualty in which she says it is downright cruel. "But you don't need me to remind you of that. You already know."

I connect the dots quickly enough. His wife. Genny just brought his *wife* into this.

My admiration for her swells within me, even as Henry unfastens my chains from the notch on the floor. I know better than to struggle free or fight his hold, but I don't exactly make it easy for him. I stay true to my role of the damaged prisoner, going limp in his grasp to where Henry must call on his reinforcements. Genny and I share a secret smile at the fact before they carry me into the bright hallway and shut the door, sealing her back in the darkness.

They trudge us towards what I assume is one of the outer edges of the castle, and as we ascend a set of stairs, Henry's breath starts to come out labored. "You'd think slowly starving you out would make you a bit easier to carry."

"Maybe you're just old and rundown."

The comment ought to earn me a kick in the ribs, but Henry seems to find my audacity laughable. "Makes sense, now. Genny never had a mean streak, not before you."

"Go pout about it after you throw me over the balcony," I retort, guessing at the fate I'm swiftly approaching.

But that, too, gets Henry to laughing. Then, we pass through a connecting pathway from the stairs and into one of the wisteria-lined promenades. The guards throw me onto the floor, and when I glance upwards, I realize that falling to my death would be a mercy compared to what I must face now.

The gold shimmer of an illustrious crown perched upon a dark, royal brow.

And then, in her complete formal regalia, the Queen Inherit of the Damocles crouches down to my level and bares her teeth like an animal. "What the hell have you done to my sister?"

That is perhaps the most loaded question on the planet.

In my mind, there's two ways that I can go about answering this—the first being brazenly. That involves me telling Venus Deragon *exactly* what I've done to Genny, particularly when we were in the Sacred City. The devil on my shoulder grins manically at the thought, especially knowing Genny would get a kick out of seeing the look on her sister's face.

To my dismay, rationality kicks in and I choose option number two. "Is there something in particular you're referencing?"

"My guards informed me that you were aiding the duchess in escaping our forces, who were attempting to bring her home safely—"

"Guard," I correct.

"What?"

"*One* guard, Your Majesty. We picked off the rest easily enough."

The remark has her fuming, and despite never hating the Urovian monarchs the way most Mosacians do, the loathing in her eyes feels like pure bliss.

"But when Tolcher got to you first," she seethes, "Duchess Geneva came running after you. She insisted that the two of you be treated as equals. As *traitors*."

I merely shrug.

"You're only alive right now because of her."

"I'm well aware."

"Then be aware of *this*, Mr. Satare." Her lip curls as she snarls at me, her words primal and fearsome. "You will tell me what you did that inspired Genny to turn her back on her family, or I will show her what it costs to fraternize with the enemy."

"What *I* did? You're terribly mistaken, Your Majesty—because, you see, I did not drive her into enemy lands out of desperation. I did not refuse to help her find her daughter. *You* did that. All I did was treat her with the decency she expected her family to extend to her."

Venus crosses her arms over her chest, but the unimpressed look on her face is melting into rage once more. "The way you carry yourself makes me think you did more than just lend Genny a hand."

"Maybe, but it certainly didn't start out that way. In fact, when she approached *me*—alone and at the mercy of strangers who could've easily chosen to take advantage of her—I didn't even *know* she was a Deragon. Even now, I'm not so sure. After all, how could someone as kind and sacrificial as Geneva be related to *poison* like you?"

Venus strikes me across the face, and I let her. She certainly has an arm on her, and I will myself not to ease the sting.

"You don't get to tell me about sacrifice," the queen says through her teeth. "Not when I've bled Mosacia dry to make up for the treacheries it carried out against my husband."

"And you're proud of that?" I counter.

"The truest testament of love is killing on its behalf."

"And what if you're wrong? What if the greatest act of love is showing mercy?"

The Queen Inherit of the Damocles stares at me like I've just pulled a weapon on her, like the very concept of *mercy* is foreign to her, appalling.

With lethal grace, Venus crosses the remaining distance. I physically feel the heat in her eyes as she tells me, "Merciful love always ends in defeat, but violent love conquers worlds. Tell me which you would rather place your faith in."

"Whichever ensures Geneva's and Pandora's happiness. You certainly can't say the same."

Venus smiles, but her words carry venom. "Lock him up."

46
Madden

Pandora has been suspiciously calm since I broke the news about her father.

I remember the day I learned for certain what had happened to him. Four years and seven months underground, I'd caught wind of a conversation between Jericho and Venus in their suites after Duchess Geneva had excused herself early from dinner. Their trick door was a tapestry hung on the western wall, so while I couldn't see their faces, the canvas didn't diffuse the sound of their voices.

"She looked sick," Jericho had remarked.

To which his wife had insisted, "It's nothing."

"You only say that when you know something."

"I know that you don't want to start down this path."

"I thought there were no secrets between us——"

"It's Kurt's birthday," she finally blurted out, and the room went ghastly quiet. "Or it was yesterday. It's the first year that Geneva missed it, and the guilt is eating her alive."

It had been a span of several minutes before either of them spoke again to the point where I feared they'd heard my breathing somehow. Jericho eventually broke the silence. "She told me she forgave me. Was she lying?"

Venus pondered on the thought for a minute. "No, my love. If she were lying, she wouldn't still be bothering to hide the truth from Pandora; she'd poison her against you. Deep down, I think it's herself she can't forgive, because it's one thing to look past your choices. It's another thing entirely to rationalize what she's done for us already in addition to what she's unknowingly doing now."

Jericho made a noise as if to say, "And what is that?"

"She's forgetting him, Jericho—and maybe that's a good thing. For your sake, I recommend you forget about him, too."

My heart shattered for a girl I hadn't gotten to share a conversation with, yet I knew her so intimately. I pictured how Pandora's lips would quiver before they gave way to tears. I wondered how foul her language would turn as she rattled the sky with her rage.

And yet, when I revealed the final, terrible truth I'd gathered from underground . . . nothing.

In fact, Pandora insisted that she was fine. That the news felt like a drop of water in a very deep bucket. That she never knew him anyway, so what did it matter how he died if everyone else had moved on.

Only I *know* it matters. They never offered Pandora the chance to have closure—and given that her entire upbringing was impacted by Kurt Prokium's death, she *deserved* to know.

I know better than to be greedy or handsy with Pandora after news like this, especially when there's likely a visceral reaction building beneath the surface. Maybe she doesn't know it yet, but I do. I sense what I cannot see, what she does a stellar job of hiding. But I also know better than to bring her back to Andromeda

House too soon.

So instead, I take her back to the docks to fish, or to the gardens to pick berries. Despite never having picked up the former hobby, she's surprisingly good at reeling in a few sizable cod—likely because she's patient, but also because she's strong. Stronger than anybody gives her credit for.

Pandora Deragon proves to be most formidable when she's quiet. The kind of woman people ought to silence themselves for when she stops participating in discussions. The kind of woman who could summon a storm with a single word—and with the blessing she inherited from Marzipan, I can only imagine the devastation and weight each of her words carry now.

And it's that understanding that now has me leading the two of us into the massive library on property. I was just beginning to learn how to read when everything had come crashing down, so it took me a few tries to find this place, but Pandora didn't seem to mind. In fact, she seemed at home within the extra bouts of silence as we perused the halls.

The moment she crosses the threshold, however, Pandora hurdles for the oldest looking tomes, likely to test theories her newfound blessing has already proven factual. Sure enough, the minute I come behind her and scan the pages, I confirm they aren't printed in either of our native languages.

"Fascinating," Pandora sighs, no tinge of sadness lingering there. Only curiosity.

"What does it say, angel?"

My name for her makes her cheeks pinken. "I'm not truly *reading* yet, just . . . getting used to seeing foreign text with my eyes even though my brain comprehends everything so flawlessly." She goes quiet for a moment before shutting the book and sliding it back into its spot. She fans at the dust that scatters in response.

"Say something in your language, Madden."

"*Non ci sono limiti al mio amore per te*," I tell her seamlessly.

A small sound reminiscent to a hiccup bubbles out of her in surprise, and the blush in her face deepens. "*Stai attento, Madden. La tua voce in questa lingua mi fa delle cose.*"

"I bet it does," I whisper before stealing a kiss. I lean in too far and tip her backwards, but I catch her just as she loses her balance. The feel of her tightly grasping my shoulders reminds me so much of the way she'd clung to me days before, pleading with me to keep her this happy and unhinged forever. A wicked smile creeps across my lips at the memory. "Maybe I'll tell you how good you feel in *my* language next time."

"Don't tempt me," she whispers before coming back for more—

Something groans from a faraway corridor, and the sound has Pandora ducking out of my arms. On high alert, she waits for something else to alert its presence, but all that remains is silence.

"Maybe something fell over," I reason.

Pandora isn't entirely convinced, but when we both straighten out, she looks over me again. Her eyes snag on my casual state of dress save for the sword on my back. I'd given her my fishing pole this morning and resorted to spearing whatever I could catch, but I can tell that she's still enthralled by it. "Were you hiding that thing under your cloaks all this time?"

The innocence in her voice makes my grin deepen. "Perhaps."

"It's beautiful."

"You think so?"

She nods eagerly. "What's its name? I assume you name all your weapons?"

Of course she remembers, my heart beams, and I unsheathe the weapon from behind my back. She assesses its density upon first touch, but her intrigue only sparks further as she wraps her fist around the hilt. "Hellfire."

"Named after what the pain feels like to face it head-on?"

"Precisely."

Pandora pauses for a moment, looking over the sword with a dark reverence that I can't read clearly. All I know is her studious gaze pierces something within me. "Maybe I ought to have one, too," she proposes shyly.

I'm one step ahead of her, reaching into my jacket. "I agree, you should have something to protect you, but nothing as overtly large as Hellfire. Something you can conceal easily."

When her eyes befall the weapon I have in mind, Pandora quickly trades Hellfire for the gleaming dagger I present her.

She studies the blade with an expert's eye, assessing the gleam of the silvery, sharp end. The golden hilt flickers in the faint, evening sun, but it's the bloodred jewel in its center that truly fascinates Pandora. The mythical prism stares back at her, and when her eyes go wide, I almost fear that she knows exactly where I found it.

But she shakes her head, as if to convince herself that whatever thoughts started to arise in her mind, they were ridiculous and did not deserve any more of her attention. "Crimson," she mumbles.

"I thought a piece of home would comfort you, even if the object itself isn't comforting."

Though her responding laugh is subdued, it sends warmth through my aching bones. "Why give me this now?" she asks hesitantly.

"I feel confident enough that you won't disembowel me with it."

"You thought I'd be able to successfully take *you* down?"

She has no clue. Pandora has no earthly idea that she didn't need a weapon to best me. She could sink me with a song. She *did*—the first night she played the harp I commissioned for her and sang for me—it was a miracle I didn't surrender right there and then.

"Don't act so modest. I saw you train in Broadcove. I may have you in size and in stealth, but you have me in speed."

You just have me, my lungs beg me to speak aloud.

Then, Pandora mutters to herself, her voice wistful and contemplative, "Perhaps I should name mine, too."

I refasten Hellfire and give her the necessary quiet she desires to comb through her initial ideas, swallowing the urge to provide any suggestions. It's not that I think she'll come up with something *bad*, per se, but I fear the prospect of her naming a dagger something painstakingly unoriginal. Ruby, for instance, after the glimmering stone in the center of its hilt.

Then again, perhaps I should just be thankful that Pandora didn't immediately recognize the blade from her aunt's jewelry trove.

"Heart Punisher," Pandora finally settles on.

Pride swells within me at the name, and Hellfire grazes the slope of my shoulder in equal acknowledgement. "It's perfect."

I wake up shivering, and when I reach for Pandora, my hands fumble with sheets and empty space.

"Angel?" I yawn, hoping my head deceives me, still in the haze of sleep.

But a passing glance towards the rusted nightside table—to the vacant surface where Heart Punisher used to lie—sends me skyrocketing out of bed. I don't bother hunting down a shirt or a pair of shoes before I start tearing through the dusty halls.

"Pandora!" I don't bother keeping my voice calm. "Pandora—"

Suddenly, a voice drifts from down the hall, its words unintelligible, but distinctly frantic. A beat later, I make light of its tone—pleading.

"*Pandora!*" I roar. "Tell me that you're safe!"

The voice cries out again, the words more distinct this time. Right as I make them out, I realize that they don't belong to Pandora at all. The next ones do, though, and whatever they are, they're said on a vicious sneer.

She's making one last stand.

"*PANDORA—*"

A gruesome noise echoes from the hallway to my right, and I dive headfirst towards the source in hopes of reaching Pandora before she starts screaming or gushing blood. The door flies off its hinges as I burst into the room.

Pandora doesn't lay crumpled on the floor nor trapped in the corner.

No, she stands with her back turned, Heart Punisher pointing down in a death grip, scarlet dripping from the tip of the blade.

"What happened?" I ask roughly.

Pandora says nothing, merely turning her head to look me in the eyes—revealing the blood coating her beautiful face crimson.

"I got even."

I sidestep her to see who she's slain in the night, only to thrum with horrified excitement as I take in the body.

Thatcher Chumley aged rather poorly after jumping ship to the Urovian cause, but seeing the traitor in a bloodied heap on the ground fills me with an undeniable sense of pride. Pandora had all the control in this altercation, all the power. I don't know how Chumley found us here, nor *why* he thought it'd be smart to intervene, but Pandora standing tall amidst her first kill is . . . electrifying.

I got even.

I shot Ardian Asticova—a man born of Mosacian blood and bred into Urovia. In a way, I slaughtered one of my own, but I did it for her. To get her away from them.

But Pandora . . . she didn't kill for me like I did for her. She did it for *herself.* And somehow, that's a hundred times more enticing.

Pandora stares after me, her eyes unblinking and smoldering, and it's only then that I remember she might be in shock.

"Are you okay?"

"They have my mother."

All the air drains out of the room.

"Venus and Jericho have my mother locked in their cells, awaiting trial alongside her companion. Then, Chumley told me that if I cooperated—if I went with him and abandoned you— they would agree to grant Mother a full pardon."

And then, Pandora Deragon's blood-drenched frown curves upward, into a disturbed smile.

"Funny how quickly they forget what they taught me. *We don't negotiate with people who think threatening us earns them anything,*" she recites, mimicking Venus so well it's almost eerie. "If this were a rescue mission, Chumley wouldn't be transferring a message. He'd be dragging me out of this palace kicking and screaming. They've made it clear that they only care about me if I'm disobeying their orders, so I'm done playing nice. They want a ruthless heir? I'll give them one. They want me to come home? I'll come home— and I'll rain hell down on their doorstep so they know *exactly* why I've come back."

Fury scorches the kind soul I had always seen in the depths of her brown eyes, and I try to mask the awe blooming in my chest at the strength she exhibits, failing miserably. "And if anyone stands in your way?"

I don't bother saying Jericho's name aloud, not when the mere implication of him might send her spiraling further. Even so, apathy paints a seductive smile over her full lips before she presses them against my mouth, the touch warm compared to an answer that feels like frostbite.

"Let's hope their headstones will accept my condolences," she finally returns.

My angel of music, prepared for whatever battle between flesh and blood comes our way.

My angel of death.

47
Kellan

All week, Andie and I have been talking in circles regarding what transpired the night Madden confronted me on the porch. Tonight, however, is the first time I've dared to bring up loyalties, and Andie is having *none* of it.

"You turned on me."

"You turned on *her*," she counters.

"Must you insist that Pandora isn't the enemy here?"

"For the last time, Kellan. Bloodlines do not define every individual within it," she bristles, baring her teeth like a wild beast. "If that were the case, I would've let the Hive swarm you and the rest of your siblings, because Saints forbid I raise up three miniature Victor Seagraves."

A wave of wrath ripples through my entire body at the name of Urovia's naval forces, at the mention of *Saints* as opposed to gods.

My father was a man of great power . . . but of what else, I'm uncertain. Six-year-olds don't tend to fully comprehend the magnitude of what a crown symbolizes, just that they reflect the light well. I didn't know him beyond his role as a father very well, and while I wouldn't disservice him and say he was a bad father, he was always tense. Borderline hostile.

"I understand that you are heartbroken—"

"I am *not* heartbroken," I bite back. "I never let her in enough for her to break my heart, and that's for the best."

She didn't break my heart, but somehow, even at arm's length, she managed to bludgeon it.

Or maybe I did it to myself—because of course I couldn't have my cake and eat it, too. I couldn't despise the people and the culture that composed her entire life and expect her to find me endearing.

"I understand you are reeling," Andie amends. "But the fact is, you *scared* me. At best, you were going to maim the poor girl, and I was not going to have any part of it. Even now, it doesn't matter that you're the estate owner here or that you're now the first in line for a throne that was stolen from you—you will *not* treat Pandora or any other woman like that again. You're almost thirty years old, Kellan Seagrave. *Act* like it!"

It's silent for a moment as I digest the greatest bout of fury I've ever experienced from Maia Andromeda—and then, slow claps sound from down the main hall.

Speak of the devil.

Pandora leans against one of the study columns that supports the weight of the second floor, one foot crossed over the ankle with hands settled on her hips. She wears a snide smile like a well-tailored suit, and she dons an onyx gown that makes her typical dark eyes look bright with mischief.

"Nice to see another woman putting you in your place," she says by way of greeting.

I want to claw her eyes out.

Andie's attention frantically darts between me and Pandora, who appears to have ventured here unaccompanied. Brave. *Too* brave. Andie reads the urge I have to take advantage of her arrival, and quickly jumps to Pandora's unknowing rescue. "You're back! What a lovely——"

"I'm here to speak with your son."

The words are full of contempt, and Andie mouths the words, "*Oh dear.*"

"I'll just be in the kitchen if you need me," she forces out, which is code for *I'll be within earshot in case either of you try to kill each other.*

When Andie departs and the door eases shut behind her, I settle down onto the sofa in the reading room and refuse to make eye contact. "Where'd you run off to this time, Princess?" With everything out in the open, now, there's no point in pretending that her name doesn't make steam come out of my ears.

"Sevensberg Palace."

I dare not flinch at the revelation; at the way she's not even trying to beat around the bush.

"Madden told me everything," she adds.

The use of my brother's name stings like a fresh wound, but I refuse to let the sensation show. "I see. So you've come to beg me to reconsider."

"Reconsider what?"

The words taste sour in my mouth. "Not telling him where Anna's buried."

Pandora takes a suggestive step towards me, eyes full of heat and surety. "No, actually. I'm not keen on inserting myself in the middle of sibling disputes, at least not more than I already have."

She winks in a way that makes me want to set Andromeda

House on fire. "Why come back here, then?"

"I have a proposition for you."

"I don't work with people who play me for a fool—"

"Help me stage a coup against the Deragons."

Pandora's face gives away nothing, and the longer I think that she's *genuinely* proposing the bomb she just dropped, I laugh straight in her face, keeling over at the middle. "You? A *coup?*"

She nods once, her gaze unfaltering. Shock aside, I know better than to insist she's still joking around. "No uncertainty?"

"None."

"Oh, come on, princess. You can't possibly expect me to believe—"

I feel her hand at my throat before I see it, and I choke out a gasp.

"I want what you want, now, with one minor adjustment." The pulse in my neck hammers against her iron-clad grip. "*Jericho* dies, and I get to be the one to kill him."

Something cataclysmic shifts in me. Maybe it's the rage turning her blood hot beneath her skin, or maybe it's the fact that she has me pinned to the wall with one hand. Whatever it is, it empties out my mind completely. It doesn't matter what changed or why she's so insistent on Jericho as opposed to Venus—because I can see it in her eyes that she's out for blood. There's no faking it.

Pandora pulls her hand away, trusting that I won't lunge for her, and my lungs burn for the fullness of air. "What's in it for me? Because taking the final blow from me already puts you at a disadvantage."

She smiles in a way that tells me she already anticipated my rebuttal. "You help me pull this off, and I'll give you something no one else can offer you."

I cross my arms and lean back against the doorframe, feigning disinterest even as my mind whirs to life with curiosity.

"I'll translate every foreign tome you own, both here in Andromeda House and the Sevensberg Palace library."

Laughter swallows me whole again, this time to the point of shedding tears. I worried it would have something to do with the books I value so highly, but this? The fact that Pandora thinks she could accomplish that—or at least make better headway than I already have—is *absurd*. I hold out a hand, silently begging her to let me catch my breath before she gets all pouty and exclaims that she's not joking. It's short lived to say the least.

"I'm serious, Kellan."

The use of my birth name sucks all the humor out of me.

"Oh, please. Your royal tutors didn't care to teach you other languages. It would go against the whole mass assimilation blueprint your *parents* laid out."

She doesn't lash out at the dig, warning sign number two that she isn't messing around. "You're right. They didn't. But I'll prove it to you anyway. Pick any book off your shelf that's not documented in the Urovian tongue and ask me to translate it."

I point a finger towards my collection. "Second row from the top, fifth book from the left—the one with the periwinkle spine."

Obediently, Pandora climbs the sliding ladder, shifting her weight so it glides across the floor. My selection is the only item in my catalog that I know Pandora couldn't fake, because when she first started reading through my belongings, I ensured she never came across it. Tucked it away from sight.

Andie had grabbed the diary in her final moments of panic before boarding us on a getaway ship. I remember asking her about it all those years ago, noting that it looked more like a journal than an actual book, to which she had told me it was hers. Once Madden left Andromeda House and I'd grown fond of literature, however, she came clean about who the diary truly belonged to.

"Read the second paragraph of the third entry," I say to Pandora.

She opens the pages, and I watch her nose crinkle at the smell of them. Not with distaste, but with sadness. Time, it seems, did not dilute the smell of Mother's perfume—and I almost insist she close it so more of it doesn't fade away. Her mouth opens, beginning to form the first syllable. Then, she stops. Flattens her lips.

"Stumped so easily?" I dare to ask.

Her eyes narrow in defiance before she directs them back to my mother's handwriting.

"How long ago did your father lose his loving nature? I'd like to think that somewhere, floating in the realm before human birth, you might know the answer. Or perhaps I don't want to know at all. Victor's anger rears its ugly head at me the more you grow, the sicker I become. If nothing else, know that I don't blame you for how your progress has depleted my strength. That, and if I have hoisted you into a world you may grow to resent, I'm sorry. It's just that nobody needs me the way you will, and I'm not sure how much longer I can live a life of being utterly unneeded."

Pandora gently closes the diary, unwilling to read another word. I see the heartbreak of what she just voiced descend into the dark depths of her eyes—the connection she draws back to her own mother.

"How?" I say through trembling lips.

Pandora shakes her head. "I can't believe you made me read that to you."

"How did you translate that so easily? So *fluently?*"

"The Saints you hate so much," she says calmly, "they're real.

Whether you like it or not, they're *real*."

The vainglorious image of Venus and Jericho hand in hand, looming over the world they usurped for their own benefit in the name of being *blessed*, burns my eyes like a brand. I'd heard the claims—studied the histories—but never believed in it firsthand. Didn't want to.

"Marzipan had the gift before me," she continues, her voice drying up in her throat. That would explain all the books and the way she could communicate with anyone and everyone at the drop of the hat. "But she passed it down to me after the King's Guard killed her."

My stomach hollows out.

Now I know why she's going after Jericho.

But even without that context—the concrete justification that causes even the kindest of souls to pick up a sword—I succumb to the proof of what she's offering me in exchange. "I'm only agreeing because your translations will save me decades of labor and will likely uncover a lot of buried knowledge. Not because I like this version of you."

"Well, you considered killing the kinder version of me. Maybe you just don't like what you can't control."

The jab is merited, but it fills me with disdain, nonetheless. "Tell me, Pandora," I whisper, noting the way her breathing turns shallow when I use her name. "If Madden told you to stand down, to not pursue violence, would you listen?"

"He'd never ask me to put aside my feelings for what *he* thinks is best," she counters. "And it's too late for him to insert his opinion on the matter, anyways."

I stare and stare after her, my face blank amidst the sinister implication.

"I'm not sure which is worse. The fact that after all my years of fighting off my family's bloody habits, I must cave into them just to make my stand—or the fact that I'm not frightened by the consequences of doing so at all. Either way, I'll get over it eventually."

It's almost like she already has.

"That's the thing about falling in love with the villain," I tell her grimly. "You end up becoming one yourself in the process."

She raises a brow amidst an otherwise bored expression. "Spare me the lecture and help me make this happen."

Whatever Pandora Deragon I thought I had a hold on, she blew away with the wind long ago. I shake my head at the comprehension of it all, the way the aggressiveness in her eyes wears me down by the minute. "Have it your way, then. I take it the three of us are carrying this out together?"

"That's correct."

"Well . . . where is he, then?"

"Madden?" Pandora only grins back at me as she makes for the kitchen. "Taking Thatcher Chumley's head to Honeycomb Harbor."

48
Geneva

Food provisions are cut in half. We get no visitors. Time moves at a glacial pace the longer we go without seeing the movement of the sun.

But the chains that keep us bolted to the floor, just out of arm's reach of each other, sinking morale to a dangerous level. I haven't touched Ren since I covered his body with mine back on the Mosacian shoreline, and if I don't make some sort of contact soon, I'll surely spiral towards insanity.

The only thing that keeps my mind at bay are the notes.

Mysteriously filed in sporadic time increments, handwritten updates Ren and I otherwise wouldn't have known about come taped to the bottom of our stew bowls. I'd discovered the first one by accident, nearly slicing my fingers as I repositioned my soup bowl in my chained hands.

Chumley's dead. His head turned up in the Harbor. Someone's sending a message.

"A warning is more like it," Ren supposed. The message had kept us questioning things for hours. Who sent it? How did they sneak it past the staff in charge of delivering our meals? What would the next one say? Would there even be another one?

Three servings later, another one turns up.

> *Jericha and Venus do not sleep much these days*
> *—likely in fear of what they may see.*

The next two come in at the same time, one addressed to me and the other to Ren. Seconds after he receives his message, Ren slides it over to me for my own evaluation.

> *Venus convinced the guards to stop beating you. I don't know what you told her, but it worked.*

Meanwhile, I keep mine tucked in close to my chest, and don't feel an ounce of remorse about it.

> *He's cute. If you two start screwing, don't let the guards hear you.*

"Saints, Calliope," I say under my breath. Only she could make me laugh after weeks in this hellhole.

"What's that?"

"The notes are coming from my oldest sister."

Ren and I wait for a fifth message. Outside of our theories, we don't talk about our pain, our hunger, our thirst. Instead, we talk about the past—because talking about a future we may not have beyond this room might just do us in.

Today, Ren asks me, "Was there ever a time when you wanted to change your name?"

"What? My first name?"

"Mmhmm."

My face scrunches up at the idea. "I don't think so. I've always thought mine was pretty."

"It is."

I blush. "Did you?"

"Oh, yes. There were a few girls named Wren in my town, so it got confusing when young ladies would call after their friends."

"I guess, but it shouldn't matter who else shares your name if the meaning of it is something positive. Mine means juniper tree, a nod to the way our home was built around a grove full of them."

I only allow myself a few moments to drift back in time and mentally walk back through the place we once called home. I see everything as it was before tragedy struck. My father's there, doting on my mother in the kitchen. Calliope and Venus bickering by the fireplace over something so trivial. And me, perched on the lip of the lowest stair step, watching it all without the slightest inclination that we're poor—for what is poverty in the wake of such overwhelming peace?

"What does your name mean?" I rasp, returning to the present.

"Depends on the translation. Mosacian dialects say that it means honesty or cleverness. But in the Urovian tongue . . ."

"Yes?"

Ren smiles at the floor. "It means love."

It's quiet for a moment, too quiet. The silence is downright provoking, to the point where I'm on the verge of word vomiting my soul onto the floor, and—

"Did Pandora ever want a sibling?"

A whole new kaleidoscope of butterflies run amuck in my

stomach at the question. "Not at all." I laugh, the movement feels like sandpaper in my throat.

"Really?"

"Absolutely not. She got to watch her three cousins fight for attention between *two* parents, so she enjoyed being the center of my universe."

Ren chuckles, but soon groans at the way laughter brutalizes his damaged ribs. I wince for a moment, but he's always known how to distract me from his misery. "Say that her wants weren't part of the equation. Only yours. Would you have wanted another child?"

For a fleeting moment, I'm not forty years old with an adult daughter. I'm not a Urovian Duchess or the secret birth mother of its beloved, musically gifted princess. I look at Ren Satare—hear the gentleness in his curiosity—and my soul feels ageless. Invincible against every dreaded hurdle life has forced me to scale.

"Not alone, no. But in a world where I met you sooner . . ." I whisper. "Yes."

Somewhere in the movement of my bashful smile, my eyes had fluttered shut. My face had tried to hide along the curve of my hiked shoulders. But when I will myself to look at Ren again, I find tears shining at the brim of his kind eyes. His laugh lines deepen as he studies my face.

"Ren?"

"I'm so disastrously in love with you, Genny," he sighs with the same reverence one would pray with.

I go stark still at the same moment his body finally, fully relaxes. The confession frees him.

"I'd be a damned fool not to tell you how deeply I love you," he goes on. "Not because we're likely on death's doorstep or because we may never get out of here—but because you simply *need* to hear me say it. I'm a single man in my late thirties who's spent his entire life searching for adventure. But it all makes sense now, the longing that felt so useless all those years. The relentless urge to scour the world for something more. It's like my soul knew that you were out there, far from my reach but still promised to appear someday."

The words make my heart soar and swell in my chest, drawing phantom tears out from the depths of my eyes.

"From the moment you conned that cinnamon loaf and kept trying to talk to me, I knew I was in trouble. The good kind. The kind that all my buddies fell into—the kind I gave them hell for. It only got worse with time, how much you were starting to mean to me. I'll admit, most nights, I would think back on our conversations that day to ease into sleep. I'd dream of you. But the minute you bounded towards the shore, towards Pandora, I *saw* the depth of your love for her with my own two eyes, and it snapped something inside of me. To imagine a reality where you could even come to love me a *fraction*—"

Sobs burst out of him like a dam, and tears of my own steadily drip off the slope of my chin. "A fraction as much as you love her," Ren resumes, chest heaving. A piece of my soul sings at the knowledge that he can be his perfect, shattered self with me. "But then, you gave it all up. You gave *her* up, just to be with me. To rot in here with me."

"I'll never go anywhere without you, Ren," I weep. "Even into death itself, I will walk with you, hand in hand."

We struggle against our restraints, and for the first time since our arrival, Ren and I manage to intertwine our fingers. The touch unravels us all over again.

"I know most people anticipate finding the love of their life by the time they turn thirty, but there were days—years, really—

where I figured the great love of my life would be nothing more than the world I'd get to explore. But all it took was you," Ren laughs, "initiating this crazy cross-country chase to find your daughter for me to realize that you *are* the world. *My* world."

There will be time to tell him everything later. How he showed himself to me in the temple's sanctuary, and how I've been a lost cause ever since. How my heart fused to his own that night we shared in Vesta. How, if I'm being honest with myself, I was doomed from the very first look. But for now, I offer him the truest thing I know.

"My love for you transcends every struggle I've faced, every year I endured unknowingly waiting for you. There's nothing in my life that fulfills me more than being with you, Ren. Than loving you—"

The feeding slot opens again, and Ren and I go ghastly still.

No food. No bowls. No cutlery.

Just a set of fiery eyes staring at me through the gap. Eyes I'd recognize anywhere.

"Calliope?"

Beneath dark lashes, her eyes dart over the two of us, likely assessing any lasting damage we've endured. And then, she whispers in warning, "Cover your heads," before dropping what I first think is a rock through the feeder and bolting backwards. Ticking fills the room.

This time, it's Ren who rushes to shield me. Metal groans and gives way as his chains snap free, and his body plasters itself above mine. His warmth and friction destroy me in the best way imaginable.

And then, the bomb goes off.

The force of it shakes the room, and I hear Ren groan in surprise rather than pain. Smoke clouds coat the room in ash, us included. Suddenly, a slender piece of metal fiddles with the part of my chains that keep me pinned to the floor, going free moments later.

Calliope hauls me over her entire frame, fearing that the blast rendered me immobile, and Ren doesn't move to tear her away from me—even with how badly he wants to touch me again. "Calliope," I mumble again, my eyes trying to adjust to the sunlight coming in from the windows. But it appears as though the smoke has followed us out here, and my lungs ache.

"The kids are out. Eli's out. But I had to come back for you."

My head swims. "Out? What do you—"

A horrible, crumbling noise further down the wing shudders in response, and Calliope presses a kiss to my temple, crying in earnest. "I should've done more for you both, and I should've done it sooner. I shouldn't have been so worried about what they'd do to me if they found the notes I sneaked in with your food. I was a *coward*."

"No, Calliope—"

"It's happening, Genny," my sister tells me with such alarm in her eyes, her voice. "The vision that sent Venus over the edge all those years ago, it's happening *now*. And if you don't get out of here, it'll take you both with it."

Calliope means to make a run for it, but I clamp my hands down on her wrist, not wanting to let her go.

"*Genny*," Ren says in a tone that makes my skin prickle with nerves.

Another blast sounds from somewhere deep in the castle, and that's when I see it—flames clawing up the columns beyond the window panes, ash streaming towards the sky and tarnishing the otherwise beautiful sunset.

Broadcove is burning.

"We need to go," Ren mutters.

Calliope assesses Ren with unwavering authority—the eldest daughter within her shining through. "Go through the tunnels. Genny knows the way, and fire won't penetrate the stone down there."

Just like that, Calliope fearlessly runs into the chaos, darting around the flames that threaten to lick up her legs and consume her. And with a tight squeeze of Ren's hand, I will myself to tear through the castle until we reach the trick door into the tunnels.

49
Pandora

Kellan, Madden, and I had discussed the plan several times over, ensuring there were no margins for error. But no matter our preparation efforts, nothing prepares me for the real thing.

To go unrecognized, Madden supplied us with some of his personal items. Dark cloaks, hooded sweaters, leather gloves, and midnight-black boots—along with skeletal masks to match his previous masquerade. We sail into Honeycomb Harbor in an unassuming ship, whereby Kellan emerges first, Hellfire slung across his back. I don't allow myself to watch him make his course uphill—whether he must use Hellfire against anyone standing in his way. As Kellan uses the maps Madden and I drew up of the Broadcove tunnels to create a diversion, Madden and I scale the sloping hill and split up at its peak. There, Madden waits for the signal to know that Jericho has been separated from Venus, and then—with Whisper's prompting—Madden will bring him to me.

And I wait here, hyperaware of every sound in the cathedral

and beyond it.

The stain glass windows within Zayanya are notched open, letting the early autumn air stream into the hallowed space. It grazes my arms through my sleeves, chilling me to the bone. I'm on guard here, but I knew this would be the spot—the one place in Broadcove that guards couldn't intervene in. Sacred in the way Vesta is back in Mosacia.

I never basked in the glory of this place before. The one time I came here, I felt like I was trespassing on holy ground, able to sense the ghost of something divine but not able to experience it fully. The only thing that kept me from running out of the cathedral was Venus. I couldn't have been older than seven, but she brought me here so that she could perform the ritual needed to summon her Patron Saint. It was the first and only time I was able to lay eyes on my grandmother.

Correction, my great aunt. After years playing along with a lie, it's hard to discern the truth. Lies felt like laws I had to abide by, and back then, if nothing else, I knew for certain that Venus and I were two very different people. Not just because of our personalities, but because her blood on an altar could summon spirits. All mine could do was stain the pristine craftsmanship.

But not anymore.

It isn't lost on me that as I stride down the aisle towards the basin of water, I'm refuting a long-instilled image of me getting married here—walking towards my groom. I'd grown up under the impression that I'd marry a nobleman of reputable status and civilized character. Would it have been for love? Younger me certainly hoped and prayed so. Present tense me, despite the apprehensions of what today may bring, still believes she found something infinitely better.

I shed my Madman mask, dropping the hood of my cape as

I do, and remove one of my thick gloves. Then, I dislodge Heart Punisher from where I sheathed it against my pants, grasping the hilt before I can chicken out of drawing blood. I pierce my palm. Dark red pools instantly, dripping into the bowl, and delicately, I run the pad of my finger over the open wound. Paint it across my mouth.

I do not recite the words that litter the star-speckled ceiling, nor do I pray for a revelation I know will come. Instead, I close my eyes and call out through a tortured whisper, "I need you, Marzipan."

The water from the bowl whirls through the air, materializing into the image of my friend from beyond the grave faster than I expected it to. Streams of it are still moving upward to accentuate her frame when her voice beams, "I was hoping I'd hear from you soon."

I nod hard, swallowing with equal intensity. "I miss you."

"Is that why you summoned me?" she asks softly.

"No. I mean, yes, I miss you terribly. I think, even seeing you in this form, I'll always miss you. But . . ." Suddenly, it's hot and cold all at once. A shiver racks my body at the same time my brow begins to bead with anxious sweat. "I wanted to ask you about the way you died."

"Oh," is all she says.

Somehow, even beyond death, her voice sounds broken.

"Did it hurt?"

Her apparition drops its gaze towards the base of the altar. "Beyond compare."

Steel-cold loathing coats my veins with iron at her answer.

"The main one among the group," Marzipan adds quietly. *Henry*. "He recognized me on sight. I don't know how, but he did. And I don't . . . I don't think he wanted to kill me. He knew the laws of the Sacred City. The troops with him, though, they didn't care. Pan, they—"

"You don't have to relive it," I cut in.

But Marzipan shakes her head, droplets dotting the floor—as if insisting I *need* to hear this.

"They broke a rib for every tribe in Mosacia."

Dear Saints.

"That's pretty much all it took to take me down. You knew me. I was . . . smaller than most." It sickens me to hear her talk about herself in past tense. "And then, when they started to see that breathing was becoming unbearable, they told me to utter my last words in a language *they* could understand."

I want to rip every last one of them limb from limb. Henry Tolcher, too, given he stood by.

"What did you say?" I ask, dreading her answer.

"Nothing," she sighs. "I chose to stay silent."

"You . . . you did?"

Marzipan nods with quiet pride. "Sometimes, the wisest use of one's words is not to use them at all. Besides, I knew that far greater words of mine would live on through you."

"Marzi . . ."

"Promise me that you'll tell them everything. All that I've written. All that you know. All that you've seen and heard and cried over. Tell them about the man in a mask who tore through nations to get to you. Tell them about the friendship that destroyed me in one way but saved me in so many others—"

"*Marzi,*" I groan, crying in earnest.

"If you get out of here, Pandora, promise me you'll do that. You'll keep this legacy alive."

My heart swells and sinks at the same time. On one hand, Marzipan is offering me the one thing I've been wanting for years, a legacy that doesn't involve conforming to cruelty. A chance to be my own person and make a difference positively for both nations as opposed to one.

And on the other . . . "*If* I get out of here?"

That's when the water forming Marzipan doesn't drop into the bowl, but mists. *Evaporates.* The screams from beyond the cathedral come next, shrill and spanning from all around me. Then, an uncanny *heat* courses through the open windows.

I turn to see the horrors for myself.

Kellan assured us back at Andromeda House that the fire would be controlled. A distraction to draw in the troops stationed at the harbor, a pointed signal to let Venus and Jericho know that we meant business.

Somewhere along the way, however, Kellan Seagrave got greedy.

I flee Zayanya Cathedral with reckless abandon, my hand still bleeding beneath my glove and my pulse skyrocketing. It beats against all my dominant points like a war drum, and I feel it throughout my entire body. I jostle with my disguise, ensuring my mask is back in place before zipping up the high neck to cover the brown skin of my mouth and chin. If nothing else, it diffuses the smoky taste in the air.

The entire western section of Broadcove Castle burns, ash spiraling up towards the sky. One of the terraces crumbles in on itself, and as the masonry gives way and falls towards the grass, I pray that there are no pedestrians crushed beneath its weight. As residents of the castle bolt out of the building, members of the King's Guard run into the hellscape, swords drawn. Steel against flame will likely be a lost cause, but I refuse to pity them after

Marzipan's recounted last moments.

Let them all burn.

Just as my heart rate begins to outrun the speed of sound, I see it. The first flash of inky black amidst technicolor flame. Their cape has been singed from the blaze, and they stagger from the main entrance and down the hillside with great struggle. My stomach clenches thinking it's because they've broken a limb somehow, but when they turn—

Whichever brother lies beneath the mask, they've accomplished the impossible.

Jericho's body is limp in their hold, the smoke inhalation having done a number on him. I hurtle for them, and as I get closer, I see the soot covering his kingly face and clinging to his arms. His uniform sleeves are tattered, his stubble colored in with ash—and when the man beneath the mask recognizes me, the first thing he grits out is, "I told you I'd bring him to you. What are you *doing* here?"

Madden.

"I was worried *sick* about you in there," I croak, pointing to the fire happening yards away from us. "To the point where I was considering—"

"Don't make me picture it."

Nodding, I look down at my uncle, his disposition softer in sleep. Madden stops walking for a moment to tell me, "I figured you wouldn't want to . . . confront him while he was awake."

I nod against the lump in my throat, but we're off moments later, trudging through the lawn as best as we can and curving towards the cathedral. A quarter of a mile away, and we're home free. My hands sweat beneath my gloves, the open wound there reeling in pain as I adjust my grip on Jericho's feet. Madden heaves Jericho upwards again, tightening his hold from underneath his arms.

A sickening cry of anguish pierces through the atmosphere like a blade through canvas, and Jericho stirs awake at the sound.

Venus.

"Drop him before he starts thrashing," Madden hisses. "I've got him. Just get behind that tree."

I don't argue, ducking for cover as Jericho comes to and starts to jerk his body into violent motion. Madden's hands hold firm, unrelenting, even as Jericho starts spewing curses through clenched teeth. Even so, I note the way he does not call out to Venus. Doesn't scream her name like she's doing now.

It's like he knows this is the end, and he doesn't want her to watch.

"*Jericho!*" Venus screams again, the sound guttural to an excruciating degree. It sounds like his name alone could crack her lungs open. "*JERICHO—*"

"Shut up, *snake*," a familiar voice sneers, yanking her along with him as he emerges fully from the front of the castle. Kellan proves to be in worse shape than his brother. Cape tattered, gloves discarded, and part of his mask has melted off, revealing his left jaw and leaving the edge of his eye exposed. "I'm taking you to him right now."

Oh Saints.

"LEAVE HER BE!" Jericho finally screams. "She has nothing to do with this!"

"Doesn't she?"

Madden and Jericho turn to face me simultaneously, terror in both of their eyes as the words tumble out of me. But I don't balk. I'm done being the scared little girl who hides behind trees to escape discomfort—the one who sings at royal parties to prove she has some sort of value since she won't get her hands dirty the way Venus and Jericho did.

Fuck a mercy kill. I'll get my revenge with his eyes wide open.

Yanking Heart Punisher from its holster, I stride towards my uncle and snatch his coveted crown from off his head. Jericho's eyes surge with horrified astonishment, and where I expect him to command I return it, he barks out, gaze locked on my dagger, "Where the hell did you get that?"

"Where do you think?" Madden answers first, his voice low and lethal.

I stand upon the threshold of insanity, hacking into Jericho's crown with my dagger in hopes that the bloodlust will wear off with enough swinging. But the crown shatters with one, swift cut. Straight down the middle. And it only floods me with the desire for *more*.

"Give me the gun," I instruct Madden.

He stares after me like I've gone completely off my rocker.

"*Give me*," I enunciate, unflinching, "*the gun.*"

Madden disengages the safety before throwing it my way, and I drop the dagger into the grass in order to catch it with both hands. I assess the weight difference between the two items and revel in the way the gun grounds me to the earth somehow. The control that washes over me knowing I can take my enemies out from a greater distance endows me unlike anything I've ever felt.

For a moment, I understand my aunt and uncle on a much deeper level.

I slide the dagger towards Madden, giving him something to keep Jericho at bay with as Kellan finally drags Venus into our reach. Snarling the entire way to us. Her eyes turn misty, and her head moves on a swivel to drink in the horrors surrounding us. Broadcove ablaze, cloaked figures bearing weapons, her husband's crown cleaved in two.

And then, venom in her maw, she seethes, "Who are *you*?"

Her eyes are on me, not the brothers. She sees *me* as the leader of this operation—and it empowers me enough to remove my mask and untether my hair from the braid down my back.

Even Venus stops fighting back, going slack in Kellan's hold.

"Pandora?" Jericho says, as if believing his eyes are bearing false witness. He jolts forwards, then pulls back when Heart Punisher slices through the first layer of skin along his throat. "What . . . what are you doing with them? We thought—"

"That they killed me already?"

Jericho gulps. "My visions stopped showing me where you were after you left the Sacred City. It made me think that—"

All the loathing in the world cannot equate to the feelings that engulf me now. "You *knew* where I was this *whole time* . . . and you did *nothing*?"

Slowly, new sounds pour into the background. Countless voices, thundering footsteps, and the source of it crests over the highest point of the hill.

Uncle Eli carries Dorian over his shoulder military-style. Flora races after him, barefoot and dirty with sweat streaking her dark hair. Samuel rounds out the group, as if to ensure his sister made it out first.

"Where's Calliope?" I ask once Eli and the cousins arrive within earshot.

He's crying, sputtering his wife's name over and over as if it just dawned on him that Calliope needed help abandoning the castle, too. Not just the kids.

It's Flora who eventually answers, her words dripping with vitriol I relate to on a spiritual level. "She went back for *them*."

Her piercing gaze pins Venus further into the ground, and it appears that I'm not the only one that has turned on Aunt Venus.

And then it hits me.

Mother is still in there.

Eyes wild, I load the gun and point it towards Venus, "You left my mother in the cells to *burn* to death?"

For the first time in my entire existence, I watch as Venus weeps.

She shakes to the point of brutal convulsion, as if she were being electrocuted. Venus claws at her chest like she can rip her heart out just to keep from feeling the weight of her suffering. And I see it then: the remorse, the agony.

"You were so busy going after Jericho that you left her behind, didn't you?"

She says nothing beyond her incoherent screams, and it's answer enough.

"Don't punish her like this, Pandora. She's hurting as it is."

I erupt, hot and furious and unhinged.

"I hope she hurts, Jericho. I hope your wife never knows another day of rest or solace ever again after today. She deserves this pain. *She* wrote this story, and so did you. Jericho Deragon— the infamous dynasty deserter and the king of all nightmares. Venus Deragon—the lovesick psychopath who inadvertently put her own sister on the pyre. The happy couple who painted the world crimson with the blood of innocent people."

Disdain darkens Jericho's blue eyes. "Some nerve for a girl poised to deal us our deaths."

"This isn't just death. It's vengeance."

Though the gun still points towards Venus, I clutch it tighter with both hands, white-knuckled and shaky. My finger hovers over the tempting, silver trigger. My next words carry equal bite as a bullet would.

"How dare you *lie* to me all these years about my father?"

Jericho knows better than to be dishonest, now. His voice is parched when he says, "I don't know who told you, but you were *never* meant to know——"

"Because that would certainly be more *convenient* for you, right?" I snarl.

And then I hear it: the faint voice in my head that sounds a lot like Madden.

Everyone you know—both here on the Isle and back in Broadcove—has been lying to you.

"They all knew," I realize. "*Mother* knew, and you forced her to *keep it from me*——"

"Tell me you wouldn't feel the same as you do right now. Tell me, at what age would it have been best to confess that I killed the man you look for in me? Tell me that you would have learned to forgive me, Pandora, that you would've *understood*."

"And what about *them*?" I shout, pointing a finger at Madden and Kellan—if only to ward off the fact that I don't have an answer to every line of questioning. "What did *they* ever do to deserve all the suffering you put them through?"

"Who are you even *talking about*——"

Venus finally stops screaming, eyes wide with dread as she looks at my accomplices. "No," she says hoarsely. "*No*——"

Madden puts a hand to his chest in mocking hurt. "Is this you rejecting me, Venus? All this time I thought you'd . . . wait for me."

The hidden intentionality in his words lands like a blow, and Venus jerks backwards as both brothers drop their masks. Everyone around us goes deathly still.

"I've spent my entire life being held to silent expectations that rang loud and clear. I fought against becoming like you for *years*— so imagine my disbelief when all it took for me to conform was to learn what you had done." I glare daggers at Jericho. "To them. To my father. To Marzipan."

"That girl put a target on her own back the minute she snuck her way over to Mosacia. She's a traitor. No *Sacred City* could keep her from punishment."

The way Jericho's insulting tone stresses on the location I remember with such fondness and beauty feels like a slap in the face, and I explode.

"You cut yourselves open and are reminded of your greatness by those who gave you your power, but when *I* cut myself, all I do is bleed. You believe our faith is the true route to the divine, yet you hide it from the world and rage against *me* when I share it with people you've conquered for sport. I grew up looking to you as a *father*," I spew, seething uncontrollably. "Yet not only did you murder him, but you convinced yourself that you were worthy enough to stand in his stead." The last phrase is said with such mockery that I almost don't even sound like myself. "But hey, your pile of bodies means nothing if it means saving her, right?"

Finally, I see true fear cross both of their features.

"It'll always be worth it," Jericho states.

"That's what I thought."

I shift my stance.

Madden and Kellan release their hold on the king and queen, getting their distance.

And in a surge of blinding fury I no longer feel like fighting off, I pull the trigger and watch as Whisper takes the life of Jericho Deragon.

50
Pandora

Jericho's body crumples to the ground in a heap, and Venus's screams leech all the color out of the early evening sky.

The sound triggers a memory, one that fills me with grave fascination despite having the story told only once. A piece of history only shared between the residence of Broadcove Castle.

It was the eve of my eighteenth birthday, the night before I officially entered adulthood and became fully endowed with the rights of Urovian Monarch should any peril come to Broadcove. Jericho had summoned me from my rooms, and while I anticipated a party or some other celebratory surprise, I found him seated in the boardroom, eyes lost in a singular spot on the floor.

There was no build up. No games. Just the two of us and his opening statement of how, despite my years of preparation, there was still one, final story we needed to brief. Together.

He came right out with it. All of it.

Jericho spared no detail. In what felt like the span of one, eternal breath, he revealed every single movement between everyone who was there in the boardroom when Venus died. From the moment she first noticed Diana Seagrave poised to strike him down, all the way up until Venus's body went limp in his hold, Jericho divulged every detail surrounding the worst day of his life. Even when she came back to him from the Beyond, his joy only existed in response to the unfathomable agony that her death consumed him with.

I had nearly gagged on my tears as I watched Jericho shrink in his seat from reliving the memory of it. I could not pinpoint which part of it tore into me the deepest. Aunt Calliope's terror. Jericho's devastation. Venus coming to terms with a painful, early death. The sight of her blood *everywhere*. Misery swallowed me whole no matter where I turned regarding what Jericho confessed.

Then, just before I had reached the end of myself, Jericho had taken my hands into his own and grasped them tightly. I remember the way his hands crushed the bones in my fingers as he told me, "After I lost Venus, Calliope had tried to tell me that if I fought hard enough, I could survive the pain knowing I had a piece of her to hold onto. It was the first moment I laid eyes on you, and, Saints, you were so tiny and innocent and . . . fatherless."

The word had felt like the bullet I just lodged into Jericho's ribs.

"And I just broke. Because here you were, this perfect, beautiful little thing that your mother never *once* considered turning her back on . . . and yet, I resented you. For many reasons, but most of all, for entering the world in the same window of time that Venus left. I saw it as an equal exchange, a life for a life. And if that was the case, I knew I'd do it." He stared into my very soul, then. "Given the chance, I'd trade her life for yours in a nanosecond."

At the time, I didn't know the truth about the man who fathered me, and looking back on it, I suppose Jericho might have done me a service by staying quiet. It must have tortured him to live a life of limited truths and secrecy—to be forced to mask his immeasurable guilt beneath his benevolent uncle act for over twenty years.

I think that, had he come clean about it on top of everything else that night uncovered for me, it would've killed me. Truly, my heart would have spontaneously combusted, and he would have had to clean the splattered pieces of me off the boardroom floor like he had to do with Venus's blood.

Because my mother loved me unconditionally. She loved me as an infant, helpless to the world and dependent on her. She loved me as a child, when I was learning my morals while actively discovering that being a kid wasn't congruent to being Jericho's and Venus's princess. She loved me as an adolescent, when I would bicker with her even as the source of my anger could be traced back to someone else. She loved me as an adult, when I'd talk to her like I would my closest friend. She *was* my closest friend. And even when our existences were distanced, her love kept me sane. Kept me *alive*.

But Jericho's next words were damn near enough to eviscerate any memory of my mother's devotion.

"You are everything to me, Pandora," he whispered, fire-blue eyes locked on mine. There was no hint of mercy in them. "But you're not *her*, and you will never be. One day, when you love someone, you'll understand. The decision to choose them—to follow them down paths of ultimate treachery—will be simple. Second nature. Until then, do not do me the disservice of forcing me to choose between you and her . . . because it will *always* be Venus."

It destroyed me.

In that moment, so many horrible realizations came to fruition. All my efforts to please them had been in vain. Any future efforts would be a waste of time. If Jericho really loved me like a father—if I were *really* his daughter—he wouldn't have said what he did. No father of mine would have told me that in my purest form, I was *nothing* of worth to him if Venus hadn't been resurrected.

But most of all, it showed me the truth of how he viewed my existence.

I was never Jericho's heir. I was merely Venus's shield.

Firing Madden's gun wasn't out of anger or a rash decision. It was a *message*. A message that told him those words—*"you're not her, and you will never be"*—would come to haunt him one day, when I was ready to prove him wrong.

And today is that day.

"YOU *BITCH!*" Venus howls.

Never in my entire existence has Aunt Venus ever uttered a hateful word against me. But now, with her eye cosmetics smeared in the wake of her fiery tears, Venus doesn't even look like herself. She looks more like a mythical being who crawled out from the depths of the Damocles hellbent on plaguing the continent's population. Sweat streaks through her dark hair, and the lines along her bronze face show her true age beneath all the powder.

"You think I wanted this to become my fate?" I shout at Venus as she stoops over Jericho's body, a sob choking off the final word. Everywhere I look, all I can picture is either my aunt weeping, or Diana Seagrave somewhere in the Beyond, grinning like a cat. "I didn't want this curse to come to fruition. I just wanted—"

"You petulant, little *victim*." Another sob cracks out of her, drool lining her lips from her hysteria. "Talking to me like you're the ultimate sufferer of our bloodline. You're *dead* to me!"

The formal disownment slides right off me. "The feeling is mutual."

"You think you had it all figured out," she rages, and I see the moment she pops a blood vessel in her eye, the dark red pooling in its corner. "So convinced that *we* are the bad guys, honing you into a cold-hearted killing machine. Because that's all that Jericho and I ever were, right Pandora? Senseless murderers who got off on killing innocents?"

I say nothing, but Madden stands firm. Kellan raises Hellfire in warning.

"We didn't train you to be a weapon," Venus croaks, her voice raw. Depleted. "We only wanted to prepare you for what we foresaw. For the prophecy."

Prophecy.

I'm once more pulled through time, back to the moment I first heard them whispering about an unknown enemy coming to destroy their home and disparage our family from the tunnels. I was ten, and I remember feeling an otherworldly sense of dread—*guilt,* somehow—at the panic in Jericho's voice as he confided in Venus.

Then, I remember the gleaming smile on Diana's face, back in her namesake's sanctuary, when she proclaimed the curse she laid upon me as a baby.

"All those years of living in fear and trying to instill protection over you," Venus rasps, horror overtaking her bloodshot hazel eyes. "Only for it to be *your* fault. *Your* doing. We groomed our own destruction for decades!"

The hysterics overcome me in a sudden surge, the shock wearing off and giving way to dread as Venus clutches Jericho's body like she can bring him back to life.

But there's no holymen, now—at least none that can raise the dead, turn back time, or to make me feel good about any of this.

I've made a cataclysmic mistake.

I stumble back, and when I sink into the warm, firm body at my back—the one that helps me stay on my feet—I startle at the realization of it being Kellan. Of him quietly coaching me to take deep breaths and steady my heart rate. "I've got you. It's okay—"

A blur of color finally emerges from the incinerated castle.

"Mother!" Dorian cries, fighting Eli's hold on him.

Eli drops him in an instant, outrunning all three of his children to get to Calliope. I'm struck dumb by just how fast he gets to her, and while I can tell that he wants to throw his arms around her and assure himself that she's here, he's gentle. Assessing her. He nods once, then conceals her from view as she likely begins to forcefully expel the smoke from her lungs. Eli doesn't flinch at the sight, merely crouching down to soothe her, to encourage her through the worst of it. When she finally stills, he helps her stand, allowing Calliope to lean on him for balance. She says something indistinguishable, and even from far away, I see Eli's eyes go wide.

He cups his hands around his mouth and screams, "SHE GOT THEM OUT!"

The words hit me like a tidal wave.

She got them out.

"Thank the Saints," a voice I wasn't expecting says through a labored breath of relief.

Kellan's grip on me tightens as a curse leaves his lips. Madden goes stiff, all movement stilling as he looks towards Venus, who starts to back away from Jericho, giving his body some room.

And then, Jericho does the impossible.

He rises from the ground.

435

51
Pandora

Jericho's skin is a sheet of white and there's blood coating the inside of his mouth. He rocks off his knees, using his hands to brace himself before slowly pulling his torso upright, muscles trembling as he stands. Venus is right there beside him, an arm curled around his back in attempts to support his limp, heavy weight.

How the hell did he live through a bullet?

Jericho drinks in the horrified look on my face, bristling in answer as he pulls up the hem of his shirt. A dark layer rests underneath—a thick one, at that—and the evening sun casts a distinct sheen over the material. Rage swallows me whole at the sight.

A bulletproof breastplate.

"Well, well, well," Madden's tone cuts through the silence theatrically. He approaches the center of our gathering like the amused ringmaster of a bloody, brutal circus. "I must say, this show turned out to be far greater than I anticipated."

Kellan takes no amusement in his brother's words. "What exactly did you *anticipate?*"

No doubt he envisioned a dead king, a bereaved queen, and delicious revenge all around. As did I. The fact that Jericho's still breathing, let alone on his feet, likely burns Kellan to a spiritual depth.

"Pretty much everything that happened," Madden answers carefully, pausing for a moment, but only long enough to turn his piercing gaze towards me. It stakes me into the ground.

"I remember the look on your face when you learned the truth about your father's death. Not despair, but *ire*. Pure wrath buried beneath a neutral expression. You probably didn't even feel your face slip, but your eyes communicated to me what I feared most, that you were prepared to slaughter him for what you uncovered. You were brilliant, committed to its full execution. And had Kellan maintained some bloody self-control," he adds pointedly, eyes vicious when they land on his brother. Kellan doesn't look the least bit remorseful. "We might have made a clean getaway."

My lungs dry out with each additional breath, shriveling under the weight of the way my entire family looks at me.

"Is that *regret* I sense?" he asks me quietly. "What is it that you cannot seem to face: the fact that you pulled the trigger, or that I gave your uncle the chance to survive your retribution?"

I dare a look at the man I looked up to as a father. More specifically, I dare a glance at the vest beneath his shirt. Then, I direct the iciest of all stares at Madden. "*You* . . . you warned him?"

"Yes, angel."

"*Why?*"

"Because I *know* you, Pandora," he counters, his words intentional and stern. "Even before you knew me, I knew you.

Knew how you operated and contemplated things. You were . . . you *are* pure of heart. Good-natured. Killing wasn't a behavior you allowed yourself to acquire despite how much you longed to please your family. But when you realized what that family truly proved to be, I saw the way their past got the better of you from a mile away . . . and I knew you'd come to regret it later."

Silence falls, and while I think that his answer is enough, Jericho doesn't.

"No," he says through his teeth, still wincing, "that's not it."

"You're right," Madden says, his voice grave. "I also did it for her."

Venus's eyes flare. "Me?"

"In part, yes. Our adoptive mother was the one who took the call, the one that warned the palace to get us out in time. No matter how much you hate yourself for it, you still spared our lives. But mainly . . . I did it for Queen Merrie."

Jericho withers at the name of his long-dead mother.

"Had she not warned my mother about Ronan's wrath in her letter, I would've died as a toddler. So would Kellan and Anna and all my other siblings. My parents. Ronan wouldn't have stopped until he saw a complete massacre through. Merrie saved us. And so, just this once, I wanted to get even."

The familiar words haunt me down to the very marrow in my bones. The same thing I had said after killing Thatcher Chumley. A death for a death—my way of matching Madden's actions.

And now, mercy in exchange for mercy.

Madden then eyes Venus with the kind of intensity that would knock me clean out on the grass. "But know this, Deragon. We are far from done here. What I just did for him, for *you*—that far from cancels out what still needs attending to. I could write a list tall enough to scale the walls of Broadcove Castle regarding the life debts you owe me and what remains of the Seagrave Family."

Madden's tone is so vile and harsh that goosebumps crawl across the surface of my skin, the voice of an ousted king hellbent on claiming justice.

He turns to Jericho, now. "We stayed out of your way—let you collect the countries we could've ruled one day like they were toys—and never fought back for what was rightfully ours. We changed our *entire lives*, names included, to let you play conquerors in love!" Madden borderline screams the charges against them, now. "And if that wasn't enough, I went even further and averted direct orders from the man who rightfully would be on our throne today to assassinate Venus at Queen's Feast. *I* ensured that your heir remained safe and unharmed while in our custody, and even though you and your wife are the reason I am an *orphan*, I *still* made the choice to warn you the moment I discovered Pandora planned to murder you."

I almost worry that if any of us stand too close, Madden will crane his head and rip our throats out with his teeth.

"So here's what's going to happen. You're going to settle every life debt you owe me and my family right here, right now. You will agree to my terms, or I'll blow a hole in your head."

The way his eyes pan back and forth between Jericho and Venus is even more menacing when I realize that the threat is for both of them, but that he'll only kill one of them—forcing the other to endure their loss alone.

Jericho doesn't want to bow into Madden's threats, but Venus nods once in understanding, her eyes laden with loathing and understanding at the same time.

Madden's jaw ticks. "You're going to release Pandora from her commitments as your heir."

"Madden—" I cry out.

"Look me in the eye and tell me that you want to serve a dynasty that killed your father and forced you to be submissive all these years."

I don't bother formulating an argument.

"It doesn't matter what she *wants*." Venus gnashes her teeth at him. "She has been brought up to safeguard our legacy, and that is what she'll do."

"You know, it's one thing to force your own child to take up the torch and rule all the lands you accumulated. But to force Pandora into the role all because the two of you couldn't conceive an heir biologically? That's just heartless."

Saints above, this just took a turn for the worst.

The loaded insult lands true, because rather than reacting with fury, Venus appears struck by the words. I even think I hear a choked off sound briefly escape her lips. Jericho, on the other hand, looks ready to wrestle Madden to the ground for his gun and shoot him for his audacity.

"You'll release her on your own, living will," Madden repeats. "Or I'll liberate her following your death. It's your choice."

"The Deragon Dynasty will not be bargained away from us," Venus growls.

"Pandora is not your only option to continue your bloodline. Your possess an assortment of nieces and nephews—"

"None of which we have trained to Pandora's capacity."

"Then I suppose the child next in line will have to learn alongside someone well-versed in foreign politics, economic upkeep, and military strategy," Madden proposes eerily.

I hear a distinct rumbling from the opposite side of our gathering, and turn in time to see Flora's face flush red. "What the hell is *that* supposed to mean?"

"My second stipulation," Madden says cheerily, happy to

see that someone is catching on quickly. "Whereby my brother, Kellan, the rightful heir of Mosacia, marries *you*, as you are the first in line for the Urovian throne in Pandora's absence."

"You're crazy," Flora bites back.

"*Mad* is the term I prefer." It only hits me now that he likely spied on Flora all those years he hid from sight, too. "But you'll do it in order to serve your kingdom—to serve someone other than yourself. Won't you?"

"Like your brother would ever agree to it."

Kellan chortles under his breath, and Flora's attention flocks towards the sound. "To reclaim what is rightfully mine, I'd marry far less attractive creatures than you, doll face."

There's a heart-stalling pause in the universe that all of us fear may never lift. But then, thwarting my wildest expectations of how she'd respond to Kellan's blatant flirtation, Flora's lips curve into a traitorous smile. "Is a taste of the crown really worth the hell I'll put you through?"

She says it like a threat. A promise.

Kellan's smile deepens at the prospect. "Do your worst, Deragon."

Flora accepts the challenge in those words. And then, as if already queen herself, she decrees, "When we marry, you'll take the Deragon name as reparations for burning our castle and nearly costing my mother's life in the process."

"Will I, now?"

Madden nears my side as we watch this game of cat and mouse in real time. "You'll live here, too. In Broadcove. You'll be King-Consort as opposed to King. You want the real title? You'll have to work your way into my good graces."

Kit starts to gawk at Flora. "And what makes you think I'd *ever* agree to those terms?"

Flora's smile seeps poison. "You broke the Morgana-Grave Agreement."

I hadn't even thought about the treaty. Not once. And by the looks on Jericho's and Venus's faces, they hadn't either.

"That agreement became null and void the minute the Morgan Dynasty was dissolved—"

"Morgan is still *legally* part of Jericho's name, is it not?" she asks with enough showboat energy to make Kellan writhe. She's putting on a show of his humiliation and loving every minute of it. "The agreement stated that if a nation's people turned on their sovereign power through a rebellious act, the opposing nation could not interfere, neither to aid the rulers in charge nor assist their assailants. That means that Pandora could've come here alone and killed Jericho with no repercussions," she says before looking at our uncle and adding, "no offense. But since *both* of you aided her in the effort—as the last members of the Seagrave line—you broke the treaty."

All the facts are there, and almost verbatim to what I remember being in the Urovian historical records. Flora cocks a brow at the silence that follows, knowing she has, in fact, bested Kellan Seagrave in a battle of wits.

"What?" Her eyes rove over everyone's collective disbelief. "Am I not allowed to take up a little light reading now and then?"

Reading.

Kellan's gaze softens at the word, at the idea of him and his reluctant bride sharing something in common.

The spark in his eyes fizzles out seconds later, though, replaced by that same, daredevil grin. "Is there an I-can't-kill-you clause you care to add to this arrangement, Princess?"

Unlike me, Flora deems Kellan's use of her royal title affectionate rather than mocking.

"Not particularly. I've always liked men with a mean streak."

"It's settled, then," Madden cuts in, eyes once more on Venus and Jericho before we're subjected to more of their charged banter. "*They* will rule in your stead when you die or choose to abdicate. Not Pandora. You will not force her to dwell here any longer."

"And where will she go?"

It's Jericho who asks, and not defiantly either. He asks it as if he genuinely cares about my wellbeing, and it twists me up like a knife in my gut.

"Wherever will bring her peace," Madden answers on my behalf.

I don't know where I'm going next. The winds of fate and my patron Saint may summon me far and wide, but all I know is that wherever I go, it'll be at Madden's side. The man who just managed to negotiate a new life for me, who believes that freeing me from this place and allowing me to move forward is worth every life debt that he's owed.

He deserves so much more.

"Are you done?" I ask Madden as politely as I can manage.

He nods, the movement brief, and I gear my head at Jericho. "I'd like to negotiate a few terms of my own."

Remorse swims in the depths of his ocean eyes. "Anything you ask."

"Madden gets to rule over Mosacia again."

"No." Anger is easier for Venus to process than sadness, her stance commanding as she stares me down. "*Both* brothers broke the treaty. If Kellan forfeits his name, Madden ought to do so as well."

I want to launch myself at her, sock my fist into her teeth, and tear out her hair for thinking she *deserves* to tear Madden's family

443

name away from him after making him live under a false identity.

But it appears Madden is far more mild-mannered about things than I am now, because he lays a calming hand on my shoulder and says, "You're right. The Seagrave line broke the treaty, and in recognition of that, the name should die out and a new one should take its place."

"*Madden*," Kellan and I both snap at the same time.

"The family name I bore following our relocation was Andromeda, in honor of the woman who raised us as her own. It is that name which I shall rule under, and you can rest assured that I will do so magnanimously, considering I spared your life from a member of your own bloodline."

Venus and Jericho don't take long to weigh the pros and cons, and my uncle looks towards me again. "What else do you request, niece?"

Jericho knows better than to use the term *daughter*, but even my proper terminology burns somehow.

"I want the Hive disbanded."

That condition rocks Jericho more visibly than anything else so far. "Pandora—"

"Don't start with your excuses. They may have broken the Morgana Grave Agreement, but you? You murdered a girl in cold blood and violated the Sacred City's most absolute law. Did you forget that perpetrators of their no-tolerance to violence policy are to face a formal tribunal, or did you just not care?"

Jericho's eyes are as cold as steel when they fall over mine. "I did *not* enjoy giving the order, Pandora. Despite what you know of my past and believe about me now, you may never understand the intricacies of that situation—"

I snort, telling him *exactly* how much I understand about this situation . . . in a mixture of all seven Mosacian dialects.

It rolls off the tongue easy enough, switching between every tribal linguistic with the same simplicity as breathing. But for all Venus and Jericho know, they may think I'm hexing them, casting a dark, foreboding incantation over them. I revel in the way they jerk backwards on instinct.

"I'm willing to pardon you from an official hearing," I say with such disdain it comes out sounding like sorrow, "but only in exchange for disbanding the Hive. Knowing the sentence that would await you, however, I doubt you'll be stupid enough to decline."

His silence is answer enough.

"And then," I decide right then and there, "when Madden takes back his family's rightful throne, you're going to give the Andromeda Dynasty ownership over all maritime activities across the Damocles."

Venus calls out her husband's name, appalled by the expression on his face—the one that makes me think he's truly considering letting me win this one despite knowing why I'm reaching for it at all.

When you control the sea, you control everything.

"*Jericho*," Venus groans again.

His calm disposition is a far cry from the magnetic man she first fell in love with. "If this is the price I must pay for the pain I've caused, then I will do as she pleases."

The declaration plunges through me like a spear. I only realize then that he means the pain on all fronts. The fear I felt first leaving Broadcove with Madden. The concern for my mother. The death of Marzipan. The loss of never knowing my father. It all culminates to this agreement, and he knows it.

"Any final additions?" His words are spoken with such uncharacteristic gentleness.

I, however, have no strength left in me to be kind.

"Just one. I never want to see you again."

Samuel and Dorian begin to cry, drawing near to their parents who are sniffling, too. Venus looks at Jericho so tragically, and Flora . . . well, I think she keeps her eyes on Kellan to keep her grounded. She's the only one of the Deragons that doesn't break under the weight of my final condition.

"You don't mean that." Jericho's voice is barely audible.

"I don't want to hear about how you're doing or receive letters that detail how sorry you are. I don't want your staff crossing the sea, showing up on my doorstep urging me to reconcile, because if I do, I'll view it as a breach of peaceful conduct and will react in any manner I deem appropriate."

The threat hangs out in the open, clear as day. I swallow hard against the ache in my throat. "You want to atone for the things you've done? That's what I'm asking for."

Jericho nods, cracking his knuckles in attempts to busy his shaking hands. He says nothing, and only once he makes his mind up about something none of us can decipher, he reaches for Venus's hand.

Letting her lead them both back towards the castle, whose flames have been thoroughly doused by members of their staff, the rest of the family follows suit. Everyone except for Flora. She approaches me cautiously, worried I'll spook as easily as a horse. Once close enough, she grabs my hands in hers.

Rather than say goodbye, the new Crown Princess of Urovia, whispers, "I would've shot him, too."

52
Kellan

I will my eyes not to linger on Flora Deragon as she retreats towards the castle I intended to reduce to ash.

There's a stark difference between the two Urovian princesses. I knew both women existed, but the looming ghost of Venus's crown one day falling upon Pandora's head always drew my attention to her first. When Pandora arrived on the Isle, *really* getting to look at her stirred my heart in ways that made me feel captivated and seasick simultaneously. I mistook her kindness for weakness, overlooking the true depths of her intellect and decisiveness—and it's perhaps my greatest error yet. Because even now, in the fallout of her fury, Pandora exudes a maturity that no other woman I have ever known possesses, the kind of maturity that might have had the chance to balance out the volatility in me.

But looking at Flora . . .

She reminds me that I'm a hot-blooded man, one with a bad temper and a racing mind. She reminds me that beneath my pile of books and my years of resentment, there lives a primal creature ready to devour a woman so thoroughly they'd flee if they had the foresight to see inside my head. But Flora is no ordinary woman, and she has made it crystal clear that she's anything but scared of me. She practically *invited* me to spar wills with her. Smoky eyes alight with condescension, olive skin like a spectacular oil painting, and a slender nose that quirked ever so slightly as we dueled.

I don't think I've ever wanted a woman more.

When I come back down to earth, however, it's clear that Pandora easily understands why I haven't gone trudging after Flora just yet. So much so that I didn't even notice her ask Madden for some privacy. He pretends to busy himself with one of the bushes downhill, picking berries that don't exist. I'm so distracted by the stupidity of it that I almost miss it when Pandora says, "Guess you can't call me 'princess' anymore."

"I'll put it to good use with your cousin."

"I bet she'll *love* that."

"I don't really care what she loves after that little arrangement she facilitated."

Pandora shrugs, her smile dimming. "Flora always had more of Venus in her than I did."

"I thought this whole time you were *proud* to not be like Venus?" It was one of her most redeeming qualities, one that I gripped like a vice.

"In some senses, I am. But in others . . . I don't know. I feel like that small victory only came out of how angry I was, or how much Jericho pitied me. A win is a win, but what's the point of having a backbone if you don't have any teeth?"

"That's the difference between our two lands, I suppose. Urovia rules with dominance, always on the offensive. Mosacian rulers aren't like that. The knowledge of our strengths brings us the peace we need without picking fights."

Pandora mulls over the words for a moment. "And those strengths are?"

"All the things I already know you stand for," I say solemnly.

She thins out her lips, and for a second, I almost believe that she'll cower. That she won't speak out on the elephant in the room. But with the tip of her chin, her eyes barrel into mine with an intensity that is unmistakably *Deragon*. "You could've easily thrown Madden into the arrangement with Flora instead of going along with it."

The laugh that leaves my chest is brittle. "I know."

"Then why not rage against it?"

"You're really going to make me say it?"

The confused look on her face nearly breaks my heart, confirming what I've already seen so much of today. Whether they know it or not, everyone she's grown up around has always expected her to bend to their wishes, *their* will for her. It's never been about Pandora, and apart from singing, she's never gotten to be centerstage in her own life.

"I may be selfish," I finally confess, "but I'm not cruel. I see the way he looks at you, Pandora." My gaze casts a quick glance towards my twin. "It's clear that a crown was the furthest thing from his mind when he met you, unlike me—and that's the kind of love you deserve. The kind of benevolent ruler that Mosacia really needs."

The weight of what I've just said is not lost on her, and I watch as Pandora's eyes glaze over with an emotion I cannot read. She takes a careful step forward. "And what about you? Don't you deserve love, too?"

"Who said I'm never going to have that?"

It's true. I never said that this arrangement with Flora would be a futile one. Unexpected? Definitely. Impossible? I don't think so—not when it appears that Flora might be as stubborn as I am. Hell, she and I might make this work out of pure spite.

Deep down, I'm starting to understand Madden's instant fixation with Pandora, because after one conversation with Flora, I'm hooked. Hooked to the feeling of sparring wills and getting under each other's skin. In time, maybe our conversations can soften into something else, but for now, I'm content. I've never been good at prioritizing companionship, so for all I know, Madden may have just saved me a great deal of trouble . . . or thrust me into a heaping dose of it. We'll see.

Pandora smiles at me then, and I see just how weary she looks. Her heart has clearly been through the wringer, and as she looks over her shoulder to where Madden watches dutifully, I feel a sense of relief knowing she'll be taken care of. He'll allow her the rest and reprieve she needs. Part of me savors the fact that my brother doesn't want to leave her alone with me, whether out of concern or jealousy or deep-seeded adoration.

She breaks the silence by assuring me, "I'll see to it that your books get to you safely."

"Just so Flora can set them all on fire upon arrival? No thanks." I laugh, the sound true and maybe even a bit hopeful. Like the idea of them harassing one another until the end of time might be more fun than we're anticipating. The thought manages to numb the realization that I may not see Andromeda House again for a long time. "Really, don't worry about them, Pandora. Just . . . take care of each other."

"Don't say that for my sake if you don't really mean it."

"But I do."

"How?" she finally asks, her composure cracking. "How am I

supposed to believe you feel anything for me beyond bitterness?"

"Because I'm going to tell you something I should've told Madden a long time ago, and I'm going to trust that you take him there."

"Kellan——"

"The hardest part about leaving Sevensberg was having to explain to Anna where Greer had gone, why she wouldn't come back," I say, swallowing hard against my guilt. "You could say that the two of them were inseparable, so when her time came, I chose to keep it that way."

Pandora Deragon's body shifts in my hold. She pulls back, eyes shining with fresh tears. Then, after one cry breaks through her line of defense, she kisses my temple and darts towards my brother—then towards the royal gravesites outside Zayanya Cathedral.

53
Geneva

T he moment Ren and I emerge from the tunnels, hacking up smoke and bearing various burns across our exposed arms, the perimeter guards on duty see to it that we get a carriage ride out of Broadcove. Considering the mess that Jericho and Venus have on their hands—as evident by the spire of one of the nearby towers slowly succumbing to the raging flames—I don't bother getting the guards to swear oaths of discretion. In fact, the looks on their faces seem to show fear, as if they don't know the status of their king and queen at all.

I haven't looked upon a tragedy like this since. . . well, ever. I was never there to see death befall my middle sister right after Pandora was born. I only saw what was painted over Jericho's face. Terror—true and everlasting. That's what overcomes me now as stone crumbles beneath extreme heat and roaring fire. History is made in the death of what turns to rubble, and Ren holds my hand in his as I watch it all unfold.

Eventually, one of the onyx carriages rips down the road that lies between the top of the hill and Honeycomb Harbor and stops in front of them. Ren pulls me behind him, wary that some threat might pop out of the cabin and leap out at me, and just as I'm inclined to argue with him about it, the door opens and confirms his theory.

I lock eyes with a face that makes me want to shatter glass with my bare first.

"Get out," I sneer, but Henry Tolcher's face is unreadable, and his only movements are to offer his hand out to me in an attempt to help me board. In the simple gesture, however, I notice the way his uniform has been burnt to a crisp in some areas. Not deep enough to char his skin, but quite close.

"I may not be a duchess anymore, but as I was your friend once, and for the way you've treated me and my—" I swallow hard, not knowing exactly what to call Ren. I bare my teeth, regardless. "You ought to show me some respect and get the hell out of that carriage."

He only chokes out one word. "Genny."

It's pathetic. *Grieved.* Having known Henry a long time, hearing the way his voice trembles despite always maintaining a sunshiny disposition and even an air of self-righteousness warns me that whatever he has to say, is not good.

"What's happened?" I ask.

"Get in the carriage, Genny, and I'll tell you." The words are not that of coercion, but of pure desperation, proving that I have all control over what happens next.

So I nod, and Ren climbs in first, staring Henry down with a glare that promises eventual retribution. He accepts that, and even allows Ren to shove him aside so that *he* can offer his hand and help me from the ground and onto the step. I feel Ren's other hand fall onto the small of my back, a protective tactic as he leads me to sit across from Henry, rather than beside him. Ren shuts the carriage door and Henry pounds his fist on the roof before the coachmen leads us onward, taking a route that diverts as far from Broadcove's burning exterior as possible.

"I'm in, aren't I?" I ask after a suspended period of tense silence. Ren still hasn't taken his hands off me. "Start talking. Good news first."

Henry's eyes go cold. "There is no good news."

"My daughter—"

"Is alive," Henry assures me.

"Then *what is it*, Henry? Is she hurt? Just *tell* me—"

"He's gone, Genny."

"Who is?"

Henry swallows hard before saying, "Jericho. And I'm afraid that Pandora. . ." He's quiet for a long time, allowing me to fill in the blanks. "It was a firearm," he finishes.

A scream leaves me.

The absolute horror of what instantly comes to mind is blinding. Before a backdrop of flames, I see blood and carnage. I see my daughter holding a weapon towards a man that was the closest thing to a father she ever had—no doubt pushed to do so by emotions no person should ever succumb to. I see her tears as I taste my own, sense her trembling in the way my limbs shake disorientedly. My daughter is not a violent girl, but to take down the king? Her *uncle*?

She's branded herself as a traitor.

I picture a trial, one that Venus executes herself—aunt against niece. I hear a resounding, guilty verdict, and jury of conflicted Urovian sentences. I hear the wailing and the begging, but most of all, I picture Venus's apathy.

And I pass out cold.

I wake not long after Henry's revelation, but given the state of exhaustion and hunger Ren and I are in, I can barely form a phrase to keep conversation with Tolcher. Instead, I lie there with my head in Ren's lap for a miserable strand of hours while Henry debriefs us on everything he knows.

Pandora came with two accomplices—all three of them emerging on the hill with masks. She pulled a gun on Jericho, and then, she killed him. One shot, straight into his chest cavity.

There's more details, but my brain shields me from them, phantom water filling my ears so that his voice sounds far away and unintelligible. Eventually, just as I hit my limit on what my soul can bear, the carriage parks before a massive tree that shades us from sight.

"What is this place?" Ren asks, his eyes trained on the ramshackle building that stands preserved in its lackluster appearance despite the surrounding neighborhood being better maintained.

I recognize it instantly. "This is my old home."

One of Venus's first acts as queen was to help renovate the marshes to a more suitable economic state—one of the least grotesque initiatives throughout her reign. The only place she didn't alter—at least not on the outside—was our family home. Venus insisted that it should stand as a portrait of optimism, a testament to the fact that even the poorest of people can ascend to something greater than their present circumstances.

Inside, however, the dingy hearth has undergone serious renovations with beautiful stonework. All the floors and stairs have been restored so they don't creak beneath my body weight, and all the window panes appear freshly cleaned. There are proper kitchen utensils hung on miscellaneous hooks and cupboards stocked full of food. The interior is painted a lighter color as opposed to the faded oak that once cloaked this place in darkness, but my favorite addition rests above the mantle in the opening room.

It's a portrait of us—all three of the Deragon girls. We never posed for this photo, given we were dirt poor at the ages captured in the portrait, but it softens my heart, nonetheless. It depicts the three of us all leaning into each other: Venus on the left, Calliope on the right, and me in the middle. I've seen it once before, though. It's a replica of the one that Jericho keeps in his boardroom: the very one that he commissioned a renowned artist to draw up from collections of the few old photographs we had in our family.

I never knew he had one sent here.

My eyes burn with tears the longer I look at it, realizing that we're embracing one another in this artwork—a touch that's felt foreign to me, at least from Venus, for some time now. In a way, it's as if the portrait shows the devotion of our youth while also capturing the division of our adulthood, with each of my sisters on either side of me.

"Are you alright, my love?" Ren whispers.

No. Not in the slightest.

I think of how the man who took residency in this house is now dead. I think of how it felt to hold Calliope in my arms before running through the tunnels. I think of my daughter and the destruction she brought to a place we both called home. I think of how my daughter went on a warpath against my brother-in-law—a man I knew held a bleeding heart beneath years of jaded agony in his youth. Worst of all, I think about how the last time I interacted with him, he had stood up for me in a way, against his own wife. . . and now, he's gone forever.

All at once, I shatter.

"Genny."

It's Henry who says it, lunging for me, as if to somehow comfort me.

"Stay *away* from me," I snarl like a rabid dog, teeth bared until Henry steps back, providing me distance. I pull Ren back towards me, away from Henry's reach.

"Genny, please, I'm sorry"

"You think I want your pity after how you treated us?"

Henry doesn't relent. "My hands were tied and you know it. Ren aided your desertion, and you aided Pandora's."

Despite my rage and my overwhelming urge to weep, I close my hands into fists and stare Henry down. "I would do *anything* for them. Could you say the same for your family?"

I see Ren straighten out of the corner of my eye. The way he appears touched by the remark is the only thing that keeps my dignity and composure in one piece. Then, I watch as Henry's stoic posture slackens. "Such bravado for a woman who betrayed her sister."

"You brainwashed fool! I *loved* Venus and Jericho, but not enough to be their lapdog. Not enough to abandon my daughter like *they* did!" I'm shouting now, and I don't spare a thought for propriety or politeness. "*You*, however, may as well come with your own collar."

The pure vitriol I spew at him feels good—glorious, even. In my flesh, I feel *alive*.

But in my heart—right when I register just how cutting my words are, proven by the bleak expression on his face—I want to take it all back. All that hate I threw his way comes careening back towards me with triple the intensity. "Oh, Saints. Henry,

I—"

"Have every right," he croaks, "to say that to me. You're right. If Jericho and Venus imprisoned one of my sons, it wouldn't matter what for. I'd . . . I would do anything to get them out. And I'm sorry that I didn't do the same for you."

It's the apology I want and need, and yet, it doesn't seem to fill the void I've created.

Ren finally intercedes. "I think you should leave."

"I'm trying to make amends," Henry argues pitifully.

"You may have lost your king today, but Geneva just lost her brother. Not to mention she requires space to recover from your participation in our imprisonment and starvation. So leave. Slither back to your burning castle and leave my wife *alone*."

I wonder if I'll ever be able to stop crying or if I'll be draining this well forever.

I can feel the fierce intentionality behind his words. If we weren't in Urovia, I'd be telling myself that Ren's only calling me his wife to maintain a ruse. But that perception expired the moment my knee cracked against the boardwalk and I ran after him, and we're a long ways away from Mosacia, now.

Henry says nothing else before finally adhering to Ren's warning. The minute he's gone and shuts the door behind him, I collapse into Ren's arms, though I expected to hit the floor first. He lowers himself with me, ensuring that I don't face this pain alone, and the longer I stay there, the tighter his embrace becomes. I almost want to die like this—suffocated by his hold, my last breath used to inhale his comforting, natural scent.

"Ren—"

"I'm not going anywhere," Ren murmurs, a vow. "I promise."

"How did we get here?" I howl into the fabric of his tattered clothes. I feel my heart tangibly break within my chest, and I wait for the bleeding to show. It never does. "How is it that weeks ago, you and I . . . we were so happy and in love in a beautiful city?"

Ren presses a firm, acknowledging kiss to my temple, and I drink it up like oxygen.

"And now, Jericho is . . ." I cannot even bear to say it aloud. "And Pandora, the gentlest soul I've ever known—and I don't just say that because she's my daughter—was driven to a place low enough to fire a *gun*—"

He shushes me, stroking my hair as he kneels further into me. "Let your heart take one thing at a time. I promise we'll get to them all, but for now . . ." He pauses, his thumbs brushing the hot tears off my face. "What weighs on your heart the heaviest?"

I find it impossible to answer him right off the bat, even though I have a million reasons. Jericho, Pandora, Henry . . .

"How can you endure this with me?" I croak. Because nothing hurts like thinking I've forced him into so much lasting pain. Nothing wounds me deeper than thinking about the potential reality of Ren feeling forced to be with me.

Ren raises my chin to meet his gaze, even as my eyes glimpse up at him beneath glass. "Because my soul felt pulled towards you before I knew your name, and once I did, I knew my fate was so blissfully sealed. Blissful not because you brought me safety, but blissful because you were sure to be my peace amidst any pain and suffering. Because being together is a choice worth every possible consequence—the best choice I've ever made. It's the same way that you could endure hell at my side. You were in freedom's grasp, for the gods' sakes, and yet—" His voice breaks, and Ren yields to it willingly. "How fast did you give it up?"

I think back to the boat, back to the masked man who held tight to my daughter, and that despite the turn of fate they took together, I knew I made the right choice. Leaving Pandora in his care. Leaving them to go after Ren.

"Not fast enough."

Ren's eyes go wide. "You barely even got to hold Pandora again."

"She'll understand when she meets you."

"Genny——"

"It wouldn't have been freedom if I left without you, Ren," I tell him firmly, so that he has no choice but to know it. To accept it. "It would've been misery."

I'll never go anywhere without you, Ren, I'd told him. *Even into death itself, I will walk with you, hand in hand.*

"That's just it," he murmurs sweetly. "How you feel about me . . . that's how I feel about you, Geneva Deragon. I know you haven't had much experience with unconditional love, perhaps not any in the realm of men, but so help me, I'll prove myself worthy of you. Enough to endure what's behind us and what's still to come——the good and the bad. You hear me?"

I taste our shared tears as we kiss, and everything feels right amidst such agony. Somehow, Ren's always managed to keep me afloat that way, ensuring that our connection and the hope it brings the both of us just barely overpowers the bad things happening around us. In this kiss, I find the strength to not just be a pile on the floor, but to pull myself up to his level, to cling to him.

His kiss turns sloppy in a way that tells me all I need to know. "You think Henry will come back?" I ask breathlessly.

"I'll lock the door," Ren says, his voice low and gruff.

"He might have a key——"

A sharp ring suddenly pierces through the living space, and I make a mad dash for the Dial Line in the kitchen despite wanting to rip it off the wall. Another addition to the space I had forgotten

Jericho installed. I pick up the receiver and grit my teeth. My voice is gravel when I ask, "Who is this?"

"Genny?"

It's Eli's voice, and my heart thunders to life at the hope in his tone. I slump against the wall, gripping the receiver like a vice and fight a new wave of tears—ones of immense relief. "Calliope. Did she . . ."

"She's safe, Genny. So are the kids," he adds, though something about the way he says kids comes out sour. I hear him swallow through the line. "But . . . I didn't expect to hear your voice. Where's Tolcher?"

"In hell, hopefully," Ren sneers from beside me.

Eli clears his throat at the realization of Ren's proximity, likely having been briefed about our shared incarceration. "I was hoping to speak to him."

I muster up what little authority I have left. "You will speak to me instead."

There's a moment of silence, of him making a decision for himself. Then, just before he can decide, I hear hash rustling and static, and—

"*Geneva*," Calliope's voice says calmly once she has control of the line on their end, the one mounted in the royal boardroom. Somehow, it's still operational, not having succumbed to the fire.

And then, my sister says, "Sit down before I tell you this."

Henry waits two days before returning to the house, informing Ren and I that we've received an official pardoning. But Ren and I don't celebrate. Come to think of it, I don't think either of us even bat an eye.

What does grab my attention, however, is Henry telling me

that he knows Pandora's location. That she's safe.

Everything in my body wants to get on the water again, to cross the Damocles and find her—knowing she likely would rather rot in a coffin than linger in Urovia after everything. But one look at Ren and I know he isn't healthy enough to sail—to travel. Not yet at least. Henry knows it, too, and the look in his eyes tells me it kills him.

"Write to her," he says after a long while.

"What?"

"To Pandora. I'll deliver whatever message you want to send her myself since—" He looks at Ren again, splotches of bright color creeping up his arms, his neck. "As far as she's aware, you and Ren didn't make it out."

My nostrils flare. "Nobody's told her?"

Henry's head bows. "Part of Pandora's negotiated terms was that none of the staff makes contact with her or crosses the ocean. But I owe you two, and if she sees your handwriting—"

"Ren," I call, deciding instantly. He peeks up from where he's boiling water on the stove. "Will you find me some parchment and ink?"

"Yes, dear," he answers, heading to the master bedroom in search of what I need.

I shut my eyes, too heartsick to watch him limp his way around the house, and Henry mirrors me. Once he feels that Ren is far enough away, Henry asks me pitifully, "Will there ever be a day when you might come to forgive me?"

Though my words are true, they're heavy on my lips. "I'm already working on it."

He smiles weakly. "And the rest of your family? Venus and Jericho?"

That makes me pause, and I use Ren's return as a temporary

out. I thank him with a smile that doesn't exactly meet my eyes, sighing as my shoulders dip towards the page. "I suppose that it'll happen one of these days. But now . . . now's not that day."

I don't wait for anyone's input before beginning to write.

Pandora,

I write to you to let you know that I am alive and on the mend. The last you saw of me likely put you under great duress: perhaps enough to inspire some of the actions and emotions you embraced in Broadcove, but I assure you now: I am recovering, as is my companion, whom you saw me chase after back on the Mosacian coast.

I've been wanting to tell you about him since I met him, so until I can introduce him to you in person, I'll say this: while I may have aged in years, Ren makes my spirit stay young. When I came looking for you in Mosacia, he guided me both through the continent and my grief from losing you. He's been my solid ground and my source of adventure. However, I know that seeing him again may be a complex notion and stir up negative feelings from when I left the boat. I hope you did not see my dash for him as a desertion of you, because all that was on my mind was how I couldn't endure another loss. I'd lost my mother, my father, your father . . .

I specifically choose not to add Venus's brush with death or even Jericho's to the list.

and the way I saw it, you were safe with the masked man. But Ren? They surely would've killed him had I not chosen to stay with him—and it was an assumption I was willing to bet my life on.

Though I do not wish to further disparage the image you have of your aunt and uncle, I must inform you that I will be taking up a prolonged distance from Broadcove Castle and its inhabitants. I have not decided when or if I will ever return, as what Ren and I experienced may haunt me for years to come. What you can count on, however, is that when the time is right, I will find you again in Mosacia. Ren and I need to do some healing here first, but then, when you and I are reunited, all will be right in my world.

I consider ending the letter there and calling it a day—my wrist certainly wishes that I would. That, and Ren seems to be running out of conversation topics with Henry from where they stand on the front stoop.

And yet . . .

I'll be the first to admit that my anger is nothing to joke about. I believe that the most joyous people in life also have room for intense retaliation, and you and I are proof. Sometimes, we make choices that feel good long enough for our anger to feast, but the second we come down from that electric high, we look around and realize that it only made things messier.

Forgive yourself, my sweet girl, just as I already have, in case you're wondering. It took me two decades to finally forgive myself for bringing you up in a home without a father or even a grandfather, but the moment I did, I could tell the difference. I breathe deeper now, savor moments beyond surface level, and remind myself that I am still worthy of happiness—and so are you. I love you.

Until we meet again,

Mother

54
Pandora

Jericho granted every stipulation from that fateful day in Broadcove, all without saying a word to me. Madden likely coordinated all the details with him, but for all sakes and purposes, Jericho Deragon did not exist anymore—and for now, it was better that way.

In two months, Mosacia went from a monopolized land to a free one. Jericho issued formal decrees—the final communications from the *U. Herald* in a land that was no longer theirs—that ownership and governance would be returned to a member of the Seagrave line and that the Hive's forces would no longer occupy residence in Mosacia. Celebrations littered the streets, and when Madden and I sailed back to the Isle and Andromeda House to tell Andie the news, we could hear some of them along the coast.

Then came the symposium—the first one in Mosacia in over twenty years—where Madden laid all his cards on the table. The mutual treachery, the Morgana Grave Agreement henceforth proceeding as the Andromeda Accords, and, lastly, me. My role in helping reclaim Mosacia's independence, my negotiations, and, of course, my relationship with Madden.

Which brings me here, to my long-awaited tribunal.

Something about standing in the same courtroom that would've sentenced me to death but now having its congregants looking to me with reverence hits me like a blow. That, and knowing Madden stands yards away, his father's crown once more restored upon the brow of a family member.

"I'd like to first extend my gratitude to you, the tribunal, for welcoming me here with open-mindedness and hospitality. Your kindness is not lost on me, and it is the highest honor to speak to you today."

Polite applause arises in the room, and I smile uncomfortably at the reception. Something eases in my chest at the sights and sounds around me, and when I look back at Madden to verify if this is all real, he mouths, *"Keep going, angel."*

"Let me start by assuring you that to anyone still uncomfortable with my presence in your beautiful nation, I understand and I empathize with you. Take whatever time you need to adjust, but please know, I have found an unparalleled adoration for this continent in the time I've spent here—and I can only imagine how much more it'll grow over the years I'm granted to spend with your king."

The remark earns me some feminine coos and male sighs across the courtroom. "For any who may be wondering, I shall only rule if Madden asks me to. But should that come to pass," I say, unable to deny myself the hopeful smile that blooms across my lips. Because we know it'll be a reality someday. Someday *soon*, considering the sapphire ring he presented me with three nights ago that threatens to burn a hole in my dress pocket. "The Deragon name will not remain with me. I will vow myself to this land, to him, and to the duties required by me as your monarch.

"For now, I act as the newest Mosacian Emissary, tasked to help renovate communication efforts throughout the different tribes. It's a role that I do not take lightly and hold close to my heart for several reasons. But chief among them, I prepare to work in your favor in honor of a girl named Marzipan."

My throat bobs at the memory of her smile, still fresh in my mind from our talk last night, when Heart Punisher had pricked my finger and I dropped my blood into the Damocles coastline.

"I know it may be hard to comprehend—and with time in this role, I aim to properly explain its complexities—but Marzipan possessed the incredible gift of speaking every language known to man, one she has since passed down to me in death."

Every onlooker goes quiet, and I will myself not to clam up at the unwavering attention my revelation brings.

"It was Marzipan's intention to use that skill-set to unite Mosacia in the understanding of love, supernatural and human—and it has since become mine, too. She was the dearest friend I had ever known, despite our nationality divisions or how short of a time we shared together, and I want to honor her memory in the way I plan to honor all of you."

Slowly, I shut my eyes, pushing past any fears of coming across as performative or preachy or aggressive—and I tell them, "There is a divine presence that longs to tell you that we are loved here on earth. It has never left you, and so long as I'm alive, I will not allow it to remain hidden."

And then, I repeat the sentiment in every Mosacian language my blessing recalls.

Section by section, the courtroom starts to stir with movement. Members of the crowd begin to whisper to one another or stifle tears that spring forth, while others cross their arms over their chest and speculate whether I'm speaking truth or rattling these things from memory. And that's alright. I never expected to convince everyone, and I have plenty of time down the road to keep trying.

"Mosacian women hold so much power, and for many of them, their sacrifices changed the course of history. All that I will do as Emissary has been made possible because of Marzipan. The very existence of the Deragon Dynasty came to be because of Greer Seagrave's convictions, even if some of you believe her trust was misplaced. If it weren't Diana Seagrave's choice to instigate chaos, we might still be in an era of perpetual disagreement.

"And as for the man I stand ready to support in all realms," I say, looking back at Madden with such overwhelming love. "His love for me is no doubt inspired by the love his mothers, Harriet and Maia, showed him, as well as the devotion he gave his sister, Annabelle."

I watch as eyes in the crowd drift towards Madden, sensing the change in his disposition. I know he thinks back on it, the moment we ran like bats out of hell towards Annabelle's grave, the way we both fell to our knees before her headstone. *Loving Sister, Radiant Daughter*. Laid to rest at her sister's side—a final honoring Venus insisted on bestowing Greer. Kellan had broken his once most unconditional rule of forsaking Urovia entirely to memorialize her here. Everything about that moment tore us to shreds, because for all the hatred between our two bloodlines, there also proved to be a great deal of deep-rooted respect.

"I know I'm not a true Mosacian, but I am honored beyond measure to be adopted into your culture," I pronounce. "And I only hope that I can be half as exemplary as all the women who paved this path before me."

I barely get the words *thank you* out before the crowd erupts again, and I step down from the podium. I dare not turn my back on them as I do, a symbolic reminder of what they faced when the Morgan Dynasty became Deragon. Madden's arms stroke my own, his warmth enveloping me.

"You did beautifully," he whispers in an almost sing-song manner.

"Thank you, Madam Emissary," the High Judge calls out, taking my previous spot before the court. "Before we depart, His Majesty has requested we bear witness to a ceremony of citizenship. May I have the candidate please come forward?"

I hear the creaking of the chair before I see the person rise, and suddenly, it doesn't matter who's watching or what any of them have to say.

Not as Mother and I run towards each other with reckless abandon, gracelessly slamming into each other when the distance is fully crossed. We practically claw at one another, tears staining our cheeks and laughter spilling out of us like wine. I think I could die like this—clinging to my mom while Madden looks onto the both of us with such admiration.

The crowd likely pieces it together, but before my mother formally addresses the room, she gently whispers, "Ren's sitting in the back row trying to be inconspicuous. Feel free to terrorize him."

"I mean, if you insist—"

I'm moving at the speed of light towards the back of the room, Madden's laughter following me all the way there. Ren rolls his eyes and stands, figuring I'll stop in my tracks before crashing into him, too. But no. Shamelessly, I throw myself at him, and instinctively, Ren envelopes me in a manner that reminds me of a new father learning how to cradle a baby's head.

"It's nice to finally meet you, Pandora." I hear the smile in his greeting.

"Thank you," I say instead of hello.

He releases an unsteady breath when I grip him harder. "For what?"

I hear the faint accent in Ren's voice and realize it's not just me Mother is gaining citizenship for. The realization pulls at my heartstrings in a way that makes my next words come out choked. "For saving my mom."

"Don't you remember?" he whispers back. "Your mother was the one who saved me."

The High Judge bangs his gavel in attempts to get everyone's attention and reel in the excitement. He sighs as the noise slowly trickles back into cooperative silence. "Thank you. Now, please state your name before the court."

My mother quickly remedies her posture. "Geneva."

"*Full* name."

"Geneva Satare," she amends casually. And my jaw drops into hell.

Finale
Venus: Four Years Later

E very time I look in the mirror, part of me feels like my soul stays frozen in time, forever trapped at age twenty-four while my body keeps ticking forward. The notion weighs heavier the older I get, so I try to forget that I turned fifty last month.

The other part, though, recoils at the woman I see in the reflective glass. Guilt-ridden. Lacking balance. Burnt out from the years of grappling control.

"Aging is a beautiful thing when it's shared with you, my love," Jericho whispers to me, crossing the last of my silk sashes down the back of my dress.

He knows that it isn't the aging that summons grief to the surface, but we play pretend anyways. Despite all that we've done, we deserve one day of peace. If not any other day of the year, then at least today.

"I couldn't agree more," I tell him. "Happy birthday, old man."

"Ouch," he chuckles, placing a kiss onto the column of my

throat. Jericho looks us both over in the mirror and smiles at what he sees, clinging tighter to me. The crimson fabric of my dress dips into his touch. "You're just as beautiful of a bride as you were on this day, twenty-five years ago."

He wears the same uniform he married me in—the same one he met me in. The medallions have started to rust along the edges, and the bright threading of the ribbons they dangle from have begun to lose their luster. But not Jericho. His raven hair has just started to pepper with grays, and it only makes him more devastatingly handsome. Proof of a long, worthwhile life together. His blue eyes are just as piercing as they were all those years ago, and I drown in them daily.

We take our dinner away from the congregated guests, a tradition we've savored over the years. Then, before we stuff ourselves to the point of pain, we make our way towards the festivities. The ballroom is filled to the brim with staff, another tradition we've implemented in recent years—specifically following the prophetic fire. No fancy balls or banquet food. No catering to noble guests. Just a night of dancing and drinking the castle's liquor supply dry—two of our favorite things to do as a couple.

When we emerge, the staff cheers and raises their glasses, some of the attendees spilling their drinks in the process—mainly Tolcher's newest recruits loitering near the champagne table. The seamstresses chortle among themselves, the younger ladies among them making eyes at some of the uniformed men. The new generation of gardeners I get to oversee wave at me with the same casual nature that a friend would, and for a suspended moment in time, my soul doesn't hurt.

Until the musicians strike up their instruments and two singers approach the stage.

I don't cast more than a passing glance at the performers—a man and a woman in sweeping, ceremonial black garments—but when my eyes catch on the lady's swollen belly, I wrench my gaze away. Jericho registers the immediate distress in my bones. "Venus—"

"Just dance with me, my love."

Neither of us look towards them again, and Jericho kisses my temple before swaying us in unhurried unison. When we were younger, we ruled the dancefloor the way we ruled nations—with no room for others and in a way that stole every show. But now, as our bodies have started to slow, everyone knows to take the floor with us.

Finally, I let one tear fall down my face, unbothered by the growing audience.

"Tell me what hurts you," my husband murmurs.

"I've overcome a great deal of let-downs in my life," I say, my voice hoarse. "But no matter how many years pass, and despite knowing I'm too far-gone to change reality, it never gets easier to see women who can give their loves a baby when I never could."

Both of Jericho's hands cradle my face, and in the touch, I feel his hardened calluses—the ones he developed from rebuilding North Star after the fire.

"You gave me the world without ever having to give me a child. How remarkable is that?"

I let him blot my tears with his sleeve. "I love you."

"Do you still want one?"

"What?"

"A child?" he asks innocently.

I fall into stunned silence as we begin to dance again. "I . . ."

"Because I've been thinking about it ever since Pandora left us," he says, and for once, the mention of her only hurts for a moment. "We claimed her as our own, even though she already had an amazing mother. But what about the kids who have no one, the kids in the marshes where you grew up?"

I taste my tears as they drip down to my lips, but we're both smiling all the while.

"Your birthday has already come and gone," he points out with the quirk of his brow. "But what if, for mine, we pay a visit to the orphanage in your hometown? I bet we can find a kid or two to give a better life to."

"Or five."

Jericho barks out a laugh. "As many as we want."

The picture in my mind of the future suddenly excites me. It's no longer shrouded in persisting guilt and unrequited remorse, but rather, gray hairs and quippy conversations with all our kids at the dinner table. Days spent getting to know all their unique personalities and nights spent ingraining how much we love them into their brains. Watching the older ones orchestrate practical jokes on the staff that make the younger ones keel over in laughter. Teaching them all life skills while silently observing what hobbies set their hearts on fire. Supporting them and providing them the kind of security that allows them to slowly forget about the pain they may be swimming in right now.

"Nothing would make me happier."

I laugh into Jericho's shoulder as glass shatters across the room. Two maintenance workers point accusatory fingers at one another, but when the one on the right hiccups to where it shakes his whole body, I start to outright cackle.

"Having fun, Your Majesties?"

Calliope and Eli make a pass near us, and I nod in answer, the newfound happiness of this moment making me feel like I already have two drinks in my system. Calliope leans in towards us. "Did you like our gift?"

"Gift?" I ask.

Calliope merely points to the stage before her husband spins her away from us.

Jericho and I go slack-jawed as we take a better look at the performers.

I always knew Pandora would make for a beautiful queen, even though I assumed I would not be alive to see it for myself. But seeing her not just as a ruler, but as an expectant *mother*—even just seeing her *here* . . .

Her body has adapted so beautifully to the future they have set up for themselves, and the king of Mosacia looks towards his wife with a gentle reverence that starkly contrasts the madman I remember him to be. I briefly recall meeting Madden as a child, and I wonder if their child will look anything like him. Wonder if, by some hilarious twist of fate, she's not too far along, but rather, carrying twins.

"I can't believe they're here," Jericho sighs, eyes going glassy.

"That's not all," a new voice I've been longing to hear again says from behind us.

We barely get a good look at Genny before Jericho and I rush her with enough force to knock the wind out of her—and she takes it like a champ. All my tears and blubbering, all of Jericho's fragmented gratitude to the Saints, all the staff that swarms her to welcome her back.

And I know without her saying anything else that we'll be alright. Even if things are still imperfect and conversations still need to be had, the fact that they're all here is enough. It's all I could ever ask for and more.

Because for so long, I convinced myself that building something formidable would make me feel secure, that force was the highest form of love. But I know now how many years I wasted on being strong, because all along, what mattered most was the people that made me weak.

Genny. Pandora. Calliope and Eli. Flora, Samuel, and Dorian. Tolcher. Ardian. Merrie.

Jericho.

Even the greatest of dynasties fell short in comparison to the feeling of family.

Acknowledgements

T his story has taught me so much about myself, about love, and, most importantly, about mercy. I wrote it throughout a pretty bleak period in my life, one where it felt easier to give into grief and criticism, both from others and from myself. But through it all, I truly felt the LORD stand with me as I wrote this story—so it's Him I want to thank first and most resoundingly. Thank you, Jesus!

To my husband, who often times went to bed without me so that I could stay up and write or edit this book. Thank you for always believing in me and my dreams. I love you!

A massive thank you to my amazing editor, Caitlin. This book would not exist without you (no, seriously, thanks for talking me into writing a duology instead of a standalone!). A special shoutout to my proofreader, Jess, for stepping in and being another pair of eyes. And to my cover designer, Bianca, who absolutely nailed the vision I had in mind for this book. The three of you were truly my dream team for this duology!

To the best girls I know who poured so much encouragement,

love, and time into me and this story: Alyssa, Heather, Emma, and Makayla. The four of you genuinely kept me sane during this whole process, and I'm spoiled to have such wonderful friends in my life. A special shoutout to Kendall, Laurel, Hali, Sam, Isa, my book club pals, and all the supportive people I've met through bookstagram and booktok. Looking back, I can say that there were many days where your kindness unintentionally kept me afloat, so my gratitude for you all knows little bounds.

And lastly, I want to extend a thank you to my parents for continuously supporting me and my dreams. Everything I know about love first came from the both of you, and I hope that this story is a testament to that. I love you!

About the Author

Sydney Applegate is a lover of comfort food, Taylor Swift, all things purple, and feel-good literature. She graduated with honors from the University of North Texas, where she studied Media Arts and English, and when she's not writing, she can be curled up on the couch with her husband and their cat, Shiloh.

Want to learn about what's next now that *The Deragon Duology* is complete? Connect with Sydney on Instagram @authorsydneyapplegate or visit her website at www.booksbysydney.com to stay up to date on all her upcoming projects.

Made in the USA
Coppell, TX
10 March 2025

46895803R00281